Wolf Girl Running

A. Mariposa

Black Butterfly

Author's Note

The BLACK RIVER MOON trilogy takes place is the beautiful Adirondack wilderness in a fictional town called Black River, NY. Although names and locations might appear to represent places in real life, they are, indeed, fictional. The setting is not meant to represent Black River Village or its population as it exists in the real world. Please note this book contains adult themes and explicit material. Reader discretion is advised.

The Black River Moon Trilogy

Contents

Prologue

Deep in the Five Ponds Wilderness of the Adirondack mountains, a few miles outside the town of Black River, New York, an abandoned hunting cabin was located. The lonely cabin stood at the end of a long, potholed forestry road, lost in a thicket of red spruce and ancient dogwood trees. The peaked roof was ten feet tall, and the cabin's main room was open and spacious. Built of hardwood logs, designed with meticulous craftsmanship, it stood strong as a fortress against the elements, showing hardly any signs of decay even after years of disuse.

The spot was recommended to Kevin Montgomery by a local member of the hunter's guild. Kevin didn't know how long the cabin had stood empty. With a bit of TLC, it could be rehabilitated into a proper home, he reasoned, as he piled firewood into the ancient brick fireplace. Too bad he was just passing through. Squinted at

A few years ago, he might have considered purchasing a little place like this, somewhere secluded out in the woods, far away from society. Nowadays, he didn't see the point. He didn't stick around one place long enough to set down roots. For a man of his proclivities, the nomadic life was more convenient. This cabin would serve as temporary housing, a place to hole up for a few days, while he worked out his kill zone. He liked the darkness of abandoned places. It was a vibe, a mindset. Monster hunting didn't belong in the daylight.

He finished stacking firewood next to the hearth, then went about unpacking his bags. A black duffel bag contained two guns for hunting big game. The first was a 22" bolt-action rifle with a nice satin walnut finish. The second rifle was a semi-automatic in camo colors. His two smaller bags were full of magazines. The guns were specially designed for hunting big game, like tigers and lions down in Africa. He just so happened to use them for a different kind of hunt.

He set the guns down on the table at the side of the room beneath a single square window. Someone had thoughtfully cleaned the cabin before his arrival. They even left a pile of canned goods and a sleeping bag for his use, a stash of emergency candles, lighter fluid, a little gas burner, some pots and pans for cooking, and a towel. He saw a handful of yellow wildflowers in a vase on the windowsill. A feminine touch.

As the thought crossed his mind, his phone rang. It was a Boost Mobile prepaid flip phone, a little burner phone he used on jobs. He recognized the number. He took a seat in the chair next to the fireplace. Then he picked up.

"Oh, hi, hello," a woman's voice said nervously into the phone. "I didn't mean to disturb you, sir, just wanted to check if you found the place."

"I did."

"Oh good," the woman said quickly. "I left some supplies for you. Supposed to be a big storm blowing in. Just wanted to make sure you were comfortable. Is there anything you need?"

"Nope." There was a silent pause. Kevin realized the woman expected a little more from him. With a sigh, he added, "The place looks nice. Thanks."

"Oh, you're very welcome. It's an honor to have someone of your . . . er, *standing with the guild* . . . come to a little town like Black River. You're one of the best. Anything I can do to help. I can show you around town tomorrow, if you like, if you're free."

Kevin listened to the woman babble into the phone. It sounded like his reputation had preceded him. Twenty years of werewolf hunting had gained him the Hellstrom Medal for excellence in the field. Mostly, it was a little "Achievement" badge next to his screen name on the guild's job boards. It marked him one of the top tier werewolf hunters in the world. It was a niche community. It didn't get him a tax exemption, but it definitely got him laid.

Kevin wondered how big the woman's tits were and if she smelled nice. Maybe a night in a small town motel wouldn't be a bad thing.

He was fifty-six years old, and he had learned a lot about women over his lifetime. They liked fantasy better than reality. Some played Sims Online and struck up affairs with imaginary characters. Some became penpals with murderers and serial killers in prison. Werewolf hunters had their own little group of fangirls. Seemed like this woman had a thirst.

"Sure," he said. "Tomorrow's fine. How about we grab a drink?"

"Oh yes, I'd love to. There's a bar in town with great burgers. I wouldn't recommend the onion rings, though. They roll them in pancake batter. It's a little bready. But the sweet potato fries are good."

"Sure. I like burgers. Text me the address, and I'll meet you there tomorrow. By the way, did you get the pictures I sent over?"

"I did." The woman hesitated over the phone. "I don't recognize the man. But the girl looks . . . um, well, she looks a little like someone I work with. But I find it hard to believe she would be involved with this."

"Werewolves come in all shapes and sizes," the man grunted. "Let's talk more over a drink. I want to learn more about this girl. Maybe you can arrange a meetup this week."

"I don't really know her that well, but . . . maybe, if it's for the guild. I'll see what I can do."

"Good. Great."

The woman went quiet, waiting for him to say something else, but Kevin was tired after a long day on the mountain, and he didn't have the bandwidth to make smalltalk. He cleared his throat a few times and stared into the fire, waiting for the woman to give up.

It didn't take too long. After about a minute, she said, "Well, I should get going. I was just checking in and I'm sure you're tired. Have a nice night."

"Yup. Goodnight." Kevin hung up the phone.

One of his dogs growled from the floor next to the fireplace. His biggest boy, Bruce, barked twice. It sounded like the low huff of a bear. Kevin grinned at the dog, displaying a missing incisor on the left side of his jaw. Three massive hounds lay on a pile of mats on the floor beside the fire. The lion-like dogs were a special breed imported from Russia: a mix of Caucasian shepherd, Rhodesian Ridgeback and a bit of real wolf. The dogs all weighed more than a hundred pounds, with wiry double-coats and thick ruffs to resist werewolf jaws.

Kevin had selected and raised all three puppies for the sole purpose of werewolf hunting. For years, he had been adding wolfsbane to their food and water, so that even their blood and flesh had become poisonous to werewolves.

The two boys and one girl were from the same litter. The biggest male, Bruce, was bulky like a little bear, with a dark brown coat and beady black eyes. The smaller male, Colt, was more wolf-like in appearance, with a masked face and long snout. He was the fastest runner and the best for tracking prey through the woods.

Sitting by Kevin's feet was his pride and joy, Rosie, the only female in their little pack. She might be smaller than her brothers, but she was smarter and a lot meaner. She was a real wild card in a fight. The bitch sat near his feet while the boys piled next to the fire. She was the leader of their little pack.

He reached down and scratched his girl behind her cream-colored ears. She let out a little love sigh.

"Don't be jealous now, sweetheart, you're still my number one," he said.

Rosie whined up at him, her affection apparent in her honey-brown eyes. Her intelligent gaze almost seemed human. Kevin didn't have a daughter—but he considered Rosie better than a child. He loved his dogs; he wouldn't be one of the best hunters in the world without them. A human couldn't pace a werewolf on foot, but his hounds could track a wolf pack through the Catskill Mountains for a solid week before cornering their prey. Once they got the scent, they didn't quit.

Kevin stood up from his chair with a groan, stretching out his sore back. Then he kept unpacking his bags. Night was falling. Time to get settled in.

On the west facing wall of the cabin, he pinned up a bunch of bird photos printed out on glossy computer paper. Northern New York was a great area for birding. The list was extensive: red-winged blackbirds, swamp sparrows, Northern cardinals, warblers and waterfowl, house wrens, great blue herons, black-capped chickadees, blue jays and raptors of all kinds. Just a few days ago, he had captured a macro shot of a white-breasted nuthatch. The little sparrow-shaped bird was hanging almost upside down from a tree branch. Its startling silver wings sparkled in the sunset. Magic hour. He had already sold twelve downloads of the photo from his stock photography account online.

Next to his plethora of bird photos, Kevin pinned up a picture of his latest obsession: an Alpha wolf he had spotted on the mountainside just a few days ago. He could hardly believe his luck. Finding a lone Alpha in the wilderness was nothing short of an anomaly. It was an auspicious sign. This might just be his retirement staring him in the face.

The photo showed a large man on a hiking trail, partially obscured by foliage and pine bows. Behind him, a smaller red female crouched on a log, hidden behind a screen of green hobblebush leaves.

Both wolf shifters were in human form, but that's why Kevin kept wolfsbane on him. The fellow's little girlfriend had almost passed out from the smell. Only a werewolf would react like that to the herb. He wasn't interested in the female, though. She wouldn't gain him much of anything. But the big male oozed Alpha vitality.

Only a week ago, the job posting had gone live on the guild's board about a possible werewolf attack outside of Black River, NY, a little mountain town lost in the Adirondacks. The posting mentioned the mysterious deaths of five men outside a trailer in the woods. The police suspected a wolf attack due to the teeth marks on the bodies, even though gray wolves were not active in upstate New York. The guild member who posted the job was worried about possible werewolf activity in the area, and Kevin agreed. He had just finished up a gig in Maine and was looking for a new assignment. So he took the job on a whim.

He didn't expect to encounter an Alpha the same day he arrived in town.

Kevin ran his thumb over the smooth, hooked fang hanging from a chain on his neck. Then he tucked it under his dirty plaid shirt. It was a trophy from his first Alpha kill, almost sixteen years ago now. It had kicked off his career, but he hadn't encountered another Alpha since. This upcoming hunt might just be the capstone of his career.

Kevin stood back and crossed his arms, thoughtfully gazing at the photo pinned to the wall. Unfortunately, he hadn't gotten a clear shot of the man's face. His features were blurry and obscured by trees. The redheaded girlfriend was a lot more recognizable. Red hair would be easy to spot around a small town like Black River, and she looked young, maybe early twenties. If he tracked her down, she would lead him straight to his prize. His contact in town sounded like she recognized the girl. If that were the case, then this hunt might go a lot faster than he first thought.

After he killed the Alpha, he could sell the loot on the black market. The pelt alone was a novelty item; certain shamans and wizards would pay top dollar for Alpha fur and claws. Werewolf blood was used for all sorts of potions and elixirs among the underground paranormal community. Almost every part of the body would be salvageable, from the testes to the teeth. If he played his cards right, he was looking at a six figure bonus. And he didn't have to split it with the guild or nobody else, because the guild didn't need to know.

The guild had its own code, its own way of doing things that were "humane" and "fair" to these monsters who paraded about as men. Werewolves were a menace, but they were still part-human, with families and lives of their own. So the guild came up with a hundred and one codes and bylaws to prevent unconscientious killing. Hunters weren't murderers, after all. They followed a creed. A code. That made it all a lot more justified. The main three rules were this:

First, hard evidence must be acquired to confirm the subject was a werewolf.

Second, it had to be proven the wolf was a danger to the community.

Third, the hunt couldn't take place man-to-man. The werewolf had to be Changed, in wolf form, for the killing to be considered ethical.

About a hundred laws followed the main three: the wolf couldn't be killed in his own home, it had to be out in the woods. The body couldn't be skinned or dismembered for parts. It couldn't be sold on the black market. No trophies could be taken or kept as evidence of the kill. The hunter had to obtain a hunting permit in the local area, the gun had to be registered, and it all had to be above board.

It was a lot, so Kevin kept a healthy lack of visibility between himself and the guild. It's not like anyone was really policing them. The guild's laws were more of a formality, really. Official law enforcement and society at large didn't know anything about werewolves.

His next step would be to locate the Alpha and his mate. He liked the chase. The rush of cornering his prey. The battle of wits, the bloodplay. Yeah. In another world he might be considered a serial killer, but this was different. This was monster hunting.

Chapter 1

Black Bear Diner was located on Highway 20 just off exit 206, about halfway between Black River and Davenport. It was famous to the upriver community for its chicken and waffles. A big sign above the entrance advertised "Breakfast All Day!" and the gravel parking lot was always full.

Beyond the Black Bear Diner, a winding country road passed by a gas station, a little Baptist church, a fruit stand and a blueberry farm. Past that blip of civilization, the road continued on through cattle ranches, horse properties, farms, patches of wetland and dense woods, before disappearing into the Adirondack mountains.

On this gloomy Sunday morning, heavy rain poured down from an overcast sky. Thick curtains of mist clung to the mountains and gathered between the dark pine trees, casting the forest in a ghostly, haunted shroud. It seemed appropriate for October in Northern New York.

The parking lot of the Black Bear Diner was full, and the front of the restaurant was packed with families waiting to be seated. Maddy put her name on the waiting list and looked for a place to sit down. Several groups of people milled about the entrance of the restaurant, grumbling about the wait and the lousy weather. There really wasn't much space to sit or stand in the lobby. Maddy felt a little claustrophobic.

Gareth took her by the hand and pulled her outside. A wooden carving of a black bear stood at the entrance of the restaurant. Seeing the statue reminded Maddy of the stuffed brown bear Gareth had won for her at Beaumont Farms. He got a perfect score at the shooting gallery. She remembered him clearing out the rows of cardboard aliens with relative ease, as the local hunting community cheered him on from the sidelines. It was pretty cool, and a little frightening, to see how good he was with a toy gun. He was an Army vet, but she didn't know much about the time he spent in Iraq.

His arm slipped around her waist, interrupting the memory.

"Come on, let's stand out of the rain," he said.

Maddy shivered at the sound of his low voice. She followed him to the side of the building, where the roof's overhang provided a few feet of shelter from the rain.

Gareth wore a white T-shirt under a gray flannel button-down, with a black weather-breaker and dark jeans. Even the layered look couldn't hide his muscular shoulders and the two little mountains across his wide chest. His long black hair was pulled back into a casual bun at the base of his neck, accentuating his firm jawline and angular cheekbones. His black eyebrows gave his face a stern appearance. Long dark lashes framed his hazel eyes, which today were a greenish brown color, though sometimes they glowed yellow or gold. He looked like he belonged on the cover of GQ Magazine, modeling a new line of Fall fashion, not hanging around a backwater little burg like Black River.

Maddy still wasn't used to being together with him in public.

He leaned against the side of the building and pulled her against his body, positioning her between his legs. Her cheeks flushed pink.

Gareth was . . . a bit older than her.

And a lot more experienced.

Actually, until a day ago, she had been a virgin.

Maddy remembered waking up just a few hours ago to the sound of rain thrumming against the bedroom window.

She was alone and naked in Gareth's bed.

She rolled over. The clock above the bedroom door said it was almost 9am, but it felt like midnight. The room was dark and murky, like a little cave. Gareth's gray comforter, bedsheets and walls added to the effect. The clouds outside the window were black and ugly. Sheets of rain fell from the sky, spilling over the metal gutter that lined the roof. It felt like an angry god was determined to flood the world.

It was the day after the harrowing events at Fright Farm Haunted Manor.

The wind whipped the trees back and forth in Gareth's backyard. He owned a little postage stamp of property near the middle of town. Through the bedroom window, Maddy saw a line of pine trees and raspberry bushes running along the back of his half-acre. The side of his neighbor's blue house was barely visible through the trees and torrential downpour, then beyond that, the mountain.

Maddy gazed at the snow-capped peaks for a moment, hazy through a layer of rain. Today, the mountain wore a cloak of fine white mist about its shoulders, and a silver crown of storm clouds upon its head. It loomed, solemn and foreboding, above the town.

Maddy lay for a moment in bed, feeling the weight of the previous night settle over her shoulders. The onslaught of memories seemed as relentless as the storm outside: the haunted house, the corn field, the woods. Losing her virginity. The long drive back to Gareth's house in the rain.

Werewolves.

Holy shit.

Gareth is a werewolf, she thought. *Lobo loco,* just like his tattoos said. He was a crazy wolf.

Her memories were too vivid to be a dream. In technicolor detail, she remembered the sight of the Grayridge pack shifting into their wolf forms. The faces of the men had melted—*literally* melted—as their skulls elongated and their bodies shrank. Fur sprouted. Teeth turned into gnarled fangs. The sight was more gruesome than any concocted effect in a movie.

Gareth was no exception. She remembered the sight of him Changing into a wolf in the corn field, the sound of his bones popping and flesh contorting. She remembered his dagger-like fangs, hooked claws and sleek blue-black pelt. He was twice the size of the other wolves; he tore them up with his massive jaws. He was a fucking monster, and he had saved her life.

It was absurd. Werewolves didn't exist. It was impossible. And yet, she couldn't deny what she had seen with her own eyes. She recalled the big black Alpha standing above her in the forest, protecting her from the smaller gray wolves. Close enough for her to reach out and touch his fur.

When he shifted back into "Gareth," she had run from him. He chased her down in the woods. And then . . . .

I lost my virginity to a werewolf.

Was monster sex different from regular human sex?

She didn't have anything to compare it to.

What the hell was I thinking?

Well, that's the thing, she wasn't thinking at all. In the dark forest, after the most terrifying night of her life, an inferno of passion had consumed her. But now, in the gray morning light, she felt very sober.

Maddy felt a twinge behind her bellybutton at the memory of her first time. Gareth was . . . very large. Her muscles were tender from his deep penetration. She placed a hand on her lower belly with a wince. Somehow, she had expected the pain to be worse. She sort of liked it. The tenderness reminded her of their lovemaking.

Her hand traveled down between her legs. His seed stained her thighs where it had dripped out during the night. She pressed her fingers into her bruised flesh. She was moist and warm. A little tingly. When she pulled her fingers out, they were sticky with his seed.

This is wild, she thought. It was totally primitive. Their scents were mingled together.

She remembered him unloading into her body for a full minute. She had orgasmed twice from that feeling alone. His thick seed had overflowed down her leg into a sticky puddle on the ground. The size of his cock had kept them pinned together for a long while as he finished. When he finally slipped out, she felt fully sedated, almost drugged.

She didn't know how much a normal man ejaculated, but it seemed like Gareth's load was very large.

He isn't human, she reminded herself. *He's a werewolf.*

The more she thought about all of it, she began to feel overwhelmed. She kind of wanted to run away. Find a safe place to hide and process everything that had happened on Friday. But she was in his house, in his bed, and eventually, she needed to get up.

With a sigh, Maddy threw off the comforter and set her feet on the carpet. She stood up. She felt self-conscious walking around his house naked, despite all the intimate ways he had touched her body. She dragged on a big hoodie and sweatpants from his closet. The scent of him washed over her, all woodsy and peppery, making her skin tingle.

She frowned as she moved around the room. Then she paused, glancing down at her feet. She noticed her ankle wasn't sprained from the night before.

She wiggled it around a bit. *Okay, that's weird.*

She felt a twinge when she rotated it, but nothing terrible. The skin was a little discolored, but the bruising and swelling was mostly gone. She did a little one-two hop to the left. All good. Had she imagined busting up her ankle? Maybe the injury wasn't as bad as she remembered? Or maybe she had slept for six weeks instead of six hours?

It was super mysterious and freaky.

Swimming in his oversized clothes, Maddy walked down the hallway to the bathroom. Her thighs and core muscles were a little sore. She felt like she had done a thousand sit-ups the night before. She grimaced when she caught sight of her reflection in the bathroom mirror. Her long auburn hair was a rat's nest. She had dark circles under her eyes. She looked like shit.

Ugh. Maddy groaned at her reflection. Then she flipped the light switch on, but nothing happened. She tried the switch again a few times. The lights stayed dark. Then she turned on the sink, but the water didn't run.

The wind howled outside, reminding her of the storm.

Shit, the power must be out.

Gareth's house was probably on a well system like her trailer—not all the houses in Black River were hooked up to the city's water reservoir—which meant the well pump was out, too. The storm must have blown over a few trees downriver. It wasn't anything she hadn't dealt with before, but the timing wasn't great. It was annoying, but not a surprise.

She left the bathroom and walked through the house looking for any sign of Gareth. The hallway emptied into a living room with a big leather couch, recessed lighting and a 60" TV hanging above the fireplace. The wood-paneled walls and red brick fireplace gave it a definite 70's vibe. The floor was covered in thick brown carpet. With the lights off and the curtains drawn, the house felt similar to the bedroom: like a cool, dark cavern.

It was soothing. She stood for a moment in the living room. The dull background hum of the refrigerator and the electronics was silent. It was kind of nice.

She didn't see Gareth anywhere.

She walked from the living room into the kitchen. She passed by a big stainless steel sink and a brand new refrigerator with an ice maker. The square floor tiles were cool on her bare feet. On the other side of the kitchen, a door led through a little mudroom into the backyard. She wondered if Gareth was outside. Maybe she should check?

Just as she reached for the handle of the back door, it opened. Gareth stepped in from the rain, his black weatherbreaker drenched and dripping, an irritated scowl on his face.

He slammed into her.

"Oh!" Maddy yelped.

With a grunt, he grabbed her arms. His eyes flashed over her, widening. Then he looked again, his gaze sweeping over her from head to toe. Maddy felt self-conscious. Her long red hair looked like a crazy bird's nest. She was drowning in his hoodie, and his sweatpants ballooned around her hips, comically large. She didn't consider herself a small woman, but Gareth towered a few inches over six feet and stood as broad as a door frame. His clothes fit her like a tent.

Gareth, on the other hand, looked . . . well, stern and a little irritated, for one. But even drenched with rain, his black hair loose and tousled by the wind, she didn't think it was possible for him to look anything less than 9/10 on the hotness scale. The dramatic angles of his face were drawn into a frown; his sensual lips were pressed into a straight line. His high cheekbones gave his face an exotic appearance, and his dark tan skin was deliciously smooth. His jaw was strong and firm, with a dimpled chin and full, sensual lips. By the knot in his brow, he didn't seem to be in a great mood.

Was this the man who had taken her virginity?

Maddy felt suddenly awkward. The spell from last night was broken; the inferno of adrenaline and passion had passed. Now, in the cloudy daylight of a rainy afternoon, she felt much more sensible. When she thought back over their intimate encounter in the woods, she felt like she was watching a porno starring a smutty red-haired actress. They had mated like wild animals. She remembered her wanton cries ringing out in the quiet woods, her little mewls and whimpers, and his deep groan as he emptied himself inside of her.

She was *not* that bold.

"How's your ankle?" he asked. His gravelly baritone gave her a pleasant little shiver.

"Oh, uh, it's fine," she stuttered, "like totally better, no worries."

"Good."

He gently nudged her aside and strode past her to the sink, then turned on the water.

"Um, the power's out," she said.

"Yup, I was setting up the generator for the well pump. Water's on now."

"What's a generator?"

Gareth raised an eyebrow. "You don't have a generator for the trailer?"

"I mean, maybe? Is that like a heater?"

Gareth sighed and turned off the sink. He folded his arms and looked at her.

"It's like a bigass battery. Dean's been letting you live on the mountain all year round with no generator?"

Maddy felt a little defensive, but she didn't know why.

She explained, "We don't lose power every winter. We might have a generator, I just don't know about it."

It was a lie—the whole town lost power at least once a year during the winter storms. It was practically a tradition in the upriver community. Black River was a rural small town buried in the Adirondack mountains. They didn't have the kind of grid system or infrastructure found in larger cities or suburbs. This far in the mountains, any number of things could take out a power line or a converter. She remembered one winter, the power went out for a whole week, and Dean almost set the living room on fire because the woodburning stove wouldn't get hot enough. She didn't think Dean owned a generator. If he did, it was piled in a heap of broken appliances at the back of their property.

Silence stretched between them. Maddy felt cursed by a sudden wave of shyness. After the events of last night, making polite conversation about the weather seemed insane.

If Gareth noticed her tension, he didn't mention it.

"So will the lights work now?" she asked.

"Naw, it's not a big enough generator. It'll run the fridge and the water pump, but not much else. Why? You need to charge your phone?"

Actually, Maddy hadn't thought of her phone yet. With a little gasp, she reached for the pocket of her hoodie, then she remembered she was wearing his clothes.

"Oh, um, where is it?" she asked.

"Behind you, on the counter," Gareth nodded.

She turned and saw a brick of black plastic sitting next to the microwave. She picked up her phone, feeling a sense of relief. The screen was cracked and it wouldn't turn on—the battery was dead. But at least she hadn't lost it. Considering the chaos of last night, it was a miracle. She couldn't afford a replacement.

"I got a battery you can use," Gareth said, reading her face.

"Oh, great, um, thanks."

Nonchalant, he opened a drawer in the kitchen and took out a flat, white square of plastic with a charging port. He handed it over to her. Maddy took it, feeling its weight. It was the biggest phone battery she had ever seen.

"This is, like, industrial sized," she said.

"It's for emergencies. Should last a whole week."

"A *week?*"

"Yup, it's what the Army uses. Here."

He slipped the battery and her phone out of her hand without asking. Maddy felt a little scandalized. He plugged in her phone. Then he leaned past her and set it on the counter behind her. The screen lit up with a white lightning bolt icon. It was charging.

Maddy sucked in a breath as he leaned past her. His delicious scent filled her nose. Her stomach clenched. Despite her misgivings about the werewolf thing, and her general overwhelm about last night, her whole body reacted to his presence.

His seed was inside of her. The thought rose up in her mind, unbidden.

Maddy briefly met his eyes. His face was so close, she could reach up and bite his chin. She considered it. She wondered if he would kiss her. She waited for him to initiate. But he didn't.

Instead, Gareth rested his arms on either side of her, propped up on the counter. His big body hovered a few inches away from her own, his face intimately close. He leaned in, nuzzling her hair. She listened to him breathe deep. The strength of his presence washed over her.

She felt like a lost girl he had found on the mountainside and brought home to his den.

"I like seeing you in my clothes," he said, his voice deep in his chest.

"Sorry, I didn't have anything else . . . ." she mumbled.

"Why are you sorry? I said I like it."

He pressed his lips against her forehead. Maddy closed her eyes. He was still Gareth, despite everything she had learned about him on Friday night. If she was so freaked out, why did she fuck him? She really needed to figure out her boundaries.

"How are you feeling?" he asked in a growl.

She knew what he meant.

"Um, sore," she said.

"A little sore, huh?"

"I mean, it's not bad . . ." her voice faded as a blush grew in her cheeks. She wasn't used to talking this intimately.

Without warning, he grabbed her by the waist and boosted her up onto the counter so she was sitting with her legs astride his hips. She gasped. She was a curvaceous woman; his strength surprised her.

"Um, wow, hi," she said.

"Hi." He gazed into her eyes. "I got something for you."

"What's that?"

He pretended to reach into his back pocket like he was pulling out his wallet. Then he mimicked holding up a card between two fingers.

"Got your V card right here," he grinned.

It broke the tension. Maddy smacked his wide chest. "Oh my god, you're such a nerd! Are you serious?"

"Yup, dead serious. You dropped it in the woods Friday night. For real though, you feeling alright? No regrets? I didn't hurt you, did I?"

"No regrets," she promised. "It was really good, Gareth. I . . . uh . . . ." She really didn't have words for it. She glanced away, feeling her cheeks turning pink again, thinking of his seed still warming her body.

He searched her face, brushing her hair back from her eyes. His gaze grew warm and intimate. In a low voice, he rumbled, "You're cute, little wolf girl. I was worried about you. You slept a long time."

"I was just really tired." Maddy fell quiet, thinking of his words—*wolf girl*. It made her uncomfortable. She tried to change the subject. "So, uh, what about you? Is your back feeling better? It was pretty torn up last night."

"Friday night."

"Yeah, last night."

"It's Sunday, babygirl. You slept through Saturday."

Maddy's eyes widened. "Really?"

"Yup."

So that's what he meant by *"you slept a long time."* Maddy was amazed. She counted back the hours. Had she slept for a full day and night? No wonder her ankle felt so much better.

Now that she thought about it, she had a vague recollection of waking up on Saturday afternoon to use the bathroom and drink some water. She remembered feeling sick with exhaustion. Then she passed out again in his bed. She couldn't remember if he was asleep next to her.

"Did you sleep through Saturday, too?" she asked.

"Naw, I got up in the afternoon. Worked out. Ran some errands. Did laundry."

"Does that mean your back is healed now?" she asked, a little awkward. Talking about his werewolf healing power was a little strange.

Gareth stood up straighter, rolling out his neck and shoulders with a wince. "Honestly, I've been better, but should be good as new in a few days."

"Can I see?"

"Sure, baby."

He lifted up his shirt, revealing his muscular chest and dark tan skin. Maddy felt her mouth go dry. She did not expect him to rip off his shirt quite so quickly. He had a warrior's physique, his torso covered in long, toned muscles, his chest like two little mountains with a deep ravine down the middle. The sight of so much bare skin made her feel flushed and heated. Jeez. She wanted to run her hands up over his chest.

He turned around, pulling his hair to one side so she could see the gouges all over his back. They were caused by werewolf claws, and she was pretty sure she saw bite marks on the back of his left arm. They were mostly scabbed over. Some had healed into thin white lines. It looked a lot better than she remembered, but still painful.

Considering only a day had passed since their altercation with the Grayridge pack, he was healing with miraculous speed. Just like her ankle.

Gareth pulled his shirt back on.

"It looks a lot better, but still a little bloody," Maddy said.

"Yup."

"Does it hurt?"

He popped his neck again. "I'm stiff, but it's fine, babygirl. I've had worse."

"It's amazing how fast you can heal."

"Yeah, well, it's an Alpha thing. Comes with the territory. We call it *vitality*. The same power that allows us to Change also repairs our body fast."

"Oh. I didn't realize."

Maddy paused, remembering the size and ferocity of his wolf form. His gleaming fangs and ravendark coat. He was a lot larger than a regular wolf, almost the size of a horse. His beast form looked majestic and terrifying all at once.

"You sure you don't have regrets?" Gareth asked, trying to read her expression.

"No, not *regrets*," she stuttered. "It's just a lot to think about. Like, Friday night was my first time, and you're not even human." She felt really dumb saying that. She searched his face. She hoped she hadn't hurt his feelings. "What I mean is, you're not just a normal boyfriend, you're a . . ."

"A *monster*, Mads? A big ol' beast?"

He had a humorous glint in his eye, like he was teasing her.

"It's a big deal, Gareth!" she exclaimed.

"I agree it is," he said, leaning closer between her legs. He pressed his crotch intimately against hers. *Oh my.* He was hard. Maddy sucked in a breath. She felt his thickness through his pants. How did he fit all that inside of her? Anatomically, it just didn't make sense.

Gareth grinned, seeing her look of alarm.

"I know *it's a lot to take in*," he murmured, his words laced with implication. "But I've been like this the whole time, babygirl. You just saw a different side of me on Friday night, that's all. Nothing's changed. I'm still that boring dude who owns an auto shop up Highway 20. I just happen to be a werewolf."

"B-boring?" Maddy said, trying to pull her mind out of the gutter. "No way. There's nothing boring about you."

"Yeah, well, you'll find out soon enough, babe. I'm pretty boring."

"Why didn't you tell me sooner about the werewolf thing? Like, you could've told me when we first met."

"I wanted you to get to know me first, babe. And to be fair, I dropped plenty of hints."

Maddy bit her lip. Right. He had told her that first night on his couch that he was a lone wolf without a pack. He had been drawn to her scent: a lost little wolf on the mountain. At the time, she had thought it was a romantic kind of metaphor. She hadn't realized he was telling the truth.

And at Fright Farm, he even told her that drinking turned him into a wolf. She thought he was teasing her with a bad joke. But he was being serious.

"You saved my life," she admitted. "If you hadn't been there at Fright Farm, then those men would've . . . ." Her voice hitched.

Gareth's eyebrows lowered. "Hey," he murmured, "no one's gonna get you long as I'm around. I'll always protect you. You got that?"

She nodded.

"Now give me your pretty mouth."

He leaned forward and pressed his lips to hers, taking her off guard. She felt the brush of his five o'clock shadow against her soft skin. Within seconds, his mouth became her whole world. He kissed her slowly, patiently. Then he deepened the kiss, expertly sliding his tongue between her lips. He took his time tasting her, as though he had never kissed her before. He explored every inch of her mouth.

A swarm of butterflies kicked up in her stomach. Her hands settled on his broad shoulders. A flush of arousal grew in her cheeks. She felt a pleasant tingle in her breasts.

Fuck, she wanted him.

His hand clasped her face. He angled her head sideways. He kissed her like he meant to drown her. Maddy found her hands threading through his long hair, weaving through his silken black locks, so different from her own. She knew sex with him again would probably hurt just like the first time, he was so large. But she was very aroused. They had already crossed that line—was there any reason to stop? They could do it right there in the kitchen.

Then a loud groan from her stomach disrupted the moment. Maddy felt a sudden, gnawing sense of hunger. It had been a full day since her last meal. She was more than just hungry—she was ravenous.

Gareth broke their kiss. He pressed his forehead against hers, breathing heavily. Then he grinned at her. His tongue darted out. He licked the tip of her nose.

"Come on, little wolf girl," he growled. "Let's get you breakfast."

Then he helped her slide down from the counter.

Now, standing outside the Black Bear Diner, the rain pouring down, Gareth pulled her between his legs under the overhang of the building. He settled her against his chest, his big tatted arms looped around her body. She could feel his protectiveness as he held her, his pectoral muscles making a cushion beneath his shirt. He leaned back against the building. The rain fell in little waterfalls from the gutters along the roof. His eyes scanned over the parking lot and the trees behind the diner. Guarding her.

They stayed like that for a little while as she listened to his heartbeat. Then his cell phone buzzed in his pocket. He checked it.

"Table's ready. Come on, let's go," he said, straightening up. He guided her towards the front door of the diner with his big body. Maddy felt like she was being herded along by an overprotective guard dog. As they passed through the crowded lobby, his hand settled on her waist. His body language was clear: *this is mine.*

Chapter 2

Their hostess led them to a booth at the back of the crowded room. As they sat down, a waitress zipped out of nowhere and deposited two cups of coffee on the table.

"I'll be right back to take your order!" the woman beamed before buzzing away like a honeybee.

The wood-paneled walls of the diner almost reminded Maddy of Gareth's living room. The diner had a definite "log cabin" vibe. Pictures of black bears and other wildlife common to Northern New York decorated the walls: deer, eagles, bobcats, beavers and foxes. A picture of a gray wolf hung above their booth. Her eyes lingered on it, thinking of the Grayridge pack from Friday night.

Then she redirected her attention to the menu. She was ravenous. Her eyes combed over the long list of breakfast items: French toast, pancakes, eggs and bacon, crepes, omelets, corned beef hash . . . . It all looked delicious.

She darted a little look over the menu at Gareth. He was drinking his cup of black coffee and swiping through his phone. His shoulders took up the whole booth. His menu was closed; he must already know what he wanted to order. A stainless steel watch adorned his left wrist, and his sleeves were pushed up to reveal his colorful tattoos. His long black hair was tied at the base of his neck. A few strands of dark hair fell across his forehead, which he tucked behind one ear. A shadow of stubble showed along his strong jaw. He was a day or two overdue for a shave.

Gareth glanced up and met her eyes, and she looked back down at her menu. A beat of silence passed. She tried to read the breakfast page, but she couldn't focus on the small print. She was acutely aware of his gaze. He was staring at her. She could feel the weight of his eyes through the menu's flimsy laminated paper.

"You've been quiet," he said.

Shit.

He settled back in the booth a little bit, one arm outstretched on the table. She noticed him moving a little stiffly. His shoulders must be bothering him more than he let on. His gaze passed over her again, studying her.

"So you gonna tell me what's on your mind, little girl?"

Maddy nibbled on her lower lip. Actually, there was a lot on her mind, but it could all be summed up with one word. She took a deep breath.

"Werewolves," she said, meeting his gaze.

"Yeah, I thought so." He folded his arms across his chest. "So you wanna know more about wolves?"

"I, uh," Maddy glanced around. She supposed it wasn't too weird. Nobody was paying attention to their conversation. The restaurant was packed full, and the hubbub was a dull roar. Honestly, they could be discussing a murder and no one would overhear.

She cleared her throat and spoke up. "Yes, I *do* want to know more about wolves, but I don't want to talk about the . . . . um, the lifemate thing. You keep calling me a wolf girl, but it's making me uncomfortable. *I'm not a wolf.* I've never Changed or done anything even remotely wolfish. So I think there's been a mistake."

He considered her with a thoughtful expression on his face. His eyes wandered over her hair, then down to his hoodie that she was wearing.

"Sure thing, babygirl," he murmured in his gruff, rocky voice. "We don't have to talk about that."

"Alright, because you said you inherited the gene from your parents, but neither of my parents are wolves," Maddy pointed out. "So it's not possible."

"I thought you said you didn't want to talk about it."

"I don't. But if we *were* going to talk about it, that would be my argument. Until I sprout a tail, I'm not jumping to any conclusions."

Gareth took a sip of coffee. Set the mug down. Steepled his hands. He looked like he was preparing for an important conversation.

"What about your bio dad?" Gareth asked. "You said you never met him."

Maddy hesitated. For a split second, she had forgotten Dean wasn't her bio dad. She was five years old when he met her mother, so sometimes he felt like one.

"Well, I don't know my real dad's name or anything about him, so it doesn't matter," she said quickly. "We can't assume anything."

"You never met him? Your mom never talked about him?"

"No. I think he was just a truck driver passing through, or something like that."

Gareth gave her a skeptical look, but he remained quiet. He didn't push the subject. Maddy's heart was starting to race again. The more she thought about her bio dad possibly being a werewolf, the more she started to freak out. She didn't want to have a panic attack in the middle of a crowded diner. She needed to change the subject.

"So that group at Beaumont Farms on Friday night was pretty terrifying," she pointed out. "You called them the Grayridge pack?"

"Yup."

"So they're like a gang, then?"

"Sort of. Wolf packs are more like tribes. Every pack has its own territory and its own vibe. The Grayridge pack seems pretty lowbrow so far. Feels like they're just a bunch of thugs and petty thieves. I think they're based out of Niagara Falls."

"So you don't know them personally?" she asked.

"Naw, they're new to the area. I haven't seen them around before."

"I see."

Maddy fidgeted with the long sleeve of Gareth's sweater. She felt a little weird talking about all this stuff, like they were playing a LARP game. But after what she had witnessed in the cornfield on Friday, she knew it was all very real.

She glanced around the crowded diner. She felt like she was seeing the room for the first time. How many people in the restaurant hid a similar secret? How could she be certain of anyone's real identity? Could the table of old ladies next to them secretly be a coven of witches? What about the family with four kids packed into the corner? Maybe they were bat shifters or vampires or something?

Gareth waited, his chin resting against his hands, his big tatted forearms propped up on the table.

"So like, is that it? Just werewolves?" Maddy asked. "What about fairies or ghosts, or you know, UFO's . . . like all that stuff they talk about on the Upriver Paranormal Podcast. Does Bigfoot exist?"

He looked amused. "Come on, Mads, I don't know about all that stuff. Yeah, there's probably some weird shit out there. But I only know about wolves."

"Right, yeah, duh," Maddy laughed awkwardly. "Sorry I assumed."

"Don't be sorry, baby. You're fine."

Maddy's eyes flickered over him, thinking about everything he had told her about his life. She was starting to see it all from a new perspective. He was an NCO in the Army before moving out to Black River. She wondered if he had used his werewolf powers in Iraq.

"Does the Army know about werewolves? Like, were you sent on a bunch of secret missions?"

He grinned like she had said something cute. "This ain't Hollywood, Mads. No, the Army doesn't know about wolves."

"But how is that possible? Don't you have to take a physical before you're admitted?"

"Yeah, you do, but it's not like there's a test for being a werewolf. Some people know about wolves, sure. But it's not something widely accepted as 'real.' Like psychics or gifted folk, people just aren't ready for that kind of thing."

Maddy was disappointed. "Oh."

She sat for a moment, playing with the sleeve of his sweater. Then she asked, "So your whole family are wolves?"

"Yup."

"Will I get to meet them?" That thought was intimidating as hell.

"Someday, sure."

Someday? She wondered why he sounded vague. Didn't he want her to meet his family? She reasoned that their relationship was still very new, so maybe it was too early to talk about that kind of stuff. Then an evil little voice taunted her: maybe he was embarrassed by her. Maybe he didn't want to tell his family that he was dating a teenage girl who lived in a hoarder's trailer with an alcoholic father. Ouch.

The more she thought about it, the more self-effacing she became. He was ten years older than her, almost thirty. She was way too young for him. Why would he want to introduce someone like her to his family? She had absolutely nothing to offer, not even a high school degree.

Maddy tried to shake the disturbing thoughts from her head. It wasn't important right now. *We are supposed to be talking about werewolves.*

"So, uh, do you think the Grayridge pack is going to come around again?" she asked.

"Probably."

"What if they . . . try to kidnap me again or . . . ?"

"Then heads are gonna roll, babygirl."

His confidence made her feel a little better. Maddy recalled the pack's interest in her. Another reminder of her possible werewolf inheritance. It made her uneasy.

With some hesitation, she asked the question burning on her tongue: "Why do they care so much about me? Why target me on Friday? I know they thought I was a wolf girl. But why does that matter?"

Gareth seemed reluctant to answer.

"Gareth?" she prompted.

"Females aren't common, Mads. They're mostly used for breeding."

Maddy stared at him. "Okay. So female wolves are *used* for breeding? I don't understand. Is that like slavery?"

"It's exactly what it sounds like, Mads."

A vision flashed in her head of some campy hentai cartoon, with a bunch of women all chained up in stocks, getting banged relentlessly by a herd of men. She had stumbled across those comics online while browsing webtoons. She fought the urge to giggle. Was Gareth being serious? That kind of crap couldn't possibly be real.

She met his stern gaze. She was about to make a flippant joke about living in an anime series, but it faded from her lips. Alright, so he was serious.

"You're serious? That's a real thing?" Maddy asked with wide eyes.

He nodded.

She took a moment to dump about five packs of sugar in her coffee. She liked the caffeine, but she wasn't crazy about the bitter aftertaste. She stirred her coffee, listening to the metal spoon clink against the porcelain diner mug. Shit, even her spoon sounded nervous.

"You sure you're alright?" Gareth asked.

"I'm *just fine*," she snapped. "I just found out that there's a pack of rabid werewolves trying to mate with me. That's totally normal. Just another fucking Tuesday." Then she felt bad. "Sorry. I didn't mean to sound angry."

"It's alright, Mads. I know you need some time to figure it all out."

"Figure out what?"

"The werewolf thing. The sex. All of it. You gotta adjust, I get that."

Maddy didn't expect him to be understanding. She felt a little worse.

"The werewolf thing might take a minute," she admitted, "but . . . I like having sex with you, Gareth. I don't need to 'figure that out.'"

He grinned. "Oh yeah?"

"Yeah," she blushed, "so um . . . are we going to do it again?"

"Maybe. If you think you can handle it."

She blushed. She knew what he meant. He was very large, and she was still a little sore from Friday night, even after spending a whole day in bed. She opened her mouth, then shut it. She wanted to say something sassy and confident, but the words caught in her throat.

"Of course I can handle it, duh," she finally said. "It's just sex, it's not a big deal."

"Oh yeah? You a *sex*pert now, huh?" Gareth's leg brushed against hers under the table. "If that's the case, maybe I should take you back home and fuck you until you Change."

She stared at him, her mouth falling open at his blunt language.

"W-what?" she stuttered.

"You didn't know about that, huh?" He grinned at her, all fangs. "I'm an Alpha. My seed is potent. If you're a wolf girl, it will trigger the Change."

Maddy stared at him in shock. "Wait . . . you mean . . . your *semen* can turn me into a werewolf?"

"Like I said, if you're a wolf girl, it'll trigger it. You took a lot on Friday. Maybe I should give you more."

His words caused a shiver to run from her head down to her toes.

"And . . . uh, if it doesn't work?" she asked, a little breathless.

"I think it will."

Shit, he was really considering it.

"I think you're assuming a lot," she said softly, frightened of the idea that she might be a werewolf. "We can have *a lot* more sex, but it probably won't do anything."

"I guess we'll find out," he growled.

Maddy stared at Gareth. She was aroused by his suggestion, but also conflicted. The memory of the werewolves Changing in the corn fields was something out of a horror film. It terrified her. It looked painful. They were *monsters*. Maddy couldn't imagine experiencing anything like that herself.

But in a naughty, forbidden way, the thought of being locked up and used like a slave for his pleasure made her all hot and bothered. She rubbed her thighs together, feeling a bit of heat stir between her legs.

"What about . . . you know, if I get pregnant?" she asked, her voice dropping. "We didn't use any protection on Friday night, so isn't that a big risk? I should get on birth control."

"Werewolves have breeding seasons," Gareth explained briefly. He seemed a little uncomfortable with that question. "You gotta get through the Change first, Mads. Until then, it's not something you gotta worry about."

"But I have my time-of-the-month. I can totally get pregnant."

"Not as a wolf girl, baby. Not until you Change. Trust me."

"And what if I'm *not* a wolf girl?"

He raised an eyebrow, but he didn't say anything.

It seemed like a big risk. She was a little concerned, but also intrigued. She had a lot more questions about werewolf breeding. Did wolf girls carry litters? Were they able to Change while pregnant? Did they have babies or puppies?

I can't believe I'm having this conversation.

At that moment, the waitress appeared with her notepad in hand. Maddy blushed and bit back her questions. Their conversation wasn't exactly "diner" friendly.

The waitress beamed at her. She swept back a lock of brown hair that was half-falling out of a messy clip.

"Oh boy, what a morning! I sure appreciate your patience, folks. Alright you two, what can I get you?"

"I'll have steak and eggs," Gareth said. "And chicken and waffles."

"Both plates?" the waitress said with a cheerful smile.

"Yup."

"No problem, sir. How about you, miss?"

"I'll have a Denver omelet and a side of hash browns."

"Coming right up. You two sit tight, we'll get your food out here in a minute."

The waitress took off, darting through the crowded tables. As she walked, two or three people looked up, trying to grab her attention. Maddy wondered how much the waitress made in tips. Probably a lot more than Maddy made at the hardware store. She wondered if she could get a job at the diner; maybe Gareth would let her borrow his car? She didn't have the balls to ask him; they had only been dating a week. But if she could make more money, maybe she could start saving up for her own car.

Thinking about money reminded Maddy about bills, which reminded her about the trailer. She sighed. The hot water heater was broken, she recalled, and she still hadn't received the tickets and the fines from the Davenport police department for Dean's arrest last weekend. She felt a sudden throbbing in her temples. She desperately did not want to return to real life. Ironically, discovering that her boyfriend was a werewolf didn't excuse her from her responsibilities.

Maddy took her phone out of her pocket and turned it on. She didn't get great reception in Black River, especially during a blackout, but the diner was downriver a ways, almost into Davenport, and she got a few bars of data.

Her phone started to ping as a flood of text messages arrived.

"Who's that?" Gareth asked.

"Oh," Maddy said, scrolling through her unread messages. "It's just Bea. She sent me a bunch of texts yesterday, but my phone was dead."

Gareth grunted and took a swig of coffee.

Maddy was relieved she didn't see any texts from her stepdad. During their last confrontation, she had slapped Dean across the face in the Fright Farm parking lot. She didn't feel eager to return to the trailer anytime soon, though she supposed she would have to eventually.

Instead, she opened Bea's texts. There was a lot to read through. The first batch was from Friday night:

> Hey did you get home safe?

> I'm at the diner with Vin. HE'S SO HOT.

> Black Bear Diner is packed! It's after midnight!

> Are you still with your sugardaddy? USE A CONDOM.

> Okay, stop freaking me out and text me when you get home.

> Hello???

It was strange to think of Bea sitting with Vin, Becca and Levi in this same diner only a day ago, after the haunted house at Fright Farm. She wondered if they might have sat at this very same table beneath the wolf picture. The Black Bear Diner was a popular place. It was open 24 hours, and it was close enough to Black River that the drive wasn't too taxing.

She scrolled down to the next batch of texts from Bea, likely sent on Saturday.

> Hey, did you get home last night?

> Power's out in town so you might not get this.

> I still got your backpack at my house.

> Please text me, let me know if you're okay???

Maddy felt a sense of guilt. A full day had passed; Bea probably thought she was dead. Maddy typed out a reply.

> Hey! Sorry I didn't text you back. Friday night was wild.

Phone was dead on Saturday. I just got a charge.

I'm with Gareth. We're having breakfast at BBD.

Almost immediately, Bea texted back:

YOU'RE ALIVE

OMG I THOUGHT U GOT MURDERED.

So??? Did you do it?

Maddy grinned at the texts. From murder straight to sex. Sounded like Bea.

Yeah, no more V-card!

Definitely not murdered.

I spent yesterday at Gareth's house.

Bea sent back a devil face.

Yay you sexy wonderbitch!

I want details.

Maddy hesitated, thinking about Friday night, how Gareth had chased her through the woods after revealing his wolf form. Their totally wild romp in the bushes. Maybe she wouldn't give Bea all the details. Actually, she might have to fabricate a different version of events, one that sounded like it took place on planet earth.

Or maybe she should tell Bea everything? They had seen a ghost together at Beaumont manor, and Bea believed in a lot of paranormal stuff, so maybe she believed in werewolves, too? It would be nice to have a friend to confide in. Worst case scenario, Bea might think she was playing some sort of roleplay fantasy game with her new boyfriend.

Maddy thought about it. Should she spill the tea in a text message? Naw, if she was going to talk to Bea about werewolves, it should probably be in person.

All the tea when I see you at school tomorrow.

You're seriously going to make me wait??!

Okay fine! But I want all the details when I see you. :)

Gareth glanced up at her with a questioning look.

"Bea has my backpack, so that's good news," Maddy explained.

"Any word from Dean?"

"No, nothing yet."

"Hm," Gareth grunted.

Then three plates of food landed on their table.

Maddy was impressed by the service. Considering the crowded restaurant, their food came out pretty quick. The kitchen must be working at full steam.

True to his word, Gareth devoured his two plates of food in record time. He inhaled his steak, slurped up the eggs like candy, and chomped through the chicken in two bites. Maddy had never seen a big man eat before. He was three or four inches over six feet and packed with muscle. A whole different kind of animal. He made the plates of food look small.

Then Gareth cut his waffle in half and deposited it on Maddy's plate without asking.

"I'm . . . uh, thanks," she mumbled.

"Eat up. I know you're starving," he said.

She hesitated, then she started cutting up the waffle with her fork. Fighting off werewolves and sleeping for a full day was a great way to work up an appetite. And she was reminded, suddenly, of her fainting spells this past week. She didn't want to get dizzy again.

Which has nothing to do with Changing into a werewolf, she thought stubbornly.

They continued their meal in silence, punctuated by the scrape of forks and knives. After a few minutes, Maddy heard a muffled ringtone from Gareth's pocket: a heavy-duty metal guitar riff from a tiny speaker.

Gareth reached into his jacket and withdrew his cell phone. Maddy hadn't heard his ringtone before. Was he a metalhead? With the long hair and combat boots, she probably should've guessed.

Gareth checked the caller ID, then swiped to answer the phone.

"Hey, what's up Vin?" he said, his voice a bit more gruff than Maddy was used to. He sounded all business.

Gareth listened for a moment, then said, "Slow down, say that again?"

This time, Maddy overheard Vin's faint voice over the speaker: *"Just get over here. I'm at the shop. You gotta see this."*

"Right now? I'm eating breakfast."

"Just get over here now. It's crazy. I don't even know how to explain."

"Alright. I'm downriver a ways. Give me about forty-five minutes."

Gareth hung up the phone and slid it into his jacket pocket.

"You heard that?" he asked Maddy.

She nodded.

"Vin's freaking out about something. Guess we're going by the garage after this."

"Did Vin say what was so urgent?" Maddy asked.

"Nope. But he's calling me and not the cops, so it can't be that bad."

Gareth was a mechanic who owned a garage called Jack's Auto Repair. This would be her second time going to his workplace.

Maddy was reminded of their age gap. No matter how overwhelming she found her life, she still didn't have as many responsibilities as him. She tried not to beat herself up about it. Here she was, stressed out about homework, and he had a whole business to run.

"It's probably nothing, babe," Gareth reassured her. "I gotta check the schedule for the week anyway. I expect it to be busy."

"Why do you think it will be busy this week?" Maddy asked.

"Accidents and flooding. People drive like idiots when it rains. I'm sure the tow truck will be in high demand."

"But isn't that dangerous?"

He flashed her a roguish grin. "Why, you worried about me?"

Maddy felt a little shy. "I mean, I want you to be safe."

"Nothing you gotta worry about, little girl. Just means I get to charge extra for the weather conditions."

"That's good then," Maddy agreed, even though she was still a little worried. She had lived in Black River her whole life, and she couldn't remember the last time it had rained this hard for so long. The whole mountain would be washed away before long.

The waitress came to take their plates and drop off the check. Gareth threw down his credit card before Maddy got a chance to pull out her own. The waitress picked it up and dashed off.

Maddy opened her mouth, but she didn't know what to say. She wanted to complain, but it seemed a little dumb, considering she was flat broke and he knew it.

"Thanks," she said. "I'll pay you back with my next paycheck."

"You can try."

"Seriously, Gareth, this is the 21st century, I can pay my own way."

"If it really bothers you, hook me up with your employee discount at the hardware store."

Gareth flashed her a big grin on his handsome face, and Maddy's breath caught. Damn, why was he so good-looking? He made her forget to be upset.

"It finally makes sense," she recovered, feigning amazement. "You were after my employee discount this whole time."

"I can finally buy that new table saw," Gareth agreed.

"Wait, are you serious?"

He laughed all big and loud.

The waitress brought back the receipt and Gareth signed the check. Then he got up and held out his hand to Maddy, helping her out of the booth. Together, they navigated through the diner to the front doors. He kept a hand pressed to her lower back as he guided her through the noisy restaurant.

Chapter 3

As they walked to Gareth's Camaro, Maddy was surprised when he handed her the keys.

"What's this?" she asked.

"You up for some practice?"

Maddy realized he meant for her to practice driving. It was probably a good idea. Jack's Auto Repair was a straight shot down the highway from the diner. Easy peasy, compared to her last time behind the wheel, when she drove back from Beaumont Farms on a stormy, pitch black night.

"Okay, I'll drive," she agreed, and took his keys.

Gareth's car was not very glamorous. He was rehabbing it, and it needed a lot of work. The body of the old muscle car was partially stripped. It used to be red, but it needed a new paint job. The engine sounded like the death throes of a wounded lion. He had only just replaced the missing window on the passenger's side door last week.

Gareth reminded her to adjust the seat and the mirrors when she got in the car.

As she pulled out of the parking lot onto the highway, he cautioned her, "Leave a little extra room between you and the car ahead. Roads get slick in the rain."

The storm had let up for a bit, but the sky remained moody and overcast. It took her twenty-seven minutes to reach Jack's Auto Repair, a long, flat, gray building located just off the highway, about two miles up the road from Maddy's trailer.

Her shoulders stiff and hands tight on the wheel, she pulled into the parking lot. She made sure to throw the gear into "Park" before turning off the engine. She had forgotten to do that last time.

Gareth opened the passenger door and climbed out of the low muscle car. His boots crunched on the black asphalt. Maddy watched him scent the air in a wolflike way, his head raised to the wind, before he motioned for her to follow him. Then she undid her seatbelt and climbed out of the Camaro.

Maddy was a little on edge, so she let Gareth take the lead. Despite his easy tone in the Black Bear Diner, she had noticed him becoming more and more tense as they neared the garage. As Maddy climbed out of the car, she couldn't help but notice the graffiti sprayed all over the garage doors. That was new. It looked like tagging. The threat *"Death 2 Alpha"* was written in ugly black letters across one of the doors, along with a poorly drawn caricature of a wolf skull. Before last Friday, she wouldn't have paid much attention to it. But now she knew what "Alpha" meant, and the wolf skull seemed extra ominous.

"Did the Grayridge pack do that?" she asked, pointing at the defaced garage doors.

"Yup."

Gareth didn't seem bothered by the death threat sprayed across the front of his garage, but Maddy felt a bit more concerned. It sounded like the Grayridge pack had been harassing him for a while. She felt an eerie sense of foreboding.

Maddy followed Gareth around the back of the garage. She could smell Vin's vape on the wind like a cloud of grape-scented air freshener. It smelled like he was outside. The heavy steel chain that secured the gate to the backlot was unlocked, and the gate was a little open, allowing for a single person to slip through at a time.

Gareth turned sideways to slip through the gap, and Maddy followed him. The backlot was mostly empty except for a flatbed tow truck parked off to the side. The lettering, "Jack's Auto Repair" in rustic red font was painted on the truck's door.

Clouds of vape juice billowed into the air, mingling with the moist, drizzly rain that clung to the mountainside. The storm clouds were so low, Maddy felt like she could gather them up in her arms. A line of towering pine trees abutted the back of the car lot. A flimsy chain-link fence created a boundary between the garage and the dark, misty forest. The trees looked ominous and foreboding.

Vin was standing on the far side of the lot, his back to them. He wore a gray sweater over his work coveralls with the hood flipped up, and a black beanie under the hood. Vin was a punk kid around twenty-two or twenty-three, close to Maddy's age. He had an eyebrow piercing and black plugs in his earlobes.

Maddy's eyes traveled past Vin to a strange wooden structure erected at the very back of the lot, just on the other side of the fence. It was a little difficult to see through the chain-link barrier. At first glance, it looked like a totem pole, or maybe a scarecrow. Then the wind shifted. The sickly stench of rotting meat and the metallic tang of blood struck her nose. Maddy gagged, pulling her sweater up over her face. She felt a strange, primal stirring at that smell; it reminded her of Friday night's carnage. Morbid curiosity compelled her to step forward.

Gareth placed his broad back firmly in front of her, blocking her view, as he reached Vin's side. Maddy knew he did it on purpose.

"Well, shit," Gareth muttered.

"The fuck is that, boss?" Vin asked.

"I dunno, Vin, but it doesn't look friendly."

"I think it's some sort of pagan cult sacrifice," Vin pointed out.

Gareth crossed his big arms over his chest and shifted his weight to one leg. A brief, thoughtful pause passed between the two men. Maddy watched them from behind, trying to see around the wall of sweaters and big shoulders. She was growing a little annoyed. Every time she took a step to one side, Gareth somehow shifted to block her view. He was pretty smooth about it, but she knew he was blocking her on purpose.

"You think it's those assholes who broke in last week?" Vin asked.

"Probably," Gareth grunted.

"Alright. So what's it mean, then?"

Maddy finally shoved her way past the two men to get a clear view of whatever they were staring at. She almost wished she hadn't. Her breath caught.

Through the chain-link fence, it looked like someone had erected a scarecrow at the edge of the pine trees, like a sentinel standing between the auto shop and the woodland beyond. It was the most uniquely gruesome and terrifying scarecrow Maddy had ever seen. A putrid assortment of organs and entrails were nailed to a wooden cross. A deer skull with branchlike antlers and haunting, hollow eye sockets crowned the effigy. The corpse-creature seemed to gaze at Maddy from across the fence. Strings of intestines draped its arms like a shawl. An assortment of rib cages and limbs from various slaughtered animals formed an unholy aberration of a man.

"Is that a loggerhead turtle shell?" Vin asked, creeping closer to the fence and turning his head at an angle. "Those turtles are protected. If they killed a loggerhead for some ritual sacrifice, that's messed up. Where did they get one? Loggerheads are *sea turtles*. We're a long way from the ocean." Vin bit down on his vape pen like some punk-rock Sherlock Holmes chewing on a tobacco pipe. "This is sick."

"It's *bullshit*, is what it is," Gareth growled.

Maddy identified a few gutted rabbits, a badger, several birds, and possibly a goat's hind leg before she started to feel queasy. The meat-marionette was mounted on a wooden cross like an offering to a pagan god. Two crows sat atop the cross's horizontal arms, squabbling over a length of intestine. The rest of the flock perched in the pine trees above the sculpture, eyeing the feast greedily.

It seemed like Vin had made up his mind that it was some sort of occult artwork, but Maddy wasn't so sure.

Gareth's hand landed on her shoulder, making her jump.

"Don't stare too long, Mads," he said. "You'll get nightmares."

"It's fine," she gulped. "It's just roadkill."

A grim laugh burst from his throat. It was a harsh, unexpected sound.

"Well, you're not wrong," he agreed.

"I think I see a piece of paper nailed to it," she pointed.

Gareth cocked his head to one side, squinting through the chain-link fence. Hidden amid the gore at the heart of the scarecrow was a one-gallon plastic ziplock bag. Inside the bag was a folded piece of paper.

"Trippy," Vin muttered.

Gareth stared at the scarecrow for a long moment. He seemed nonplussed. Then, with a put-upon sigh, he grabbed the fence and hauled himself up and over it. He dropped down on the other side near the treeline. He walked up to the death totem, reached into its meaty core and pulled out a bloody plastic bag. He unzipped it and slipped out a piece of white printer paper. He read it. Then he folded the page in half and tucked it into his back pocket.

"What's that? A letter?" Vin asked as Gareth climbed back over the fence.

"Don't worry about it," Gareth said. "You got a towel?"

Vin tossed Gareth a rag from the back pocket of his coveralls. Gareth started wiping off his hands with a grimace.

"Was it a threat?" Vin asked again. "Or like, a spell of some kind? A code? Maybe I can decipher it."

"Just more bullshit. Nothing you need to worry about."

Gareth's tone was flat and unfriendly. It didn't invite more questions. Vin looked like he wanted to argue, and Maddy felt a bit of tension between the two men. Gareth stared down his younger employee until Vin finally turned away. He puffed on his vape a few times, staring resolutely at the trees, as though he expected an entire army of blue-faced Vikings to materialize out of the woods.

"Just trying to help," Vin grumbled.

"If you want to help, go grab an ax."

"An ax? Why?"

"I'm gonna pay you doubletime to cut this shit down and chuck it in the woods. Let the crows have it. I don't want customers seeing it. Crazy backwoods bullshit. Some nutter's got too much time on his hands."

"Nasty," Vin grumbled, but he didn't seem surprised. He already had his phone out before Gareth finished talking. "Alright, I'll hack it down, but first I'm going to take a few pics. I want to see if any of the paranormal community can identify it. Might be a ritual offering of some kind. Or maybe there's a cult somewhere upriver."

"You're not posting pics online," Gareth growled.

"Why not?"

"It's not great for business, Vin, and I'm superstitious."

Vin looked at Gareth skeptically. Maddy felt that tension rising between the two men again. She could tell that Vin really wanted to help Gareth, and she thought his heart was in the right place. But she also understood why Gareth didn't want him to get involved. Based on Gareth's evasive behavior, the totem probably had something to do with werewolves. It looked threatening.

The young man struggled for a moment, then finally sighed. He looked a little put out, but he kept his disappointment hidden behind a cloud of vape juice. He slipped his phone away.

"Alright. Fine. I'll clean it up," Vin grumbled.

"The ax is in the tool shed," Gareth said, pointing to a metal structure leaning against the east side of the garage. Then he repeated, "*No pictures.* If I see anything about this online, you're out of a job."

"What? Serious?"

"Dead serious."

Vin gazed after his boss as Gareth strode past Maddy. He grabbed her hand as he passed by and pulled her into step with him.

Maddy gave Vin a little goodbye wave over her shoulder, but the punk kid wasn't paying attention. He was already slinking toward the shed behind the auto shop, his hands shoved in his pockets. Maddy was pretty sure he would take a pic of the totem as soon as they rounded the corner of the garage. Heck, she kind of wanted to take a pic of the monstrosity herself. But she could tell Gareth was a lot more aggravated than he was letting on.

Gareth led her back to the Camaro. He opened the passenger side door. Maddy slid inside and slammed the door shut as Gareth climbed in behind the steering wheel. They sat for a moment in the muscle car with the rain pattering on the metal roof. She found herself staring out the windshield at the threatening graffiti on the garage doors. The caricature of the wolf skull didn't seem half as funny now. She sank down into Gareth's hoodie, discreetly sniffing the cotton fabric. His smell brought a pleasant tingle to her skin. It was comforting.

Then, with another sigh, Gareth stuck his keys into the ignition and started up the vehicle. The Camaro's engine roared to life like a waking dragon. But he didn't make any move to pull onto the highway. They sat in front of the garage with the car idling loudly.

"So?" Maddy asked. "What was all that about?"

Gareth released a slow breath. "That, Mads, was an Alpha Challenge."

He reached into his back pocket and handed her the piece of paper. Maddy unfolded it. Below his bloody fingerprints, only a few lines appeared on the page: a series of numbers that looked like coordinates on a map, the number "2100," a date, and a phone number.

"What is this?" she asked.

"Date, time and location, would be my guess. Looks like an RSVP, too," Gareth said ironically. Then he took out his cell phone from his jacket. He opened up his texting app.

"What are you doing?" she asked, numb.

"Letting them know I got their message," he said.

Maddy watched him type the anonymous phone number into his phone. Then Gareth texted two letters: *OK.*

"Okay?" she demanded. "Wait, did you just agree to this? What is an Alpha Challenge?"

"It's a fight between Alphas, babe. Just what it sounds like. The Grayridge Alpha is calling me out. It was only a matter of time. I gotta say, this guy Marquis is old school. Challenges like this were sent in colonial times. The fucker's got flair. Trying to set the mood, I guess."

Maddy gulped. She let that settle for a moment. She really didn't like the idea of more violence. She had gotten a big serving on Friday night; she really didn't need to experience any more werewolf confrontations.

"So wait, does that mean you have to fight him?" Maddy asked.

"Yup. Pretty much."

About a dozen questions occurred to her at once, but Maddy didn't know what to say. She was horrified at the thought of facing the Grayridge pack again so soon.

"Your back isn't even healed yet," she pointed out.

"The date for the challenge is on the next full moon, more than two weeks out," Gareth said. "Gives me some time to prepare."

"That's still not a lot of time," Maddy grumbled.

"Yeah, well, I didn't plan for this all to go down this way, babe, but I'm not surprised. I was thinking of issuing a Challenge myself if Marquis didn't throw down first. I know this is all new for you, but it's just werewolf business. Basic stuff. That brings me to something else on my mind, Mads. I think we need to talk."

"You call that . . . that *meat popsicle* 'basic stuff?'" Maddy demanded, her jaw dropping open. She ignored the second half of his words, the bit about "needing to talk." She was too overwhelmed. "What the hell, Gareth? That's the most gruesome, barbaric thing I've ever seen! Does becoming a werewolf mean going totally *feral?*"

Gareth shrugged, his hands propped up on the steering wheel, his big arms on full display. By the glint in his eye, she got the feeling he liked that word, "feral."

"I really don't want any part in this," she groaned. "Even if I am a wolf, I'm opting out. I'll forgo the Change. I'm going to stay a normal human girl, okay? Hit me up in two weeks. Let me know how the Alpha Challenge goes."

Maddy opened the door and swung her legs out of the car. She jumped out of the low-riding Camaro and started down the side of the road at a fast walk. Her threadbare Converse sneakers were quickly drenched, and the rain soaked straight through her cotton hoodie. Maddy didn't care. She crossed the parking lot of Jack's Auto Repair, jogged past the gas station, and kept going up Highway 20, with the ancient forest on her right hand side.

She wasn't far from her trailer, only about two miles. She wasn't keen on seeing her stepdad after all the drama at Fright Farm on Friday night, but facing Dean's wrath at home seemed safer than being around Gareth. His world terrified her. She had tried to be open-minded that morning, but after seeing all those dead animals nailed to a crucifix, coupled with the graffiti on the garage doors, she was done. She would have to be blind to miss this parade of red flags. No doubt, she would be much better off running for the hills.

The Camaro's engine roared behind her, and the car's bright headlights illuminated the rain-slicked road. Much to her chagrin, Gareth began following her down the highway. He pulled up alongside her and rolled down the passenger side window.

"Get in the car, Mads. It's raining too hard. I'll give you a ride back to the trailer."

"I'll walk, thanks," she snapped.

She could barely hear herself over the rumble of the muscle car, but Gareth had werewolf hearing, and he seemed to pick up her words just fine.

"You've got more than a mile to go. You'll be soaked. You're gonna get sick."

"I don't mind. It's fine!" Maddy barked. "I've got Dayquil at home."

Gareth looked frustrated. With a low growl, he revved the engine and pulled in front of her, then parked a little ways up the road, blocking her path. He climbed out onto the shoulder of the highway and slammed the driver's side door shut behind him.

"Babe, we gotta talk."

"I don't think so," Maddy said.

Her footsteps slowed down to a halt. How did she get past him? She eyeballed the car, his broad shoulders, and the forest at the side of the road. If she walked by too close, he would probably grab her. She kind of hated that he was so big. She could duck into the trees, but he was a wolf, and he was more than capable of following her through the brush and bramble. Her only other option was to head across the street, but she wasn't going to run out into the middle of the highway in this kind of weather. Although hardly any traffic had passed on that wet Sunday afternoon, Highway 20 was a two-lane road through the mountains, and it was never pedestrian safe.

Finally, she crossed her arms and glared at him. The rain poured down, soaking through her sweater, plastering her red hair to her forehead. The downpour was the only thing cooling her temper. She felt like she was about to explode.

"I said I'm done. Just leave me alone," she snarled.

Gareth watched her carefully, as though she might turn into a wild beast at any moment. Maddy certainly felt dangerous. She was definitely prepared for a fight. Her arms itched to strike something. This was the kind of mood that always got her in trouble at school.

But Gareth didn't engage with her. He kept his distance. Within seconds, the rain soaked through his jacket and drenched his hair. His eyes glinted a vibrant hazel color against the gray forest. Wolf eyes.

"I'm sorry, Mads, but I can't leave you alone, I gotta stay with you," he said.

"Fuck that. I don't need you hovering around."

"I think you need me more than you know right now." His eyes flickered over her.

"Oh, are you talking about the Change? Well that's never going to happen. I won't let it. I'm not a wolf!" Maddy seethed. "*I just want to go home.*"

"I know this is frightening for you—"

"Don't you dare!" Maddy howled. "You have no idea how terrifying this is! You asked me earlier if I have regrets? Well maybe I have one now: I regret ever getting in this deep without knowing what you are. You're a monster!"

Gareth flinched. His face went stoic, his jaw firm. She knew she had hurt him. She felt a little guilty, but her anger was honest. How could he withhold all this important information from her for so long? It was almost like a betrayal. If his world was this dangerous, and if she was destined to be a part of it, then why hadn't he prepared her for it?

"I screwed up, Mads. I thought we would have more time," Gareth started.

"Yeah, you really fucked up," Maddy glared, cutting off his words. She really wasn't in the mood to hear any of his excuses. She was scared, and she didn't want to go through with the werewolf Change. Was it possible to turn back time? How did she go back to Thursday night? Or better yet, two weeks ago, when he was still her fantasy crush, just a hot guy who dropped by the hardware store sometimes.

Fantasies really are too good to be true, she thought.

"I don't want to be a wolf girl," she repeated.

"I know, baby."

"I won't. I'm not going to Change."

"It's not really a choice, Mads."

Gareth took a few steps toward her. Maddy felt her feet move before she could control herself. She shot into the woods, overcome by nameless fear.

"Shit," she heard Gareth curse behind her. Then he gave chase.

Maddy was usually a fast runner, but she didn't make it very far in the pouring rain. Her old sneakers didn't have any tread, and tiny streams of rainwater runoff flooded the forest, making the ground slick and loose. She ran about fifty feet before she slipped down a muddy slope, barely catching herself on a tree trunk before she tumbled face-first into a raspberry thicket.

She gripped the tree hard, panting, her fingers digging into the rough bark. Her heart pounded in her chest. Her hearing and vision seemed crystal clear, unnaturally sharp and keen. She didn't hear any footsteps, but she knew Gareth was behind her. She didn't need to look. She could sense his presence at her back.

Maddy gritted her teeth angrily. Her Alpha. Her mate. She couldn't escape him like this. Gareth was a soldier and a survivalist. She had grown up in these woods—the forest had practically raised her—but he still knew this wilderness better than her.

Finally, she turned and faced him. She pressed her back against the tree. He stood a few feet away, outlined by a row of paperbark birch trees. He watched her warily, poised in case she tried to run again. Maddy knew it was useless to try. He had chased her down on Friday night. She was pretty fast, but his werewolf strength gave him an edge.

The rain was so loud, he called to her in a shout.

"I'll be blunt, Mads. I wasn't expecting an Alpha Challenge to get dropped on my doorstep. I wanted this to go down differently. I wanted to ease you into it. Make it fun. But it looks like we don't have that choice right now. Look," he paused, gathering a breath, "I know it's not what you want, but I need you to stay at my place until this shit gets handled. It's for your own protection. I can't protect you from the Grayridge pack if you stay in the trailer."

Maddy bit her lip. She struggled with his words, battling down her fear. That morning, she had expected a somewhat normal Sunday. The biggest news was supposed to be losing her virginity. She would call up Bea, hang out, work on homework in her friend's Hot Topic themed bedroom, and gossip to her teenage heart's content.

But it seemed like the terror of Friday night was still ongoing. Gareth's conflict with the Grayridge pack had only just begun. And in some ways, it was her fault. If Gareth hadn't rescued her from those thugs outside her trailer, he never would have crossed Marquis, and the situation wouldn't have escalated quite this far.

Maddy pulled in a deep breath. She wanted to run back home to her stepdad, but she wouldn't be safe there for multiple reasons. Gareth was right. She needed his protection.

She just really, really wanted to run away.

"Fine," she barked.

Gareth's eyebrows shot up. "For real?"

"Yeah. Fine. I get it."

Then she shoved past him and started back up the hill. He watched her stalk past, a bemused expression on his dark face, before he started following her at a short distance. Maddy could feel his quizzical eyes on her back, but he didn't say a word. He obviously didn't expect her to change her mind so quickly. The only sound was the patter of raindrops on the autumn foliage. They walked upward at a steady pace.

About halfway up the hill, Maddy's torn up sneakers betrayed her again. Her foot slipped and she lost her balance. Gareth caught her arm before she fell in the mud. She snarled at him, just like a wolf, and wrenched herself free of his grip.

"Look, I'm going home with you, but that doesn't mean I'm officially moving in. I'm *not* okay with this. I'm just doing this for protection," she snapped.

"Right. Got it," he grunted.

Maddy glared at him, then glowered down at her own feet as she trudged back up the hill. She felt ridiculous. She was totally throwing a tantrum, but she couldn't bring herself to care.

Soaked and shivering, spattered with mud, Maddy emerged from the forest a few yards away from the Camaro. Still angry, she dragged open the passenger door and slid inside. She slammed the door shut behind her.

Gareth slid into the driver's seat without a word and started up the car. Maddy glanced over at him, but he kept his eyes trained on the road as they pulled onto the highway. She wondered what he was thinking. He didn't seem angry, but his silence was a little intimidating. Was he trying to avoid a fight? Maybe he was just grateful to have her back in the car. Or maybe he didn't want to scare her off again?

Maddy spoke her thoughts aloud, "I'll stay with you for a little while, just until we figure this out. I need to grab some things from the trailer before I head back to your place. I need clothes. And I want to check on Joker."

"Alright. Sounds good."

Maddy folded her arms across her chest and slouched back in the seat. She felt childish, but still moody and irritated. And now, bubbling up from the depths of her psyche, a wave of dread was rising at the thought of seeing Dean again. She still didn't know what kind of mood her stepdad might be in. She was used to him flying off the handle at the slightest trigger. She wanted to rip off the whole ordeal like a bandaid. Hopefully Dean wouldn't be home, and she wouldn't need to confront him . . . but if he *was* home, she hoped he wasn't drunk.

Her last encounter with Dean had been pretty dramatic. She had slapped him across the face in the carnival parking lot. He hadn't texted her at all that weekend. He was either pissed or on a bender. She half expected some sort of retaliation from him. Of course, he might not be home. Maybe he was down in Davenport at the casinos. But with the power outage, it was hard to say.

Without noticing, Maddy started picking nervously at her fingernails. Then Gareth's big hand covered her own, interrupting her train of thought. She glanced over at him and briefly met his gaze. It was like he could feel the anxiety building under her skin.

"Breathe, babe," he murmured. "It's gonna be fine."

Chapter 4

The Camaro popped and growled as Gareth turned down Maddy's long gravel driveway, marked by a single red mailbox next to the road. Her doublewide mobile home was set back in the woods. Black River and the surrounding area was full of mysterious gravel roads that disappeared into the emerald forest. Some led to abandoned tweaker dens. Others led to artist communes, eccentric types, or old retired couples. Then some belonged to people like Dean, who washed ashore in the backwoods of Jefferson County like trash piling on the beach.

Honestly, Maddy didn't understand how people like Dean Harvey survived in the world. But she was beginning to see things from Gareth's perspective. Dean was an addict, and she suspected every addict had a caretaker: someone willing to buy them groceries, take care of the bills, clean vomit off the toilet and a million other things. It was hard to admit to herself, but deep down, she knew Dean treated her more like a roommate or a housemaid than a daughter.

Maddy was angry at Dean, if she had to be real with herself. She hated his drinking, but on the other hand, he was the only dad she had ever known, and the only person she could really call family. Deep down inside, she still hoped her stepdad would get help for his problems someday. But she had stopped expecting him to change. At least, that's what she kept telling herself.

Maddy's doublewide mobile home looked even sadder in the downpouring rain. The roof was covered in moss, the front porch buried in dead leaves, and the paint was peeling on the front of the house. Red leaves littered the long driveway, and a big puddle spread out in front of the house like a miniature lake. The Camaro rolled through it, kicking up a spray of muddy water.

Gareth parked on the grass at the side of the property, on a slight incline, so Maddy didn't step out into the mud.

"I'm coming in with you," he said.

Maddy felt a jolt of alarm.

"No, wait," she said. If Dean was home and he saw Gareth with her, it would definitely lead to another fight. Her stepdad hated Gareth, and after the altercation at the carnival, he would get belligerent.

"I just want to check on Joker and pack a bag of clothes. I'll be in and out," Maddy said.

A stern frown settled on Gareth's face. He looked displeased. Especially after the Alpha Challenge at the garage, he was in protector mode. But Maddy didn't want more drama with her stepdad. She knew Dean was probably home. Her stepdad might be passed out on the couch, sleeping off a late night. If he was up, they might talk about what happened Friday in the parking lot, or they might not. Hard to say.

"I don't like you going in alone," Gareth said.

"I'll be fine, really," Maddy reassured him. "It'll probably make things worse if my dad sees you. You really don't need to come in. I'll be five minutes, tops."

Gareth's hands tightened on the steering wheel, but he didn't push it. Maddy was grateful. She knew Gareth was protective, but she didn't think Dean would do anything extreme.

Suddenly, Gareth leaned over and grabbed her chin. He pressed a kiss to her lips, taking Maddy off guard. She felt a storm of butterflies kick up in her stomach. The kiss was short and rough; she felt the heat of his mouth and the graze of his stubble across her cheek. Then he released her.

"Get on, then," he growled.

"Okay. I'll be right back."

Maddy unfastened her seatbelt and climbed out of the car into the rain. She gave Gareth a little wave. He raised his big hand in return. Then he settled back behind the steering wheel to wait, his elbow propped up against the door, his head against his hand, watching her through the windshield.

Maddy started walking up the side of the house, around the back of the mobile home. She always used the back door. It was a habit. Actually, pretty much anyone who knew

Dean would come around back. Often enough, he was sitting outside having a beer and a smoke, but probably not on a day like this.

The rain poured down as she started around the trailer. Her shoes squelched in the wet earth. The yard was a soupy mess of unmowed grass and sticky mud. Pineneedles clung to Maddy's high-top sneakers. A cold gust of wind blasted a flurry of rain in her face. She pulled up the hood on Gareth's big sweater.

As she approached the back of the trailer, she couldn't help but notice the sliding glass door was open—*wide* open, not cracked like Dean sometimes left it. The sight gave Maddy an eerie, empty feeling. A guest might have accidentally left the door open, but not on a day like this, when half the county was drowning under a curtain of rain. Something was wrong.

Her footsteps slowed down. She hesitated.

"Dean?" she called, uncertain.

No one answered her call, which made her even more anxious. Dean was an asshole, but he usually responded to her. She also didn't hear Joker at all. The trailer was silent.

Maddy stepped up onto the wooden deck. She walked over to the sliding glass door and poked her head inside. She sniffed a little, like she could use Gareth's special werewolf senses and discern who had been in the trailer an hour ago. But her nose, while keen, was overwhelmed by the trailer's stench: the sour hops of spilled beer, the tang of moldy trash, and musty cigarette smoke baked into the walls. She didn't see Dean in his usual spot on the couch. The power was out, so maybe he wasn't home, but it still didn't seem right.

Her gaze traveled to a spilled beer on the floor next to the couch. It still looked partially full. Not like Dean to leave a beer half-empty.

Then she saw a cushion that looked like it had been slashed open with a knife. No, not a knife, *claws*.

Her breathing hitched. Yeah, something was *very wrong*.

"Mads," a voice came from behind her.

Maddy whirled around, facing Gareth across the deck. He was drenched in rain, his black hair slicked against his face. She didn't know how long he had been standing there, gazing over her shoulder into the trailer.

"What?" she asked, her voice harsher than she intended.

"The woods stink of wolves."

Maddy gulped visibly. "Okay. Well, Dean isn't in the trailer."

"He wouldn't be. He ran into the woods."

Maddy stared at Gareth. "How can you know that?"

"I can smell him, baby. If you want, I can go look."

"No, no, I'll go . . . I have to go," Maddy said, feeling a little shell-shocked, a little jittery. A week ago, the Grayridge pack had come to her trailer to rough up Dean and get back their missing drugs. They had found Maddy instead and almost raped her if Gareth hadn't intervened. Had the Grayridge pack returned to finish their work? That seemed to be the obvious explanation. Considering the Alpha Challenge left at Gareth's garage, Maddy couldn't help but feel like it was all connected somehow. Like this was all one big retaliation for Gareth decimating the Grayridge pack on Friday night.

Shit. None of this would be happening if Dean hadn't stolen those drugs. She had no illusion over what she would find in the woods. The more she looked around the trailer, the more it became apparent that something violent and terrible had happened here just a few hours ago.

"Do you think this has to do with the Alpha Challenge?" she asked, unable to hide the tremble in her voice. Whether caused by fear or anger, she really couldn't say.

"I think the Grayridge pack has been busy in this neck of the woods, is what I think," Gareth rumbled.

Feeling a little sick, Maddy crossed the deck and jumped down into the wet, squishy yard. Then she started across the grass, her feet automatically carrying her to the hiking trail that cut through the back of her forested property.

Gareth caught her arm.

"This way," he said, pointing to a thicket of spruce trees.

"There's no trail that way," Maddy said.

"I think your stepdad was in a panic, babygirl," Gareth said. "His scent leads in that direction. My guess is, this all went down last night."

"A panic . . . ?" Maddy's voice trailed off.

By Gareth's grim demeanor, he already guessed where Dean's trail ended. But Maddy needed to see it for herself. Over the past five years, she had spent countless days and nights waiting for Dean to come home from his benders. If Dean became a missing person now, it would be one last sick joke of the universe. She would never know if he was about to walk through that door again, roaring drunk, ready to drag her back into his chaos.

She needed to know if he was dead.

Maddy walked through the wet green forest with Gareth behind her. She realized, belatedly, that he was holding a gun in one hand. She felt a little better about that. He moved quietly through the woods, his footsteps almost inaudible. She was reminded of his military training. He obviously knew how to handle himself in the woods.

She focused on the path ahead of her through the dark evergreen bramble. Now she could discern a pattern of snapped branches and crushed autumn leaves. She saw paw prints in the mud. Large ones. Too big to be coyotes or dogs. Definitely wolf tracks, though she wasn't trained to identify them. Some of the pawprints were full of rain, creating puddles along the makeshift forest trail. She picked up a bright yellow maple leaf that had been partially trampled. A bit of blood smeared the back of it. Whoever had run this way was already bleeding. She found a few skid marks where it looked like a person, probably Dean, had fallen down.

Then a pungent stench caught her nose. It was a familiar smell, but it was not welcomed.

"Oh shit," Maddy murmured.

Up ahead, the tracks in the mud led through a copse of young maple trees, then downhill to a babbling, rain-swollen brook. Moldy star-shaped leaves littered the ground. Protruding from behind one of the grayish-brown trunks, she saw the sleeve of a gray jacket she recognized.

"Maddy, you don't have to—" Gareth started to say, and tried to pull her back, but she pulled away from him before he could get a firm grip on her arm.

Maddy dashed through the maple trees, bounding over roots and rocks, her sneakers sinking in the soft ground. When she reached her stepdad's side, she knelt down by his body and touched his arm.

The body was stiff with rigor mortis. Dean's face was scrunched up in a look of terror. His head was angled to one side in an unnatural way—a broken neck. That wasn't the worst of it, unfortunately. His stomach was ripped open. The wound was gruesome, like a wild animal had torn him to shreds. His guts were pulled out onto the ground.

Maddy stumbled back when she saw the full extent of the carnage. She threw her sleeve up over her nose, gagging. The whole scene looked like a NatGeo documentary about lions on the savannah, and Dean was the unlucky gazelle.

She stumbled away from Dean and caught herself on another maple tree in the grove. Suddenly the smell, the sight, the sounds of the forest were all too intense. She found herself bent over, upchucking her breakfast all over the muddy ground.

Then she crouched close to the ground and rested her back against the maple tree's smooth trunk. Her eyes felt grainy. She struggled to pull in a breath as her heart raced in her chest. It was the quietest, most covert panic attack she had ever experienced. She leaned over, her breath heaving, her arms wrapped around her legs.

Gareth knelt down by her side.

"Hey little girl, you're alright," he said in a deep, soothing tone. He reached into his pocket. Then he offered her a little black pen.

"You brought my CBD pen?" Maddy panted.

"I keep one on me now, because you always forget yours," Gareth flashed her a grin. "Go on, stoner, smoke up."

"It's not weed . . . ."

"I know. Just teasing."

How he could act so cool, so nonchalant, with a dead body only ten feet away, amazed her. But he was a soldier. In Iraq, he must have seen death like this on a regular basis. Their lives were so different, it was a little shocking.

She took a hit off the CBD pen and blew it out. Then she muttered, "I'm sorry for . . ."

"Don't be. Come on, let's get back to the trailer."

Maddy gripped Gareth's arms and rose to her feet on shaky legs. Then she pushed away from him. Despite her better judgment, she turned back to face Dean's corpse. She stared for a long, morbid moment, entranced by the gruesome sight. Gareth started to say something, but thought better of it, and shut his mouth. He hung back as she approached Dean's body again. Maddy didn't know why she did it. She stared down at her stepdad's gray corpse in fascination. She knew she would get nightmares from this, but she didn't care. He was dead. Dean was gone.

Then her eyes caught on a folded square of white paper sticking out of his breast pocket. Somehow, despite the decimation of the corpse, the bit of paper looked clean and white. It must have been placed on the body after Dean's violent demise. Maddy felt sick again at the thought.

Feeling numb, she reached down and gingerly plucked the envelope out of Dean's jacket. It looked eerily similar to the Alpha Challenge. She unfolded it.

In blue ballpoint pen, the following message was written:

Dean Harvey's debts are paid. I'll collect yours next. Blood for blood.

~gm

A cold chill ran down her spine and she read the message over again. Gareth came to peer over her shoulder at the message.

"What does this mean?" Maddy asked. "I don't owe any debts. And who's G. M.? I'm guessing it doesn't refer to 'General Manager.'" The dark irony in her voice didn't carry over very well. She sounded bitter and afraid.

"I think the letter is for me, Mads," Gareth said, his voice solemn. "And I'm pretty sure it's referring to the debt I owe the Grayridge pack for the deaths of their men."

"So the letter is meant for you, not me? So the Grayridge pack knew you'd be here?" Maddy worried her bottom lip. "Then they know we're all related: you, me, Dean, and Friday night."

"Yup. I'm guessing Marquis put it all together. Took him long enough."

Maddy felt like she was going to have a second panic attack. She finally turned away from Dean's corpse and walked a few yards away, her sneakers squelching in the thick mud. She folded up the letter and shoved it into the pocket of her hoodie. It felt like the weekend's nightmare had only just begun. Was she ever going to find her way back out of this horror film?

"So what do we do now?" she asked, numb. She looked around the woods. "What about the Grayridge pack? What if they come back?"

"This all happened early in the morning. I don't think they're around anymore," Gareth reassured her. "Let's head back to the trailer. We gotta report him dead, Mads. I'm gonna call it in."

Maddy's eyes returned to the gutted corpse of her stepdad. It seemed wrong, somehow, to just abandon Dean's body by the tree. In the movies, someone always laid a discreet jacket or a bedsheet over the corpse, hiding the image from the camera. But this wasn't a TV show. She wasn't wearing any clothes under Gareth's hoodie except her bra, and he didn't look eager to leave his jacket behind.

Her mind flashed back to the auto garage and the death totem near the woods.

"Do you think . . ." she started to ask, then paused.

Gareth glanced down at her, waiting for her to finish her sentence. It was so gross, Maddy almost couldn't make herself say it.

"Do you think the Grayridge pack used some of his . . . ." She cleared her throat, disgusted at herself for even pondering such a thing. "You know, maybe the effigy behind the garage wasn't just animal parts."

"We don't need to think about that, Mads," Gareth said.

Maddy felt another chill go down her spine. He didn't deny it. So, maybe, yes. A few human bits might have been mixed in with all the animal carcasses nailed to the scarecrow. She almost puked all over again.

Gareth's hand landed on the back of her neck. He started walking with her through the woods, away from Dean's corpse. Maddy felt like she had entered a dream. The misty forest seemed strange and foreboding, the trees skeletal and unfamiliar. Every rustle of the wind felt like a threat. She kept close to Gareth's side, their earlier spat in the car forgotten. She didn't know what came next, but she knew that her life would never be the same.

The trek back to the trailer seemed twice as long as their initial walk through the woods. So much longer, in fact, that Maddy wondered if Gareth had taken her by a different route. But she was too shocked to care. The CBD pen took the edge off her anxiety, but she still felt like another panic attack swimming beneath the surface of her skin, ready to overwhelm her.

"The cops will probably blame another wolf attack—and they wouldn't be wrong," Gareth explained as they walked. "It's probably better this way. I don't want to complicate the situation. I'm not gonna mention Dean's stash or his business down at the casinos. Nothing you need to worry about, babe. I'll talk to them."

Maddy nodded. She felt a little grim. Dean's death was a drug related execution, but of course, the cops wouldn't know that. They would just see a body gnawed on by wild animals. No bullet wound. No blunt force trauma. Just teeth and claw marks.

It felt like it took a whole hour to walk back to the trailer, though in all likelihood it was more like twenty minutes. Gareth took out his phone when they reached her backyard. Maddy sat in the rain on the back porch, feeling despondent. She placed her head in her hands. She didn't know how she was supposed to be feeling right now. She listened to Gareth call-in the "accident" and talk to the operator over the phone. It sounded like the Black River Police were overloaded from all the weather-related emergencies, so they were sending out a few rangers in the area.

Dean was dead. The last time she had seen him alive was in the parking lot at Fright Farm. He had apologized for the drugs and for being a shitty parent. Little had she known at the time, that would be their last conversation.

Would she grieve his death?

He was her abuser. She had countless scars all over her body inflicted by his drunken hands. Her entire life revolved around his alcoholism. Protecting herself. Appeasing him. Catering to him. She often felt more like a slave than a daughter. And now, suddenly, today, it was over.

As the fog lifted a bit from her mind, she felt a flicker of relief.

Oh no. A wave of guilt and horror struck her. Dean was gutted and used as scarecrow fodder, and she was *relieved?*

I'm a fucking sociopath.

She felt the urge to vomit again, this time out of disgust at herself. Gareth might be a werewolf, but *she* was the real monster. She didn't deserve to be called a human being. While Dean was brutally murdered on Saturday night, she was sleeping peacefully in Gareth's bed, oblivious to the world. She hated herself. If they hadn't encountered the Grayridge pack at Fright Farm, then Dean might still be alive. His death was obviously a retaliation. Shit, this was her fault, too.

The guilt was overwhelming. She was having another panic attack. Her heart raced; she couldn't catch her breath. Hot, fiery pain shot up her spine. She gasped as her muscles spasmed up her back.

"*Oh shit,*" Gareth said suddenly. He hung up the phone, dashed across the yard, grabbed Maddy by the shoulders and pulled her up to her feet. "Shit, Mads, *not now,* this is a really bad time."

"What . . . what's happening . . . ." Maddy tried to say, but her words were cut off by another spasm of pain, this time down her left side. Her teeth seemed a little too big for her mouth. Why did her tongue feel different?

"Fuck, Mads, not with the cops coming!" Gareth groaned. "Alright. We gotta get you calmed down. Come with me. Let's go inside."

He pulled her into the trailer, then down the hallway into her bedroom. Maddy caught a whiff of Joker's doggy scent inside the house. Realization hit her over the head—the dog was still missing. She hadn't thought at all to check on Joker since Friday, and she hadn't looked for the dog in the woods. Fuck, she was a worthless dog owner, too. Maddy felt another stab of guilt over losing track of the pitbull puppy. Then another excruciating burst of pain traveled from her tailbone up to the base of her skull.

"Ah!" Maddy gasped. "We have to find Joker!"

"I'll look for the dog," Gareth said. "But you gotta chill out."

He pulled her into her bedroom, then he sat her down on the tiny twin mattress. He was such a big man, he barely fit inside her closet-sized room. He took a seat next to her on the bed, and the whole mattress sagged. The wooden frame creaked. Maddy thought it might break under his weight. Apparently Gareth had the same concern, because he stiffened for a moment, glancing down at the bed.

"What's going on?" Maddy asked. Another muscle spasm started in her leg. Her foot suddenly went numb. "Am I having a stroke?"

"No, babe. You're fine. Look, the cops will be here soon. Just relax here for a bit. I'll look for the dog outside," he promised.

Gareth's hand gently stroked down her cheek as he gazed into her eyes. Then he reached behind her for something on the bed. The white stuffed bear he had given her a week ago, just before their first date, was sitting on her pillow. He picked up the bear and pressed it into her arms.

"Here, this'll help. Deep breaths. Hug the bear."

"Okay, I can do that."

"Get yourself calmed down, puff on this CBD pen. I'll talk to the cops. Just chill in here, alright?"

Maddy nodded numbly. Another burst of fire shot up her spine, making her groan. She leaned forward and clutched at Gareth's shirt.

"It *hurts*," she gasped. "What is wrong with me? Is this a panic attack?"

"Sorta," Gareth grunted, "You're wolfing out."

"I'm *what?*"

Their conversation was interrupted by the sudden blast of a siren down the highway. The high-pitched wail shattered the serenity of the rainy forest. It sounded like the rangers were just up the road.

Gareth gave her hand a little squeeze, then he stood up.

"Just stay put," he repeated.

Then he slipped back through the bedroom door and shut it firmly behind him.

Maddy clutched the white bear to her chest. She flopped back on her bed and stared at the ceiling, her eyes tracing over the pattern of glow-in-the-dark stars. She remembered putting the stars up there in 6th grade with her mom. She had followed the same pattern with her eyes a million times before, but this time, it seemed different.

Shit. Dean was dead. Not down at The B Joint. Not missing on a bender. He was *dead-dead*, so now what?

How many debts did he owe? She wasn't naive. People were petty about money. Folk would come knocking on the trailer door as soon as word got out. The Grayridge pack collected their debt in the form of Dean's life, but Dean had a lot of buddies down at the casino, and someone else was bound to show up, too. She would rather not be at the trailer to greet them.

The rangers were outside taking down a report; she could see an officer in a green uniform speaking to Gareth in the backyard. She needed to calm down and pull it together if she wanted to go outside and see what the rangers had to say.

Maddy climbed to her feet, still clutching the bear, and reached for the bedroom door. As she passed by the mirror in her closet, she caught sight of her reflection, and paused. Or, more accurately, her feet became glued to the carpet. She sucked in a short breath. Her eyes were yellow, and not in the cirrhosis way. Her usual bright-blue corneas were a fascinating yellow-gold, like the wild Coreopsis that sprinkled the side of the highway at summertime. She noted a ring of dark amber around her pupil. Wolf eyes.

"Oh fuck," she said.

No wonder Gareth had asked her to stay in the trailer.

Maddy closed her eyes and pulled in another calming breath. She tried to think of something peaceful and soothing, like a full moon over a glossy lake. Or the Monarch butterflies in summertime. Or the mist over the river at dawn. Yeah. She wasn't a wolf girl, she was *human* Maddy.

When she looked back into the mirror, her eyes were blue again.

"I imagined it," she said. "See? You're fine. You're not a werewolf. That's crazy."

In the dreary light from the bedroom window, Maddy stared at her reflection again. She leaned in close to the mirror, inspecting her bright blue eyes. Then she curled back her lips to look at her teeth.

Don't be ridiculous, she told herself. *You're not a wolf.*

Her eyes weren't yellow. She didn't have fangs or a fluffy tail. She was just an average nineteen-year-old girl living in small town America. Actually, she was less than average. She was dirt poor and utterly forgettable, except for her massive wonder-tits, which attracted all sorts of obnoxious attention. She had no exceptional talents and very few hobbies. Between work and school, she really didn't have the bandwidth for anything else.

But . . . Gareth called her his lifemate.

It's impossible. There's been some sort of mistake.

If she was a wolf, wouldn't she know it by now? She had never Changed before. Watching Gareth and the Grayridge pack shift into their wolf forms was terrifying. It looked painful. She just wanted to graduate high school and move out of Black River. Where did becoming a werewolf fit in with any of that?

Forget it, Maddy thought. *There's no way.*

With a determined nod to her *perfectly normal* reflection, she opened her bedroom door and stepped out into the hallway.

She started through the trailer with a quick step. As she passed through the living room, she realized she was still carrying the stuffed bear. Ugh. How embarrassing!

She turned to toss it onto the couch, but she hesitated when she saw the big claw marks on the cushions. Maddy flinched at the sight. She instinctively clutched at the soft bear again. Maybe she preferred to hold onto it for now.

She opened the door and stepped outside.

Chapter 5

A s Maddy exited the trailer, a high, feminine laugh met her ears. It wasn't a sound she expected to hear.

She blinked. Gareth was standing in the middle of a muddy backyard with his arms folded across his big chest. Across from him, a female ranger was taking down an incident report. She looked around his same age. The ranger had a special little grin on her face and a sparkle in her eye. She looked fit and athletic. Being a ranger, she was probably out on the mountain a lot. Her skin was lightly tanned by the sun.

Maddy recognized the way the woman was leaning toward Gareth, with her weight shifted onto one hip and a small curl to her lips. She was flirting.

Gareth was hands down the hottest guy in Black River, but Maddy still wasn't used to all the attention he got from women. A sudden, irrational wave of jealousy flooded her. Her back muscles twinged. Shit. She squeezed the bear.

Calm down! she told herself.

As though sensing her jealousy—or maybe he could smell it—Gareth glanced up. He frowned when he caught sight of her hovering on the back deck.

"Feeling better?" he called.

The female ranger followed his gaze. A sweet, professional smile spread across her face. With a start, Maddy recognized the woman as a local who came through the hardware store on occasion. Cassie? Callie? She couldn't quite remember the woman's name, but

Maddy knew she was married, she had seen the female ranger with her husband around town.

Maddy's hackles went down a little bit.

Gareth explained to Ranger Cassie, "This is Madeline Donovan, Dean Harvey's daughter. She was a bit shaken up after finding her dad's body, so she went to lie down."

"Oh no! She found her father like that? Poor girl, this must be very traumatizing for her," Cassie gasped.

As the ranger's soft brown eyes flickered over Maddy, the woman's expression changed. A sad, sympathetic frown formed on her lips. Ranger Cassie obviously saw Maddy as the very image of a shell-shocked teen: a girl with messy hair and tear-stained eyes, wearing a borrowed hoodie. Maddy knew it was too late to hide the stuffed bear behind her back and try to look like an adult. Maybe Ranger Cassie's assessment wasn't far off.

"How are you feeling, sweety?" the ranger cooed. "I'm really sorry about your dad. That must have been a shock for you. We're all pretty upset. I was telling Mr. Delarosa that Dean did some handyman work on our house a few years back. He did a good job."

"It's . . . uh . . . ." Maddy mumbled, a sense of unreality settling over her.

"You found him out in the woods?" Cassie asked.

"Yeah."

The ranger jotted down a note in her report.

"Is there anyone you need us to call?" she asked sweetly. "Maybe an aunt or relative who can pick you up? I don't recommend staying in this trailer for the time being. Looks like a dangerous animal is on the loose. You're not injured, are you?"

"No, I'm fine," Maddy mumbled.

Cassie gazed at her for another long moment, like she wanted to do more to help. Then she turned back to Gareth.

"I've called an ambulance. They'll remove the body and take it to the local morgue for a coroner's report. Unfortunately, we won't be able to release Mr. Harvey's body until the investigation is complete. A few folk from Wildlife Control are also on their way to check the area for signs of large predators. This is all very unusual. We haven't found evidence of any escaped animals from nearby zoos or reserves. Our current working theory is that someone's illegal pet got loose."

"I see," Gareth grunted. "So do you still suspect a wolf?"

"We are trying not to limit ourselves to just one animal. But, *yes*, that's what we suspect, a wolf. The bite marks on the previous victims are a match for wolf teeth, and the last attack was also in this area."

Three more rangers emerged from the woods at that moment, all men. They looked solemn and a little pale. The lead ranger, a gruff man with a gray buzz cut, took off his hat and walked up to Gareth. His badge read "McCoy."

"Well, I suppose you already know it was an animal attack," Ranger McCoy said. "We found five bodies in this area just a week ago. Probably a wolf. Looking like this might turn into a real crisis. We need to catch this animal before anyone else gets hurt."

"I was just giving Mr. Delarosa the rundown on what we know so far. Wildlife Control is on their way," Cassie added. She cast a little smile in Gareth's direction, and Maddy felt another flare of jealousy.

"Is there anything else I can help you with?" Gareth asked the rangers.

"No, Mr. Delarosa, we got it from here," McCoy replied. "We'll call you with any more questions."

"Alright. You all be careful out there," Gareth said. Then to Cassie, he added, "You and your husband got a 2003 Jeep Wrangler, right? Bring it to the shop for an oil change, I'll give you a discount."

"Sure thing, Gareth. It's good seeing you again," Cassie said and shook his hand.

"Yup."

Gareth waved casually as the rangers walked away, lifting his big arm up in the air. Then he turned back to the trailer. He came to stand in front of Maddy on the deck. He gazed down at her with his hands shoved in his pockets.

"Thought I told you to chill in your room," he rumbled in a low voice.

"I wanted to help," Maddy said.

"Yeah, well, not much to do now. The rangers will handle the rest. Let's stay out of their way." Gareth nodded to the back door. "Grab your stuff. Get what you need for the week. I'm gonna look around for Joker real quick. I'll see if I can pick up her trail in the woods."

Maddy nodded, a little uncomfortable, her mind preoccupied with jealousy. She couldn't help herself. She looked over at Ranger Cassie across the yard.

"Do you know her?" she asked, cringing at her blatant insecurity.

Gareth followed her gaze, half-turning to glance over his shoulder. "Donahue? Yup. She was an airforce pilot before moving out here. I've done some work for her and her husband. Nice people. Why?"

It took a moment for Maddy to realize he was talking about their cars. Cassie must be his customer at the garage. Well, that explained how they knew each other. She felt dumb for getting so defensive over a few harmless smiles from Cassie. Maybe she was just one of those women who always came off like they were flirting.

"I don't know. Forget I asked," she grumbled.

Gareth flashed her a knowing grin. "You gettin' attached to me, little girl?"

"No, it's not that," Maddy balked, feeling embarrassed. Jeez. After their violent afternoon and all the werewolf drama, she wasn't in the mood to be playful with him. Getting attached to him could be a lot more dangerous than she first thought.

"I'm not 'attached.' I'm not clingy like that, okay? Just forget it," she glared.

"Maybe I like clingy," Gareth's grin widened.

"Well, I'm *not that*."

Then Maddy climbed to her feet and walked back inside the trailer. Gareth chuckled behind her as she walked away.

The living room was full of boxes of junk. Dean was an epic hoarder and held onto all sorts of "useful" little things, like coffee tins, garage-sale DVD's, old magazines, coupon books and Amazon boxes. Her eyes flickered from one pile of trash to the next. Really, she needed to rent a dumpster and just throw everything out. But that would happen at another time. For now, she wanted to grab her essentials for the week ahead. She had school tomorrow, and if she was going to be staying at Gareth's house, she would figure out the rest later.

Maddy ducked under the kitchen sink and grabbed two black trash bags. Then she salvaged three more cardboard boxes from the hoard in the living room. She stopped briefly in the bathroom to grab her hairbrush, bathrobe and other toiletries and toss it into one of the bags. Then, with a heavy sigh, Maddy entered her bedroom and dumped the boxes and bags onto her bed. Now to start filling them up.

She inspected her closet. It was messy and disorganized. A lot of old stuff could probably be thrown out. But she would save that task for another day. She started ripping down shirts, sweaters, bras and pants and tossing them into one of the plastic bags.

She was so caught up in her work, she didn't hear Gareth's heavy boots as he walked down the hallway. She didn't notice him at first when he leaned up against the doorway of her bedroom.

"Did you draw those?" Gareth asked.

"What do you mean?"

He pointed to a bunch of ink portraits of Monarch butterflies on the wall. Maddy followed his hand. She had drawn the illustrations a few years ago, when a big cloud of Monarchs swept through Northern New York one summer. She spent hours trying to draw their wings. She didn't know why, but the butterflies fascinated her, they were so beautiful and delicate.

She remembered Dean liked the art as well. Like everything in her life, he made it about himself.

"Got a little hobby, huh? Not just a dumb lump on your cell phone all day. Good job, using your brain. Hey, maybe you can sell it online. If you get famous, I can retire."

"Yeah, I drew those," Maddy said. "They're not very good."

"I think they're great. You should bring them."

Maddy considered the pictures on the wall. Then she unpinned them and put them in her bag. She grabbed her sketchbook from under her bed and stuck it in the bag, as well.

Gareth encouraged her, "What else do you need to pack? Homework? Laptop? Let's focus on one thing at a time."

Maddy was relieved to shut off her brain for a moment and just focus on his direction. Gareth was ten years older than her, which technically wasn't old enough to be her father, but sometimes she got that vibe from him, like she was getting now. It helped her stay focused.

Her bedroom wasn't really big enough for two people to stand side-by-side, especially someone Gareth's size, so he waited at the door. He glanced around her room, taking note of the glow-in-the-dark stars on the ceiling, her little bookcase shoved under the window, her twin bed and her closet. Her furniture was old. The carpet was stained and ripped up near the door. She had duct taped it down so it didn't catch.

He watched her pull up the carpet in the corner of the room. Underneath the fold in the carpet, a flat envelope with a wad of cash was hidden: about three-hundred dollars for emergencies. She shoved the money in the pocket of her hoodie.

Gareth raised an eyebrow, but she didn't need to explain.

Maddy tossed more items into the cardboard boxes: her laptop, bedside lamp, makeup box, favorite books and school supplies. She would sort through it all later, when her head didn't feel like a beehive. She opened her dresser and pulled out a little box of mementos from the bottom drawer. She didn't have much left of her mother, just a few pictures and birthday cards from when she was little.

She didn't remember a lot from her early childhood, but she recalled playing hide-and-seek in the backyard with her mother. Maddy would pretend she was a wolf, and her mom would chase her through the woods, trying to find her.

Maddy paused, thinking about that game. *Wolf girl.*

It was crazy. Her mom couldn't have possibly known about werewolves. She shook off the strange, unnerving memories. Then she put the shoebox full of mementos in the black trash bag. She looked around the room. Nothing else seemed important to grab. It was all old stuff that should have been donated a long time ago.

"Is that it? You ready to go?" Gareth asked.

"Yeah, that's it."

He picked up two boxes from the bed, then grabbed one of the black trash bags. She would carry the second bag and the last box. Together, they headed out to the car. Maddy followed Gareth through the trailer, then out onto the deck. She set down her trash bag for a moment and locked the back door. Then she followed him across the muddy backyard. She circled the side of the house with her trash bag in hand. It looked like Wildlife Control had just arrived. A group of five or six men and women passed her on their way to the backyard, their hats pulled low over their faces, their conversation tense. One of them held a big tranquilizer gun. Another carried a backpack full of electronic equipment. They looked like they were ready to catch bigfoot.

Maddy walked past the group, a little awkward and self-conscious.

In the driveway, Gareth was loading her boxes into the backseat of his Camaro. An ambulance was parked in front of her house. She didn't remember the ambulance arriving; there was no siren. As Maddy watched, she saw two EMP's in blue uniforms wheeling a gurney out of the woods. Her stomach sank as her eyes landed on the black body bag strapped to the gurney. Was that Dean?

"Hey," Gareth distracted her. "Help me with this box?"

Maddy knew that Gareth didn't *really* need her help, but she went to his side, anyway. She pushed the cardboard box a little farther into the backseat of the car, then shoved her bag in after it. He reached past her to rearrange her stuff to fit a little better. The Camaro's backseat wasn't very large.

"Did you find any sign of Joker?" she asked.

"I caught her scent in the woods, but I didn't find her."

"Oh no," Maddy groaned.

"Hey, babe, I think it's a good thing. Better than finding her all mauled up by a wolf, right? I gave Wildlife Control and the rangers a heads up. There's a whole team of people looking for her now. If she's out in those woods, she'll turn up."

Maddy nodded, feeling unexpectedly teary eyed. She couldn't yet summon tears for Dean, but crying over Joker seemed a lot easier.

"I don't think she'll stray far from the trailer. I put a bowl of food out on the porch just in case," Gareth added.

"Okay," Maddy murmured, the knot tightening in her stomach.

Then Gareth helped Maddy into the passenger seat. The sound of heavy rain pounding on the metal roof filled her ears. Tiny waterfalls cascaded down the windshield.

Gareth opened the driver's side door and slid into the car. He turned his key in the ignition. They rolled out of the driveway, waiving to the EMP's as they passed by the ambulance. Then they turned onto the open highway.

As though on cue, a flash of lightning split the sky. The storm redoubled its onslaught. Big heavy drops of rain spattered across the windshield. The wipers flipped back and forth at full speed.

"I never expected this to happen," Maddy mumbled as Gareth sped toward town.

She settled deeper into his hoodie. If she sank down deep enough, maybe she would disappear completely.

"Yeah, well, I got no words, Mads. It's a shitty situation. You doin' alright?"

A beat of silence stretched between them.

"Can I tell you something?" she asked.

"Sure, babe."

"I'm not sad."

Gareth reached over and took her hand, his rough thumb feathering over her knuckles.

"Actually," Maddy admitted, feeling that lump of guilt lodge in her throat, "I'm kind of relieved."

Gareth raised her hand to his lips and pressed it against his mouth, warming her cold fingers with his breath.

"Just feel whatever you feel, babe," he said.

The rain poured down. Gareth kept his grip on her hand and his eyes fastened on the road. His eyebrows were drawn low. His jaw was tight, and tension ran through his big arms and shoulders. Maddy noticed a slight tick in his cheek. Was he upset?

She tried to suppress the sense of shame rising within her. Maybe she should have kept her thoughts to herself. She must be really fucked up, admitting her lack of remorse over Dean's murder. Now Gareth knew her messed up, selfish, sociopathic thoughts. That's probably why he was silent.

Maddy focused on her reflection in the window. Her eyes glinted back at her: blue, not yellow. Had she imagined all that in the bedroom mirror? What about the fangs in her mouth? Had she imagined those, too?

Shit.

Why wasn't Gareth saying anything?

Chapter 6

Gareth's Camaro passed through the quiet streets of Black River.

Due to the power outage, the intersections were empty, the street lights were all down, and Maddy didn't see any porch lights or glowy residential windows as they drove through the silent neighborhoods. It was just after 3pm but it felt like evening. The houses were lost in the torrential rain. She didn't see anybody out and about on the sidewalks around town. Maddy felt like they were driving through an abandoned ghost town in the middle of the mountains.

Gareth pulled into his driveway at 1110 South Bickford Ave. He parked in the driveway in front of the house and turned off the car. He carried Maddy's boxes through the front door.

"Take off your shoes," he said.

She did, leaving them just inside the door so she didn't track mud onto the carpet. The house was cold and quiet without any electricity. The wind howled outside, leaking through the gap in the weatherstripping of the backdoor. It was an eerie sound. The house was full of shadows and unnervingly silent. Maddy felt like she had entered a library of sorts. She followed him through the dark living room and down the hallway.

Was she . . . moving in?

She didn't really have any other options. Maybe Bea would put her up for a while, but her mom had a full house with four other siblings living at home. Maddy supposed she could always move back into the trailer if she was desperate, but for now, it was too dangerous. The Grayridge pack had killed Dean in cold blood. She could easily become their next victim. The stark reality of her situation was beginning to dawn on her. These were dangerous monsters, werewolves, and Gareth had just accepted an Alpha Challenge.

Her gaze traveled to his wide back. She was suddenly frightened. How was Gareth supposed to put down an entire pack of enemy wolves and their Alpha? It seemed like an impossible feat. What if she found his body in the woods someday, torn to pieces? The thought left her cold. She almost stopped walking.

Oblivious to her dark thoughts, Gareth entered the small bedroom that he used for storage. He took her boxes to the closet and stacked them on top of his plastic totes. Maddy set her black bag down on the floor just inside the doorway. She looked around the ten-by-ten square foot room. It didn't have any furniture. She recalled seeing an old mattress in the bedroom a week ago, when she first visited his house, but she didn't see it anywhere now. The walls were an off-white cream color; the carpet was the same shag brown as the hallway and the living room. Compared to her bedroom back at the trailer, it was practically a master suite.

"What happened to the mattress?" she asked.

"Got rid of it. My old roommate left it behind. You wouldn't want to sleep on it. He had bad hygiene."

"Oh." Maddy was quiet again. She hadn't thought of Gareth having a roommate before. It struck her again how little she knew about him. They were barely acquainted, and yet, she was moving into his house. The whole situation felt surreal.

"Did he move out a long time ago?" Maddy asked.

"Yeah, like June."

"Why did he move out?"

"He stopped paying rent, so I had to evict him."

Gareth finished with the boxes and brushed his hands off on his jeans. He sighed and turned away from the closet. Maddy noticed how her cardboard boxes were all neatly stacked on top of his storage totes. He kept his house well-organized. She wondered if it was a military thing.

"Right," Gareth said in his gruff baritone. "So, I figure you might need a desk and a dresser, maybe a few other items. Make me a list and I'll see what I can put together. We can paint the walls, too, if you like."

It took Maddy a moment to realize what he meant.

"Wait, are you giving me this room?" she asked.

"Yup."

"I . . . uh, I can pay you rent," she said, thinking of his last roommate.

"No need, babygirl. Keep your money. Save up."

Maddy picked at one of her nails, suffering from a lowkey sense of anxiety. She didn't know what she was supposed to do in this situation, but she felt like he was treating her like a kid. She had been paying her own bills around the trailer since she was sixteen. She was used to it. It felt wrong to live in his house for free.

"Really, I can pay my own way," she insisted. "I don't want you to treat me any differently, just because of Dean . . . um, or what happened to him. I paid half the bills for the trailer. So I can pay here, too. Just let me know how much."

Gareth folded his arms across his chest and raised an eyebrow, but he didn't try to argue with her.

Maddy continued, "I don't want to take advantage of your kindness. This isn't how I imagined moving in. I really didn't expect to . . . uh . . . ." She felt a tear slip down her cheek. Shit. She didn't want to cry about this. Dean was an asshole. He didn't deserve her tears. But here she was, getting all shaky and teary-eyed for no good reason.

"He got what was coming to him," she muttered, wiping an angry hand across her eyes. "He made a stupid deal with the wrong people. It's his own dumb fault."

Still, the image of Dean's mutilated body was hard to dismiss. The tears kept coming.

Gareth frowned when her voice hitched. He crossed the distance between them. He stopped a few inches away, his big body leaning over hers, then he pulled her into a firm hug, crushing her against his chest. Maddy struggled to breathe.

"Mads," he said, his voice gruff, "Let it out. I know you're in shock."

Maddy clung to him for several minutes, angry at herself for being so weak. It wasn't a full cry, but a slow stream of tears that wouldn't stop. She took several deep, steadying breaths. She avoided his gaze; she didn't want to see the pity on his face.

When the tears slowed, he took her by the hand and pulled her into the hallway.

"Where are we going?" she sniffled.

"To light a fire, baby. The house is freezing."

With the power out and black clouds smothering the late-afternoon sky, the interior of the house was murky and cold. Gareth stepped into the laundry room, where he pulled out a handful of emergency candles and a few camping lanterns from the cupboard above the washing machine. Power outages were nothing new in Black River, and it looked like his house was well stocked.

She followed Gareth around the living room like a little shadow. He set out the LED lanterns in the kitchen, then deposited the candles around the house and lit them one by one. She didn't really know what to do with herself. She felt a little displaced. She had a bedroom but no furniture, and her clothes were all in bags. She couldn't put her things away yet, because there was nowhere to put them.

She sat cross-legged next to Gareth in front of the fireplace when he knelt down to start a fire. She watched him stack logs inside the hearth and prep the kindling. He worked quietly, his brows low and his gaze focused. She wondered if he was used to having company. He lived by himself, and he didn't seem to have any friends besides Vin. She had never really thought about it before, but in that moment, he seemed even more solitary than her.

"Am I bothering you?" she asked on impulse.

He glanced sideways at her. "No."

The kindling caught fire and the fragile flames started to spread across the logs. Gareth sat back with a sigh. His big hand landed on her foot.

"Why'd you ask me that?" he said.

"You just looked . . . I don't know," Maddy paused. "I just realized you're probably used to living alone."

"Yeah, well, I like the house better with you in it."

"Even though my life is a fucking mess." Maddy's lips curled into a self-deprecating smile. "How does it feel, having a homeless, orphaned girlfriend?"

"You're not homeless, Mads. I'd rather you be here than at that trailer, and no offense to Dean, but he wasn't much of a parent. It's a shit way to go, but maybe some good will come out of it."

Maddy fell silent. The golden light from the fire struck Gareth's eyes, making them flicker eerily, just like a wolf. He sat back on the brown carpet. He rested his hands on his knees and looked at her.

"Think of it this way. You got this festering wound. It's all big and nasty. And you gotta cut it open and let all that gunk out before it can heal. So it's gonna get messy before it gets better, you know what I mean, Mads?"

"I think so."

"Maybe this had to happen, in order for things to heal up right."

Maddy nodded, surprised to feel tears sting her eyes again. She didn't think Dean *had to die* in order for her life to improve; that was a bit over-the-top. And yet, she knew her life would be easier without him. She felt that mingled sense of guilt and relief all over again. She had known since meeting Gareth that her days at the trailer were numbered. She had been toying with the idea of moving out all week, since he first brought it up. But she hadn't planned for it to happen this way. The rug had been ripped out from under her feet.

"Have you ever been in my situation before, Gareth?" she asked.

"Sort of. Right around your age, actually, I got kicked out. I didn't have anywhere to go. That's why I went into the Army."

"I didn't know that. Was it hard?"

"Sure, at first. But then it got better, once I embraced it." He shook his head at himself, an ironic smile on his face. "But I wasn't like you, Mads. I was a dumbass kid. Out of control. Anger issues. The Army beat it out of me when my dad couldn't. I see kids like you and Vin, and I think y'all got it rough for no reason. You're better than I ever was. I wasn't a good guy back then."

Maddy considered his words. She hadn't realized that about Gareth's past. She didn't know that much about him and his family.

"So when did you become a better person?" Maddy asked.

"I don't know, baby," Gareth shrugged. "I think I just learned self-restraint."

"I don't think you were ever a 'bad guy,' Gareth."

"Yeah, well, you didn't know me back then." Gareth shrugged and flashed her a grin. "Lucky me, huh?"

Then he reached for her. Seated on the living room floor, Maddy leaned forward instinctively, allowing him to draw her into his chest. He kissed her in front of the growing fire. His lips were gentle, almost chaste. His touch, so brief and fleeting, awakened a hunger in her blood. She wanted to feel his body pressing her down.

Before things could get more heated, he broke away.

"Mads, we gotta talk about the trailer. You started to wolf out," Gareth said.

"What do you mean?"

"You started to Change. Your eyes turned yellow. I know you felt it: the *vitality*. That spark."

Ah, yes, the fire that shot up her spine. It didn't feel very good at all. Maddy leaned back on her hands, a skeptical frown on her face. "*That* was the Change? Those muscle spasms? I thought I was having a panic attack."

"Yeah, babe, that was the Change. To be honest, I noticed it starting at Fright Farm in the haunted manor. But it was subtle. I wasn't sure."

Maddy glanced at the fire, gnawing on her bottom lip in thought. Of course, she didn't want to belly up and admit that he was right, and she was a wolf girl, after all the fuss she had made that morning. But denying it was getting harder and harder. She remembered seeing her eyes turn yellow in the trailer mirror, and she had touched her pointed fangs. Still no fluffy tail, but maybe that would come next? Well, shit. If she decided to accept this new part of her identity, a lot about her life was going to change. She would no longer be "Small Town Maddy Donovan," a struggling high school student and daughter of a local bartender. No, she would become someone she didn't recognize. She wouldn't know herself at all anymore, and everything she had taken for granted would become a lie. It meant her mother wasn't just a bartender—she must have been a werewolf, too. Which meant her mother had lied about Maddy's past and her family, and maybe even Maddy's father's identity. The realization was so immense, Maddy felt a little dizzy.

"So, you've known about this all along?" she asked Gareth softly. "That I'm a wolf?"

"I'm your lifemate, Mads."

"I barely know what that means."

"I know," he said, "but just wait until you shift the first time. Then you'll understand. It was always gonna be this way."

Gareth's confidence alarmed her more than his words. Despite all of her protestations, he hadn't wavered once. Her eyes passed over him, searching for some sign of doubt, some misgiving, but his gaze remained hard and intense. He sat across from her in front of the fire, his legs casually crossed, one big arm propped up on the coffee table. The soft firelight played off his smooth tan skin, highlighting the dramatic angles of his face, making him appear younger than his twenty-nine years. Shit, yeah, twenty-*nine*. She reminded herself of his age. He wasn't some kid making a mad guess about her werewolf heritage. He was a grown ass man with life experience. He knew she was a wolf. He was waiting for her to accept it. His patience was plain as day. Shit, this was really happening.

Okay. She needed to get a handle on herself.

"Alright, so, if I'm a wolf girl, what do I need to know? Like, what happens now?"

Gareth's eyes glinted. "You done runnin'?"

"We'll see," Maddy snapped, feeling irritated by his smug expression, like he had brought her to heel. "I don't want to go through a 'Change,' but if it's inevitable, I might as well know what I'm dealing with. And I don't want to become some breeder bitch for the Grayridge pack. So tell me what I need to know."

Gareth snorted. "Alright. So this is you all raw."

"What is that supposed to mean?"

He shifted his position, turning toward her more fully. "I'm used to seeing you all timid, tiptoeing around Dean with your belly to the ground, second-guessing yourself. But now you're gettin' all puffed up. Not a caretaker anymore, huh? So is this the real you?"

Somehow, she felt annoyed by his observation. Last week, he had accused her of acting like a caretaker toward Dean, like she was codependent because of her stepfather's alcoholism, and maybe he was right. She really didn't know how all that worked. But now Dean was dead, and she had a whole lot of other crap to deal with. She couldn't even begin to fathom how she was going to adjust to this new situation. Gareth acted like he knew her so well, but they had only just started spending time together.

"I'm angry, if that's what you mean by *raw*," she glared. "I'm pretty fucking *pissed*, actually. My whole life has turned upside down since I met you. Now Dean is dead? I can't even . . . If it weren't for you, then none of this . . . ." Maddy stopped. Her brow darkened.

"If it weren't for me, *then what*, Mads?"

"I'm just saying, all this trouble started last week when we met," she pointed out. At his silence, she grew bolder. "I never would have encountered the Grayridge pack if you hadn't shown up. Maybe I still wouldn't know about the Change, either. My life would be totally normal. I didn't sign up for any of this werewolf stuff when we started dating. Like, that wasn't part of the picture. I don't take back what I said before. I wish I'd known about all this before I got involved with you. You hid it from me. That's fucked up."

Gareth grunted deep in his throat. He didn't look happy, but he took her outburst in stride.

"We met a long time ago, Mads, and the trouble with the Grayridge pack all started with Dean. They were gonna rape you at the trailer that night. It was gonna happen whether I was there or not. I'm just the lucky guy who got to rescue your fine ass."

Maddy's mouth dropped open, shocked by his bluntness. Gareth's head dipped forward. He surprised her with a brief, powerful kiss. His hand caught her jaw, and he held her mouth as his tongue slid between her parted lips. Maddy struggled to breathe. This was a different kind of kiss: dominant and possessive. His teeth sank into her lower lip. She felt her breasts tingle. The flame of desire stirred in her blood.

When Gareth broke their kiss, he kept a firm grip on her jaw. He gazed into her eyes as he spoke.

"The Change is gonna start one way or another. Keeping you safe is my job, little girl. You gonna listen to me, or you gonna be a brat about this?"

When he released her, Maddy swallowed a big gulp of air. It took her a moment to recover from their brief battle of wills. Gareth might be a dominant man, but she wasn't a pushover, either.

"You're coming off like a controlling boyfriend," she glared.

"I'm not your boyfriend, Mads. I'm your lifemate. And I'm your Alpha."

"Wait, so you're *not* my boyfriend?"

"Not the way you understand it, baby. I'm a werewolf. We do things different."

Maddy was confused and a little hurt. She really didn't know what he meant by that. She pushed away from him.

"I don't get it," she said. "I thought . . . ."

"Being your Alpha makes me responsible for you," he explained in a patient tone. "That means by wolf law, I answer for *everything* you do. If you kill someone, it falls on me. If you *get killed* during your first Change, that falls on me too. Wolf world has laws, babygirl. We got kingdoms and councils and prisons and all that shit."

Maddy's eyes widened. "I didn't realize . . . ."

"Yeah, well, there's a lot you don't know yet. But first thing's first. The Change is gonna come on hard and fast, and you're gonna get all caught up in it. A lot of werewolves kill or get killed their first time, if they don't have a pack to control them. So be a team player, yeah? Follow the rules and no one gets hurt."

Maddy sat back with an angry sigh. She thought about the Change and his warning. Her arms wrapped around her waist defensively. The thought that her body might betray her at any moment, like something wild and deadly inside of her might jump out, was terrifying. She thought of the Grayridge pack and their gruesome transformation in the corn maze. She didn't think she would ever get the harrowing vision out of her head. What would it feel like, to have her flesh rearrange itself so completely?

Her memories from that afternoon weren't very pleasant. She remembered the terrible cramping in her back and legs.

"It was . . . painful," she admitted. "Is it supposed to hurt like that?"

When he didn't answer, she felt a creeping sense of dread.

"Gareth?" she repeated, less certain.

"The first time can hurt pretty bad, sweetheart," he admitted. "It's different for everyone. It's a bit like sex. At first it's all painful and uncomfortable, then after a while, it starts to feel good. I don't know how it will be for you. But . . . you're a bit late. So it might be a little rough."

So she was a bit late? Just like everything else in her life. Maddy shrank back and pulled her knees up to her chin. How painful would it be? Like surgery? Or childbirth? What if she couldn't handle it?

Gareth searched her eyes, noticing her panicked look and her short, shallow breaths.

"Okay, you're freaking out. Hold on."

He stood up and strode into the hallway. Maddy listened to him enter the bedroom and start rummaging through one of the drawers in his dresser. She was incredibly irritated at herself. Why was she having an anxiety attack over this? She hated feeling out of control. Shit, what if all her panic attacks were related to the Change?

No, don't think like that, she fought herself.

But her panic attacks had gotten a lot more frequent since meeting Gareth. She had blamed it on the break-in at the trailer and her chronic anxiety. She had experienced some unusual and extraordinary situations this past week. But maybe it wasn't her anxiety driving the panic attacks at all. Maybe it was all the repressed werewolf vitality trying to explode out of her body.

Gareth returned with the CBD pen in hand and her white stuffed bear from Zippy's. He handed them both to her. Then he stepped away for a minute, giving her some space.

Maddy took a few puffs off the pen. It helped a bit. She was pretty sure the CBD oil contained a little bit of THC, because she felt a slight mood lift, too. She liked it. She felt more relaxed. Then she wrapped her arms around the stuffed bear and pressed it up against her chest, feeling her heart race.

Gareth hovered over the couch, his hands shoved into his pockets.

"You all chilled out now?" he asked with a half-grin.

"Yeah. Better." She sighed. Then she asked cautiously, "So . . . What rules are you talking about?"

"Every wolf has to learn them, Mads. Just basic stuff."

"Like what?"

"Like you can't tell anyone you're a wolf. Some people know about werewolves, and they're not all our friends. So keep that business to yourself."

Maddy was quiet for a moment, considering his words. It sounded reasonable. She found herself growing more curious.

"What else?" she asked.

"You may have noticed I don't have any alcohol in the house. I don't drink. It's hard to control the Change when you're drunk, Maddy. You can lose your shit and really make a mess of things."

"I've never had a beer in my life."

"Yeah, well, you're at that age, so it might come up. So that's rule number two: no alcohol. A sip or two might be fine. But don't get drunk. Changing in the middle of a bar or at a party can cause a lot of problems."

"Well, that makes sense," Maddy said. "Alright, no drinking."

Gareth carried on, "Last rule: *no fighting*. The Change is more likely to kick in when your fight-or-flight gets triggered, so keep it lowkey."

Maddy's thoughts immediately flew to Kaylee Mackovich and the Varsity jackets. What if another confrontation happened? Those girls were always harassing her.

Gareth seemed to anticipate her question.

"If those girls try to fight you again, I want you to run," he said. "Better a coward than an accidental murderer, yeah?"

Maddy felt a little offended. "I'm not some monster like the Grayridge pack. I'm not going to go crazy and start hurting people just because I'm a werewolf. *I'm not like that.*"

"Unfortunately, Mads, you're not the first young shifter to say that. Trust me. That's the wolf talking. The wolf's gonna tell you all sorts of things. You're gonna feel invincible, but you're gonna have to learn your limitations."

Maddy kept quiet, considering everything he had said. He really lived in a whole other world. She felt like she had traveled to another country and now she had to learn the customs.

"Okay, I can keep it lowkey and follow the rules," she agreed. "I've been trying to stay out of fights this year, anyway. I really want to graduate."

"I want you to graduate, too," Gareth murmured, but something about his tone of voice caught her attention. He seemed doubtful.

"What's wrong?" she asked.

"Look, Mads, I'm not gonna lie, a lot of werewolves drop outta high school and complete their GED later. My younger brother Antony was homeschooled for a semester during his Change. It's kind of a big risk, leaving you in school while all this is happening. It might be better if you dropped out."

Maddy bit her lip. She found his words a little triggering. Since last summer, Dean had been nagging her to drop out of school and get a job down at the Sapphire Club as a stripper. Kaylee Mackovich had already spread a rumor around the school that Maddy worked at the strip club. Dropping out felt like admitting defeat. She wanted to walk across the stage and receive her diploma with her robes on. It was a point of pride.

"I think I'll be fine if I stay in school," she insisted. "I tend to avoid people, anyway. I'll be extra careful."

Gareth still looked grim, his dark eyebrows drawn into a stern frown.

"You can't force me to quit school," she said. "That's psycho."

"I don't care if it's 'psycho,' Mads. My job is to protect you. If I was doing this right, I'd lock you up in my bedroom until you wolfed out, let you get all wild and crazy, then teach you how to control it. I'm still considering it."

"Fuck that! I'd call the cops."

"Yeah, well, we'll see how it all shakes down."

Maddy searched his eyes. Shit, he was serious, he would really do it. She felt her heart quicken in her chest as the enormity of their conversation sank in.

I'm not a wolf, she argued with herself.

Yeah, you are, her conscience echoed back.

Shit, I'm not like the Grayridge pack. I'm not like that!

"So you understand the rules?" Gareth asked. "You got questions?"

Maddy opened her mouth, then shut it. What was she supposed to say? It wasn't rocket science. She just didn't like all these sudden restrictions. Becoming a werewolf sounded like a pain in the ass. She felt an invisible collar tightening around her neck.

"So I'm basically your prisoner until I can control the Change," she said, her voice tinged with bitterness. "What happens if I break the rules and do my own thing?"

"There'll be consequences, Mads."

"So I'm supposed to sit around your house and wait until I wolf out?" she asked, an angry bite to her voice.

"Yup. If you like, I can help it along."

Chapter 7

Maddy saw the heat in Gareth's eyes. She knew what his words insinuated. For some reason, it scared her. He was part of a violent world that she didn't understand, and she was under his roof, in his power. He wanted her to wait around until she Changed, but how could she trust him, after everything she had witnessed that weekend?

Maddy leapt up to her feet without thinking. She must have taken Gareth off guard, because he didn't react immediately. She lunged across the living room, heading for the front door. She didn't know where she was going, but she needed to leave the house. She craved the shelter of the woods.

He was faster than her. He overtook her in two bounds and slammed the door shut as she started to open it.

"Where you think you're gonna run off to, little wolf girl?"

Maddy trembled, her back pressed to the door as his big body leaned over her. His scent filled her nose, potent and masculine. Delicious heat flared between them. She grew unexpectedly shy when she met his gaze; she couldn't hide her physical reaction to him. His eyes dilated as he gazed down at her. Then his hand found her neck. His thumb feathered along her jaw.

"You really wanna go?" he asked in a dark voice.

She nodded, her heart quickening in her chest.

His lips hovered close to hers, so close she thought he might dip his head down and kiss her. But after standing over her for a moment, he turned the door knob. He moved out of her way and opened the door.

"Go, then," he growled.

She gazed up at him with wide eyes. "Wait, really?"

"Yeah. If you wanna leave so bad, then go. Figure yourself out. Do what you gotta do, babygirl."

Maddy glared up at his patronizing tone. Why did he always act like he was in control? She didn't need his permission to leave; she was going to head out, anyway. With a huff of anger, she broke away from him, ducked under his big arm, and slipped through the doorway into the dark, rainy night. The cool evening air bit through her sweater.

Gareth shut the door behind her.

Maddy stood for a moment out on the porch, listening to the pounding rain. It soothed her nerves. She sucked in a deep breath. Then she pulled her hood up and stepped off the front porch. At first her steps were quick and agitated as she walked down the driveway to the sidewalk. The downpouring rain drenched through her sweater after only a few minutes. She made it to the edge of Gareth's property before she came to a stop. She stood on the sidewalk, hovering between his fence and the neighbor's lot. The dark night spread around her like a vast and silent ocean. She wondered where she was going. Her mind was in the forest, but the woods were far away. With the Grayridge pack stalking around her trailer, her usual refuge was no longer safe.

She hung her head, and her hands curled into little stubborn fists. She wanted to run, but where could she go? The only person she could think of was Bea, but her little Goth friend didn't know anything about werewolves, and Gareth's "rules" were pretty clear. Could Bea really help her against a vicious wolf pack? No, of course not.

Maddy fought with herself. She might be scared, but she didn't want to be alone right now, and she didn't really want to push Gareth away. His world frightened her, but in truth, she couldn't imagine her life without him. She wanted to be with him, in his house, in his arms. The situation was terrifying, but he was the only person who could protect her. And here she was, storming off like a child having a tantrum.

Maddy groaned. Ugh. Why did her temper always have to get the best of her?

"I'm such an idiot," she grumbled at herself.

With another harsh sigh, she turned around and stomped back up Gareth's driveway. Her cheeks heated with embarrassment. She reached the front porch. It took a lot of guts to drag her feet up the doorstep. She supposed she could have opened the door and let herself in, but it still didn't feel like her house. She hesitated, then she knocked.

The door opened almost immediately, and Gareth's bulky shadow leaned up against the frame, silhouetted by the flickering fire in the living room. He crossed his arms.

"Alright," he said. "Then it's decided."

"What's decided?"

"You're a brat," he murmured, a dark grin in his ironic voice.

Maddy rolled her eyes. "Alright, so maybe I overreacted. Are you going to let me in?"

"Sure, babygirl, on one condition."

"What's that?"

"You let me hold you."

His words shook her. Maddy felt her throat close unexpectedly. She wasn't used to people taking care of her. Actually, she expected him to be angry, subconsciously bracing herself for a Dean-like explosion. But Gareth remained calm. He reached out and took her hands, drawing her into the house, then he shut the door behind them and locked it against the night. He pulled her into his chest, wrapping her up in his strong embrace. He had thick, calloused hands, used to working on cars and handling guns, but he cradled her head gently.

"I'm sorry I ran off like that," Maddy mumbled into his broad chest. Silent tears stained her cheeks. "It's just . . . *a lot*."

"I know."

He leaned down and captured her lips with his own. She leaned into him, desperately seeking his warmth and the comfort of his touch. He left a trail of little bites across her cheek, then teased her earlobe with his lips. She drew in a shaky breath as her face grew flushed. Was it wrong that she craved this? She was still angry at him and the whole situation. She still had her misgivings about moving in so fast. But she wanted the comfort of his body, and he seemed to understand that instinctively. His hand trailed down her back, resting upon her hip, over the mass of scar tissue on her lower back. It's like he had memorized the location even through her clothes.

"I know you don't understand how this works," he growled against her ear, sending a delicious shiver down her neck. "But I'm your Alpha, sweetheart. You're the little one, I'm the big one, so I'll keep you safe. I'll teach you how to be a wolf."

"You're not my keeper, Gareth," she murmured.

"I am now, babygirl. Who else are you gonna run to?"

Then he slipped his hand beneath the band of her sweatpants. His calloused thumb pressed against her panties, skillfully finding her clit, drawing a little gasp from between her lips. He rubbed her in slow circles through her panties. Maddy felt her hips rock forward against his hand as he tortured her with slow, sweet circles of his thumb.

"Mm," he grunted. "So the brat likes a good petting."

"I'm not a . . . a brat," she panted.

"*You are.*" He grinned, watching her meltdown in his hands. "Just means we're gonna have a lot of fun."

Another gasp of pleasure escaped her lips. He grinned wickedly, watching her with burning eyes. "I know you're used to doing things on your own," he growled, "but you got me now. I was meant to find you on that mountain, and I'm gonna take care of you. Let me help you turn into a wolf. I'll give you my vitality. It's what I've been doing all along."

Maddy nodded, gazing up at him, leaning into his touch, her knees weakening as he stroked her. She gripped his biceps as her legs trembled. Then she sighed when he removed his hand from her pants. He brushed his lips across her forehead, almost fatherly, then he pulled her deeper into the living room. There, he settled her onto the cushions of the soft leather couch.

Silhouetted by golden firelight, Gareth pulled off his shirt, revealing his chiseled physique. Maddy's mouth went dry. His tan skin glowed, and the flickering flames danced off his tattoos. The grinning skull of Dia de los Muertos looked like it was moving. A massive scorpion crawled down his right arm, its stinger wrapped around his muscular shoulder. He untied his hair and shook out his long, black mane. Then Gareth gazed down at her on the leather couch. A devilish grin curved on his lips. He stood directly before her.

"Go on," he murmured, his throat thick with lust. "Touch me like you want to."

Maddy hesitated, frozen, unsure of what to do. She suddenly felt very much like an inexperienced virgin. Touch him? How? What if she messed up? Ugh, why did she have to feel so awkward at a time like this?

Then Gareth took her hands and placed them on his well-defined abdomen.

Maddy almost panicked. Her cheeks flushed with giddy embarrassment. Although he had touched her many times before, she had never done anything like this to him, face-to-face, in his living room.

"Where's all that attitude, little brat?" he murmured down at her with a cocked eyebrow.

Maddy knew he meant to tease her, but she couldn't hide her shyness. She had lost her virginity to him only two days ago, and she knew hardly anything about sex. Her cheeks heated, turning bright pink. She cast her eyes down, self-conscious beneath his gaze. She thought, maybe, that he liked seeing her so vulnerable. She found his naked body intimidating as hell. The sight of all that manly muscle made her stupid flustered.

After a little hesitation, she ran her hands over his broad chest, her heart fluttering erratically as she pressed her fingers against the sturdy cushion of his pectoral muscles.

Her embarrassment slowly faded as her fascination with his body grew. He was built nothing like the boys she went to school with. His physique was so masculine, he was like a whole other species. She grew a little bolder. Her hands traveled down his lean torso to the dusting of hair beneath his bellybutton. Her hands wandered down and down. His skin was a little rough to the touch and very warm. Feeling brave, she leaned forward and pressed a kiss to the flat plain of his lower abdomen. His muscles tightened and he sucked in a quick breath. Hearing his reaction was strangely erotic. She felt a little burst of confidence. A little zing of power.

She started to unbuckle his belt. He watched her with lustful eyes. After a minute, he took over, gently pushing her nervous hands aside. He unfastened the length of leather and slid his jeans down his hips. He wore a pair of loose, black boxers underneath his pants. As he stepped clear of his jeans, Maddy found her eyes fixed on the bulge of his erection and the outline of his massive, heavy balls, visible even through the loose fabric. She gulped. His cock was obscenely large. More intimidating than its length was its meaty thickness. She almost moaned as her blood heated. She didn't know how she had taken him on Friday night, and she didn't know if she could do it again, but she was more than willing to try.

Gareth seemed to sense her uncertainty. He sat down next to her on the couch and pulled her legs onto his lap, her feet brushing against his massive erection. Then he leaned over and kissed her. His hand sank into her wet hair, cradling the back of her head. His hot mouth quickly became the focus of her small world. His tongue slid between her lips, exploring her cheeks, running over her teeth, then pressing deep down her throat, utterly dominating. Maddy lost sight of the room, completely absorbed by his wicked mouth.

Then his hands hooked the bottom of her sweater. He drew it up over her head, exposing her breasts and her padded sports bra. Maddy wished she had sexy lingerie to wear, something feminine and silky to impress him. He didn't seem to care. As the cold air struck her smooth torso, he gently ran his hand down her ribs, then over her bare stomach, leaving a trail of fire in his wake. She felt her nipples swell pleasantly. He reached around and undid the clasps on her bra with dexterous fingers. Her breasts sprang free as the flimsy bit of clothing slipped to the ground.

Maddy watched Gareth's expression as he gazed down at her tits. His jaw twitched. Hunger flickered in his gaze. He took one of her breasts into his mouth and sucked on it, drawing a gasp of pleasure from her lips. He groaned in response. After spending several minutes lavishing attention on her large breasts, he slid further down her body on the couch. With a shrug, he boosted her knees up on his shoulders, giving him full access to the apex of her thighs. His hands cupped her ass, then he leaned forward and pressed a gentle bite against her lower lips. She shivered. She felt the brush of his sandpaper stubble against her sensitive skin. He kissed her cunt several times through her panties, his lips feathering over her most intimate parts, making her wet. Then his hands hooked the edge of her underwear, and he pulled her panties down her legs. A minute later, his hot tongue dipped between her folds to taste her.

Maddy gasped wantonly. Her back arched and she almost sat up. Gareth groaned deep in his throat.

"You taste like candy," he murmured. "Fuck."

His finger slipped inside, opening her tight flesh. He slid his long middle finger in and out, in and out. When he pushed two fingers up inside of her, she moaned.

"Easy, sweetheart . . . ."

Maddy's fists clenched, her back pressed to the couch, her legs spread across his shoulders, her eyes closed, overwhelmed by the sensation. His fingers curled forward, touching that sweet bundle of nerves behind her bellybutton that gave her so much pleasure. *Lifemate.* Her Alpha. Fuck, she could feel his hunger. His strong hand controlled her body, his thick arm flexed between her legs. She gazed down drunkenly at his tattoos, at the glint in his eye as he pleasured her.

She was utterly at his mercy.

Outside, the wind howled past the chimney, and rain pounded against the windows. The fire cast mysterious shadows throughout the room. She stared upward, watching strange shapes and half-faces form in the dancing light across the ceiling. How had she come to be here, on a night like this? How many times had he found her out on the mountain during such a storm? She remembered when she first met him. He had appeared through the woods on a dark night, a homeless hitchhiker backpacking through the mountains, his hair tangled, his face obscured by a month's worth of unshaven scruff. After that, for the longest time, she had thought he lived in the woods, where she always encountered him.

She shuddered as his long tongue penetrated her, as his lips suckled her clit. She whimpered and gasped. She thought, maybe, his teeth seemed sharper than they were before, his tongue longer than it should be. She bit her wrist, choking back a sweet little mewl of pleasure as she neared her peak. Now, the tables were turned. She was the homeless one. She was trapped in his den. She had nowhere else to go. She was under his roof and under him, too. She couldn't return to her trailer, couldn't afford her own place, couldn't pay him rent. She was a lost girl, a stray he had collared up on the mountain, and now he could do whatever he wanted to her.

Maddy gasped and arched off the couch with a little cry. She gushed into his mouth, feeling a flutter behind her bellybutton as he made her come with his devilish tongue.

Fuck, she was homeless under his power and he was going to eat her up like this every night.

He lapped her up like a starving wolf, his long tongue sliding up and down as she undulated against him. After she came, he held her hips steady and kept licking and biting her sensitive parts, driving her insane. Maddy started to sob. She wiggled against his mouth, chasing another release, then—*"Ah!"* He brought her into a third peak. Maddy arced off the couch with another moan, riding so high on the wave that she left her body for a few seconds. Fuck, how was he this good?

Then she collapsed back on the couch.

Gareth raised his head to look up at her. He stretched out his jaw. Then he licked his lips. His mouth was glistening and sloppy with her juices. His eyes blazed bright yellow. His incisors seemed a little too long, more like fangs than regular teeth. His wolf was showing.

She probably should have been afraid, but he was a handsome monster, and she felt so warm and wonderfully satiated, she couldn't make herself care. Maddy gazed down at him between her legs. She felt docile, her limbs like butter.

"Are you ..." she mumbled, a little fearful at what he might do next. "Are we ...." Her eyes flickered down to the thick bulge in his pants.

"I'm gonna make you come until you faint."

"W-hat?"

Then he shifted positions. His massive shoulders spread her legs open wide again. He pushed his fingers deep inside and curled around her G-spot. He leaned forward, giving his strong arms more leverage.

A deeper moan of pleasure escaped her throat as he massaged inside her body, rubbing her thoroughly with strong hands. Maddy bucked her hips, losing control. She felt that flutter start again. Then a tremble. She found herself arching off the couch, her hands gripping his broad shoulders as her muscles clenched down on his penetrating fingers. She climaxed, her legs wrapping around his neck, her hips thrusting against him. Then he pressed his mouth to her clit again.

Her orgasms came closer together. Sometimes they were soft and sweet, sometimes deep and gut-wrenching. He tortured her until she was barely aware of the room, until the couch was covered in sweat, until her body felt like a sponge cake. The vision of him from that first night they met kept returning to her mind. His bearded face. His wild hair. The smell of pine and wet earth. She hadn't known it then, but he had already claimed her as his own, leaving his mark the moment he lifted her off the ground and settled her against his broad chest.

Maybe an hour later, when she was close to unconscious, he sat back with a deep groan and licked his fingers like he'd just eaten three plates at a buffet. Maddy felt like she was floating on a cloud above her body. As the minutes stretched, she slowly returned to herself. Her cunt was vibrating. She could feel her pulse in her clit and her lower lips. The fluid on the couch was a lot more than just sweat. Gareth didn't seem to care; he laughed deep in his throat whenever she started gushing uncontrollably, like it was all some sick game to make her lose control.

Then Gareth slid off the couch.

She slitted open her eyes, glancing around the shadowy living room. Her gaze landed on his broad shoulders, outlined by golden light as he knelt in front of the fireplace and threw another log on the fire. Unable to form a coherent thought, she drank in his physique, the slope of his mountainous shoulders tapering down to a lean waist.

He turned slightly, catching her sultry gaze.

"You dead yet?" he asked.

Maddy couldn't speak. She moaned a little.

"Not quite? Alright."

Fuck, was he *not* done? She couldn't endure any more orgasms. She tried to crawl away across the couch, but she couldn't. She barely rolled over and almost fell on the floor. She felt the cushions dip next to her. Gareth's big arms wrapped around her waist, scooping her into his lap.

"Where you think you goin'?" he laughed. "Come here, little wolf girl, I'm not done with you yet."

Maddy could barely follow what he was saying, she felt drugged. She tried to slide down from his lap, but he easily restrained her with one hand wrapped around her wrist.

"You're so cute," he murmured, gazing down at her with lustful golden eyes, his black hair draped over his shoulder in a long, dark curtain. She gazed at him deliriously in his lap, her lips gently parted.

"Is this . . . my rent?" she mumbled.

"Rent?" his voice caught, then he laughed. "Sure, yeah, call it that. Pay up, baby."

With his big arms, he maneuvered her so that she was sitting astride his hips, facing him on the couch, his cock pressed between her legs. Her eyes widened slightly when she realized his intention. Was he going to fuck her like this? Holding her in his lap? It was a new angle for her. She was wet and aching for him, but she wasn't very experienced, and his size intimidated her. Her legs quivered as his member slid back and forth against her lower lips. He teased her with his head, rubbing himself in her juices, boldly pushing against her entrance. She was soaked. Maddy squirmed, a little uncomfortable, her muscles unused to his angle of penetration. Even adequately prepared, she was still narrow.

"Gareth! *Ah! It's too big!*"

"You're doing good, just relax, I'll help you," he murmured, kissing her sweaty temple. "It's gonna be like this the first few times, until you get used to me."

He lifted her up a little higher on her knees. Then he pressed his cock deeper between her legs with a guttural groan. The head of his cock wedged snuggly into her tight canal. He pressed his hips upward as he guided her down along his shaft. With just the first few inches inside, she felt filled to the brim. She flexed her hips and whimpered a little as he sank in another half-inch. Fuck, she was so full.

"I'm gonna come," he groaned. Then, with little other warning, he spilled into her tight core.

It surprised her. Maddy gasped, feeling his thick seed spurt into her tight flesh. The head of his cock twitched as he emptied into her. His seed filled her up like warm honey, up and up, until a trickle spilled down her inner thigh. A flush of warmth traveled up her body, beginning at the place of their joining, then creeping up through her bellybutton, her breasts, her arms and legs.

Maddy remembered something he had told her on Friday night: *Werewolf cum is an aphrodisiac.*

Maybe it was true. It seemed to have a drug-like effect on her body. Her nipples swelled and tightened. The tension inside of her loosened, replaced by a soothing warmth. His member softened a little bit, but remained semi-erect, allowing her to sink down further onto his cock after his orgasm. He gripped her hips and held her for a moment as he caught his breath. He kept her pressed flush against him, his cock tucked deep inside her canal. She could feel his swollen balls twitch against her ass cheeks every time he shot into her.

"Are you finished?" she asked, confused.

"I'm just getting started, baby."

His cock swelled up again, growing rigid inside of her body. Her eyes widened helplessly as his full length and width stretched her. It was a whole different sensation. Their bodies fit snugly together like a lock and key.

He grinned, watching her expression. He pushed a lock of hair back from her face. His finger and thumb pinched her chin, and he pulled her face close to his, placing a chaste kiss to her lips as his cock swelled up to its full size, buried inside her tight virgin flesh. Maddy's eyes widened. He was so deep, she felt his head behind her bellybutton, tickling where she didn't expect to feel pleasure. She shifted her hips a little, staring helplessly into his eyes, barely able to move.

"Look at you," he murmured, "taking all of this big cock. It's a lot for you, hm?"

She couldn't answer. Her lips parted in a silent gasp of pleasure.

He dipped his head to kiss her, his voice low and crooning. "Yeah, I'm deep in there, little girl. You're alright. Just feel me, baby. I feel you, too."

His arms looped around her hips, pulling her snug against him. Then he began to rock into her, moving her hips with his big hands, teaching her how to ride him. At first, all Maddy could do was gasp with each stroke of his cock. She wiggled a little, scared it would hurt, but all she felt was pleasure. Tentatively, she started to match his rhythm. He released her waist and gripped her hands as she went up onto her knees. Then she started sliding up and down his length. Her breath came in short, hoarse gasps. It felt really good, and she was in total control. She could sit down as far as she wanted, taking him deep, squeezing her muscles, then releasing him as she slid back up.

She was so absorbed in their dance, she didn't notice him gazing at her, his eyes full of smoky heat, a satisfied smirk on his face as he watched her take her pleasure.

Unexpectedly, she felt tears in her eyes. Big wet tears began sliding down her cheeks. A sob escaped her throat. More than just a few stiff muscles were being released. As her orgasm neared, finally breaking over her body in a wave of bliss, Maddy found herself overcome by tears. She gripped Gareth's shoulders and ground her hips, taking his cock deep inside, as racking sobs escaped her throat. Fuck, she was balling.

Gareth watched her cry with dark, amber-gold eyes. His eyebrows grew stern. He raised a hand and stroked her wet cheek.

"Does it hurt?" he murmured. "We can stop if it hurts."

"No . . . no, it doesn't hurt. It's not that."

Maddy felt another sob working its way up her throat. She didn't understand why, but with his cock buried so deep between her legs, forcing her physically open, she felt something deeper opening as well. It felt like years of pent up fear and grief were suddenly being released from her body. The deep emotions started in her hips and rolled upward, spilling out of her in big wet tears.

"Fuck," Maddy murmured as she sobbed. Fuck Dean. Fuck the trailer. Fuck that awful prison. She was finally free. Free of the terrible weight she'd been living under for so many years. Free of the monster who had terrorized her childhood. Her tears were deep and cleansing, a waterfall of suppressed grief finally being unleashed.

"*Gareth*," she sobbed.

"I'm here, baby."

"Gareth—*daddy, ah!*—please don't let me go," she cried out. She kept grinding her hips, feeling another orgasm building inside. She started to come on him, grinding back and forth, gripping his hands, their bodies locked together against the couch.

"I won't let go, baby," he murmured, kissing her chin, her jaw, her neck. "You're mine. You're safe now."

"*Ah . . .*" she moaned as her body clenched around him. "*Please . . . .*"

"Good girl," he murmured, licking the sweat from her temple. "*I got you. Just let go.*"

He watched her mindlessly melt against him, riding a wave of pleasure. Through tear-stained eyes, she gazed at the gaunt angles of his face, outlined by golden firelight.

"You're under me now, babygirl," he growled low in his throat. "So just stay under me, yeah? I'll take good care of you."

Then Gareth shifted down slightly on the couch, pulling her forward against his chest. His hands gripped her ass and he began thrusting, filling her with the full length of his thick cock. She gasped as he took control, sobbing at the delicious pull of flesh every time he pushed in, stretching her wide. She bit into his shoulder, her hands clawing into his biceps as he bounced her up and down. His cock slid against her G-spot, tickling her deep inside. She couldn't stop coming; she had never felt anything like it before. She moaned and gushed all over the couch, over and over, losing control of her body. She could hear the squishy wet sounds of him sliding in and out.

"I like you like this," he murmured. "*Just a wet, hot mess.*"

Her whole body spasmed as she clutched at him. A tidal wave of pleasure rolled through her. She felt herself dissolving into him as he thrust into her.

"Gareth . . . ah, Gareth!" she moaned. She was drowning. "*Ah . . . please . . . .*"

"*That's my little brat,*" he murmured when he saw her expression go wide and glassy. He put his face next to hers, his hot tongue licking the sweat from her cheek. "*I'm gonna fill up your sweet little womb.*"

His cock began to swell up. Maddy's lower lips fluttered and twitched. She wanted his cum inside. She craved it.

With a deep groan and a shudder, he climaxed into her body, filling her a second time with his seed. Maddy shuddered when she felt him spurt into her, warm and thick, his cock pulsing inside her tight canal, dumping his generous load into her little womb. His balls twitched against her ass with each eruption. She moaned as her muscles gripped him, milking him with gentle thrusts of her hips. She stared at his face, entranced by his intense focus, his stern expression. She pressed a kiss to his cheek as he unloaded. He grunted, meeting her eyes. Was he surprised by her little kiss?

He came a lot. Gareth held himself inside of her, rigid for several minutes as he finished. Maddy rested against his chest, lost in the sensation, so full she thought she would burst. That's when she felt the knot. She hadn't noticed it the first time they made love, when she lost her virginity back in the forest. A hard, round bulge of flesh wedged against her wet lips, throbbing at the base of his cock, far too large to fit into her virgin canal. It felt good to grind against it, about the size of both her fists pressed together, or a large grapefruit.

She didn't know if it was a normal part of male anatomy. He was her first, and he wasn't human.

His big hands traveled down to where their bodies were locked together, his calloused fingers rubbing her slick lips as his cum dripped around the base of his cock.

"What . . . what is that?" she asked, barely able to speak.

He didn't answer her; his jaw was clenched tight. His back was tense and his face was drawn into a passionate scowl. He was covered in sweat. The veins stood out in his arms and chest; he looked like he had just spent a few hours at the gym. He groaned as he spurted his last few rounds into her body. Then he collapsed back against the couch. He wrapped her up tight in his arms, cradling her against his chest. He lazily licked her collarbone. His tongue traveled up her neck to her ear, tasting her sweat.

Maddy couldn't move. She struggled to catch her breath. Her whole body was sweetly humming. Several minutes passed until she felt him soften and finally slip free, the strange bulge deflating from the base of his cock. His limp member rested against her inner thigh as his seed gushed down her leg. She felt utterly spent and exhausted. She loved it.

"Come on, let's take a shower," he said.

Gareth slid his arms under her legs and lifted her off the couch. Maddy gasped in surprise and clung to his neck, wondering where he got his energy. He carried her across the living room, down the dark hallway, then into the bathroom. He set her down in the tub. Her legs were a little wobbly, but she stood upright, one hand propped against the shower stall.

Gareth lit a candle in the bathroom for light. Then he rinsed her down in the shower, only running the water in short bursts because of the generator. It was lukewarm at best, and Maddy flinched under the cool stream. Better than ice cold, she supposed. Nothing really to be done about that until the power came back on.

Maddy let him clean her off; he seemed to like the little ritual, and she enjoyed the intimacy. Then he started rinsing himself off. Maddy watched little rivulets of water run down his muscles. Fuck, he was so tall and broad, he was like a mountain. She fought the urge to reach out and touch his rigid abdomen. Her eyes flickered over his limp cock. It looked totally normal, if a little thicker than average, in its unaroused state. Maybe she had imagined the strange knot of flesh? She put it from her mind and averted her eyes, a pink tinge to her cheeks. She was scared if she stared at his cock too long, it would grow hard again. If he tried to fuck her again so soon, she was pretty sure she would break into pieces.

She found herself wiping a wet washcloth over her face, her eyes swollen and tear-stung. She wondered what had gotten into her. It was kind of embarrassing. Why did she cry in the middle of sex?

She knew it had to do with Dean, with the trailer, with all the pent up fear she had stored inside from the abuse. She knew she was only scratching the surface. Years of physical abuse wouldn't wash off overnight. But she felt way more relaxed than she could ever remember, like a heavy weight had been released from her body. Shit, was she going to cry now every time they *did it?* Just her luck. She was a sex crier. Goddammit.

Maddy lowered the washcloth and noticed Gareth gazing down at her from the corner of his eye.

"What?" she asked.

"You okay?" he growled. His big hand reached out and pinched her chin gently. "I didn't hurt you, did I?"

"No, no, I . . . ."

"Cried cuz it felt so good?"

She laughed unexpectedly. "Um, yeah. That's why. It was some kind of release."

"Good. Cuz if I hurt you, I'd never forgive myself."

"No, it's not that. I think it was a good thing. Did it bother you?"

"Not at all, babygirl. I know you're a mess right now. You just work it out on my cock, yeah? I'll help you get right."

Maddy rolled her eyes. "You're such a guy sometimes."

Gareth let out a big ol' laugh in his deep baritone voice. Then he brushed his lips against the top of her head.

"I'm *your* guy," he murmured.

Gareth turned off the shower and climbed out of the tub. He grabbed a towel from the rack and wrapped it around her shoulders, then grabbed one for himself.

Your guy.

Maddy blushed, strangely pleased. Yeah. Even before they were together, he had always felt like *her guy.*

After drying off, Gareth reached over and started toweling her down, too. She remembered the little ritual from Friday night. He seemed to like taking care of her this way. After patting the water out of her hair and gently rubbing her down, he reached up and pinched her chin, gazing into her eyes.

"You had a big day, huh? How're you feeling, little wolf girl? You still scared of me?"

"No, I mean . . ." she released a breath. "It's still a bit overwhelming, but I feel a lot better."

"Yeah, good sex'll do that."

She snorted. "You're so full of yourself."

"Hey, where's the lie?" he grinned at her.

She smiled back, her eyes sparkling. Then a thought occurred to her.

"Um . . ." Maddy's hand slid over her abdomen, where she could feel the warmth of his seed filling her belly, making her calm and sedated. "So this is your vitality? Will it really help with the werewolf Change?"

"Like I said, babe, it'll move things along."

Maddy glanced at her reflection in the mirror. Maybe her eyes looked a little yellow? She was probably imagining it. She briefly wondered what she would tell Bea at school. Tomorrow was Monday. Her friend was going to want all the details about her "first time," but all this was starting to sound like an elaborate fantasy. Maddy couldn't imagine trying to explain all this. She felt like she had gone to Wonderland for the weekend.

"You're certain I won't get pregnant?" she asked, gazing at her reflection next to Gareth in the mirror.

"Female wolves have breeding seasons. Your Change has to come first. That's just how it works, babe, but I can understand why you're skeptical. Seems too good to be true, huh?"

"Yeah, it does, but . . . alright," Maddy said, choosing to trust him. She was a wolf girl. She needed to embrace it somehow, but it was going to take a minute.

Gareth opened the bathroom door and walked into the hallway. The house was cold. He crossed to his bedroom, where she heard him rummaging through his closet. He came back with a bundle of clothes in his arms, and tossed her a T-shirt and sweatpants. It looked like she would be wearing his clothes again. She didn't mind. Her stuff was still in bags.

"Now what do you want to do?" Gareth asked.

Maddy folded her arms around herself. It was still too early to go to bed. Technically, it was around dinner time, but food was the last thing on her mind. Back at her trailer, she would curl up in bed and scroll on her phone a bit, or go on a walk through the woods to clear her head. At Gareth's house, she didn't really know what to do with herself.

"I . . . uh, I don't know. Usually I'm up for a walk or something, but we can't really go out," she said. Then she got a little sad, thinking of her missing dog. "Shit, what about Joker? She's out in the forest right now. She's probably starving. I feel terrible. We should go look for her."

"Right," Gareth also looked concerned; he glanced at the clock. "It's getting late, babe, and the Grayridge pack is probably still in those mountains. I'll go looking for her tomorrow, I promise."

Maddy still felt tearful. "I have work after school, so I can't go with you . . . we really need to find her."

"I'll handle it, I promise. I'll shift tomorrow and go hunting for her again. I doubt she'll wander far from the trailer."

Maddy heard the sincerity in his voice.

"In the meantime, I got board games," Gareth suggested. "You want to play something?"

"Really? You have board games?"

"Yep. You like chess or Scrabble?"

For some reason, playing Scrabble with someone like Gareth—all bulked out and covered in tattoos—made her want to laugh hysterically. So now he was suddenly acting like a normal, everyday boyfriend? She didn't quite believe it.

"I've never played Scrabble," she admitted.

Maddy expected Gareth to tease her or make a dumb comment like Dean would do, but he didn't. Instead he took her hand and led her into the living room, where he deposited her on the floor in front of the fire, next to where they had made love just a half-hour ago. Then he got up and walked down the hallway. He returned a few minutes later with a stack of board games in hand, including Battleship, chess, Scrabble, Clue and a few others.

"Which one do you want to play first?" he asked.

"Isn't chess really hard?"

"It's not that bad. I'm no pro, my brothers always beat me. You want to learn?"

"Yeah." A little self-conscious, she asked, "Can you teach me?"

"Sure. You want to be black or white?"

Then Maddy spent the next few hours learning chess from her werewolf boyfriend.

As unlikely as it seemed, in the warm firelight of the living room, with the storm raging outside the windows, she found herself forgetting about the impending werewolf Change, the Alpha Challenge or the murder outside her trailer. She felt like she had entered a glowy bubble of security. Even with the power out, it felt so . . . *normal*. Gareth showed her how to move the pawns, the rooks, and the knights. He waited patiently as she studied the board before each move. He even let her take his queen.

"Second round, I won't go as easy on you," he said.

"Good. I don't like it when you go easy on me."

"You've said that before. Guess I'll keep it in mind." He flashed her a suggestive grin.

They played a few more rounds, then they made dinner: canned soup and Ritz crackers. It felt like camping. After a little while, Maddy found herself growing exhausted. The fire was warm and comforting. It became harder and harder to keep her eyes open. She found herself leaning against the coffee table and laying her head in her arms, as she waited for Gareth to make the next move on the chess board. She didn't notice when she started to doze.

She was vaguely aware of Gareth's arms sliding under her legs, of being picked up and lifted into the air. She murmured sleepily and turned her head toward his shoulder. Then she drifted off to sleep.

***

Later in the evening, Gareth settled Maddy into bed. The day's stress had caught up with her hours ago. He watched her lean up against the coffee table and rest her head against her arm. He reset the chess board. When he looked back up, she was asleep.

He picked her up and carried her to his bedroom. He laid her down in bed, pressing the white stuffed bear into her arms when she stirred. Then he stayed up for a bit, putting away the board games and clearing his stuff out of the closet in the spare bedroom. He moved his storage totes into the garage. His house was a decent size, around sixteen hundred square feet, but he always seemed to be lacking storage.

As he picked up the house, he thought back over the events of the weekend. A lot had gone down. For a moment, he was back in the forest on Friday night, feeling her small, soft body beneath him, submitting to his strength. The sound of her moans mingled with the rustling woods as he took her virginity. It was everything he had imagined and more—her muscles gripping down on his shaft. Her little sounds, her smooth skin, her curves, her bounce, her delicious scent filling his nose. He wanted to eat her like a cake. He took a few bites, sinking his teeth into her breasts, the soft meat of her inner arms, her beautiful long neck. He left little love bites all over her body, marking his territory. He was a hungry wolf, and she was exactly what he craved.

And now she was under his roof. Yeah. He had to be careful not to wear her out. He had a lot of energy, and she was only just beginning to Change.

Then his mind returned to the rest of Friday night—the less pleasurable part—when Maddy was thrown headfirst into his world. She saw him go full wolf and witnessed a bunch of gory shit she probably wouldn't forget anytime soon. He felt a little guilty about all of that. He had hoped to break the news to her about werewolves another way. Something fun and playful, not horrifying. Any normal teenage girl would run screaming for the hills. She might still run.

He needed to keep her close. She was on the verge of the Change, and this situation with the Grayridge pack would only get worse before it got better. He needed to keep her safe.

Gareth felt no remorse for Dean Harvey; he was a petty criminal who crawled through life like a rat through garbage, and it looked like his karma had finally caught up with him. When Gareth thought of the abuse Maddy had endured at Dean's hands, physical and emotional, his jaw clenched and a vein popped out in his neck. He really should have collared Maddy and yanked her out when she turned eighteen. By werewolf law, she was his mate, and he had every right to take her under his protection. But wolf law was a lot different than human law. Soon, she would have to learn. Everything about their relationship was about to change. As a wolf, she would feel the bond between them more strongly. She would recognize him in a new way. And she would learn what it meant to be mated to an Alpha. She was a den mother. A fucking queen. But she didn't understand anything at all. She was only just stepping into his world.

It got him thinking, who were her parents? How did she end up in Black River all alone, with no pack? Gareth was Arizona royalty. Second in line to the Sonoran wolf kingdom. When he brought her home, his family would want to know her pack lines, where she came from, her parents, her history. But Maddy was an orphan.

He had no idea how he was going to find out more information about her family. But maybe that was a problem for another day.

Gareth blew out the candles around the house and stoked the fire. Then he joined Maddy under the thick gray comforter. He pulled his lifemate into his arms, spooning her from behind, wrapping himself around her. He loved feeling her soft body pressed against him like this, the curve of her ass cheeks gently cradling his shaft. Fuck. He could easily slip up inside of her from this angle. The thought made his cock twitch. He sighed in frustration. Werewolf libido was a fucking curse. He felt like a man let out of prison. Years of pent up yearning and tension, wet dreams and daydreams and stolen looks at the hardware store . . . . She was intoxicating. Her sweet scent made his head buzz. He could run a marathon with all his pent up energy. His wolf wanted out. He wanted to run in the woods. Hunt down a caribou. Taste hot blood. He felt wild.

His lifemate.

Of course, he also wanted to protect her. Take care of her. Keep her safe. All those well-intentioned warrior things. But when he pressed against her like this . . . .

Gareth sighed. Finally, she was safe in his bed, under his roof. She would adjust soon enough, and they could get on with their lives.

Their lives. Together.

Fucking finally.

Chapter 8

Maddy woke up alone in Gareth's bed on Monday morning. His scent assailed her nose. It clung to everything—the bedding, the pillows, the entire room. She felt like she had woken up in his den in the woods. It wasn't a den, it was his house, but still.

Then she checked her phone, only to discover a half-dozen texts from Bea.

> I have your backpack.

> Are you still coming to school today?

> My mom heard the news down at The B Joint.

> It's fucked up. I'm sorry for your loss.

> Are you okay?

Maddy felt a little pale reading the text. The last thing she wanted to think about was Dean's body in the woods. She had dreamed about it all night. Gory, disgusting, terrifying dreams had haunted her, where she took the place of her stepfather, running out of the trailer with the Grayridge pack on her heels, stumbling through the misty forest. She woke up just as a wolf lunged at her throat. In another version of the dream, she fell at the feet of a carrion-covered scarecrow, sobbing and begging for some sort of protection as the eerie deer skull gazed down at her, unmoved. In a third version, she tripped over Dean's body on the ground. It was terrible, and now awake in the early morning light, she felt exhausted.

She read Bea's texts again and sighed. News spread fast in a small town. The B Joint was a popular local watering hole, and Dean was a regular customer. One of the rangers probably let it slip while having a drink after their shift.

She texted back:

> yeah, I'm staying at Gareth's house.

> I'm okay. I'm coming to school.

> Meet you at my locker in an hour

ok

Of course, Maddy had forgotten all about her homework assignments over the weekend. It was going to be a painful day showing up empty-handed in class.

Maddy crawled free of her comforter and wandered into the hallway. In the cloudy morning light, she walked into the bathroom, rubbing sleep from her eyes. She reached for the light switch and flipped it on, but it seemed the power was still out. Day two, no electricity. Ugh. She tested the sink in the bathroom. It seemed like Gareth's generator was still running the well pump, because the water turned on. That was a small relief. The bathroom was clean and quiet. No mold, urine or vomit caked the toilet. No dirty socks or discarded underwear left behind by her slob of a stepfather. No beer bottle forgotten next to the sink. There was a little rack with towels colored gray, black and Navy blue.

It was so . . . normal.

No need to tiptoe around a passed-out, hungover Dean in the living room. No stepping over piles of fast food trash or spilled beer on the rug. It was a brand new experience.

Maddy turned on the shower, but it looked like the water heater needed electricity to run, and the water stayed cold. It sucked, but she had dealt with this kind of thing before. Losing power was part of Black River's charm. She stripped down quickly and took a very fast, very cold shower, applying minimal shampoo and conditioner to her hair, then toweling off. The whole process took less than five minutes. She felt much more awake after that.

As she walked across the hallway into her new bedroom, she thought of the night before. Sleeping next to Gareth had been a whole other experience. She had woken up around midnight to the sound of another storm raging outside. Sweat poured from her brow, the fringes of a nightmare still in her vision. Her heart raced in her chest. For a moment, she had thought she was still in the trailer. She had almost launched to her feet, certain she had heard someone breaking in through the front door. She clutched the blanket to her chest, sick to her stomach, paralyzed in fear, wondering if she should check on her stepdad in the living room—wondering what she would find.

But, no. Wait. This wasn't the trailer. The bed was much too large, and someone was sleeping next to her. Gareth rolled over, his weight making the mattress dip as his big arms wrapped around her, spooning her, clasping her against his body. With a sigh, she felt the tension ease from her muscles.

She rolled over to gaze up at him. Gareth was sleeping on his side, turned toward her, his black hair spread across the pillow, his face stern even in his sleep. He was shirtless. Her eyes traveled over the deep indent of his chest, then to the tattoos on his arms. She had never looked at them up close before. She studied the intricate details and patterns on each sleeve. His left shoulder bore a sinister, grinning skull in the style of Dia de los Muertos. This close, she could see that one eye was a rose, while the other was a black, gaping hole. There was a cross in the middle of the skull's forehead, a surprisingly religious symbol, and the teeth were fangs. Was he Catholic? They hadn't talked about personal beliefs yet.

Beneath the skull, the tattoo dissolved into geometric patterns and linework that traveled down his thick biceps to the word "*loco,*" in rustic Southwest font, on his forearm. She had never noticed the small dates woven into the tattoo's shading on his dark skin. They were from eight years ago, probably from his time in Iraq, if she had to guess. She wondered what they meant. Were they his deployment dates? Or commemorating fallen friends?

His other arm was less visible beneath the blankets, but she remembered the big scorpion tattoo on his right bicep. She was pretty sure it was a zodiac sign. She remembered him saying his birthday was next month, which was November. So yeah, that would be a Scorpio. She would have to look up more about his sign. She believed in the zodiac, even if some people thought it was silly. She was born on August 5th, which made her a Leo. Her sign was supposed to be charismatic and social, but Maddy didn't feel it. A lion was a symbol of courage, but most of the time, she just felt scared.

As she gazed closely at Gareth's sleeve of tattoos, she thought she saw a line of raised skin underneath the colorful ink. She squinted in the dark bedroom. Was it . . . a scar?

Maddy felt her fingers itch. She wanted to touch the white, raised line beneath the artwork. As she looked more closely, she thought she saw a few more silvery ridges of skin. Her curiosity grew. It looked like he had several long scars across his bicep.

Maddy could relate. She had a scar on her back from when she fell on a broken bottle when she was fifteen. She had planned to get it covered up with a tattoo someday. It looked like the idea wasn't very original. The skin beneath the ink of Gareth's tattoos looked crisscrossed with scars. It seemed unusual. Shouldn't his werewolf vitality allow him to heal?

A sense of curiosity filled her. Maddy finally reached out and ran her fingers gently up his arm, feeling the ridges of raised skin.

When she glanced back up at his face, she started. She saw a glimmer of gold through his dark lashes. He watched her through slitted eyes. The dark bedroom was quiet except for the gentle tap of rain against the window. Her eyes slid over his thick, masculine neck and Adam's apple, his strong jaw and the rugged shadow of stubble on his gaunt cheeks. She didn't know how a man could look so rugged and beautiful at the same time.

Then he reached up and ran the back of his big hand against her soft cheek. He was so gentle. When he spoke, he sounded half asleep, his voice all low and grumbly.

"You okay?"

"Yeah," she whispered back. "Just a bad dream."

He gathered her up in his arms, pulling her against his large, warm body. She felt the rigid length of his member press against her belly; its size startled her once again. He was obviously aroused. He rubbed his face into her neck, placing a row of kisses along her bare skin down to her shoulder.

"Nothing bad's gonna get you here," he rumbled.

She thought, maybe, he would try to initiate something, considering the beast of an erection in his pants. Anticipation filled her. She waited, his lips resting against the nook of her shoulder as he inhaled her scent.

"Do you . . ." she started quietly, "do you want to, *you know*, again?"

"Not tonight. You got school. You should sleep."

"But . . . ."

He pressed his lips against her ear. "Rest up, sweetheart."

His dark words sent a pleasurable shiver down her spine. Somehow, they intensified her need. Her body felt flushed and warm. His lips grazed her forehead, then he settled back down, holding her against him. His breathing deepened once again.

Maddy shivered pleasantly at the memory. Then she sighed. She really needed to hurry up and get ready for school.

After getting dressed for the day, Maddy walked into the kitchen. She recalled Gareth's generator also ran the fridge, so she opened the fridge to make herself lunch—only to discover a sandwich and a can of soda sitting on the top shelf.

She picked up the sandwich: cheese and turkey on white bread. As far as sandwiches went, it looked pretty beasty. It was packed full of extra thick turkey slices. Did Gareth also make her lunch?

She stared at it maybe too long. Well, shit. She was not going to cry over a sandwich. She didn't know why the sight of it struck her so hard. Maddy placed a hand over her stomach and sucked in a deep breath.

It's alright. This is what normal life is like, she told herself. People doing nice things for other people. So what if no one had made her lunch before? Not since her mom died, anyway.

Maddy shoved the sandwich in a paper bag and told herself to stop being so sentimental. Then she flipped up her hoodie and headed out the door.

Despite the insanity of the day before, it was the most perfectly normal morning ever.

It took half the time to walk to school from Gareth's place than it did from her trailer. The streets of Black River were shrouded in hazy mountain fog. Hardly a single car passed on the road. The town felt deserted. She reached the school a lot faster than she was used to, which was the most incredible thing ever, because it was damp and cold outside. Gareth's house was a lot closer to campus than her trailer in the woods.

Down the hallway in front of her, she saw Bea leaning against her locker with two backpacks slung over her tiny shoulders. Her Goth friend wore her hair in two black buns, one on each side of her head, like little panda ears. Her outfit consisted of a velvet choker, a black T-shirt dress, purple and black pinstripe leggings, and her Doc Martens. She looked like a character out of a Tim Burton film.

When Bea saw her, she opened her arms and embraced Maddy in a fierce hug.

"You crazy wonderbitch, I was worried about you," Bea said.

"I'm really sorry, my phone died on Friday night," Maddy replied, a little sheepish. "I didn't mean to scare you."

"It's cool, I get it. You've had one hell of a weekend." Bea released Maddy and gave her arm a sympathetic squeeze. "I'm so, so sorry about Dean. How are you holding up?"

"It's, uh, a bit of a shock," Maddy admitted.

"My mom found out last night at work; apparently it's all anyone would talk about at the bar. She said after midnight, a few really drunk people stood up on the counter and said a eulogy. You'd think he was a local celebrity or something; I guess he had a lot of friends down at the bar. Anyway, my mom heard from a ranger that it was another animal attack. I'm really sorry."

"Yeah, it was an attack," Maddy confirmed. "We, uh, found him out in the woods yesterday."

"Here, I wanted to show you this," Bea said, as she opened up her cell phone's browser. She shoved the screen under Maddy's nose. "I saw this was posted on the Black River Village website about an hour ago. You want to read it?"

Maddy scrolled through the post. It was only a paragraph long, with a photo of a closed-off hiking trail. The reporter described, *"Another tragic victim of a wild animal attack found just outside the town of Black River, NY. Local hiking trails and campsites will remain closed until further notice. This is the second animal attack in the Black River area. If residents of Jefferson County see any signs of a large predator, such as a wolf or bear, please contact the Wildlife Control service at . . . ."*

The article was followed by a statement from the Black River mayor asking for residents to "stay vigilant and take precautions," and "keep out of the woods at night." Dean Harvey's name wasn't mentioned, or the location of Maddy's trailer, which was a blessing. Last week, her name was announced on the local news as a "missing person," and Maddy didn't want any more attention after all that. She was a bit relieved, actually, to see the warning only posted on the town's website. She didn't think many of the kids at school checked the site, probably only Bea and a few teachers, which meant she wouldn't be the subject of more gossip. She felt a bit less tense; she needed a break from all that drama.

"You sure you're alright?" Bea asked again. "Maybe you should head back home. You look pale."

"It's fine. Really. I'd rather be at school than sitting around doing nothing."

Maddy didn't disclose her honest reasoning. She was struggling to feel a sense of remorse over Dean's death. How was she supposed to grieve for someone who had made her life a living hell? It wasn't black and white. On the other hand, no one deserved to die in such a violent way. It was deeply unsettling. She didn't really know what else to say to Bea. She had a lot of conflicting feelings over Dean's death, and she didn't feel like hashing it all out right now.

Then Bea handed Maddy her backpack. After a slight hesitation, the spunky Goth girl shared her thoughts out loud.

"Remember last week, you said you saw that black wolf in the woods? Well, now there's been six victims of a 'large animal' attack. Do you think it might have been that wolf you saw?"

"No, I really don't."

"It just seems odd, all these people getting attacked near your trailer. The rangers think it's a wolf, and *you said you saw a wolf.* Maybe you should report it."

Maddy gritted her teeth, her mouth clamping shut. She really didn't want to talk about that. When she saw the big black wolf last week, that was before she knew about Gareth's secret. She didn't expect Bea to bring up Dean and the whole incident first thing in the morning, and it was stressing her out.

"I'll think about it," Maddy said. "I'm sure Wildlife Control will find the beast, whatever it is. They're also looking for my lost dog. Um, Joker got out during the . . . *attack*. We can't find her. I think she ran off into the woods."

"I didn't know you had a dog, Maddy! That's so sad!"

"Yeah, she's a pitbull lab mix," Maddy explained. "I have a few pictures of her on my phone. Maybe your mom can put up a 'Missing Dog' poster around The B Joint?"

"Of course, just text me the pic. I can print it out at home, once the power comes back. Do you want to go looking for your dog after school? I can help you. It's the least I can do. Please let me help? I feel like I need to do something to make this better."

"Thanks, Bea, that's really sweet, but I have work after school, so I don't have any free time today."

"Then let's go looking tomorrow. Highway 20 is super dangerous for pets. People don't pay attention when they're speeding through the mountains. It's really sad."

Maddy winced. She wished Bea hadn't said that; now she felt twice as worried about Joker.

"You're right, let's definitely go tomorrow. I would take off work today, but I need the paycheck."

"Hey, I get it. Don't feel bad. We'll find your dog, don't worry."

At that moment, a piercing whistle blasted down the hallway, ricocheting obnoxiously off the tile floors and metal lockers. All the students in the hall flinched and looked around, grumbling with bleary, early-morning confusion. Maddy looked up as well, squinting down the dark, cold corridor.

Principal Rodriguez strolled down the hallway in his fancy cowboy boots, wearing a brown ten-gallon hat. He wore a whistle around his neck, which he blew again to get the students' attention. Maddy winced and put her hands over her ears. It was very annoying.

Rodriguez' voice echoed down the hallway: "Come on now, buckaroos, this isn't our first rodeo. We're not canceling classes just because the lights are out. Power might be back as early as this afternoon. Go to your homeroom just like any other day. Take your seats. Listen to your teachers. No shenanigans!"

A little after 8am, Maddy found herself sitting in her usual homeroom seat with most of the class present. A substitute teacher grumbled about the lack of heating or lights, and the misguided decision *not* to close down the school for a day. She waited for the students to settle in, then the sub read the morning announcements off a white sheet of computer paper. Due to the power outage, they had a modified schedule. P.E. classes would be held in the gym, the library was closed, and "Computer Lab" would be used as a "Study Period" due to the power outage. The bells weren't working, so teachers would inform the students when to go to their next class.

"Be prepared for a chaotic day!" The substitute teacher ended the announcements with an ominous laugh.

Maddy listened with half an ear as she played with her phone, flipping it around in her hands, tempted to text Gareth, though she didn't know what to say. She wanted to thank him for the sandwich, but for some reason, probably her dumb anxiety, she felt inexplicably shy. She sighed. Even after their passionate night, she still felt like a guest in his house, like any day she would return to the trailer, and her life would go back to normal.

That claustrophobic feeling began to close in. This was her first relationship. She hadn't even said "I love you" yet, or sent him a heart emoji, and she was living under his roof. She had cried on his dick last night, sobbing in catharsis as he impaled her on his meaty monster rod, and she hadn't even sent him a hug over text. Like, when was that supposed to happen? It all seemed so backward.

Then her screen lit up. Her heart leapt a little when she saw his name on her notifications. Holding her cell phone discreetly under her desk, she read the message.

> *you in class?*

He was checking on her. She released a quiet sigh. That meant he was okay, too. Despite her mixed feelings, she was relieved to hear from him. Jeez, how many conflicting emotions could she feel at the same time? Shit, she was a mess.

> *Yes, dad.*

She followed up with a little eye roll emoji. Sarcasm, of course. She didn't want him to know how vulnerable she felt.

> *how'd you sleep last night?*

Maddy stared at the screen, surprised. Didn't he know how she slept? He was next to her the whole time. Why would he ask about that? If she had to be honest, she had slept like shit, trapped in a nightmare hellscape for six hours, but she didn't want to complain to him about that. He had already done so much for her, and he was probably busy at work. She should let him get on with his day.

> I slept good.

> School's starting, g2g

Maddy slipped her phone back into her pocket.

***

Lunch was a disorganized mess on campus. It was raining again, and part of the quad was flooded, so most of the students packed themselves inside the cafeteria. A few ate in the halls, which wasn't usually allowed, but nobody seemed to care. There was a lot of grumbling and discontent from the school staff about being forced to work with the power out. Maddy saw about a half dozen angry teachers gathering in the doorway of the Administration Building, their cell phones out, calling the local union. Yeah. Something was up.

At first Maddy wandered the quad, trying to find Bea. She was pretty sure her little friend would be outside somewhere, where she could smoke. But Maddy gave up her hunt after a few minutes. A strange, pensive mood had settled over her, and she decided to spend lunchtime alone at a secluded table near the gym. Between the football field and the basketball courts, a tool shed for the janitor was screened by a line of white birch trees. Behind the tool shed, an inconspicuous picnic table was located where the groundskeeper sometimes took his lunch. Students weren't really allowed to eat there, but Maddy scoped out the spot Freshman year and took advantage of it when it wasn't being used. So far, no one had caught her or complained.

It wasn't her only private lunch retreat. She had several little spots all to herself around campus. One was on the steps behind the shabby auditorium where school assemblies and plays were held. Another was between the new Science Hall and the regular classrooms, where an unhappy beech tree, crammed between two buildings, created a sheltered nook at the edge of the grounds. Another hidden spot was behind the bleachers, but a lot of kids went back there during football games, so it wasn't really a big secret.

As she ate her sandwich that Gareth had packed for her, Maddy scrolled on Picplace, looking at photos her friends had posted over the weekend. Bea had uploaded a ton of pics and videos from Fright Farm. With a blush, Maddy found a photo of her and Gareth standing in line for the haunted house, leaning close together, looking pretty cozy. He looked older and dashing in his leather jacket; she looked cute in an oversized flannel jacket and crop top. She felt a little flutter, remembering their date at the carnival. It felt like eons ago. Then she swiped through more of the photos. She saw a lot of pics of Bea and Vin. She wondered if they were dating yet, but they hadn't posted each other publicly on Picplace, so maybe not.

Then her cell phone pinged.

> *you making it okay?*

Wow, Gareth checking on her twice in one day? He must be worried.

Maddy chewed on her sandwich and frowned at the text. Her restless night was catching up to her, and she felt exhausted and numbed out. She wanted to go home, or go look for Joker, but she had work after school. And after work, she needed to catch up on homework assignments she had missed over the strange weekend. She groaned. Could life slow down just for a minute? Safe to say, her mood was about as dark as the weather.

She texted back:

> *Yeah, eating lunch, I'm alright*

> *I'm heading down to Davenport*

> *Gotta pick up a few things*

> *You want pizza for dinner?*

She squirmed for a moment. Right. They would be eating dinner together, every night, for the foreseeable future. She was a little excited, a little nervous, about that thought.

> *Yeah, pizza sounds good*

> *How's your day? Any word on the Alpha Challenge?*

Nope. No contact from Marquis.

Tow calls and complaints, the usual

Vin called out sick

When are you off work tonight?

The usual time, 9 o'clock.

Gotcha. Hang in there. Don't fall asleep in class.

Yeah, so he knew she slept like shit. Actually, he probably knew she was a shaky, fragile mess today. After all those tears she had shed in his arms? Of course he would know.

Her mind traveled back to the night before, and she blushed thinking about her sob session on his couch, embarrassed over the whole thing. She had cried during sex *like a baby*. She couldn't imagine a more virginal, inexperienced, *non-sexy-thing* to do. Ugh, he probably thought she couldn't handle him physically. And he might be right. Any guy would have second thoughts after that little display of waterworks. She had cried harder than she had in a long time. It was scary. How long had she been carrying around all that hidden pain? How much more was locked away? The memory made her a little queasy. He probably wouldn't want to make love to her again any time soon. He wouldn't say anything outright to spare her feelings, so maybe she should just avoid having sex with him, if this was going to be a thing. His cock did strange and frightening things to her body.

"So you're living with him now?"

Maddy looked up in shock. She almost dropped her cell phone on the ground. Bea was peering around the back of the tool shed, a pack of cigarettes in hand, pinching a match between two black acrylic nails. At Maddy's look, Bea stepped out into the open and tossed her pack of smokes on the picnic table.

"You want one?" she asked.

Maddy hesitated. She wasn't really a smoker, though she had shared a cigarette or two with Bea before. Gareth had mentioned no drinking for werewolves, but he hadn't said anything about tobacco. She knew the health risks. Like who didn't? Even thinking the word "cigarettes" caused cancer—along with birth control, food preservatives, car exhaust, bathroom cleaners, fast food and about every other modern convenience—but she figured a few puffs couldn't hurt. She wasn't exactly a role model of good behavior these days.

"Sure, thanks," she said, and pulled a smoke out of the pack.

"So how long are you going to live with him?" Bea asked as she handed over her matches. "Like, I get why you're doing it. I mean, I wouldn't want to stay in your trailer either after everything that's gone down. But is this a permanent thing, or . . . ?" Bea quirked an eyebrow curiously.

Maddy shrugged. "I don't know. I haven't really figured it all out yet. Honestly, I have no idea what I'm doing."

"So what, are you paying him rent?"

"Um, not yet."

Beatrice's other eyebrow raised up. "Alright, so he's *really* your sugardaddy now. I mean, free rent and all that eye candy, every day? I think you're making the best of a shitty situation. Girl, I'm worried for you, but also, like, good job."

Maddy released an unexpected laugh. "Wow, Bea, you make it sound like I planned all this."

"I'm just saying, I know Becca gave you shit at Fright Farm about your age gap, but I saw how he looked at you. Remember when you had that freakout in the haunted house? Yeah, I don't think he's just playing games. He's serious."

Maddy bit her lip. She thought of the lifemate thing. Her little Goth friend had *no idea*. Beatrice leaned against the table in her platform boots, puffing on her cigarette.

"So is that why you're hiding back here? Trying to decompress from your weekend?"

"I'm not hiding. Well, sort of." Maddy sighed. "I think staying with Gareth is safer for me right now. I guess if it doesn't work out, I can always try to find another place to stay, but the trailer isn't really . . . um . . . ." Maddy swerved away from that subject, because she didn't know how to explain the threat of the Grayridge pack. "I can't really afford my own apartment with only part-time work, and there's not a lot of housing in Black River, you know? I've already looked into this. If it was that easy, I would've moved out a long time ago. So I guess I'm staying with Gareth for now."

"I agree, it seems like the best choice. But you can always stay at my place if you need to."

"Thanks," Maddy said with a grateful smile. "But I wouldn't want to put your mom out. She has a lot of kids at home."

"Don't I know it." Bea sighed and looked back toward the school. "So how was it Friday night? Losing your virginity?"

"It was . . . an experience, for sure," Maddy said, taken aback by the question.

"So, did you go back to his place? Or did you guys get a hotel room or something? Or . . . was it in his car?"

Bea grinned knowingly, as though she had done all of the above. Maddy had to wonder at that. She had no idea what her cute, tiny friend got up to, but she knew Beatrice was a lot more promiscuous than her.

"We, uh . . . ." Maddy's cheeks started to burn as her mind flashed back to the forest. "We kind of . . . well . . . ." Maddy thought of Gareth's weight pressing her down into the soft moss, her senseless moans of pleasure as he pushed another orgasm through her body, his deep golden eyes watching her shudder and writhe and cry out . . . *daddy, ah!*

His lips pressed against her sweaty temple, his dark voice in her ear: *Say it again, babygirl.*

A sweet tendril of warmth moved through her belly.

Stop right there, Maddy thought, freaked out by her lusty thoughts.

Bea's eyes narrowed at her long pause. "It's okay if you don't want to share, but you two *did it*, right? He didn't back out at the last minute? If that fucker turned you down again—"

"No, no, we, uh, *yes*. We definitely *did it*."

"Wow, okay." Bea looked a little shocked, like she had expected Maddy to change her story last minute. "So, good experience? Bad experience?"

Maddy really couldn't sum it up easily.

"It was . . . it was cool," she finally said.

"It was *cool?*" Bea exclaimed, horrified. "Okay, I hope that means it blew your mind."

"Yeah, like that," Maddy blushed. "It was good. Like, *really* good."

Bea looked relieved. "Did you come?"

"Yeah, a few times," Maddy grinned, a bit shy. She fumbled for more details. She really sucked at talking about this stuff. Plus, when she thought of Gareth's lovemaking, it was really hard to remember anything besides a series of mind-melting orgasms.

"It wasn't as painful as I thought it would be," she added. "I mean, it hurt, but it was good, too."

"Yeah, sex is weird like that. Well, I'm glad he made it good for you. I mean, I figured he would. Older guys are way better at foreplay."

Maddy nodded. She didn't really have anything to compare it to, so she took Bea's word for it. Still thinking of Friday night, Maddy asked Bea, "So are you still talking to Vin? How's that going?"

"We're just friends right now."

Maddy was surprised. "You two got super friendly at Fright Farm. Didn't he ask you out?"

"That boy is hella fine," Bea replied with a fond expression. Then her face soured. "Unfortunately, I found out he's talking to someone else."

"Talking to someone? You mean, on Picplace?"

"No, I mean, he already has a girlfriend."

Maddy's mouth dropped open. She couldn't believe it. Vin and Bea were arm-in-arm at the Halloween carnival. They liked the same podcast, and they listened to the same oldschool bands. Vin's punk vibe fit well with Bea's edgy aesthetic. The two deviants seemed like a perfect match. Maddy had fully expected them to start dating.

Come to think of it, though, she recalled Gareth saying something about Vin already having a girl.

"How did you find out he has a girlfriend?" Maddy asked.

"He told me Friday night, after we hung out at the diner."

"That's really not cool. He led you on."

"I don't think he meant to," Bea said quickly. "Sometimes shit happens, you know? You never know who you're going to meet. I don't know, Maddy. Have you ever met someone and it feels like you've always known them?"

Maddy felt a little chill. Like Gareth. She nodded.

Bea continued wistfully, "I just feel like Vin and I . . . This is gonna sound sappy, and you know I'm not some starry-eyed romantic, but . . . I feel like I've met him before. Like maybe we knew each other in a past life."

Maddy looked up at her little Goth friend. Bea took a drag on her cigarette and flicked it, then glanced away. She seemed bashful. It was a new look for her, one Maddy hadn't seen before.

"You really like him, huh?" Maddy asked.

Bea sighed. She gazed across the basketball courts, her eyes fixed on the gray horizon, momentarily pensive. Then she shook herself. She stood up and put out her cigarette.

"Yeah, but oh well. He's just another dumb boy. Trust me, he can't handle this." She stuck her thumb in her chest.

Maddy let the subject go, but she didn't believe Bea was "cool" with Vin dating another girl. Not in the least. Her little friend was all spice and vinegar where dating was concerned. Bea could pretend not to care, but Maddy knew her pride was wounded.

The distant sound of a whistle reached Maddy's ears, and she groaned, thinking of Principal Rodriguez in his stupid cowboy hat. She put out her cigarette as well. It seemed like lunchtime was over. Bea waited for her to gather up her backpack, then the two girls walked across the quad to the Science Hall.

***

After school, Maddy headed to Hawkins' Hardware for her afternoon shift. It wasn't a long walk. Black River was a small town—more of a village, really—in the foothills of the Adirondack mountains on the edge of the Five Ponds Wilderness. Many of the houses were fifty to a hundred years old. Maddy had learned a little bit of the town's history over the years, especially working at the hardware store, where a lot of locals came through. People liked to spend a minute chatting with the cashiers.

She knew the settlement of Black River began back in 1806, when a mill was built on the south side of the river—a mill that still stood to this day, though it was nothing more than a stub of rotten timbers. Eventually, the mill turned into a profitable logging venture, which grew from an intersection in the road into a post office and a general store. Eventually, bungalows appeared for the forestry workers. Around that time, the Beaumont family arrived as more French settlers migrated south from Canada. Already wealthy fur traders, the Beaumont family bought up most of the land that eventually became the town, though the town itself wasn't incorporated until around 1890.

The historic plaque outside Town Hall described a fire that swept through the town that same year—1890—burning down the post office, a hotel, several outbuildings and even an opera house. The next year, 1891, was when the Black River Fire Department was founded, which still served the upriver area to that day.

Maddy passed by the fire department, post office and town hall on her way to work. The intersection at Main Street and Herst was flooded, and the street light was broken. An obstacle course of orange cones and "Caution" signs was set up through the busy intersection. A police officer in a bright yellow vest was directing traffic.

The officer blew on his whistle, waving for Maddy to cross the street. She trotted through the crosswalk, which was submerged in several inches of water. By the time she walked into the parking lot behind Hawkins' Hardware, her Converse sneakers were soaked through. She traversed a giant puddle behind the warehouse, then walked through the back door of the building.

When she got to the employee break room, she took a moment to scuff her shoes on the floor mats, trying to get the water out. At this rate, she would be squeaking all over the linoleum floors.

The door to the employee restroom opened, almost smacking her in the face. Maddy leapt back with a little gasp.

"Oh hey, Maddy," Gabby said, darting out of the restroom. "Sorry about that, I'm on my second Red Bull. How's your day? Did you lose power at your trailer?"

Gabby's box-blond hair was wrapped up under a handkerchief, and she was chewing a stick of gum at manic speed. She was clutching a sugar-free Red Bull in her right hand. She didn't mention anything about Dean or a second animal attack, which meant word of the incident hadn't spread very far outside The B Joint, probably due to the power outage. Maddy felt relieved. Last week, everyone at work had been asking her about the wolf attack at her trailer, when five men were found dead in the woods. She really didn't need to relive all those conversations with the addition of Dean's death.

Before Maddy could answer her question, Gabby said, "Just a heads up, we're closing early. One of the registers is down and it's cash only. What a nightmare! I think Mr. Hawkins put you on cleanup, we got a big leak in the back. Watch out, he's on a rampage. Anyway, I gotta run. I'm not on break, I just couldn't hold it. See you out there."

Gabby flew past her down the hallway, heading to the front of the shop. Maddy watched her go, a little bemused. Then she checked the schedule again. With a flood of relief, she saw that she was on cleanup duty like Gabby said, which meant minimal contact with customers. Thank goodness. She needed an easy day.

Then she frowned. It looked like she wasn't scheduled for the rest of the week. She wondered if Mr. Hawkins had made a mistake. Each employee was listed out on the grid. Sundays were always closed during the Fall. But it looked like the rest of her week had a big "X" blocking out every day. No shifts. No job assignment.

"Marci, is this the right schedule?" she asked.

Marciella, another lifer at the hardware store, was taking lunch. She was sitting at the break room table listening to an audiobook in Spanish on her phone.

"What's that, Maddy?" Marciella asked in her cute, lilting accent. "I t'ink so. It's the only schedule posted."

"But I'm only working one day this week," Maddy said. "Usually I'm Monday through Thursday."

Marci shrugged. "I don't know, maybe Señor Hawkins changed it?"

Marciella didn't seem very invested in the conversation. She went back to her audiobook.

Maddy put on a red work apron and headed for the front of the store. As she walked out onto the floor, she changed her mind about having an "easy day." The storefront of Hawkin's Hardware was hectic. Piles of half-sorted products were stacked around the registers in a chaotic maze. She soon found out why. It looked like a roof leak had flooded the back corner of the store. The damage was extensive. Three whole aisles were barricaded off.

Her boss, Archie Hawkins, saw her from the front of the shop. He was a tall and lanky man in his late forties, with a patchy, blondish-grayish beard and a shaved head. He always wore a pair of plastic shop glasses. Today, a stress-out frown pinched his thin face. He waved at her, then he pointed at a mop and bucket propped against one of the shelves.

"We got most of the water cleaned up, but there's all sorts of spills in the back," he yelled across the store. "The leak was right over the bird seed and plant fertilizer. Start on Aisle 7 and work your way up. Try to get everything off the floor."

"Got it, no problem, right away!" Maddy said, taking the bucket and mop in hand. Wet bird seed and plant fertilizer? Sounded like a mess.

Then, hesitating, she called back, "I'm only on the schedule for today. Am I working the rest of the week?"

"Sarah did the scheduling. Take it up with her," Mr. Hawkins said, then he turned away to help Gabby with a broken register. He looked busy and distracted.

Maddy liked her boss okay, but he could be blunt and short-tempered. She opened her mouth to call after him again, then she sighed. Sarah worked in the office next door. She was in her late thirties and a mom of three boys. She always seemed frazzled and a little overworked. Maddy decided to go talk to her about the schedule on break.

Then she fumbled her way to the back of the store, trying to juggle her mop, trash bags and cleaning supplies in two hands. Monday evenings were usually pretty busy, but with weather this bad, the store was dead. Mr. Hawkins left the generators running, but only half the fluorescent lights in the building had power, and there was no heat.

Maddy set down her mop and bucket at the back of the store and started cleaning up piles of wet, gooey birdseed. She moved from one mess to the next, scooping up the spilled product and then scrubbing down the linoleum. She threw away a bunch of ruined cardboard boxes of plant food. She tried to be as thorough as possible. She appreciated the mindless, repetitive task of cleaning. As her hands worked, she thought of what to do about the trailer. If she left it empty for too long, then someone might come by and steal the appliances, or set up camp and squat on her property. She would have to check on the trailer periodically, and she still needed to haul all that trash to the dump.

She didn't know when Dean's body would be released from the morgue. Law enforcement could keep him indefinitely, as far as she was concerned. She had never met Dean's family. She didn't know if his parents were still alive, or if he had siblings or cousins or anything. They never visited the trailer. His family wasn't really her kin, anyway. She didn't know anyone she could notify about his death. Part of her wanted to toss all of Dean's things into the river and pretend like he had never existed. Just let the whole situation float away into Lake Ontario. Then a terrible thought struck her. What if his family showed up? Or worse, what if he owed them money?

I suppose we'll cross that bridge when we get there, she told herself.

Maddy wiped a Clorox-scented hand across her forehead. She thought of the girls at school with their neat, color-coded binders and streamlined notes. She wasn't like that at all. She had never suffered from perfectionism. Getting a firm grip on her life was all she wanted. But it looked like that goal was still out of reach.

Before she knew it, six o'clock had rolled around and it was time for her ten minute break. Maddy set down her cleaning supplies and washed off her hands in the employee restroom. Then she ran out into the parking lot, shivering in the autumn wind.

A rich layer of red and golden leaves covered the wet asphalt of the parking lot. Faded lines of white paint marked the different parking spots. A little secondhand boutique called Calico's Vintage Wares stood next door to the hardware store. Archie Hawkins rented the apartment on the second floor, above the thrift store, for his office space: a one-bedroom with a kitchenette. That's where Sarah worked. Maddy had gone inside only a few times over the years. She remembered the carpet was a creamy beige, the walls were white, and the cabinets were basic IKEA quality. A series of desks and computers lined one wall, while a bunch of metal filing cabinets stood at the back. The single bedroom was used as a conference room, but Archie Hawkins kept it closed and locked most of the time.

As Maddy climbed the staircase to the apartment door, she overheard a man's voice carry through the open window: "I'm telling you, we need to lure him out. It's the only way."

Maddy paused, listening. She didn't recognize the man's voice. It was low, gruff, and a little croaky.

A woman's voice, definitely Sarah, answered him, "I know you have a lot of experience with this, but are you sure? I don't want to put anyone in danger."

"The girl is our best shot," the man answered.

"But I've known her for years. It can't be her. I won't believe it," Sarah protested.

Maddy's eyes widened curiously. Two people were whispering to each other inside the office, but it didn't sound like the usual business drama. *But I've known her for years.* Who were they talking about?

"Denial is pretty common in these situations," the man insisted. "Think about it—the attack happened on her property. It's not a coincidence. Just look at the photo. You can see them standing next to each other on the trail."

Maddy felt a little jolt of alarm. Did they mean the attack on Dean? Growing more suspicious, she crept up to the landing outside the apartment door. She leaned forward, her ears strained.

"Alright, I see the resemblance," Sarah relented. "But we have to be sure. If we're wrong, then this could backfire in a really bad way. You said you can test them, but how close do you have to get to her to be certain?"

Suddenly, a truck missing a muffler roared down the street. Maddy gave a start of surprise at the loud engine. She gripped the metal railing for balance, and it rattled loudly. *Shit!* She winced. Now what? She waited for the man and woman to continue their conversation, but no more words drifted through the open window.

Instead, the door cracked open. Sarah stood with one hand on the knob, the other on the door frame. Her long red hair was loose and messy, and her cheeks were a little flushed. Her makeup seemed thicker today than usual. Her eyeliner and mascara made her eyes pop. The top few buttons on her shirt were undone, displaying a wide view of her freckled cleavage. She definitely wasn't wearing a bra.

Maddy was taken aback. Was Sarah hooking up with someone in the office? She had a flash of a thought that it might be Mr. Hawkins, but no way, her boss was back in the store. And that didn't explain the strange conversation about "the attack." What was going on?

The secretary looked shocked to see her.

"Oh, Maddy!" Sarah exclaimed. "What are you doing here? Is something wrong?"

"Hi?" Maddy said. She tried to see over Sarah's shoulder. She thought she saw someone else inside the apartment, but the person moved out of sight.

Sarah quickly stepped onto the landing and closed the office door behind her. She crossed her arms over her chest, trying to look casual. A chill autumn wind blew her long red hair over her shoulder. She looked cold.

"So what's up?" she barked, suddenly brusque. "You need something?"

"I wanted to know the schedule. I don't have any shifts for the rest of the week. Was there a mistake? I usually work Monday through Thursday."

"Oh right, I forgot to tell you, I probably should have texted," Sarah said, slapping her hand against her forehead. Somehow, it seemed performative. "I had to adjust everyone's schedule because of the power outage. Mr. Hawkins needs to fix the roof leak, and it's not cheap, so the budget is pretty tight this month. He doesn't need any extra hands on deck."

Maddy didn't know what to say. "So you're taking me off the schedule, but you're keeping on Marci and Gabby?"

"They're full-time employees and you're only part time, Maddy. I don't know what else to say. That's how it works."

"What about next week? Will the schedule go back to normal then?"

Sarah looked uncomfortable. "I don't know. I'll let you know when Archie is ready to have you back."

Maddy felt the stairs tilt a little beneath her. She needed those hours, and she needed a paycheck. Just because Dean was dead didn't mean bills around the trailer would stop accruing. What was she supposed to do about the property taxes or the insurance? What was she going to do without any money? Tears stung her eyes, and she tried to pull herself together.

"Well, I-I could really use the hours," she stuttered. "Are you sure you don't need someone to help clean up or organize things? I can do itinerary."

"No, no, Mr. Hawkins has that handled. I know it's tough. We're all struggling right now. The roof repairs are looking pretty expensive."

Sarah's eyes swept over Maddy a few times. Her expression seemed a little intense. Maddy found herself glancing down, wondering if she had a big stain on her sweater or something.

Then Sarah forced a laugh. "Hopefully power's back up by tomorrow. Remember the year before last, when that winter storm blew in? The power went out for a whole week. It was a nightmare. I remember the pipes froze on my house. I'm dreading it might happen again. I moved the boys down to my mother-in-law's place in Davenport. She's driving us all bonkers. It's a hassle-and-a-half getting out here for work, and I can't even do anything in the office. It's freezing and my laptop died a while ago. I'm trying to talk Mr. Hawkins into letting me work remote tomorrow."

"Yeah, I remember that storm," Maddy said, still irritated. "It was pretty rough. That was a cold year." She started to turn back down the stairs, then paused. "If anything changes about the schedule, can you give me a call? I could really use the hours."

"I'll definitely keep you in mind, Maddy," Sarah said with a little salute. "Hey, maybe you can use this time to catch up on school work and friends. You know, be a kid for a while."

"Yeah sure," Maddy mumbled.

As she turned around on the stairs and headed back down to the parking lot, Maddy tried to keep a firm grasp over her emotions. Gareth had said to keep things lowkey and not get too upset, or she might trigger the Change. She shoved down a rising wave of fear and frustration. Her hands balled into fists. This wasn't the first time Mr. Hawkins had cut back her hours. Last year, business had slowed way down after the summer rush, so her schedule got cut to two days a week. She picked up a canvassing gig to make ends meet, but it was a lot of walking, and she didn't think the company was still in business.

She thought of the unpaid utility bill waiting for her back at the trailer. Property taxes would be due at the end of the year. Dean had met an untimely end, but she was still responsible for cremating him and the ambulance fees. Fuck, how much was that going to cost? Funny how that sort of stuff never came up on TV shows. Maddy's thoughts began to spiral. What was she going to do? Maybe Gareth could help her out? No, she didn't want to use him for money. Despite Bea's nickname for him, Maddy had no intention of making him a real 'sugar daddy.' She shouldn't have to rely on him for everything. She needed to figure this out by herself.

There's always the Sapphire Club, she thought ironically.

"Ugh, pull it together, Maddy!" she groaned. "You'll think of something."

Her break was finished, so she headed back into the store to collect her bucket and cleaning supplies, anxiety curdling her stomach like a spoiled apple. She went back to mopping up the spilled plant food. She finished with Aisle 7 and worked her way down Aisle 6. She scrubbed extra hard at the linoleum floor, trying to work out her frustration on the off-white tiles. She couldn't help but feel like Sarah's scheduling decisions were somehow personal. The office manager had looked at her several times with a strange little scowl, like Maddy was an unwelcome stranger on her doorstep. She wondered about the mysterious conversation she had overheard in Sarah's office. The attack? It sounded like they were talking about Dean. But then, why didn't Sarah say anything to her face? Who was the mysterious man? Was Sarah having an affair? Was the secretary really bold enough to hook-up with someone at work, with Mr. Hawkins next door?

Maddy's thoughts were interrupted by her boss strolling up behind her with a dolly.

"Madeline, can you organize these cans of plumbers putty and roof patch at the front of the store? They're going to be in high demand this week, I guarantee you."

"Sure, no problem," Maddy agreed automatically.

She set down her cleaning supplies and took the dolly to the front of the store. There, Gabby stood at the only working register, price-marking a box of Halloween decor as she waited for a customer to come through. Maddy crouched down next to the wide window at the storefront. She started arranging cans of *Durham's Rock Hard Water Putty* in a little pyramid. Twenty minutes slid by. She struggled with the strangely sized cans; she wasn't a brilliant window display artisan. Marciella was the talented one—she made their products into castles or hearts or rainbows. Maddy's pyramid looked like a lumpy snail shell. She tried to make the stack more symmetrical, but the rows wouldn't line up right.

Maddy remembered one Christmas, a few years back, when Marciella was out sick. Mr. Hawkins had assigned her the task of setting up a Christmas village display in the front window. It had been a disaster. She recalled spending her entire eight hour shift slaving over the front window, creating little snowy hills out of cotton, and arranging all the buildings in a row. Except she didn't realize the town was supposed to mimic Main Street, and she got the row of storefronts all wrong. The fairy lights were strung in the wrong direction, so they didn't reach the extension cord. Mr. Hawkins had taken the whole thing down after her shift.

About halfway through that stressful Saturday, when she took her allotted ten minute break, she remembered catching sight of Gareth in the aisle with the Christmas lights. He was wearing a heavy tan coat, snow dusting his shoulders, comparing a few different boxes of outdoor lights side-by-side. She paused for a moment at the end of the aisle, hiding behind a large inflatable snowman. She watched him from a distance, admiring his height and manly jawline. Back then, she only knew him from the mountain, and she rarely caught a glimpse of him around town. Knowing what she knew now, it was probably his first Christmas on Bickford Ave. He would have just bought his house.

She remembered wanting to go up and speak to him, but she didn't know what to say, so she held back. Now she wondered what he would have done, if she had approached him boldly. She was underage, so he probably would have backed off. But maybe . . . maybe they could have struck up a friendship? She could have gone over to his house. Hung out in his garage as he worked on his car in the driveway. Played videogames in front of his giant TV. Yeah, it would've been weird, and nobody would be on board with that, but maybe it could've been good, too.

Reflecting back on that time, he must have already known she was a wolf girl. Must have already claimed her as his pack. Must have, even in those early days, already thought of himself as her Alpha. Her keeper. Actually, she probably would have been quite safe spending time with him in his backyard, or going over to his house alone. He probably would've been a decent guy and tried to make her feel comfortable.

Had he come by the hardware store just to check on her? Had he sensed her standing at the end of the aisle on that winter day? Smelled her through the vanilla air fresheners and cinnamon-scented holiday candles?

Lost in memory, stacking cans of plumber's putty in the window, Maddy didn't notice a shadow fall across her, until she felt a prickle of alarm on the back of her neck.

She looked up.

Startled, she almost gasped. A man stood behind her who she didn't recognize. He didn't look local, but that didn't mean anything. He seemed to be around her manager's age or a little older, maybe mid-fifties. Maddy stood up, straightening her apron, a little taken aback. He wore a red baseball cap pulled low over his face. He had a leathery, weathered kind of appearance, like he spent a lot of time outdoors, and his clothes seemed a little dirty and faded, like he wore them a lot. He might be homeless, except he didn't stink of sweat or B.O. Actually, as he leaned in close, a different sort of smell stung Maddy's nose. It was very unpleasant. It reminded her of a skunk. It seemed to grow stronger as the man loomed over her.

Maddy gagged, a little dizzy, and leaned away from him. The stench made her eyes water. She couldn't help but raise a hand to her nose, struggling to breathe.

"Ugh, sorry," she muttered.

Surprising her, the strange customer looked pleased by her reaction. He stepped a little closer, like he wanted to suffocate her with the horrible smell, and fixed her with a wide grin.

"Well, don't you have beautiful red hair?" he said. "What's your name, sweety?"

"Uh, Madeline," Maddy choked, indicating the name badge on her work uniform. "Can I help you?"

"Sure you can, young lady. Do you have a camping section?"

Maddy pointed. "It's down Aisle 9. Careful of water on the floor. There was a roof leak."

"Can you show me? I'm new to the area—haven't been in here before."

Maddy hesitated, trying to figure out how to turn down the customer. Something about the fellow seemed *off*. He didn't blink enough, and his grin was too wide. Plus, he seemed more than comfortable invading her personal space. From a customer service perspective, those were a lot of red flags.

Luckily, Gabby came to her rescue.

"Hello sir! Are you looking for something?" Gabby said, her heeled boots tapping across the linoleum at a fast pace. "Maddy is finishing up a window display, but I can help you."

"I'd much prefer the assistance of this young lady–"

"It's no problem," Gabby insisted. She hooked the stranger's arm, seemingly immune to the strange herbal stench, then she started walking down the nearest aisle.

"Camping equipment is this way," Gabby sang. "So where are you going? Doing some hunting? You know, this really isn't great weather for camping. There's a lot of flooding in the area. I wouldn't recommend it. They've probably closed most of the sites around here . . . ."

If Gabby thought anything was weird about the fellow, she didn't show it. She kept chatting as she led him away. Maddy saw the man glance back over his shoulder at her, before they both disappeared down an aisle, heading to the back of the store. Maddy sighed in relief when the man was gone from sight. It definitely wasn't the creepiest thing to happen at the hardware store, but it left her feeling unnerved.

Maddy checked the clock, eager for her shift to be over, but she had another hour to go. Then she went back to stacking her little pyramid of roof putty.

Chapter 9

It was close to nine o'clock in the evening when Maddy emptied the bins around the store, tied up all the plastic bags, and wheeled the trash out to the dumpsters behind the warehouse.

Gabby was counting out the register, and Marciella had already gone home for the day. Mr. Hawkins was next door talking to Sarah. Maddy smirked when she saw him climbing the staircase to his office above Calico's Vintage Wares. No doubt Sarah's secret paramore had already left. She wondered who the man had been, but she supposed she would never find out now, since today was her last day on the schedule.

Somehow, Maddy had pushed through the rest of her shift without succumbing to an anxiety attack. Money troubles were heavy on her mind. She still hadn't figured out what she was going to do. Black River wasn't exactly a booming center of commerce, and she didn't have a driver's license yet. She was desperate enough to drive without a license, but her school schedule would make getting down to Davenport difficult, and she didn't own a car.

A weekend night shift at the Sapphire Club was starting to look more and more appealing. She wondered what Gareth would say if she tried out as a dancer. She could already imagine his reaction. Yeah, he would hate it. But she knew the tips were good, and she was feeling more desperate than usual. She wondered if she had the guts to sneak around his back. He would notice eventually, but maybe she could pick up a shift for a month or two, make enough tips to pay her property taxes. Maybe getting up on stage wasn't that scary? Maybe she didn't have to go topless or do anything extreme. Maybe she could keep it tame, like wearing a leotard?

She sighed. Who was she kidding? Realistically, she didn't know how to dance, and pole dancing was a whole other level. Plus, if the club served alcohol, she would have to be over twenty-one. She hadn't thought of that before. She didn't know much about the establishment. But maybe it was worth inquiring?

Her phone pinged in her pocket. Maddy set down her trash bags and fished the lump of black plastic out of her hoodie. A text from Gareth was waiting for her.

Where are you?

Maddy sighed. A bit of her worry eased from her brow. She texted back.

About to get off work

Heading to your place in a few minutes

Our place

I'm just down the street

I'll pick you up

Maddy smiled when she saw his text. *Yeah, our place.*

Then she dragged the four heavy black trash bags up to the side of the large industrial-sized dumpster. A cold wind blew across the dark, damp parking lot. The streetlights were still out. It was pretty creepy. Her eyes combed the darkness, feeling a strange chill on the back of her neck, but besides the wind, the night remained uneventful and quiet.

Gareth's Camaro rolled into the parking lot a few minutes later. Maddy breathed a sigh of relief, feeling a knot of tension loosen between her shoulder blades. The old muscle car rumbled to a halt. Gareth opened the door and climbed out as she ran to him across the cracked asphalt. She threw herself into his arms and embraced him in a tight hug.

"Aww," he grumbled in his low baritone, leaning into her hug. "I missed you too, baby."

She pressed her face into his chest and inhaled his scent. Yeah, she needed that. Then she looked up at him. "Can you hold on a moment? I still need to clock out from work. I'll be right back."

Gareth's jaw clenched, his expression changing, becoming firm and focused. His head lifted. His eyes focused on the willow trees that lined the back of the lot, separating the parking area from an undeveloped parcel of land behind the hardware store. He gazed at the trees, unblinking. Maddy wondered if he smelled anything unusual. He looked suddenly grim.

His hand caught her upper arm.

"Wait, Mads," he murmured.

"What is it?"

She sniffed the air, trying to mimic his werewolf senses, but her nose wasn't as keen as his. She felt a little silly. She just smelled the Camaro's exhaust. She tried to pull away, but his grip remained firm on her upper arm. Then the wind shifted, and with a jolt of alarm, Maddy caught the stench of werewolves. She would never forget that smell from the corn fields at Fright Farm. It made her viscerally ill.

Maddy trembled as three men materialized out of the shadows at the back of the parking lot. The air vanished from her lungs. She thought she might suffocate. The men—obviously werewolves—strode onto the asphalt, appearing through the drooping branches of the willow trees.

Maddy wanted to run, but her legs seemed frozen to the ground. Shit, she was terrified. Gareth seemed a lot more calm. Of course, he would. He had decimated a dozen wolves on Friday night. She doubted he was scared of anything.

Slowly, Gareth drew her behind him, placing his body between her and the approaching men. Their leader stopped about fifteen feet away. Maddy's eyes flickered over the tall stranger curiously. It was difficult to discern his features in the shadowy parking lot; she couldn't tell his age. He wore a double-breasted, tan trench coat with a black hoodie underneath, the hood pulled up. He was as tall as Gareth, though probably not as broad-chested underneath all those clothes, and he smelled like a rangy mutt.

Maddy's eyes darted from the trench-coated man to the back doors of the hardware store. The back of the shop was still open, technically, but the doors were about fifty feet away. She didn't know if she could run fast enough to get back inside, if these wolves decided to pounce.

"Don't worry," the man before them said. "I'm not here to fight."

He had a deep, warm voice with a sing-song accent. He sounded unexpectedly French. It took Maddy off guard. Perhaps he was from Quebec? Her mouth had gone dry with fear, and she tried to summon enough saliva to speak.

"What do you want?" Gareth called. He didn't sound friendly in the least.

The man folded his arms across his chest, his legs planted in a wide stance. His head cocked to one side.

"Just wanted to get a look at my prize."

My prize.

Maddy didn't understand what he meant. His prize? She sensed Gareth stiffen next to her. She glanced up at her Alpha, but she couldn't read the expression on his face with his back turned to her.

"I am Gabriel Marquis," the stranger said, "Alpha of the Grayridge pack."

Maddy felt the world tip a little to the left. Shit. Marquis? She clutched at Gareth's back, shaken by the sound of the enemy Alpha's name. So this was the man who had killed Dean in cold blood, and left the scarecrow outside of Gareth's garage. His initials were *G. M.*, just like the letter they found pinned to Dean's body. She should have known Marquis would still be lurking around Black River, but she never expected to see him here, at her workplace. It was unnerving. That meant the Grayridge pack had followed her around town, keeping tabs on her daily routine. For how long had they lurked around, watching her?

Her eyes raked over the Alpha again, trying to discern his features, but his face was mostly hidden by the shadows of the parking lot. She thought she saw an outline like a goatee around his mouth. Was his hair long or short beneath his hood? His jaw, narrow or broad? She really couldn't tell. It was difficult to reconcile all that violence with his fluid, lyrical Québécois accent.

Marquis cocked his head to one side, returning her curious look, but Gareth planted his body between them.

"Madeline Donovan, isn't it?" Marquis grinned. He said her name like *Madeleena*, with a very soft "ah" at the end.

"One more step, and I'll rip out your eyes," Gareth snarled.

Of course, Marquis took a step forward. Maddy jumped back and rammed her shoulder into the side of the car. Her heart pounded in her chest, drumming against her ribcage. She could tell this Alpha was strong by his potent wolf-stench, but Marquis' smell didn't appeal to her the way Gareth's did. She wrinkled her nose. Shit, why wasn't Gareth doing anything? She glanced up at him. His fists were clenched at his sides. The muscles bulged along his arms. He looked ready for a fight. But when Marquis took yet another step forward, he didn't retaliate.

"Why don't you get gone, before I lose my patience," Gareth said threateningly.

"I want to give you a choice," Marquis said. "Hand over your precious breeder, and I'll consider your debts paid. I'll drop the Challenge. I'll even let you join our pack, if you want. You can still enjoy her, but . . . you'll have to share her with the rest of my men."

"Fuck off," Gareth snarled.

"Oh? I know you're alone out here. You don't have many other options. So I thought I would be fair. Join the Grayridge pack and I'll call off the Alpha Challenge. Hand over your breeder. Nobody has to die."

Maddy's mouth gaped open, shocked and outraged by Marquis' offer. She wasn't a piece of meat to be bargained over. She felt a burst of pure rage. Before Gareth could respond, she jumped to the attack.

"Fuck you!" Maddy yelled, surprising both the men. Gareth reached out an arm to block her when she lunged forward. He caught her around the waist, holding her back.

"You killed my stepdad! You're nothing but a murderer!" Maddy screamed.

Marquis laughed. He genuinely sounded amused. "You mean, Dean Harvey? He was your father? I suppose even cockroaches have families. Sorry for your loss, but you must understand, I'm a businessman, and Mr. Harvey was a bad investment. It's not personal. He became more trouble than he was worth. You can blame your Alpha for that."

Maddy felt another surge of rage. This was the bastard who had ruined her life. His men had chased her into the woods and tried to rape her. Then they attempted to kidnap her at Fright Farm. Now she was homeless, all because of the Grayridge pack, and their Alpha was standing right in front of her, sneering. She felt a surge of fire shoot up her spine. She thought, maybe, her feet grew a little more pointed.

"*You* killed Dean, you disgusting bastard!" she screamed. "You ruined my life. You're a mangey, stinking, ugly *coward*. I would *never* join your pack."

"That's enough, Mads," Gareth said softly, his grip tight on her arm as she struggled to break free.

Marquis scoffed. "Feisty little wolf, eh? I'll forgive your outburst . . . *this time*. Consider my offer: a pack can give you protection. Money. Security. We keep our breeders well. It's not a bad life. Some females get a power trip from it, all those randy males eager to mate. You can take your pick. I can offer you pleasure like you've never experienced before."

Gareth snarled. A deep and ferocious sound rumbled from his chest, loud as a lion. The hair stood up on Maddy's arms. She stared at the Grayridge Alpha, hardly able to believe his words. Did he really just promise her *pleasure* if she came willingly? Did he expect her to betray Gareth that easily? It made her absolutely livid.

"I'll never be your breeder bitch," she seethed.

Marquis' smirk widened. His gaze returned to Gareth. "She is young, so maybe she doesn't understand her full potential. You should educate her—then let the bitch choose." He flicked a business card onto the ground. "Think about my offer, yeah? I'll give you a week to consider it. You've got my number. I'll be waiting for your text."

With a snarl, Gareth reached under his jacket, pulling his pistol out of the band of his pants. It was tucked against the small of his back. Maddy gasped in surprise. She hadn't realized he was armed all this time. Gareth held the gun out before him with both hands and clicked off the safety.

"Get the fuck out of my sight," he growled menacingly, "before I end the Challenge right here."

The wolves behind Marquis froze. No one moved. They looked just as surprised as Maddy to see Gareth wielding a sleek black Glock. Marquis' hands slowly rose into the air. He grinned one last time at Maddy, his eyes gleaming in the dark like a nocturnal animal, visible beneath his hood. Then he made a little motion with his wrists, and the three wolves turned away, swiftly retreating across the parking lot. Within a minute, they had vanished once again under the willow trees.

Maddy gazed after the Grayridge wolves, still anxious, her eyes straining to pierce the shadows under the grove of weeping willows. Without the light from the parking lot's streetlamps, she couldn't see much of anything, but she didn't think Marquis and his wolves had gone far. She shivered in disgust and rage.

Gareth kept his pistol held at ready as he walked over to the business card on the ground. He picked it up and glanced over it. Maddy caught sight of the logo on the card, which looked familiar. She craned her neck a bit, then she grimaced. It was for the River King Casino, Dean's favorite spot to throw away a paycheck. She wrinkled her nose, remembering all the times her stepdad had stumbled home in the evening, liquor heavy on his breath, ranting about his lost winnings. It was always the same story: he won a fortune on his first five dollars in the slots, then he lost it all at the tables. And of course, the games were all rigged.

Maddy glanced up at Gareth, waiting for his reaction to the whole ordeal, but he remained quiet, turning the business card over in his hands.

Suddenly, the tension was interrupted by Gabby's high-pitched, feminine voice hollering across the parking lot: "Maddy? Is that you? Did you finish taking the trash out?"

Maddy jumped, startled. She whirled around, facing the hardware store, her heart unexpectedly in her throat. Shit, how much had Gabby seen? She had totally forgotten about her coworkers in the hardware store.

Gabby was standing at the back door, her arms crossed over her employee uniform, looking concerned. The middle-aged blond lady turned her head back and forth, peering around the dark parking lot. The perm had fallen out of her hair, which tumbled around her shoulders in a messy tangle. As Maddy watched, Gabby pulled a scrunchy out of her pocket and tied her hair back in a high ponytail.

Then Gabby yelled, "What's going on out here? I thought I heard voices. Everything alright?" After a pause, she added, "Is that a gun?"

Gareth clicked the safety on his pistol and tucked it back under his jacket. Then he shifted his weight onto one hip, adopting a much more casual stance, his hands shoved in his pockets.

"Nope, it's nothing, not at all," Maddy said quickly, forcing out an awkward laugh. "Uh, my ride's here, but I forgot to clock out. Are you locking the doors?"

"Yeah, come in and punch out, then I'll lock up." Gabby's narrow eyes swept over Gareth with a flicker of recognition. He was a local, after all, and he had come around the hardware store plenty of times. She relaxed slightly. "Sir, we're closed for the evening, so I can't let you in," Gabby called.

He raised a hand to her. "No worries. I'll wait out here."

Maddy shared a quick glance with Gareth. He saw the unspoken question in her gaze, and he gave her a slight nod. Then Maddy started for the back doors of the hardware store. She was halfway across the parking lot before she realized what she had done, and she groaned inwardly at herself. Did she really just ask his permission to go inside and clock out? Like, really?

Gabby moved aside to give her room as she ran through the glass double doors. The blond shopkeeper held a lanyard full of keys in hand. She looked frazzled and ready to go home for the day.

"Oh hey, Maddy?" Gabby called as she rushed past.

Maddy slowed her step and glanced over her shoulder. She felt a little jittery and distracted after the confrontation in the parking lot. "Yeah, what is it?" she asked.

Gabby continued, "I'm really sorry to tell you this, hon, but Sarah wanted you to clear out your stuff from the back. I don't know if you have anything important in the break room, but just make sure you take everything with you. It's probably going to be like last year. Mr. Hawkins will bring you back closer to Christmas, when the rush picks up again. I'll give you a call when I see your name back on the schedule."

Maddy had almost forgotten her conversation with Sarah earlier that day, she was so sidetracked by Marquis' unexpected visit. Right. No more job. Tons of bills. Life falling apart. She sucked in a deep breath, feeling her pulse begin to pound in her temples.

"Sure, I get it, no problem," Maddy said with a weak voice. Actually, *big problem*, but not like Gabby could do anything to help her.

Then Maddy continued through the store. Only the front was lit, and she used her phone light to guide her way through the dark aisles to the employee break room. Punching out her timecard felt like a mundane way to end the evening, especially after the sudden appearance of the Grayridge Alpha. Then she opened her little square cubby and grabbed her backpack. She had a few snacks stashed away, and a stack of little cards, notes and inside jokes the team had written for her. She took them all down without blinking an eye. It was silly to get sentimental over leaving a job. This wasn't her first rodeo. She knew Mr. Hawkins would probably put her back on the schedule around the holidays, but she couldn't help but feel a little sad.

With her backpack slung over one shoulder, she left the building. Gabby gave her a friendly wave before locking the door behind her.

"Goodbye, Hawkins' Hardware," Maddy mumbled under her breath as she waved back.

Then Maddy dashed to Gareth's car. A few raindrops struck her face. It looked like the storm was starting up again. In relief, she found the parking lot still empty. No epic Alpha battle had broken out while she was clearing out her things. Gareth was leaning against the Camaro, looking vigilant but relaxed.

When she reached the car, Maddy asked, "Is the Grayridge pack still hanging around?"

"They're not far off, I can smell them," Gareth growled. "But I don't think they're gonna do much other than lurk around. Get in. Let's go home."

Home.

Maddy climbed into the car and Gareth started up the Camaro. They rolled through the silent streets of Black River at a slow pace, Gareth keeping an eye on the rearview mirror, but they weren't being followed. She noticed him taking a different route home, heading in the opposite direction of his house. He was probably being extra careful.

As they drove through the silent, empty streets, her eyes remained focused outside the window. She scanned the alleyways, the spaces between houses, the shadowy front porches and vacant lots. She couldn't help but feel like the Grayridge pack was lurking just beyond her line of sight. But she didn't see anyone walking around on a night like this, with the power out and the storm looming ominously overhead.

Minutes passed in tense silence. Maddy waited until the tick in his right cheek disappeared, and his arms didn't bulge quite so much.

Then, finally, she said, "So that was . . . um, interesting."

Gareth remained focused on the road, his hands clenched on the wheel.

"What do you think that was about?" she probed again.

"It's just another way to fuck with me, Mads," he sighed, his voice laced with irritation. "Marquis meant to taunt me. He wants me to know he can access you whenever he wants. It's a head game, babygirl."

"So, Gabriel Marquis asked you to join the Grayridge pack?" she asked cautiously. "Like, I didn't miss that. He said . . . if you hand me over, he'll forgive your debts."

"I don't owe that bastard anything."

Maddy licked her dry lips. Her eyes traveled to the window. She gazed outside at the dark, wet night, thinking of Marquis' strangely threatening French accent. "He said he wanted to *see his prize*. What does that mean?"

Gareth reached a stop sign at a residential intersection. Usually he rolled through stop signs like they were mere suggestions, but this time, he put the car in park. He turned to look at her. Maddy braced herself. He looked serious.

"If he wins the Alpha Challenge, by wolf law, he lays claim to what's mine. My territory. My finances. My mate."

Maddy's eyes widened. "That's . . . barbaric."

"Yeah, baby, but it's real."

"I'm your *lifemate*. Doesn't that mean anything?"

Gareth's expression softened. His hand landed on her leg. He gave it a reassuring squeeze.

"It means a lot, babe, but that doesn't stop bastards like Marquis from trying to claim whatever they want. He's looking at Black River like a place to set up business and sell drugs through the casino. Snagging a new breeder for his pack is just a bonus. Keeps his men happy. You're like the cherry on top of a chocolate shitcake."

Maddy almost laughed at his dark humor, even while she hated the thought of being a breeder. She wasn't anyone's property to be passed around or bargained with, but it seemed like the Grayridge pack didn't see her that way. She didn't want to imagine what Marquis would do with her, if she somehow fell into his hands.

Gareth continued, "Don't worry. Wolf law protects us up to a point. Marquis issued an Alpha Challenge, so technically, he can't make a move against me until the day of the fight. Talking to us in a parking lot is about the worst he can do. He probably hoped I would lose my temper and throw a few punches. That would give him leeway to fight back, and I'd be at a disadvantage."

"I didn't realize it was all so complicated."

"Yup. Likewise, if he tries to lay a finger on you, he forfeits the Challenge and I can take him out however I like. It works both ways. The Alpha Challenge is an old tradition, maybe the oldest, between wolf packs. Wolf world has laws and councils. My father is on one of those councils. Marquis has no idea who he's messing with. He better play by the rules; otherwise, he'll have hell to pay."

Maddy felt a little reassured, though she still found the entire situation terrifying.

Gareth squeezed her leg again. "Don't worry. I'll protect you. I'm not gonna lose this fight."

Maddy couldn't hold his gaze any longer, but turned away to stare out the window. She felt totally numb.

"There has to be something I can do to prepare for all this," she said.

"You just stay focused on school and getting through the Change. I'll handle Marquis. That's my job."

Gareth put the car back into gear and rolled through the intersection, continuing to his house. Maddy scowled at her reflection in the window. As much as she hated to admit it, maybe she needed to master the Change. At least then, she could face the Grayridge pack as a wolf. She could flee or fight, or whatever she needed to do to protect herself.

Her eyes slid back to Gareth, her mind lingering on his vitality and his promise to help her with her first Change. She was still scared of becoming a werewolf, but . . . it might be her only option to survive.

Chapter 10

Tuesday morning, half of the classrooms at Black River High School didn't have lights or heat. Two of the five buildings on campus were still without power. A lot of teachers and students were complaining, and an atmosphere of discontent had settled over the whole campus. Maddy sat in a dark, cold homeroom while another substitute teacher read off the announcements for the day. All the kids looked a little tired and disgruntled.

As the substitute teacher read off the different bullet points, Maddy's mind wandered. Last night, Gareth had surprised her after they got home from the hardware store. Her room was filled with new-used furniture: a desk, a dresser and a bookcase. The set was posted online at a thrift shop in downtown Davenport. He went to pick it up for her after work.

Maddy didn't expect to feel the sting of tears in her eyes when she saw the new furniture. She was momentarily overwhelmed by his generosity. She leaned up on her tiptoes to kiss Gareth's cheek.

"*Thank you*," she said sincerely.

"*Aw, you're cute*," he growled in his low, grumbly baritone.

Finally, she could put away her clothes and set up her lamp and laptop on her new desk. A thimble of normalcy was restored to her life. Even that little bit made a difference.

Still, she had tossed and turned last night, unable to fall asleep in his giant bed. Worries over her finances filled her mind. Then more worries over the Grayridge pack. When Gareth first warned her about breeders, she hadn't taken him very seriously. The whole idea was pretty outlandish. Almost silly. But now, her new reality was becoming more clear. She was afraid of what might happen if Gareth lost the Alpha Challenge. She wouldn't go with Marquis willingly, of course, but how was she supposed to escape him if she couldn't even drive? She felt utterly helpless, and she hated it. Being captured and used by a pack of werewolves was far from a sexy, erotic fantasy in her book.

The morning flew by at school. At lunch, students and teachers were encouraged to eat inside the cafeteria, where temporary heat lamps and lighting were set up. As Maddy looked around for a spot to eat her lunch, she almost ran headlong into Kaylee Mackovitch and the Varsity jacket crew, who were walking inside the warm cafeteria. One of the girls pushed Maddy out of way with an aggressive shove, knocking her into the wall of the building. Maddy scraped her hand on the rough brick.

"*Move*," the girl sneered.

Kaylee passed by next. The blond princess kept her nose in the air as she strode through the door, arm-in-arm with her closest bestie, Amy Higgins. Amy glanced at Maddy with a malicious little glare as they walked by.

Maddy swallowed down her anger. She stared after the group of girls, feeling a tingle of red vitality begin at the base of her spine. It made her fingers itch, like they might sprout claws at any minute. She was beginning to recognize the first glimmers of the Change, even if she couldn't control it at all. She wanted to tackle Amy to the ground and drag her nails down the girl's back. For a moment, she let herself fantasize about it. She clenched and unclenched her fists, stretching out her itchy fingers. Then she sighed. She should find somewhere else to eat, in a more secluded place, where she wouldn't be triggered by a bunch of mean girls.

At least she wasn't fainting anymore, which was an improvement from last week, but after her wave of anger had faded, Maddy felt a little dizzy. She needed to eat something. Ugh. She didn't like feeling so out-of-control in her own body.

"Maddy! Hey! Over here!"

She looked up as Bea's voice caught her attention. It looked like Bea's group was sitting outside at a picnic table, sheltered under an ancient beech tree in the middle of the quad. It had stopped raining for the moment. Bea was smoking a cigarette, which technically wasn't allowed on campus, but in the chaos of the day, no one seemed to notice or care.

Maddy started across the quad to join the girls under the tree. Bea was accompanied by her two eccentric friends, Rachelle and Andie. Maddy had met them once before. Andie was very punk rock geek, with two green bangs hanging down either side of her face, and a pair of black-framed glasses. Rachelle was more "pastel Goth," with bubblegum pink hair and bright purple eyeshadow. Today she wore a fuzzy black sweater over a pink chiffon fairy skirt. Her dramatic makeup made her look like a fae queen.

Bea's eyeliner was super thick today, too, and her foundation was extra pasty white.

Maddy slid into the seat across from Bea and gave Andie a little wave.

Rachelle was on the phone talking to her mom: *"Look, it's just a B minus, I'll do better on the next one . . . I know you want me to keep a 4.0 GPA, but A. P. Chemistry is really hard, the teacher has a reputation."*

It sounded like Rachelle's mom had high standards for her daughter, which was unsurprising of the Beaumont family. They were one of the founding families of Black River, with a prestigious reputation to uphold. Rachelle lived out in Elk Haven like the Mackovich family and the other bougie types.

Bea lit up a cigarette and fixed Maddy with a suspicious look.

"You're moody today," she remarked as Maddy flipped up her hood and slouched down at the table.

"I don't feel great," Maddy said, exhausted from another restless night.

"If you're sick, I don't want to catch it," Bea scooted away.

"I'm not sick, I'm just not feeling . . . *right.*"

"Yeah, well, considering everything going on in your life, I'm shocked you're at school."

Maddy glanced around the table, a little self-conscious. The other girls were listening curiously.

"What are you two talking about?" Andie asked.

Maddy shot Bea a desperate look. She didn't want to talk about her stepdad, the trailer, or the animal attack. She really didn't want the whole school knowing about her personal life.

Apparently Bea had some tact, because after blowing out a big cloud of smoke, she said loudly, "Maddy lost her V last Friday! Congratulations, Maddy!"

"Bea!" Maddy gasped, mortified. She wanted to wring her little friend by the neck. "That's private!"

"Oh, who cares? It's just sex," Bea smirked.

"I thought you *lost it* a while ago, Maddy," Andie said. "Like Sophomore year? I'm pretty sure Kendal Sterling said that you guys, um . . . ."

Maddy stared at Andie, her mouth agape. She tried to remember that particular rumor, but Kaylee had spread so many stories about her, it was hard to keep track. Maddy was pretty sure Kendal Sterling was on the football team. He was part of Kaylee's flying monkey crowd.

"Was he the guy who said I had an STD?" Maddy finally remembered.

"Maybe?" Andie hedged.

"Yeah, it was him," Rachelle confirmed. "He said you had sex with him and you gave him an STD. Which is obviously not true."

Great. Maddy didn't like thinking about Sophomore year. That was the same year her breasts decided to explode overnight, and everyone started calling her Porno Titties. Kaylee's bullying had escalated, and the two girls got into so many fights, Maddy almost got expelled from the school district.

"So you *didn't* have sex Sophomore year?" Andie asked cautiously.

"No. I didn't fuck Kendal Sterling, if that's what you mean, and I don't have an STD," Maddy said with a sour tone. "Did you two really think I had sex in Sophomore year?"

"Everyone at school thinks that," Rachelle answered, "thanks to Kaylee, of course. Now she's got half the campus believing you work as a dancer at the Sapphire Club, nevermind the condom incident last week. Ugh, I can't believe I was ever friends with her."

"Yeah, I can't stand her," Bea cut in.

Maddy felt hurt and a little pissed off. She was so sick of Kaylee's insidious rumors. She knew the Varsity jackets were bad news, but she hadn't realized the whole campus believed Kaylee without question. She thrummed her fingers on the metal table, thinking of what it would feel like to rake her nails across Kaylee's stupid pixie face. Why did the thought make her feel so happy?

"Speaking of Kaylee, I saw she RSVP'd to the Halloween Haunt event. We're still friends on Picplace," Rachelle explained.

Bea snorted. "Are you serious? She's going to the Halloween Haunt? What, does she think she's a badass now?"

"It's senior year, so she's probably trying to live it up." Rachelle rolled her eyes. "Last year she wouldn't go with me because she didn't want to get her boots muddy. I think she just didn't want to hang out with, you know, uh . . . ."

"Poor people?" Maddy offered.

Rachelle had the decency to look a little embarrassed. She shrugged. Yeah, the real problem was that Kaylee thought she was better than everyone because she had more money. It was no secret. Unfortunately, a lot of people thought like that, which was part of the reason why the campus put her on a pedestal.

"Wait, what's the Halloween Haunt?" Maddy asked. She didn't know anything about the Halloween Haunt and she had never been invited before. She felt a bit like an outcast.

"You don't know?" Bea looked surprised. "It's, like, an upriver tradition. Every Halloween, there's a big bonfire party somewhere on the mountainside. They change the location every year to keep it anonymous. It's a real rager. Becca took me during Freshman year, back when she was cool, before she got all weird and strict. The party is 'invite only' because there's a lot of underage drinking and stuff."

"Yeah," Rachelle agreed. "Details just posted on Picplace. It's a private event. Looks like they're holding it at Devil's Tower this year."

"Devil's Tower? That's kind of dangerous, isn't it?" Maddy said, a little skeptical.

"That's what makes it fun," Bea grinned.

Then Rachelle showed them the event page on her phone screen. Maddy looked at the list of RSVP's. It looked like over a hundred kids were attending. Some pictures were posted of the party from last year, which looked like it took place at an old barn out in the countryside. Maddy saw a lot of kegs, and a lot of people in costume dancing around a bonfire. Alright, so it looked pretty fun, even though she wasn't into large crowded events.

As Rachelle scrolled through the attendee list, Maddy recognized a bunch of names from their high school. Some of the students had graduated in the last year or two.

"What's the Devil's Tower?" Andie asked.

"It's an abandoned cement factory up on the mountain, kind of out toward Elk Haven. It's fenced off. There's 'No Trespassing' signs and everything," Maddy explained. She had hiked up there last summer when she didn't have anything better to do. She hadn't gone into the tower itself, just looked at the outside of the building. The exterior cement walls were covered in vibrant graffiti murals, but she wasn't brave enough to explore any deeper on her own. The building was over fifty years old, with a lot of loose stairwells and sagging floors that could crumble under a wrong step. Never mind all the broken glass, old needles and other trash that had accumulated over the years.

"That seems like a really risky place to hold a party," Maddy repeated.

"Yeah, well, they're probably not going to light all the bonfires *inside* the tower. The party will be held outside somewhere. The cement factory will be in the background, like ambiance," Bea said, lighting up a second cigarette. She held it low under the table, like the whole quad couldn't smell the stink of burning tobacco.

"It's this Saturday," Rachelle sighed. "Well, I can't go because I'll be in the City shopping with my mom."

"I'm going," Bea said. "Do you want to go with me, Maddy?"

"Maybe. I don't know. I probably shouldn't," Maddy mumbled. She supposed she could go with Bea, but considering all the werewolf drama going on, it probably wasn't a good idea.

"I'll go with you," Andie offered. "I'm free this Saturday."

"Oh, awesome. Yay! I didn't want to go alone," Bea looked relieved. "Do you have a costume?"

"I was going to cosplay as this anime character. Do you think it's too much?"

Andie took out her phone and opened her photos. She showed Bea a picture of an anime girl with teal hair, dressed in a schoolgirl uniform with a short blue skirt, a big bow on her chest, and knee-high teal boots. She was making a peace sign over her forehead. Maddy didn't recognize the character.

"It's Sailor Mercury from Sailor Moon Crystal, the reboot," Andie explained. "Have you seen it? I think I can keep my hair the same. But I don't know which version of the sailor scout uniform I should wear."

Bea leaned over the pic, nodding sagely as she shared her opinion, while Maddy picked at her fingernails. She wished she could join Bea and Andie. She hadn't dressed up for Halloween since eighth grade. Even with the threat of the Grayridge pack hanging over her head, she wanted to join her new friends, but she knew Gareth would be against it. What if she Changed into a werewolf in the middle of a Halloween-bonfire-rager? It would be on theme, but it probably wouldn't go over well.

"I'm going to the cafeteria, it's cold out here," Rachelle said, standing and picking up her backpack.

"I'll go with you, I'm freezing," Andie added. "How about you guys?"

"I'm going to finish my cigarette," Bea said.

"I'll stay outside, too," Maddy waved goodbye.

The girls waved back and headed toward the cafeteria. Bea puffed on her cigarette for a moment. Then she glanced at Maddy.

"So, do you still want to look for your dog after school?" she asked.

Shit, Joker. Maddy's eyes widened. She had almost forgotten about their plans to find the dog. Well, that was one benefit of losing her job—she didn't need to worry about her work schedule anymore.

"Yes, for sure, let's go," she agreed.

Bea glanced around the quad, which was mostly empty. She leaned forward conspiratorially, catching Maddy's eye. "So I overheard some teachers talking in the hallway this morning. There's going to be a campus walk-off after lunch today. I guess the teachers are protesting having to work without power. So a bunch of kids are going to head home, too. I was thinking of ditching this afternoon."

Maddy's eyebrows went up. "Really?" She fiddled with her phone for a moment, considering it.

"I mean, a lot of people are going home. If you haven't noticed, it's already pretty empty."

Maddy glanced around. She had assumed everyone was in the cafeteria, but she saw Bea's point. They were the only two students still outside, except for a couple holding hands near the basketball courts. Across the quad, she saw Principal Rodriguez stalking toward the Administration Building with a scowl on his face. Two teachers followed behind him, talking at his back. One of them held a clipboard. It looked like an argument. So maybe Bea was telling the truth.

Well, if the teachers were leaving, then students might be released for the rest of the day, too.

"Alright, I guess I'll head home with you."

"Awesome!" Bea grinned. "Do you want to walk to your trailer? I think we should start by looking around your house. I read online that it's the best place to look. A lot of lost pets are found under the porch, or near the trash cans around your home, and like, there's a lot of trash in your yard."

"Uh, thanks, yeah," Maddy grimaced. Sometimes Bea's honesty was a bit much.

Maddy felt a little shiver of dread at the thought of returning to her trailer, but she pushed it down. She knew she would have to go back eventually. She should really check on the property and make sure no one had broken into her house. Still, the memory of Dean's gruesome demise haunted her thoughts. She didn't like the idea of returning to the location of his death.

Be real, she told herself. Marquis had already approached Gareth outside the hardware store. If the Grayridge pack wanted to kidnap her, they would have done so last night. *Nothing bad is going to happen.* Still, she should probably talk to Gareth before heading over.

"Let me text Gareth. I'll let him know the plan."

"Do you think he'll help us search?" Bea asked. "Maybe Vin can come, too?"

"Uh, they're working today," Maddy hesitated, "but I can ask."

"Cool. Hey, the garage is next to Tiny Costco, isn't it? Your sugardaddy should pick up some pepperoni sticks and peanut butter to lure out the dog. If he wants to help, I mean."

"I'll see what he says."

Tiny Costco was the local name for Sunshine Grocery, a little convenience store attached to a gas station next to Jack's Auto Repair. The owners of Sunshine Grocery bought up Costco goods downriver and sold them at a markup. It was too expensive for Maddy to shop there, but she bought ice cream bars from them during the summer.

Maddy unlocked her screen and started texting Gareth the new plan. Then she hesitated. It might be better if she called him. She stood up from the table. "Just a minute," she said to Bea.

Her friend was scrolling through reels on Picplace and waved her off.

Maddy walked over to an empty part of the quad and hit the "Call" button. She felt a little squirmy, calling Gareth in the middle of the day at work. It rang several times. He picked up on the fourth ring, right before it went to voicemail.

"Hey babe," he grunted into the phone.

Maddy sucked in a breath, suddenly nervous. "Uh, hi."

"You alright?" There was a pause, and Maddy could imagine Gareth checking the time. "You at school?"

"Um, yeah, I'm fine, nothing's wrong," she said. "So, a lot of students and teachers are leaving campus early today. The power is still out. Bea and I want to go looking for Joker. We were thinking of going to the trailer this afternoon."

He didn't answer immediately. Maddy heard a rustling sound as Gareth shifted the phone around in his hands. She heard a clunk as he set down something heavy. Then his deep baritone resonated through the speaker, *"Hey Vin, gimme a moment."*

"Is that your girl, boss?"

"Yup."

It sounded like Vin was standing right next to him. They must have been working on a car together. More shuffling and crackling over the phone's speaker. She imagined Gareth walking through the auto garage, wiping grease off his hands on a rag as he tucked his phone into his breast pocket. She waited, feeling a little more awkward.

The acoustics changed subtly as he stepped into his office and shut the door.

"I don't want you around the trailer after last night," he said.

Maddy frowned. "But I don't think Marquis is going to bother us again. Didn't you say the laws of the Alpha Challenge protect us?"

"I did, but . . . I dunno, Mads. I don't trust the Grayridge pack to follow the rules. A lot of bad shit keeps happening around your place."

"Well, we have to find Joker." Maddy heard the stubbornness in her voice. "I promised Bea we would go today. She really wants to help."

Another beat of silence passed. She chewed on her lip. She could sense Gareth's resistance, but she knew he cared about the dog, too. Then, finally, he sighed. "Alright. When are you planning to be there?"

"We're going to walk over after school."

"So like, an hour?"

"Yeah."

"I guess Vin can drive the tow truck this afternoon. I'll close up shop and help you look. I don't want you wandering around alone in those woods."

Maddy felt a flood of relief. This was a much safer idea than going alone with Bea. With Gareth helping them, she felt a lot more confident that they would find the missing dog.

He could use his werewolf senses to sniff out Joker's trail in the woods. With all the rain this week, it might be hard to track down a single pitbull in a large forest, but it would be a lot more effective than wandering around with a jar of peanut butter.

"Okay, I'll text you when we get to the trailer," Maddy said.

"Alright. Be safe." There was a pause, like he was about to add something, but he held back. Maddy filled in the words in her head: *love you*. He didn't say it. She gripped the phone, hesitating. Maybe she should say it first? Was this the right time? A casual "*love you*" over the phone seemed harmless and lowkey. Maybe even a little whimsical.

But then the moment passed.

"Okay, uh, see you," she mumbled. She hung up the phone.

***

Gareth stared at the cell phone screen for a moment in thought. Then he set down the brick of plastic with a sigh. He leaned back against his metal computer desk in his small office. Well, shit. Fucked that one up. Should've said the words lingering on his tongue, but he over-thought it. Maddy could tell. She had sounded a little sad hanging up the phone. That was his fault. Damn, he was dumb.

He didn't think he had ever said, "*I love you,*" to a girl. He was an amateur like that. His life had been pretty chaotic since getting out of the military, and hitchhiking across the U. S. wasn't exactly a sexy occupation. He didn't really have time for more than a hookup here and there, and after finding his lifemate in Black River, he hadn't dated seriously.

So yeah, he knew women liked that mushy stuff, but the last few days, he'd been more focused on keeping Maddy safe. He was good at that. As for romance, he was learning right along with her. He knew he should say something. She probably needed to hear it. But . . . they were just getting to know each other. If he blurted out all his feelings, wouldn't he just be putting more weight on her shoulders?

Buying new bedroom furniture for her was like an apology, the least he could do after dumping this shitstorm on her life. He knew her current predicament was entirely his fault, and he felt a good amount of guilt over it. He had spent a lot of time thinking about Sunday night on his drive down to Davenport, remembering her meltdown in his arms, her body twitching and shivering around his cock as hard sobs ripped from her throat. It surprised him. He knew his cock was a lot to handle. He still wasn't convinced he hadn't hurt her. Not every woman liked his size; some women clutched their pearls and turned him down. Maddy was a wolf girl, but she was also a virgin. After seeing her cry like that, he wondered if he had opened her up too soon, fucked her too deep, showed too much of his monster. She was getting attached, which he wanted, but he didn't want to stir up all that pain. Maybe he should slow his roll on the sex and coast for a while?

He sighed and leaned back on his hands. Well, shit. *Not* fucking her would also be a challenge. He needed to give her his vitality somehow, and this was the easiest, fastest way to stimulate her wolf blood. That, and her sensual curves drove him wild. He wanted to smack that sweet ass every time she walked past him. He didn't know if he could control himself, especially if she initiated.

Sleeping next to her like a decent, respectful boyfriend was *hard*, in more ways than one. His cock just wouldn't quit. Talk about a special kind of torture. If she knew how much he wanted to fuck her in her sleep, press himself inside her all nice and cozy, keep her impaled on him all night long like a comfortable, warm, drippy little pillow, she'd probably sleep on the floor.

Ah, he hadn't even started doing half the things he craved. But . . . werewolf sex was the big leagues. She wasn't ready for it. He groaned, thinking of Sunday night again. Her passionate tears had been strangely erotic. His knot had swelled up. It did that, when he was really enjoying himself, and rough sex could trigger the Change. Yeah. He had never gone full wolf on a girl—that would be a little too bestial—but werewolf cock had a following on the internet. Some of the stuff on Rule 34 wasn't just a fantasy. Fucking a monster was a whole different kind of ride.

He wondered if Maddy would ever cross that line. If she'd be cool with it. Or if he'd have to rein in the wolf every time they got frisky. Hard to say. But if she was going to be part of his world—a world she belonged to—she would get a taste of it sooner or later. Hopefully then, her tears would be pure pleasure.

Gareth glanced out the window of his office at the forest behind the car lot. A gentle mist clung between the trees. He thought of the bloody, roadkill-covered scarecrow that Vin had dismantled and thrown into the woods. A bonafide Alpha Challenge, right in his backyard. Marquis probably hoped to scare him off, but Gareth wasn't going anywhere. He liked living this far away from the city. He grew up in Phoenix, in the heavy heat of the Sonoran desert, and he found life in Black River to be a nice change of pace. After his stint serving in the Army, he enjoyed the relative peace and seclusion of the mountains, plus his business was finally turning a profit. This year, he was doing really good. He didn't plan on leaving the backwoods of Jefferson County anytime soon.

Which meant he needed to win this Challenge.

It seemed clear that the Grayridge Alpha, Marquis, was now lurking around Black River. He really shouldn't be surprised that Marquis had finally made his way to town, though he had hoped the shit weather would delay him another week or two. At least enough time for Gareth to wrap his head around the whole situation. He didn't know where the bastard was headquartered, if he hailed from Ontario or Quebec or Niagara Falls, or wherever. It didn't matter. The business card he gave Maddy was for the River King Casino. As far as Gareth knew, Marquis kept an office there.

Gabriel Marquis showing up last night at the hardware store to harass Maddy was an unexpected surprise. It was a bold move, and it left a bad taste in Gareth's mouth. He didn't like other Alphas trying to move on his girl. He knew Marquis just wanted to piss him off; his enemy liked to play head games. Marquis wanted to keep Gareth off balance, wondering what he might do next. Well, it wasn't going to work.

Gareth shifted to his computer chair and sat down. He propped his legs up onto his metal desk. Then he opened his phone and scrolled through his contacts. He landed on his younger brother's contact info.

He hadn't talked to Antony in five years. But if he was going up against an enemy Alpha, he needed someone to protect Maddy if the worst happened. He didn't plan on losing to a shaggy bastard like Marquis, but he also knew the risk. Alpha fights could get out of hand. Lots of drugs existed on the black market, potions and serums and strength-enhancing steroids, brewed by shamans and shifters alike, to aid a wolf in battle. He didn't expect a clean fight.

Asking for help was not Gareth's strong suit. But this was a special case. He wondered briefly if his brother had changed his number. Guess he was about to find out.

Gareth hit the "Call" button.

The phone rang a few times. Then someone picked up.

"Hey bro, long time no talk."

Gareth was relieved. It was strange, hearing his brother's voice after so many years. Antony sounded nonchalant, as though they had just spoken a week ago.

"Yeah, been a minute," Gareth said.

"Let me guess. You're calling to wish me 'happy birthday?'" Antony asked.

"Shit, is it really . . . ?"

"Just kidding, bro," Antony laughed. "The fuck is up?"

"Asshole," Gareth grinned. So maybe some things hadn't changed over the last five years. "Look, I got a problem on my hands, and I thought maybe you could help me out."

"A problem, huh? *No fucking way.* The infamous Lobo Loco got himself in trouble? I don't believe it."

"Cut that shit out."

"You still out on the East coast?" Antony asked.

Gareth was a little taken aback, but maybe he shouldn't be surprised. "Did mom tell you that?"

"No, she doesn't know where you live. I helped her setup the money transfer for the downpayment on your house, and you know, titles are listed under public records. Don't get mad. You weren't hard to track."

Gareth sighed. Tony was whip smart. He recalled his little brother taking college-level programming classes in 8th grade.

"Alright, so you know where I live," Gareth said. "Look, there's a wolf pack out here giving me problems. When I first moved to the area, there weren't any other shifters around. But a group showed up recently and–"

"Let me guess. They issued an Alpha Challenge?"

"How did you know?"

"It's posted on the wolf web."

Gareth groaned and put a hand to his temples. Bullshit. No wonder Antony acted like they had just spoken yesterday. His tech-savvy younger brother was keeping tabs on him. He really shouldn't be surprised. Antony worked in data security, so he knew how to dig up information about people.

"The Alpha Challenge is on the wolf web?" Gareth said. "Didn't realize that was a thing."

"Yeah, it's the new law. They instituted it last year. Every challenge has to be posted a week in advance on an official site for it to be considered binding. This guy must be serious; he wants you off his turf. What was his name again? *Something* Marquis? He knows all about you, too. The challenge went live yesterday and he listed your name, lineage, everything. You're lucky dad is old school and never uses his wolf web credentials. Otherwise he'd be pissed his name got attached to all this."

"I see. Well, shit. Glad I called you, then," Gareth growled. "I need info on this Alpha. His pack is a bunch of drug-dealing scumbags. Nasty, violent fuckers. I don't think this is gonna be a fair fight."

"Got it. Maybe I'll help, but first I gotta ask, why all the drama? What's keeping you up in Northern New York? You know, Mom's all excited about some girl you called her about. You dating someone?" Tony paused. "She a wolf?"

Gareth didn't say anything. He suddenly felt protective.

Tony's voice went a notch deeper. "Holy shit. You got a mate, bro? Is that why you're not leaving the area? You know, dad's gonna want to know if you're making babies."

"Shit, Tony, this is not why I called you," Gareth said. "No babies yet."

"*Yet?* Then it's true. You met a wolf girl way out in the twigs. You're starting your own pack. Dad's gonna—"

"I don't give a shit what Dad is gonna do," Gareth growled.

Antony went quiet. At first Gareth thought he might be upset, but then he heard an intense clicking and clacking at a keyboard. He frowned as the noise persisted.

"Are you playing a videogame right now?" he asked.

"Yeah, I'm on a dungeon raid with my guild." After another long, obnoxious pause, Antony asked, "So does your mate have a name?"

"Yeah, uh, it's Madeline. Goes by Maddy." Then he added, "I'd rather you not pass all this along to the family just yet."

"No worries, bro. Your secret breeder is safe with me."

"She's not a breeder."

"Oh? So you didn't buy her off the black market?" He could hear the smirk in Antony's voice. "Good on you, big bro, sticking to your principles. You know Diego bought one at an auction."

"No shit?"

"Yup. Just a few months ago. I don't think it's going well, though. She ran off. He's been looking for her."

"What does Mom think of that, after Roselia?" Gareth asked.

"Oh, she was pissed. Pretty sure Mom had something to do with the girl disappearing. But you know, Diego's always been . . . ."

"A bastard?"

"Yeah, to put it nicely."

Their older brother, Diego, was heir to the Sonoran wolf kingdom, which made him very rich and also very much an asshole. Buying a personal breeder was basically participating in sex trafficking, and it made Gareth's temper flare. His family should know better than that. Their *tía*, Roselia, had been kidnapped at fifteen and sold into slavery at a breeder's auction. His mother finally located Roselia more than twenty years later, living with a pack in North Hollywood. Then, at his mom's begging, his psychopathic father went to recover her. That's when the war started.

Those were crazy years. His father rescued his aunt and little cousins in a bloodbath that triggered a war with the LA wolf kingdom. Which should make his dad a hero, but really, he was just a scary motherfucker.

Gareth remembered all the Alphas in the LA Empire making their separate challenges against his father. Lots of fighting, Alpha-to-Alpha. His mom was a wreck. He and his brothers went into hiding. His dad was gone a lot, traveling to California "on business." Their family never knew when or if he would come home. Oddly enough, it was also the most peaceful time he could remember living with his mom and brothers, with his father out of the house.

After his pops won the day, the LA Empire fractured and fell apart, but then his dad suddenly lost interest and settled down in Phoenix. So he single-handedly dismantled the LA wolf kingdom, and after all that, he left the territory in shambles without a head.

Out of all the brothers, Diego was probably the most like their father. He was certainly the most ruthless. He probably bought himself a breeder because he didn't understand the concept of dating, courtship, or any of it. In werewolf terms, he was a lot more wolf than man. Actually, Gareth couldn't recall Diego ever bringing home a girl. He was pretty aloof. This breeder might have been his first.

"So now that you know about Maddy," Gareth said, "what I'm about to ask probably won't come as much surprise. The Alpha Challenge puts her at risk. The Grayridge pack has been harassing her. So, I need to make sure she is protected. Would you be my Beta in this fight?"

Antony was silent. Gareth waited, letting the awkward pause draw out. Well, maybe he had hoped for too much. He heard the vicious clacking of a keyboard in the background.

"You don't gotta help me, Tony. I know it's a lot to ask, and I haven't exactly been around," Gareth started.

"Sorry, dungeon boss. My guild just beat it! Fucking finally, a new armor upgrade. Loot drop! *Nice*. To your question—of course I'll be your Beta for the fight. Pack is pack, brother. You and Dad had a falling out, but that's got nothing to do with me."

Gareth was more than a little surprised. "Thank you," he grunted.

"For sure. It'll be good to see you again, at the very least. Don't worry, I have no doubt you're gonna win. This Grayridge Alpha has a death wish; nobody walks away from *el lobo loco*." Antony's grin was audible. "So when is this fight?"

"Next weekend."

"I'll buy my plane ticket today. Where am I heading? Black City, New York?"

"Black River."

"Right. Cute town. I'm looking at pictures right now. I'll probably fly in a day or two beforehand to catch up. Let's say, next Thursday night?"

"Sounds good. I'll let Maddy know. You need me to pick you up at the airport?"

"No need, I'll get a rental car. So what's the weather like out there? How should I dress? Jackets? Warm socks?"

Antony was living in Arizona, so he was probably in 90-degree weather right now.

"Sounds about right," Gareth said. "Dress for it to be fucking cold."

Antony laughed again. Then, after a slight hesitation, he added, "You know, you're going to have to deal with Dad if you're starting a new pack."

Gareth flinched. Starting a new pack? He hadn't thought about it that way; he was just trying to keep his head above water and get the Grayridge pack off his back. But he supposed, if he won the Alpha Challenge, then he would have claim to Marquis' territory. He was pretty sure that extended all the way up through Canada.

Perhaps even more significant, he had a lifemate. Their bond was the perfect foundation for a new pack. Maddy was mated to an Alpha, which meant that someday, she would be a den mother. Other wolves would come to join them eventually. It was the natural order of things.

If all of that came to pass, and this Alpha Challenge ended with Gareth taking control of the Grayridge pack, then his father would want an oath of allegiance. His father wasn't a fool. He reigned over the Sonoran wolf kingdom with an iron claw, and he wouldn't tolerate one of his sons competing with him, even if it was from the other side of the continent.

Gareth felt a new headache coming on. Shit. How long until word of all this reached his father? If the Alpha Challenge was public information, all his dad had to do was look it up on the internet.

"It's too soon to talk about any of that," Gareth finally said. "I'll deal with Dad when the time comes. Let's put down this Alpha first."

"I'll do some research on this guy. Give me your email address. I'll send you all the important stuff: age, pack history, affiliations, fighting style."

Gareth gave Tony his email address. Then he glanced at the clock on his wall. He needed to start opening up the shop, but it seemed too soon to hang up the phone.

"What else is new with you? You still into bikes?" Gareth asked, leaning back in his office chair.

He heard Tony's grin on the phone. "Yeah, I just bought a new Kawasaki Ninja . . . ."

As Antony talked about his new motorcycle, Gareth reflected on how good it was to talk to his brother again, despite the circumstances.

They chatted for another twenty minutes or so before Antony had to go. Then Gareth stood up from his desk and started roving restlessly around the shop, randomly straightening shelves and tools as he went. It sounded like his mom and Antony were still close. Tony lived in the bottom part of their family's mansion out in Arizona. He doubted Tony would keep his secret about Maddy for long. His mom was going to find out the full story sooner or later.

It stressed him out. Maddy had just learned about werewolves. She was still struggling with her new identity. Meeting his family was a lot of pressure. He hadn't figured out yet how he was going to introduce Maddy to everyone. He was hoping to get her through the Change first. Maybe even figure out something about her lineage. Shit, he hadn't even started digging into that yet.

One thing at a fucking time, he thought.

He needed to get a handle on the Alpha Challenge. And he still needed to keep up with work. He was closing up shop this afternoon, but he couldn't close down the garage for two weeks straight while he handled all this. Vin needed a paycheck, too. Jefferson County was drowning under the torrential rain. Flood warnings were posted all over the news. He expected road closures up and down Highway 20 as the river swelled. He expected another day of being slammed with emergency tow calls from people stranded in the downpour. And on top of it all, Joker was missing.

Yeah, he had his hands full.

Chapter 11

Usually, Maddy was a little nervous about running into Kaylee and her flying monkeys outside of school. They always walked in a big group to the football field for cheer practice. But with the gray weather and power outage, sports and extracurricular activities were canceled, so the Varsity jackets were nowhere to be seen.

Bea met up with her outside the school's gated entrance. Her little friend hadn't been exaggerating—a herd of students were being picked up at the loading zone outside the school, and a bunch of teachers were walking to their cars. It looked like everyone was fed up with the power outage.

Maddy slouched under her hoodie as she started down the sidewalk with Bea. A flat sheet of clouds covered the sky, and a brisk wind carried a flurry of leaves down the street. It was cold, but the rain was holding off for now. Searching for Joker in the woods would be a damp, muddy adventure, and she was eager to find her dog and get it all over with. She hoped Joker was close to the trailer and uninjured, but considering how her week was going, she expected the worst.

It took them about forty-five minutes to walk from the school to Maddy's trailer. Bea was good company. She talked about the last few episodes of the Upriver Paranormal Podcast, then gushed about Vin for a bit. He was a graffiti artist, and he had promised to take her to all the spots around Black River where people went to tag. The Devil's Tower was a popular place for backwoods street artists. He had painted a few murals in the old, abandoned cement factory. Bea showed Maddy some pictures of his artwork on her phone. Maddy had to admit, Vin was really good at stylized letters and patterns. One of her favorites was a mural of an electric guitar, with all sorts of crazy waves and swirls flowing out of it. Big, orange, dripping letters spelled "MUSE" across the Fender. Her second figure was a larger-than-life, green and purple version of the grim reaper.

The two girls cut through the woods to get to Maddy's trailer. Maddy recognized the trees bordering her property and felt a little spike of anxiety, but she managed to control her fear. As Bea carried on her one-sided conversation about Vin's impressive art portfolio, Maddy's ears strained to catch any sounds in the woods. She didn't think anyone was following them, and she didn't smell werewolves, which put her somewhat at ease. So far, so good.

Finally, they entered her backyard. Maddy took a moment to text Gareth on her phone, letting him know they had arrived safely at the trailer. Then she looked around. The pile of broken appliances remained near the trees at the edge of the yard, undisturbed. The wind had blown her trash cans over, and it looked like a few animals had gone through it. Plastic wrappers and spoiled food was littered around the yard. By the tracks in the mud, it was probably a family of raccoons.

Dean's stash of 12-packs were missing from the porch, so someone must have come by and picked them up. But nothing else seemed out of place. Maddy didn't know what she had expected, but as she climbed up the back deck, she felt a little silly. Of course there wouldn't be a wolf pack waiting for her in the backyard. She was being jumpy for no reason.

"I'm going to check the house real quick," she said, taking out her keys. She unlocked the back door and wrinkled her nose at the stale air. She stepped inside her home and looked around.

Well, shit. The front door was busted open, and it looked like someone had made off with the refrigerator and microwave.

"Fucking for real?" she muttered as she stalked through the house, stepping around boxes of hoarder's junk. She slammed the front door, but the knob was busted and it wouldn't click shut. With a groan, Maddy looked around for a solution, and finally slid a heavy armchair in front of the door.

"Wow, that didn't take long," Bea said from behind her, looking around the trailer. "That sucks. Someone broke in?"

"Yeah, I'm not surprised. It was probably one of Dean's buddies."

She noticed the box of porno DVD's missing from next to the TV, too. Yeah, definitely one of Dean's friends from the bar. Real classy types. She sighed. Then she walked through the rest of the house. The bathroom cabinets had been rummaged through, probably someone looking for pills, and the closet door was open. Maddy considered herself lucky that Gareth had made her pack up all her things before heading to his place. Even if the appliances were missing from the kitchen, at least nothing truly valuable had been stolen. She didn't think she owned anything worth over $500.

At that moment, Maddy heard the low rumble of Gareth's Camaro down the driveway. She glanced out the front window as the red muscle car came into view through the trees. Bea came to stand next to her.

"His car is pretty cool," she admitted.

"Yeah, he's rebuilding it," Maddy said with a little grin. "Let's go meet him out front."

On their way out of the trailer, Maddy stopped to collect the mail from the coffee table in the living room. Too bad the thieves hadn't stolen all of her unpaid bills. She saw several pink envelopes and a letter from the Davenport Police Department, likely the fines for Dean's last harrah. A week ago, he had broken a car window after a weekend of partying down at the casinos. She sighed. Maybe she didn't have to pay for it? She wasn't sure if her mom and Dean ever got married. She still had a lot to figure out. She shoved the letters into the pocket of her hoodie and went to meet Gareth in the driveway.

Gareth climbed out of the Camaro as Maddy and Bea rounded the corner of the trailer. He lifted a big arm at the girls in greeting, and flashed Maddy a grin. His hair was tied back. He wore a padded flannel jacket over a graphic T-shirt and a pair of ripped jeans. Black grease stained his pants and his fingernails, and when Maddy hugged him, he smelled like a mixture of sweat, deodorant and oil. Yeah, he had definitely come straight from work.

Maddy explained what she had found inside the house, and Gareth didn't seem surprised to hear about the break-in or the stolen appliances. He took a moment to go inside and look around. He checked all the windows, then he helped her secure the front door. He frowned at the busted knob and latch combo.

"I'll have to come by with my drill later, see if I can't fix that," he muttered. Then he circled around the house, checking for any sign of Joker. He paused next to the spilled trash cans.

"She was around here yesterday," he said.

"I thought raccoons did that."

"Naw, they came later. See these prints right here," he said, pointing to the soft ground next to the back deck. "They lead straight to the trash can."

"Wow, that's cool you can track stuff," Bea said.

He glanced at the little Goth girl with a raised eyebrow, then he turned back to Maddy. "Why don't you two girls search down the hiking trail at the back of the property? Joker might come if you call her. I'll see if I can find more tracks through the woods."

Maddy nodded. She met his eyes, searching their hazel depths, trying to gauge his intentions. She was pretty sure he planned on Changing into his wolf form, and he didn't want Bea anywhere close by when he did that.

Gareth walked with them to the trail that cut through the back of Maddy's yard, then handed her a pack of dog treats from his jacket pocket.

"Try to lure her out with these. If you need help, just yell. I'll hear you."

"We have cell phones," Bea pointed out, waving her iPhone in the air.

Gareth met Maddy's eyes again, giving her a significant look, and she got the hint.

"Yeah, no worries, we'll holler," she said. Gareth couldn't answer his phone if he was in wolf form. That would be a little tricky.

Bea looked confused as she slid her phone back into her pocket. She glanced back and forth between them, a little frown on her face. Gareth ignored her. Before they parted ways, he pulled Maddy against him and brushed a chaste kiss against her forehead.

"Be careful," he murmured.

Maddy nodded. The brief, full-body contact made her heart flutter. Without thinking, she reached up and planted a warm kiss on his lips. He licked out his tongue at the last minute, playfully catching her across the mouth, and she half-gasped, half-laughed.

"You taste good, baby," he said. "Meet you back here in an hour?"

"Yeah, sounds good," she blushed.

Bea sighed loudly, kicking a pile of dead leaves on the ground, and generally making a lot of noise. "Gee, I wish I had a boyfriend to kiss me goodbye, all cute and sweet," she gushed, sticking out her pierced tongue.

Maddy shrugged, a little awkward, and went to join her friend as Gareth headed into the woods. He waved to them once, then he vanished between the trees.

"Is he like a ranger or something?" Bea asked, sounding impressed.

"He was in the Army, remember?" Maddy said. "He knows his way around the forest."

"I guess so. He doesn't care about sticking to the trail at all . . . kind of like you," Bea pointed out.

"Yeah, well, we both know the area pretty well," Maddy agreed. She tried to act nonchalant, but she couldn't keep the little smile off her face.

The two girls started up the hiking trail, equipped with a bag of dog treats. After a few minutes, Bea started calling Joker's name at the top of her lungs. Her voice echoed through the trees of the quiet forest. It was a bit alarming. At first, Maddy felt reluctant to join her friend. She was scared the Grayridge pack would overhear her. But how was Joker supposed to find them if she didn't cry out?

Don't be afraid, dummy, she told herself. Gareth was in the woods, too, and the laws of the Alpha Challenge protected her. She had nothing to worry about.

Then she raised her voice as well: "Joker! Joker, come out! Here, Joker!"

The girls climbed up the muddy trail, wandering deeper into the wilderness.

Chapter 12

The rain held off while Bea and Maddy walked the switchbacks of the hiking trail. The stormy weather had taken its toll on the dirt path. Ten to twenty foot lengths of trail had dissolved into black mud pits from the week's deluge of rain. Maddy and Bea threw down logs and branches to walk across the worst of it, but within twenty minutes, their shoes were caked with mud and dead leaves.

Eventually, the trail led them along the mountainside to a small lake. Maddy knew the area, though she didn't often walk down this far. It was a popular spot to go swimming in the summer. The trail led them past a few benches and picnic tables, barbeque pits and a narrow dock poking out over the water. The shoreline was deserted except for a flock of crows and a very lost seagull circling around.

The two girls followed the path through the woods that bordered the lake. They kept calling for Joker at the top of their lungs. Maddy couldn't help but feel like the whole search was futile. Considering the size of the Adirondack wilderness, part of her doubted she would ever see the pitbull puppy again. But she tried to keep her hopes up. Dogs were resilient. Even if it took all month, she would keep coming out to the area to search for Joker. The little pit was bound to turn up eventually.

They finally reached the other side of the lake, where the trail hooked into the wilderness again. It climbed up the side of a bluff that overlooked the water. Maddy followed along with dogged determination. From the top of the bluff, the two girls stopped to catch their breath. Together, they gazed out over the silvery lake.

"I can't believe I've never been out here," Bea said, looking down at the water. "This is beautiful."

"Do you go hiking a lot, Bea?"

"I'm not really a woodsy girl," she admitted. "Like, I would hike more, if I had people to go with."

"There's a lot of nice spots on the mountain," Maddy said. "We can go together, if you like, once the weather improves. Maybe Vin would like to go hiking, too."

Bea perked up at that. "Yeah, I'm all for it! So, do you and your sugardaddy go hiking a lot? I mean, it seems like you have that in common. You said you guys met at the hardware store, right?"

Maddy hesitated, thinking back to how she and Gareth had actually met. She had never told anyone their true story. It was . . . pretty unconventional. She wondered if she should tell Bea the truth. She glanced over at her friend out of the corner of her eye, wondering if Bea would judge her relationship. She didn't think so. Her little Goth friend had secrets of her own. Maddy remembered, maybe three years ago, walking in on Bea having sex in the PE locker room. She was definitely underage. Her partner didn't look like a high school student, but Maddy didn't think it was a teacher, either. Maybe someone's older brother? It was after school during a football event. Maddy had been so shocked, she had shut the door and run away. She still remembered that glimpse of a pale, round, male ass flexing against her friend's tiny body. And the moans.

She had never asked Bea about it, and she didn't know if she would ever feel bold enough to bring it up.

"Um, actually, we met in the woods," Maddy admitted, answering Bea's questioning look.

"Wait, really? You met Gareth in the woods? But that's not what you told me." After a long pause, she asked, "So, you said you crushed on him for a while before you started dating. Like, a *few years*. How old were you when you guys met?"

Maddy blushed, glancing back over the lake. "Um . . . I was fourteen."

Bea was quiet. "Okay. That's cool. I mean, you don't have to tell me all the details, if you're uncomfortable."

"No, I . . . I've just never told anyone before. I was running away from home and he found me. It's not what you think. He didn't do anything. He just helped me get back home when I was lost."

Bea gave her a reassuring sort of grin. "Wow, that's it? That was anticlimactic. Alright, so you got a crush on an older guy who rescued you. I mean, Mads, that's pretty tame.

Nothing to be ashamed of. It's not like you kept sneaking off into the woods to meet up with him."

Maddy released a breath. She kind of laughed. "Yeah, I guess you're right." Even though she had totally met up with Gareth several times in the woods after that.

"It's cool you're dating now," Bea continued. "Not a lot of couples have a story like that."

"I guess not. Thanks for understanding, Bea. You're a good friend."

"Yeah, well, I've heard a lot of crazy shit around town. My mom has some good stories from The B Joint. I'd rate yours a five out of ten on the shocker scale."

Maddy wondered if Bea would change that rating, if she heard about the werewolf thing. But Maddy couldn't really talk about that. The two girls hugged. Then Maddy looked back down at the lake. Her eyes combed the wilderness as she gripped the dog treats in her hands. It was a nice view, but so far, she hadn't seen any sign of Joker. She tried not to feel disheartened at the size of the forest. Maybe Gareth was having better luck, wherever he had gone.

Then a distant noise caught her attention.

"Do you hear barking?" Maddy said, turning and listening.

"I don't hear anything," Bea said.

The two girls went quiet. Maddy's heart squeezed in her chest. Was it Joker?

After a pause, the distant sound of barking continued. Bea's eyes went wide.

"Oh! Now I hear it!" she gasped. She cupped her hands around her mouth and yelled off the top of the hill, "Hey Joker! Here girl! Come here, Joker!"

Maddy's heart leapt, and she started yelling for Joker, too. She looked down at the lake from her vantage point upon the bluff. After searching for a minute, she spotted the furry forms of three large dogs bolting along the shoreline. She didn't see anyone with them.

Three dogs? That didn't seem right.

Maddy stopped calling Joker's name and went quiet. It was an eerie feeling, seeing three big dogs off-leash without any man or woman around. At first she thought the dogs were chasing after a frisbee or a ball. But they kept barreling along the beach, following the exact same path Bea and Maddy had taken just a few minutes ago. As they got closer, their vocals changed from baying to snarling. Maddy knew what a playful dog sounded like, but these hounds were growling as they ran. They looked big, too, like Saint Bernards. One was frothing at the mouth.

Actually, it looked like the dogs were headed straight for them.

"Bea, that's not Joker," Maddy said, as the hair stood up on the back of her neck.

The dogs rounded the side of the lake, running at manic speed. They looked aggressive, like they meant to attack.

"Maddy, uh, those dogs are pretty big," Bea said.

"I think we should run," Maddy agreed.

"What the *heck*. People need to keep their mutts on a leash!"

Then Maddy grabbed Bea's hand and pulled her along the hiking trail. At first they walked quickly, then they broke into a run when the dogs didn't slow down. Maddy's confusion turned to fear as the dogs neared. They were a lot bigger up close, and their faces looked a little unusual. One had nasty scars all over its snout, and another had a big chunk missing out of one ear. Maddy gagged when the wind shifted, carrying a nasty odor to her nose. The dogs reeked like dead skunk.

The trail led to a giant tree with a forked trunk and many thick branches spreading into the sky. Maddy ran to the base of the ancient beech tree and started climbing upward. The hounds were coming up behind them too fast; she had to make a quick decision. After climbing into the crotch of the tree, she took Bea's hand and dragged her little friend up behind her. Bea scrambled onto a higher branch.

The dogs reached the base of the tree, a frenzy of teeth and matted, oily fur. Maddy pulled her legs up to her chest. Thankfully, the dogs couldn't jump high enough to reach the two girls. The hounds circled around on the forest floor, snarling and barking. In a desperate attempt to distract the dogs, Maddy threw the bag of treats on the ground. It burst open, and little bone-shaped biscuits went flying everywhere. One of the dogs went sniffing through the mud, snatching up the little treats in his thick snout, but the other two didn't seem to notice.

"We're fucked!" Bea said.

"No, we're *treed*," Maddy said ironically. Then, thinking of Gareth's promise, she yelled at the top of her lungs, "Help! Gareth, help!"

"Somebody help us!" Bea took up the cry.

The two girls kept calling for help, clinging to the tree branches as the vicious dogs circled down below. After finishing the spilled treats, the largest one started baying. The two smaller dogs took up the call. They sounded like hunting hounds signaling to their master. It surprised Maddy, because they looked more like big shaggy shepherds than hunting dogs. One of them had a mask similar to a husky.

That's when a piercing whistle split Maddy's head. She gasped in pain and threw her hands over her ears. What the heck?

"What's wrong?" Bea asked, looking at her in alarm. "Are you okay?"

"The hell is that sound?" Maddy gasped.

"I don't hear anything."

The whistle blasted again, and the dogs stopped barking. Then a man appeared, walking down the trail from the direction of the lake. He didn't seem to be in much of a hurry. He strolled up the path in an orange jacket with a big pair of birding binoculars strung around his neck. Maddy wasn't great at telling age, but he seemed like he might be in his fifties. He was lean with a leathery face, like he spent a lot of time outdoors. His red baseball cap looked a little familiar. It took her a moment, but with a little gasp, Maddy recognized him from the hardware store.

He blew again on his whistle, and the shaggy dogs ran to his side, tails down, whining. He halted a dozen feet away from the base of the tree. He scratched one of the dogs on the head, the smallest one, which Maddy thought might be a female.

He must have used a dog whistle to call them off, Maddy thought. She shouldn't be able to hear the whistle, except for her increasingly keen werewolf senses. No wonder Bea seemed unaffected by the high-pitched sound.

The man looked up at the two girls curiously.

"Now this is quite a sight," he mused. "What are you two girls doing all the way out here? Hiking trails are closed. I'll admit I'm surprised. These dogs are only trained to hunt a *special breed of wolf,* not little girls."

"We're searching for a lost dog," Bea called down from the tree. "It's a pitbull mix. Have you seen one?"

"I'm afraid not," the man answered. He folded his arms across his chest and looked up at them with a humorous grin. "Seems like you two are in quite a predicament."

Maddy felt a strange chill at those words. Her sense of relief was replaced with dread. The man gave them a long, slow, poisonous grin. His eyes glinted. It was creepy. Something about the fellow seemed familiar, and after a long, tense moment, she recognized the man from the hardware store yesterday.

"Hey, I remember you," Maddy called down to the hunter. "We spoke yesterday at Hawkins' Hardware."

"Yes, I recognize that pretty red hair," the man leered. "Why don't you girls come down, and we can have a chat? I've called off my dogs. They won't bother you now."

Maddy and Bea shared a glance. Bea leaned close to her ear and whispered, "I kinda want to stay in the tree."

Maddy nodded. She felt the same way. But how were they going to escape? She wondered if Gareth had heard their cries. Maybe he was on his way? She couldn't be certain. Her hand went to her cell phone, but she didn't know who she would call. Her mind raced, trying to come up with a plan. Maybe, if she asked the strange man a few questions, she could buy them some time for Gareth to arrive.

"A special breed of wolf? What are you talking about?" Maddy's voice carried an edge.

The fellow called back, "I'm talking about *werewolves*, little lady. These dogs hunt *werewolves*. You haven't seen one around, by chance? Seems like there's a lot of activity in this area."

"Hah!" Bea scoffed. "Trust me, mister, I might look like I have otherworldly abilities, but I am *not* a werewolf. And this girl here is *definitely* not a werewolf. She's more like a cowardly lion."

"Wow, Bea, thanks," Maddy muttered under her breath. A hard knot formed in her stomach. Was this guy really a werewolf hunter? That was absurd. People didn't hunt werewolves, did they? Well, maybe. If wolf parts were sold on the black market, then someone must be sourcing them. So maybe it wasn't that crazy. But why would a werewolf hunter be hanging out around Black River, of all places? Did this man know about the Grayridge pack?

"Why don't you girls come down?" the man called up to them. "I don't bite."

"We're good," Bea said. "Why don't you just walk away with your dogs?"

The man's grin changed into a scowl. He glared up at them, his face becoming cold and hard. Maddy and Bea exchanged a frightened glance. Shit, this really wasn't good. Then the man's eyes dropped to the trail. His expression changed, becoming even more menacing. One of the dogs started whining, but the hunter hushed the hound with a downward motion of his hand. The smallest one, the female, held her teeth bared in a silent growl.

Maddy looked down at the ground beneath the tree. At first her eyes passed right over the black wolf standing like a shadow amid the ferns and bramble. But then she noticed the sheen of a blue-black coat. She gasped. Even though she knew it was Gareth, the size and ferocity of the werewolf made her limbs turn to liquid. He was almost the size of a horse. She clutched hard at the tree branches. He stood perfectly still and silent. How long had he been there? It seemed like he had taken the hunter off guard, as well.

"Bea, look!" she hissed.

Gareth emerged from the bushes and faced the three dogs in Alpha form. He planted himself in front of the tree beneath the two girls. He looked fierce, his hackles raised, his fangs gleaming. A rumble began in his throat, a sound so deep, she could feel it in her chest.

"Holy shit, Maddy!" Bea whispered. "Is that . . . *your wolf?*"

Maddy couldn't respond. She didn't know if the dogs would attack him or not. Her heart was in her throat. The hunter's gaze passed over the werewolf. The man looked more calculating than afraid.

"Well, look at his handsome beast. Is this your missing dog? Looks like he has some wolf in him," the man said with an evil smile. He sounded sarcastic, like he knew exactly what Gareth was.

"Uh, yeah, that's my dog," Maddy called down, thinking fast.

Bea gave her a *"what the fuck?"* look, but stayed quiet.

Maddy's grip tightened on Bea's hand. This guy was looking more and more like a nutter. She didn't want to provoke him, even with Gareth standing right there. What if the hunter had a gun on him? Her eyes flickered over the fellow, looking for a weapon, but all she saw were his obnoxiously large birding binoculars strung around his neck.

Then Gareth broke his protective stance and glanced up at Maddy. It seemed like he wanted them to get down from the tree. Maddy gazed into his golden wolf eyes for a long moment, trying to discern the meaning of his look. Then she slowly slid down from her hiding place. She leapt the last few feet to the ground, landing with a soft thud in a cushion of autumn leaves. Bea followed after her.

Gareth walked to her side, where he sat at her feet like an obedient guard dog. It was pretty comical, because he was so big. His head almost reached her shoulder, and his massive jaws could have snapped her arm in half. He very much looked like a wild animal pretending to be a pet.

Maddy reached over and placed her hand on Gareth's ruff. Her fingers sank into the bristly fur along the ridge of his neck. It made her feel a bit more confident.

She called to the hunter, "Your dogs almost attacked us. You should put them on a leash."

"Hard to hunt with your dogs on a leash. But sure. I'll keep it in mind," he sneered in reply.

Gareth fixed his golden eyes on the stranger. Their gazes locked. Hunter and wolf stared at each other. The man's attention shifted between Maddy and the big black beast, then over to Bea, who huddled behind Maddy's shoulder.

Finally, the man said, "I'll be on my way. You girls have a nice evening."

The hunter started up the trail, his nasty mutts following at his heels. He gave Gareth a wide berth as he passed under the ancient beech tree. The fellow walked with an easy stride. He didn't seem scared of the werewolf at all. Maddy's eyes narrowed as he grew farther away. Eventually, he disappeared from view through the pine trees.

She was left with an ominous, uncomfortable feeling in her gut.

"Have you ever seen that guy before?" Bea asked.

"He was in the hardware store yesterday. He was weird then, too."

"I've never seen him or his dogs around town before," Bea said. "I don't think he's local."

Maddy nodded in agreement. In a small town like Black River, those big hulking beasts would be memorable.

"I think it's time to go now," Maddy announced.

She grabbed Bea's hand in her own. The two girls started down the trail together, back toward the lake, in the opposite direction of the hunter. Despite her bravado, Bea's hand was shaking. Maddy was nervous that Gareth had appeared in his wolf form in front of a self-proclaimed "werewolf hunter," for the sake of protecting her. It seemed like a big risk to take, showing himself like that in broad daylight. She didn't know how to explain his presence to Bea: where a hulking black wolf had appeared from, and why it was acting like her pet dog.

Bea walked silently by her side, lost in her own thoughts. Maddy didn't know what to say to disperse the ominous cloud that seemed to have fallen over their little group. Gareth walked in front of them at a slow pace, his black tail sweeping the ground. Maddy tried not to admire his powerful, beastly presence. Even as a wolf, he was built like a tank, with meaty shoulders and a barrel chest, a thick neck and paws the size of dinner plates. He looked big enough to ride into battle.

She tried not to stare at the anatomy tucked under his tail, though from this angle, his balls were pretty obvious. She found her mind wandering to her own wolf form. She hadn't Changed yet, so she had no idea what she would look like. Would she be big and tough like him? Or smaller, like the regular wolves of the Grayridge pack? She had never seen a female werewolf before. He had mentioned that females had mating seasons. What would that be like?

She felt a bit of heat in her cheeks. Wow, she didn't need to imagine that. It was all a bit too National Geographic.

They circled the lake and continued up the hiking trail as the sky darkened overhead. Despite all of the excitement, they still hadn't found Joker, which was a disappointment. As they neared Maddy's trailer, Gareth changed course. He took off into the woods without warning. Maddy watched the black wolf disappear into the forest.

She and Bea exchanged a glance.

They reached the part of the trail that cut through Maddy's backyard. Bea's footsteps slowed down and Maddy released the tight grip on her hand. They paused for a moment under the trees as Bea took out a pack of cigarettes from her cargo pants. Her hands were still shaking. It took her several tries to light one.

"You probably don't know this about me," she admitted, "but I'm scared of dogs."

"What, really? I didn't realize. If I had known that, I wouldn't have asked you to help me look for Joker."

"It's alright, it was my idea, I wanted to help you. Anyway, yeah, I got tackled by a big Rottweiler when I was in third grade and needed seven stitches on my arm. I'm okay with small dogs, but big mutts like that . . . ." She shuddered.

Maddy didn't blame her little friend. Those aggressive hounds made her nervous, too.

"So was that your wolf, Maddy? The one you told me about before?" Bea asked after she took a few pulls on her cigarette.

"Um, yeah," Maddy said.

"I guess I didn't totally believe you," Bea admitted.

"It's okay," Maddy mumbled, bracing herself for the inevitable stream of questions. She didn't have to wait long.

"So where did it come from?" Bea asked, flicking a bit of ash on the ground. "Does that *thing* just follow you around? Kind of a coincidence, don't you think? And now there's some nutter in the woods calling himself a hunter? This is too much. Obviously there's something suspicious going down. I'm going to tell Vin about this. After that pagan sacrifice he found near the garage, I wouldn't be surprised if it's some sort of cult activity."

Maddy bit her lip. So, Vin had told Bea about the death-totem. She didn't know what to say. She really didn't have a reasonable excuse for any of it.

Bea gave her a suspicious look. "What do you know? Are you holding out on me?"

Maddy shoved her hands in the pocket of her hoodie.

"Come on, Maddy! We saw a ghost together in the Beaumont Manor, didn't we? Nobody believed me but you. Don't gaslight me now! You're like, the Scooby to my Shaggy."

"Don't you mean we're like Velma and Daphne?"

"No, they were boring." Bea blew out another puff of smoke. "I mean, do you feed that monster? Did you tame a werewolf, Maddy? Shit. I bet you did, living out in the woods like you do. You're a werewolf whisperer. I should've known. It's always the quiet ones you gotta watch out for!"

Maddy broke into a laugh. "No, I didn't tame a werewolf, Bea."

"Then what's the deal with that big wolf in the woods?"

Maddy really didn't know what else to say, but just then, another bark caught her attention, this one much more familiar. Her eyes widened. She turned around to see Gareth emerging from the forest on the other side of the trailer. His hair was loose where it had been tied back before, falling in a glossy mess down his shoulders, but that was the only sign he might have Changed. He held a rope in hand. A fawn-colored pitbull mix tugged at the end of the leash.

The moment Joker saw Maddy, the dog started lunging and barking frantically. Maddy's heart leapt as well. She found herself tearing up a bit. She couldn't describe her relief at seeing Joker alive and unharmed.

"Oh shit," Bea said, backing up. "Is that your dog? She's a lot bigger than I expected."

"Don't worry, she isn't aggressive," Maddy reassured her little friend. Then she started across the parking lot to meet Gareth next to the Camaro. She ran up to Joker and embraced the dog, laughing as the big puppy licked her face.

"Where did you find her?" she asked Gareth, who was looking a little smug.

"She was hiding off over that way," he said, pointing into the forest. "Made herself a nice little den of trash in the woods. Waiting for you to find her, of course."

"Hey, girl, hey," Maddy laughed, hugging the big puppy around her thick, sleek neck. "You doing alright? You okay?" She grabbed the puppies paws and looked at them, checking for scratches.

"She's alright. She's a little hungry and dirty, but none the worse for wear," Gareth reassured her. Maddy looked up and met his eyes. His gaze gentled when he saw the gratitude written plainly on her face.

Bea finished her cigarette and came to stand next to them. She frowned up at Gareth, then at Joker, her forehead wrinkling up like a prune. Her eyes returned to Gareth suspiciously, her gaze lingering on his black hair.

"Craziest thing, we just saw a big black wolf in the woods," Bea said.

Gareth glanced down at Bea, then back to Maddy. Smooth as silk, he said, "A wolf sighting seems pretty rare out here. You sure it wasn't a coyote?"

"Definitely too big to be a coyote," Bea answered him. "It was more like a grizzly bear. It scared off some dogs that were chasing us. They belonged to a guy who called himself a werewolf hunter."

"Dang, really? All that happened? That's messed up," Gareth sounded surprised.

"Yeah, didn't you hear us yelling for you?" Bea asked, a hint of sarcasm in her voice. She folded her arms and shifted her weight on one leg, like she wasn't buying it.

"Nope, guess I didn't. So where is this guy now? I can go talk to him."

"He walked off," Bea said. "Disappeared into the woods like a crazy serial killer. We're lucky we weren't abducted. So, do you believe in werewolves, Gareth?"

Maddy interrupted, "Let's just drop the whole werewolf thing. That guy was crazy."

There was a pregnant pause. Bea looked back and forth from Gareth to Maddy. Her gaze was so sharp, Maddy felt like it might peel her skin. She stared down at Joker, trying to hide her terrible sense of guilt. She hated lying like this.

"Come on, it's getting late. Let's head back to town," Gareth said. "I can drop you off, Bea."

"Alright, sure."

Maddy took Joker's leash and walked back to the Camaro a little too fast, circling around the trailer at a fast trot. Gareth followed at a more leisurely pace with his hands shoved in his pockets. Bea hung back a bit as well. She kept giving Gareth the side-eye, like she expected him to sprout a tail or start howling.

You're imagining it, Maddy scolded herself. Her little friend couldn't be that quick to figure it all out, could she?

Maddy opened up the Camaro's passenger door and ushered Joker into the front seat, where the dog could ride next to Gareth. Then she slid into the backseat. She indicated for Bea to sit next to her. If Bea was scared of large dogs, she didn't want to force her friend to sit next to the pitbull. Gareth got in behind the steering wheel and started up the engine. He cracked the window for Joker before pulling onto the highway.

The drive back to Bea's place was tense and quiet.

"You know, animal control is looking all over for a killer wolf in the area," Bea interrupted the awkward silence. "Maybe we should report the wolf we saw today, Maddy. It could be dangerous. I mean, I don't mean to be rude, but just think of what happened to Dean. Someone needs to report it."

Maddy cleared her throat, wishing Bea would just drop it. "I mean, you're right, but I don't think—"

"Yeah, we'll report it," Gareth interjected. "I don't want a man-killing wolf wandering around in these woods."

Bea crossed her arms in the backseat and glared at Gareth, but she didn't say anything more. Maddy glanced out the window. How long would it take for Bea to put it all together? And what were they supposed to do about a werewolf hunter? Was the creepy guy a threat, or just some eccentric old man with a pack of scary dogs? She really couldn't say, but she had a feeling Gareth would want to talk more about it once they were alone.

Chapter 13

The sky opened as they cruised up the street to Bea's house, and the rain started to pour down again with renewed vigor. It looked like the storm had caught its breath and was ready for a second round. Maddy felt lucky they had found Joker in time to avoid the worst of the weather.

Bea's neighborhood might have been beautiful if the houses weren't so rundown. They passed by old craftsman-style homes with wide front porches and bay windows. Most yards were buried in weeds and bramble, and broken down cars filled the long gravel driveways. Ancient beech trees, a century old, lined the streets. Red and yellow autumn leaves adorned the sprawling branches. The whole neighborhood looked like a Fall painting.

Gareth pulled in front of Bea's house and turned off the car.

"Well, this is me," Bea said, picking up her backpack. "Thanks for the ride."

"Here, I'll walk you," Maddy rushed to say. She felt a little guilty about how the afternoon had gone down. She didn't know what to say to Bea, but it didn't seem right to drop her friend off without trying to smooth things over. Bea had been silent most of the ride back from the trailer, and the tension was pretty uncomfortable.

Maddy cracked open the door of the Camaro and put her foot down on the asphalt street. Then a commotion in Bea's front yard caught her attention. She heard the cadence of angry voices. The two girls both looked up to see Becca, Bea's older sister, storming across the yard with a heavy box in her hands. Becca's voice was loud enough to carry across the street.

"Fuck you!" Becca screamed at her mother.

"Becca, listen to me—" her mother, Ms. Almut, called from the front porch.

"Fuck you and your *woowoo* bullshit!" Becca repeated furiously. "Levi is my boyfriend. How dare you say he's going to cheat on me, just because of some vision you saw smoking peyote? Our relationship is none of your business. *I'm out!*"

Becca charged across the front yard to her ancient black Range Rover parked in the driveway. She was carrying a big cardboard box in both hands, and her black purse was slung over one shoulder. Levi followed after her with two more cardboard boxes, his blond hair mussed and slanted to one side. He looked disheveled and confused. He was wearing a gray wool cardigan with a fancy knit weave and white tennis shoes. Very prep. Maddy had met him at Fright Farm, and she recalled him being a pretty chill dude.

Becca shoved her cardboard box into the backseat of the Range Rover, and jumped into the car before slamming the door shut. Levi climbed into the passenger seat, a lot more calm. Then Becca reversed out of the driveway at breakneck speed, hardly glancing in the rearview mirror. She turned the wheel too soon and rolled off the curb, the big SUV bouncing back and forth, nearly colliding with Gareth's Camaro. Then, with a puff of gray exhaust, the old Rover flew off down the street.

"That's a lot of smoke," Gareth pointed out, watching the car speed off through the rear window. "That motor doesn't sound great. She should bring it by the shop. Might be a transmission leak."

"I'll . . . uh, I'll mention it to her," Bea said.

Gareth seemed unphased by the dramatic scene they had just witnessed, but Maddy was more concerned. She stared at Bea's house curiously. It looked like her mom was standing on the front porch. As she watched, Ms. Almut lit up a cigarette.

The two girls shared a *"What the heck?"* look in the backseat. Then Maddy fumbled with her seatbelt, unfastened it, and climbed out of the car behind Bea. Together, the two girls walked up to the front porch.

"Hey mom, you alright?" Bea called as she climbed up the front porch. Their two-story house was painted brown with white trim. The porch had a distinct sagging feel about it, and the front steps were recently rebuilt. An ancient maple tree fanned out across the front yard, creating a canopy of fiery red leaves against the heavy rain. Moss caked the shingles on the roof, and the wrap-around porch was covered in old chairs, little outdoor tables, weedy planters, forgotten doormats and a few buckets that had found their way outside. Like most houses in Black River, the yard was not well defined. It bled into the neighbor's yard, and instead of a fence, the property line was marked by a pile of used tires.

Maddy climbed the front steps of Bea's house. A sparkling sun catcher hanging from the front porch caught her eye. She hadn't noticed it before. As she looked, she saw a few more decorations hanging from the eaves: a couple of old wind chimes, a hummingbird feeder and some stained glass ornaments.

Bea's mom waved to them as they approached. "Oh, hello girls. Sorry you had to see that. I think Becca's having a hard day."

"She's always upset over something," Bea rolled her eyes. "What was all that about a peyote-fueled vision?"

"That's between your sister and me," her mom hedged. "Anyway, nothing to worry about, I'll talk to her later. Did you girls find the lost dog?"

"Yes," Bea said. "The dog was out by Maddy's trailer, just like you said."

"Good. I'm glad."

Maddy looked questioningly at Ms. Almut. She knew Bea's mother from The B Joint, a little dive bar up Highway 20 not far past Gareth's auto shop. She was divorced from Bea's dad, who was incarcerated for a gang execution about five years ago.

"You guessed where my dog was?" Maddy asked curiously.

"Oh, well, I just had a hunch."

Maddy felt a little unnerved. Bea came from a family of shamans. It seemed like Ms. Almut had more psychic potential than met the eye. The middle-aged Native woman was sitting on the porch, smoking an extra long Pall Mall. She looked good for her age, with a healthy shine to her dark hair and skin. She was a tiny woman like Bea, with an oval face, high cheekbones and bright, almond-shaped eyes. Hardly a wrinkle creased her smooth skin. Her luxurious hair, long and thick like both of her daughters, was dyed black with a good inch of gray roots showing along the crown. She was wearing a knit sweater with vague tribal patterns, probably bought at a discount department store in Davenport, and a pair of bright orange crocs.

If Maddy understood Bea's heritage correctly, then Ms. Almut was half Native, while Bea's grandmother was full Seneca. She had met Bea's bossy older sister, Becca, at the Halloween carnival on Friday night. Becca was twenty-three or twenty-four, and like most older siblings, she was a little militant and parentified.

Ms. Almut surprised Maddy with a question: "I've seen that Camaro before. That's the man who runs the car garage up on Highway 20, isn't it?"

"That's Maddy's *boyfriend*," Bea said loudly. "Don't give Maddy any shit, mom. Gareth is cool, he went to Fright Farm with us, he isn't creepy or anything. We had a good time. And hey, Maddy's dog likes him. That's always a good sign."

Ms. Almut mused, "I recall him moving to town a few years ago. He stops in for lunch at The B Joint every now and then. I never see him in the evenings, though. Kind of a quiet fellow. Bit of a loner, I think."

"He doesn't drink," Maddy pointed out.

"You're right, he doesn't. I only see him with the lunch crowd." Ms. Almut looked thoughtful again. "Strange that someone like him would move out here."

Someone like him. Maddy felt a jolt of shock. Ms. Almut's dark eyes landed on her, searching her face for some mutual understanding. Her eyes were a beautiful deep brown, almost totally black. It seemed like the middle-aged mom saw too much. Maddy suddenly felt certain that Ms. Almut was aware of Gareth's true identity—that he was a werewolf.

"How long have you two been dating?" Ms. Almut asked.

"Like two weeks? But we've known each other a while," Maddy replied.

"A while, hm? How long?"

Maddy licked her lips nervously. It was an innocent enough question, but now she felt guarded.

"Like a few years," she said, purposefully vague.

"I see. So maybe he had a reason to move to town, after all."

Maddy stared at Bea's mom. Did Ms. Almut know about her and Gareth's strange connection? How he had found her on the mountainside when she was fourteen, lost in a rainstorm? That was ridiculous. How could Bea's mom know about any of that?

"If you have a few minutes, Madeline, there's something I found in storage that I wanted to give you. Can you come inside?"

"Oh, uh, sure," Maddy said. She glanced back at the Camaro. She could see Joker pushing her pink nose against the car's window. She slipped her cell phone out of her pocket and texted Gareth, *"Be right back."*

***

As they entered through the front door, Ms. Almut reiterated, "I'd like to speak to Maddy alone, Beatrice. Would you give us a few minutes?"

Bea looked surprised. Maddy could tell her friend didn't like being left out, but she couldn't refuse her mother. After a moment of struggling with herself, Bea sighed.

"Alright mom, fine, I'll head up to my room. I got homework, anyway."

"Uh, thanks for your help with Joker," Maddy said lamely.

"No worries. It was fun. I'm glad we found her."

Bea's response was a little stilted and formal. Maddy could tell her friend was still annoyed about something—probably the mystery of the big black wolf, and Gareth's evasive behavior. Maddy wanted to say something to fix it, but the words didn't come, especially with Bea's mom standing right next to them.

Beatrice shouldered her backpack and disappeared upstairs, leaving Maddy alone with Ms. Almut in the living room.

"Come with me, Madline," Ms. Almut said with a kind smile. Then she led Maddy deeper into the house. The power was partially restored in town, but it looked like Bea's house was still waiting for their part of the grid to be repaired. As Maddy followed Ms. Almut through the craftsman-style home, she felt like she had stepped into the old pioneer days: an oil lamp illuminated every room; white emergency candles flickered on bookshelves and end tables; a few battery powered string lights hung around the center island in the kitchen. It was kind of magical. The whole house was lit up like a Christmas tree, all sparkly and romantic.

A hallway led from the living room through a small dining area, then opened into a large family room at the back of the house. One wall was transformed into a giant entertainment unit with videogames, DVD boxes, and controllers scattered about. Kids' toys were piled into a big wicker basket in the corner.

The den was separated from the kitchen and dining room by a butcher block countertop island. Along one wall, a massive hutch was filled with old pottery and stoneware. Maddy saw a few Native-themed decorations on the walls, but she didn't know much about Native artwork in the New York area, so she couldn't identify which tribe it might be from. Probably Seneca, like their heritage.

About twenty cardboard boxes and totes were stacked at the far side of the den. Maddy stared at the sight in surprise. It looked like a lot to sort through. Her eyes traveled across all the different labels, written in black sharpie: *Christmas decor, glassware, grandma's stuff, baby clothes, photo albums, old tech* . . . . Some of the boxes were only labeled with dates.

"Are you clearing out your whole storage unit?" she asked Ms. Almut curiously.

"Yes, I thought I'd save some money. I can't afford the extra expense anymore with Joey needing braces. My boyfriend and his kids helped me clear out the unit last week. It's not very organized, and most of that stuff is too heavy for me to lift."

"Well, if you need any help, I can always lend a hand," Maddy offered.

Ms. Almut didn't say anything. She gazed at the pile of boxes thoughtfully, then the middle-aged mom turned toward Maddy with a sympathetic frown.

"I'm really sorry to hear about Dean," she said. "I feel like I should give you a heads up. The owner at The B Joint is probably going to send over a bill for his tab. Are you handling all that or . . . ?"

Maddy felt her anxiety spike. Great, more bills? She should have known this would be about Dean's bar tab.

"Um, just mail it to the trailer. I'm still figuring it out," she said.

"Alright. I'll tell the owner to do that." Ms. Almut's voice softened. "We heard it was another animal attack."

"Yeah, it happened Saturday night. I found him out in the woods."

"I'm so sorry. If there's anything we can do to help, just let me know. Are you staying with family right now?"

"Um, with my boyfriend," Maddy said, as she stepped gingerly around the stacks of boxes. She really didn't want to talk about Dean.

"That's good. Well, the timing is a little serendipitous. I found a box of your mom's things in storage this weekend. I set it aside for you. It's over here. I figured you'd want it."

"From my mom?" Maddy echoed in disbelief.

Ms. Almut pointed to a legal-sized cardboard box with a white lid sitting on the butcher block counter, between the den and the kitchen. Maddy's eyes immediately spotted her mom's name scribbled on the side in black ink: *Jonine Donovan*.

With a lurch, she recognized her mom's handwriting. Oh wow. How long had it been since she saw her mother's signature?

Maddy stepped gingerly over to the box and tried to pick it up. Despite being a relatively small box, it was very heavy. It felt like it was full of papers. Maddy had a sudden flash of dread. Was it a bunch of documents and old mail? Oh god. She *did not* want to sort through her mom's old bills. What if she discovered some ancient, past due bill with a million years' worth of late fees? It was the stuff of nightmares.

"So that's it? Just one box?" Maddy asked Ms. Almut.

"Yes. I forgot I had a box of her stuff in storage. Otherwise I would've given it to you sooner."

"I appreciate you telling me. Some people would've thrown it out after so long."

"Nonsense. I would've given it to you sooner, dear, had I remembered."

Despite Maddy's suspicion that she had just inherited a stack of bills, she looked forward to sorting through some of her mom's old memorabilia. She had lost almost everything belonging to her mother after she died. Dean had thrown out a lot of stuff and sold the rest. The timing did seem special. With all the changes going on in her life, she felt like she needed her mother more than ever. And now here was a box of her things.

Then Ms. Almut said cautiously, "Madeline, I know you don't know me very well, but your mother and I were friends. I was wondering if we could speak in private? I think you know what I want to talk about."

Maddy met Ms. Almut's gaze, feeling a little apprehensive.

"Um . . . ."

"It's about *shifters*, Maddy," Ms. Almut said in a low voice.

Maddy's eyes widened. Ms. Almut waited for her to say something. The longer the silence stretched, the more nervous Maddy felt. She thought of Gareth's rule, *"Just keep that business to yourself,"* but there didn't seem much point in lying to Ms. Almut. It seemed like she already knew about Gareth's identity. The cat was already out-of-the-bag . . . or, the wolf was out-of-the-woods.

"Sure, we can talk," Maddy said weakly.

A door slammed somewhere upstairs, interrupting their hushed conversation. The sound made her jump. Maddy listened to a flurry of footsteps across the second floor.

A boy's voice cried out, "Not fair, Bea! I was using those headphones! Give them back!"

"They're mine, little dude. Did you get these out of my room?"

"I found them downstairs," the boy complained.

"Bullshit," Bea's muffled voice drifted from the second floor. "I was just using them yesterday, and I know I left them in my room. Don't snoop through my things!"

Ms. Almut glanced upward, listening to her children squabble. Then, with a sigh, she said, "Come with me, Madeline. Let's speak in private, where we won't be disturbed."

Then Ms. Almut motioned for her to follow her, and walked into the kitchen. After a hesitant pause, Maddy followed.

Bea's mom led Maddy to a door in the kitchen between two tall cupboards. Maddy thought it was a walk-in pantry, but when Ms. Almut opened the door, she revealed a tiny workshop. Ms. Almut started lighting candles, illuminating the small room with a mystical ambiance. Crystals of various colors and sizes filled the shelves that lined the room: pink rose quartz, moonstone, blue and red jade, black obsidian, and bright green malachite. The pantry had been converted into a workshop of sorts, a curiosity closet full of rocks, feathers, lizard tails, bundles of white sage and dreamcatchers. All sorts of dried herbs and other natural items were hang-drying from the ceiling. Handwoven mats hung from the walls. It smelled pleasantly like dried flowers. The air tingled with a strange sort of electricity. It all looked beautiful and mysterious. It was a beautiful sight.

Ms. Almut caught Maddy's sleeve and pulled her a little ways forward, then shut the door behind them. She locked it with a little latch that dangled at eye level. Then she indicated a stool where Maddy could sit down. She took the seat across from her.

Maddy glanced around. Directly above the door, Maddy saw a big vinyl decal sticker for the Upriver Community Paranormal Podcast. It had a little UFO on it. Alright. So maybe Bea wasn't alone in her obsession.

Ms. Almut sat across from Maddy in a wingback chair, upholstered in brown and white cowhide. She clasped her hands thoughtfully in her lap and leaned a bit forward, looking Maddy up and down. The candlelight glinted off her dark eyes. She looked curious, but not threatening.

"So, how long?" Ms. Almut asked.

"How long . . . ?" Maddy echoed, a bit more slowly.

"How long since you became the Alpha's mate?"

That got her attention. "*What?*"

"No need to hide it from me, sweetheart. I remember when that Alpha came to town. Alpha werewolves are dangerous beasts. A lot of the paranormal community won't tolerate them, but I figured he wasn't harming anyone, so I didn't report it."

"Oh," Maddy stuttered, surprised. This wasn't the exact topic of conversation she had expected.

"Now I'm connecting the dots," Ms. Almut continued, a special glint entering her eye. "I didn't know how much you took after your mother, but you look just like her. It makes sense you would share her *heritage*."

A beat of silence passed while Maddy struggled to understand.

"You mean, my mother was a werewolf?"

"'Werewolf' sounds so medieval, doesn't it?" Ms. Almut said gently. "I prefer 'wolf shifter.' Yes, dear. Your mother was a wolf shifter, just like you."

Maddy already had her suspicions, but still, hearing it out loud was a shock to her system. The news was still hard to swallow. *It's like I didn't know her at all.* Her mother had passed away when she was thirteen. She had a few good childhood memories of her: birthday parties, Christmas, camping in the summer. But Maddy didn't remember anything about werewolves. And she definitely didn't remember her mother ever Changing into a wolf.

"I found out by accident," Ms. Almut continued. "She missed a few days of work right after she started at The B Joint. I thought she was sick, so I drove by your place—out near Whitehorse Falls, you know, that little apartment community—and found her stuck in the Change. I didn't know a wolf could get stuck."

"I thought my mom grew up in Black River," Maddy said, a little hoarse.

"Oh no, she moved here when you were little. I remember she struggled with you wetting the bed at night. I don't know where she moved from, she never told me."

Maddy was totally embarrassed. Bed wetting? Why would Ms. Almut remember that details, of all things?

The shaman continued her tale, "I really didn't know much about werewolves back then. But I believed the usual bias and horror stories circulating around the paranormal community. Wolf shifters aren't very well liked, you should know. People think your kind is violent and unpredictable. Now, thanks to your mom, I think differently. Your mother never hurt anyone. She was a kind soul and a good friend."

Maddy nodded, falling silent. Ms. Almut waited as she grappled with all this new information. It wasn't easy.

"So then, you know Gareth is an Alpha," Maddy said, lowering her voice a little. The door was shut and locked, but she still felt self-conscious saying the words out loud.

"Yes, dear. It's pretty obvious, once you know what to look for. Alphas have this aura about them. At least, that's how Nana used to describe them. My mother was a powerful shaman, I'm sure Bea told you. Alphas have auras that look like rupturing volcanoes. Lots of vitality. They're one of the top predators in the supernatural world. Last thing you want to encounter on a dark night is an Alpha wolf."

Maddy gripped the seat of the stool with her hands. She remained silent, processing what Ms. Almut had said.

"Sorry," the shaman woman apologized, noticing Maddy's shell-shocked expression. "I thought you must know, considering that man you're with . . . ."

"Well, I knew some of it, but . . . are Alpha wolves really that dangerous?"

"Oh yes, dear. *Very* dangerous. I would caution you about him, but . . . well, it's probably too late for that, if he's already claimed you."

Maddy started tugging at a lock of her long red hair. Claimed her? She thought back to her wild night in the woods with Gareth, when she lost her virginity. When she got down on her knees before him and tasted him. Offered herself to him. She felt like an idiot. She had barely batted an eye when Gareth called himself an Alpha. She remembered wondering if it was some sort of slang for a big dick. Jeez. So he wasn't just a werewolf—he was a whole other level of monster?

"You mentioned *vitality*," Maddy said, pulling her mind back to the present. "What is that, exactly?"

"Just another word for mystical energy, like the Taoist 'chi' or Hindu 'prana.' *Vitality* is a wolf's magical *essence,* for lack of a better word. It allows them to Change. Other shifters have it, too. If you want the big picture, *vitality* is in everything. It's the life force of the universe itself."

That was a pretty big concept for Maddy to wrap her mind around. She considered it for a moment, gnawing on her bottom lip. So vitality was in everything?

"So then, not just shifters have vitality?" Maddy asked cautiously.

"No, dear. As I said, vitality is in everything. Shifters just have a larger amount, and their bodies process it differently. Humans can cultivate their own vitality to develop psychic abilities. But not a lot of people bother with that. I really thought you knew about all this," Ms. Almut said. She looked appropriately embarrassed. "When Bea said that man was your boyfriend, I thought . . . well, I assumed a lot. I didn't realize this is all so new to you."

"I just found out about werewolves this past Friday," Maddy admitted. "My mom never told me anything, so I guess I'm learning about it now."

"I'm sure Jonine is relieved her daughter is finally coming into her own. The years really fly by, don't they?"

"Yeah, I guess so," Maddy said. It still seemed like yesterday her mom had passed away. She felt a little awkward talking about her mom's death. It was a sore spot. She sucked in a deep breath, trying to release the uncomfortable feelings. She glanced around the workshop, inhaling the scent of dried chamomile and jasmine.

"So, you're a shaman?" she asked.

"I dabble. I don't have many clients anymore, but sometimes people find me. Do you know what being a shaman truly means, Madeline? More than psychic powers and energy healing."

Maddy shook her head. "No, I don't."

"A shaman, in the highest sense, is becoming a Mother or Father to all life, and honoring the kinship within all creatures. So I would never take action to harm anyone, unless I was protecting an innocent life. That's why I never reported your Alpha to the guild." Ms. Almut's face darkened. "Some shamans don't see their practice that way. They swindle people out of money, or try to get famous, or act as mercenaries, hiring out their gifts to the highest bidder. They give all of us a bad name. You should be careful. Not every shaman is a friend to shifters. Some shamans believe a shifter's vitality can enhance their gifts. There's a big market out there for shifter blood, pelts, teeth—it's all underground."

Maddy's mind leapt to the man in the woods, and before she could stop herself, she blurted out, "Werewolf hunters."

"Yes." Ms. Almut frowned at her. "Have you encountered one?"

"Um, I don't know," Maddy dodged the question. "Are there a lot of, um, hunters?"

"There are some," Ms. Almut admitted, but with a reassuring smile, she added, "I don't think you need to worry about that. Black River is pretty secluded. I can't imagine a hunter coming all the way out here. But I would keep your shifter powers a secret. It's just safer that way."

"Right, I know that, I'll be careful," Maddy said, her mind filled with new information. "I'm glad you told me all this. Really. I don't know how else I would've found out that my mom was a shifter."

"Of course, my dear. I'm sorry I didn't say anything sooner, the opportunity just never presented itself. I don't think it was a coincidence that we got a chance to speak today, Madeline. Rest assured, your secret is safe with me."

"Thank you for everything. I mean it." She glanced at her phone, looking at the time and thinking about Gareth waiting in the Camaro outside. Her visit with Bea's mom had already taken longer than anticipated. "I should really get going. My, uh, Alpha is waiting for me."

The shaman woman stood up and embraced Maddy in a warm, strong hug.

"Be careful," Ms. Almut repeated. "For your mom's sake, just be careful."

"I will. I promise," Maddy said.

Then Ms. Almut stood up, picked a stray feather off her shirt, and opened the pantry door.

Bea yelped.

She was standing on the other side of the pantry door, looking guilty as hell. At her feet, little six-year-old Joey was crouched on his hands and knees, very obviously trying to see under the crack.

"Good lord," Ms. Almut groaned, "is there no such thing as privacy in this house? Do yourself a favor, Madeline, and don't have kids."

Maddy laughed self-consciously.

"I wasn't eavesdropping! You were just in there a long time," Bea protested. "So, what were you two talking about?"

"Another time, Beatrice."

"Mom, that's not fair! You always do all the cool shaman stuff with my friends."

Ms. Almut put her hands on her hips. "I thought you said you had homework to finish."

Bea groaned. "Fine. But first, I'm going to walk Maddy to the door." With an angry scowl, Bea picked up the heavy box of Jonine Donovan's things and started through the house. Maddy rushed after her, waving goodbye to Ms. Almut. She grabbed the box before Bea could drop it.

"The heck is *in* that thing?" Bea gasped as Maddy took it from her hands.

"Probably a decade's worth of insurance policies," Maddy said with some irony. Then she started for the front door.

Chapter 14

Maddy slid her heavy box into the backseat of the Camaro and climbed into the car after it. Then Gareth revved up the engine and started down the road back to his place.

"What's that?" he asked, glancing in the rearview mirror.

"It's my mom's things," Maddy said, taking a peek under the lid. Yeah, it looked like a bunch of statements and other legal papers. Nice.

"Anything interesting?" he asked.

"I don't know yet. I'm not super eager to sort through it. Looks like random paperwork."

Maddy stuffed her mail and unpaid bills under the lid of the box, then shut it firmly. There. She would go through this all later when she had a bit of quiet time. For now, it was too much to think about.

Then she gazed out the window, watching the gray, dreary streets of Black River pass by in the rain. She knew she should tell Gareth about her meeting with Ms. Almut and her mom being a werewolf. Really, there was no reason to hide it from him. He probably wouldn't be surprised by the news, but she held back. The information about her mother's shifter identity seemed precious, like a little pearl she wanted to keep close to her chest for the time being. As usual, she had a lot to think about. If her mother wasn't born in Black River, then where did she come from? Did she flee from her wolf pack? Or perhaps she ran away from some other threat? Could Maddy possibly have grandparents, aunts, uncles and cousins living somewhere nearby?

The flood of questions was confusing, and left her conflicted. Did she dare to hope that she might have family searching for her somewhere?

If so, why did they never visit? Why did her mother never tell her about her family? A sense of ominous foreboding plagued her thoughts. Something must have gone very wrong in her mother's life, to choose to raise Maddy alone out in Black River, separated from her pack.

As Gareth drove, she studied him from the backseat of the car, thinking about Ms. Almut's warning about Alpha wolves. Considering Gareth was a top predator of the supernatural community, he kept things pretty lowkey. She didn't think she had any reason to be afraid of him. But . . . there was also a lot she didn't know.

She wondered when exactly he had claimed her as his mate. Was it last Friday? Or was it even before that? She remembered, suddenly, a conversation they had had last week over the phone. She was lying in bed in the trailer, the TV blaring in the living room.

"Well, Mads, look, you're a young girl in a bad situation. Ain't nobody looking out for you, not from what I can see, anyway. So maybe I just kinda claimed you back then."

"You can't just claim people, Gareth."

"Why not?"

"Well, it's gotta be mutual."

"You saying you didn't claim me, too?"

Maybe she had claimed him first?

Maddy wrapped her arms around herself, gnawing on her bottom lip in thought. Gareth was silent, too. He looked like he had something serious on his mind. After a few minutes, they turned up Bickford Ave. He pulled up to his house and parked in the slanted driveway. A river of rain water flowed down the side of his driveway into a storm drain in the street. Joker whined from the front seat.

"You eaten yet?" Gareth asked as he turned off the car.

Maddy didn't expect his question.

"Um, no, I haven't eaten anything, not yet," she admitted.

"I picked up some tri-tip sandwiches from Tiny Costco. They're in the fridge. Let's get the dog settled and have dinner."

"Okay?" Maddy asked, waiting for him to add something else, like a comment about the creepy hunter in the woods, or maybe her mom's box. But he was thinking about tri-tip sandwiches?

Gareth climbed out of the car and unlocked the front door. Maddy followed him up the front drive as Joker pulled on the leash. When she entered the house, Maddy removed her shoes and slipped the leash off of Joker's collar. The big, fawn-colored pitbull puppy bounded across the living room and down the dark hallway, sniffing around and exploring the new space, oblivious to the solemn mood.

Gareth reached over and flipped on the light in the kitchen.

"It works!" Maddy gasped in relief. "Does that mean the power is back?"

"Yup. They're still fixing a few converters down on Main Street, but the town has partial power. I think we're good for now." Gareth paused, watching Joker sniff around the living room with her skinny tail arched in the air. "We should let her out into the yard," he suggested.

He whistled to the dog, and led Joker through the kitchen to the back door. Maddy dropped off her mom's box in her bedroom, along with the stack of bills, then followed behind him.

"I got a request," he said as they walked through the kitchen.

"What's that?"

"So, if Joker's gonna live here, I think she needs a new name. Dean picked it, and it's dumb as hell."

An unexpected laugh escaped Maddy's throat. It took her off guard. But she felt the same way: "Joker" just didn't match the puppy's personality at all. She had already been brainstorming ideas for a new name before the terrible events of the weekend.

"So, I've been thinking about Buttercup," she suggested, "because she's so sweet, and her coat is that buttery yellow color."

"Buttercup it is, then."

Maddy felt a little more grounded. She took a deep breath and let it out slowly. She was moving in with her boyfriend and naming their dog. She had a room all to herself with new furniture. She was out of the trailer and safe in Gareth's house. Normal. *Just focus on normal.*

Buttercup shot outside when Gareth opened the door. The big puppy jumped up and down excitedly, spattering wet leaves all over the place. Her coat was already slick with rain.

The sky was a deep violet-gray, the clouds heavy and immobile. Spatters of rain fell every few minutes, with little intervals in between, like a faucet that wouldn't quite run. Through the trees at the back of Gareth's yard, Maddy caught a glimpse of the neighbor's porch light.

She watched for a moment as Joker ran back and forth through the grass. She had never been in Gareth's backyard before, though she had seen it a few times through his bedroom window. It felt larger compared to her own yard, even though it was half the size, because her property was surrounded by dense woods. Gareth's house was close to the center of town, a rectangular postage stamp of land that slanted slightly downward into a ditch at the back. On the other side of the ditch was a chain-link fence, then a wooden fence, then a row of pine trees, then his neighbor's house.

Joker would be hard-pressed to find a way out of the yard. The young pitbull mix seemed more interested in a woodpile on the south side of the house than escaping. There was probably a critter living under all that wood.

Maddy watched the dog investigate the wood pile for a minute. When she glanced up at Gareth, she discovered that he was watching her. He leaned up against the backdoor's wooden frame, his arms folded across his big chest. His hazel eyes glinted in the soft gray light. Raindrops thrummed down on the roof's gutter, punctuating the silence.

"You alright?" he asked.

Maddy nodded. She thought of telling him about her mom, or about her conversation with Ms. Almut, but maybe it wasn't all such a big deal.

"That guy with the dogs was pretty creepy," she admitted.

"I know."

"I saw him around the hardware store yesterday. He was looking for camping equipment. Did you hear him talking to me and Bea out on the trail? He called himself a werewolf hunter."

"Yup, I heard that," Gareth growled.

"So, do you think he was being serious?"

"Yup."

Maddy blinked. "Really? I thought he might have been crazy."

"There's a whole guild called Hellstrom International. They used to hold conferences once a year out in Vegas. Not sure if they do that anymore. Most of them are bored bastards just looking for a taste of the supernatural. But some of them take the job seriously. There's a lot of money in it if you're good, and you don't get caught," Gareth explained.

Maddy took a moment to drink that down. Alright, so on top of everything else, there was a hunter in Black River? Right after Ms. Almut reassured her, too. Gareth acted like they were talking about the weather. How could he sound so casual about an entire guild of people out to kill werewolves?

"But . . . that makes you a target," Maddy said, concerned.

"It makes us both targets, babe. But nothing you gotta worry about. He's probably after bigger game."

"Like Alphas?"

"Yeah."

Maddy cleared her throat. "Um . . . so Alpha wolves are kind of a big deal, then."

His eyes glinted in the hazy light, a slight frown on his lips, but he didn't respond to her comment. Instead, he asked, "Did you catch his name, by any chance?"

"No, he didn't introduce himself."

"Alright. Well, if you see that guy or his dogs again, you tell me, alright? Don't go anywhere near him. It's probably better if you don't go wandering through the woods for a while."

Maddy glanced up at the mountain looming on the horizon. She felt a little wistful. She knew Gareth meant well, but the woods were her sanctuary. It sucked, feeling like the mountain wasn't a safe place anymore.

"The hunter and his dogs had a weird smell," she recalled. "They stank like skunks. Why is that?"

"They smelled like wolfsbane," Gareth explained. "It's poisonous to werewolves in large doses. Hunters feed it to their dogs to give them an edge."

"An edge?"

"It makes them poisonous if you bite them. As a wolf, I mean. Too much of that bad blood can paralyze you. It's an old trick, but very effective."

Wolfsbane. The name of the plant sounded familiar. After a moment, Maddy recalled her driving lesson last week with Gareth. They had encountered a stranger in the woods who also smelled of wolfsbane. Her eyes widened at the memory of the terrible stench.

"Oh my gosh," she gasped. "Do you think this is the same guy we saw on the hiking trail last week?"

"Yes," Gareth said with certainty. "I recognized his scent."

Maddy recalled the birding binoculars with sudden clarity.

"So then, is he stalking us?"

"I don't know, Mads. He probably heard about the unexplained animal attacks and came to investigate. Or someone reported the incident to the guild. This is likely all my fault. I should've kept a low profile. I didn't think a hunter would show up."

Maddy saw the solemn look on his face and felt a little echoing pang in her heart.

"Don't blame yourself, Gareth," she said softly. "You couldn't have known."

"Yeah, well, you're not wrong, what you said before. I brought all this trouble into your life. Looks like there's more to come. All I want is to keep you safe."

"I didn't mean that, what I said before," Maddy rushed to say. "Really. I don't blame you for any of this."

He released a long, slow breath. "I'm glad you feel that way."

Suddenly, the newly christened Buttercup came bounding across the yard. It looked like she had found one of Gareth's old boots to chew on; the workboot was ripped in half and utterly destroyed.

Maddy groaned when the dog dropped the decimated boot on the deck.

"It was trash anyway," Gareth said. He scooped up the ruined boot and stepped off the back deck. He walked around the side of the house to toss the mangled wad of leather and rubber into a trash can. In the meantime, Maddy turned to the dog.

"Alright, I got big news for you," she said. "We're giving you a new name. What do you think of Buttercup?"

The pitbull mix barked twice and wagged her tail. She looked happy?

"It might take some getting used to, but I think it's more your style. You're not some joker, are you? No, you're a sweet dog. You're a total Buttercup."

The big pitbull puppy—who would probably tip 100 pounds fully grown—cocked her head to one side. She looked like she was sincerely trying to understand Maddy's words. Then she tried to give Maddy her paw. Maddy laughed and almost fell on her ass.

Gareth strode back onto the deck. When she looked up, she saw warmth filling his hazel eyes.

"You hungry?" he asked.

"Yeah, starving," she admitted.

He opened the back door. Maddy stood up and followed Gareth into the quiet house. In the kitchen, Gareth pulled three hefty sub sandwiches out of the fridge. He set them down on the counter. Maddy could already smell the tangy-sweet barbeque sauce through the wax paper. Her stomach growled. She took one of the sandwiches and started unwrapping it.

"Wow, there has to be a half-pound of meat on this thing," she said when she saw the size of the sandwich.

"Trick is to ask Johnny to hollow out the bread before he makes it," Gareth said. "Then he packs on more tri-tip."

"Wait, did you buy yourself two sandwiches?" she asked.

"Protein. Gotta feed these muscles, babygirl," he grinned. Then he took a massive bite out of his first sandwich. Maddy watched almost a third of the footlong sub disappear into his mouth. She didn't think she would ever get used to seeing him eat.

Tiny Costco had pretty good sandwiches. Maddy took a few bites, then she glanced around the kitchen, her eyes combing over the magnets on the fridge. She pointed to one that read "Phoenix, AZ" in fiesta-style lettering.

"I saw that magnet last time I was here. Did you grow up in Arizona?" she asked.

"Yeah, born and raised in Phoenix."

"So that's, like, the desert."

"Mmhm." His murmur was low in his throat, like a growl. He talked around a mouthful of steak. "Not as hot as Iraq. Hot as balls over there."

"How hot does it get in Phoenix?"

"Average in the summer? I'd say like 110."

Maddy tried to imagine it, but couldn't. The hottest day in Black River was usually around the end of August, and it might get up to 100 degrees.

"So why'd you come out here? Like, what brought you to the East Coast?"

Gareth seemed a little uncomfortable with the question. He paused before answering. "Fucked up with my family, I guess."

"What happened?"

"I got into a fight with my old man. I wanted to start over somewhere far from Arizona. My family and I don't really get along."

Maddy's ears perked. She didn't know anything about his family except that they were werewolves.

"Why don't you get along?" she asked.

"It's complicated," he shrugged. "I lived with them a bit after I was discharged from the Army. I've never seen eye to eye with my old man, so we got into a few fights. It kept happening, so I figured it would be easier on everyone if I left."

"Your dad's an Alpha, right?" she asked.

"Yeah, me and all my brothers are Alphas."

Maddy sensed there was more to the story, but Gareth seemed uncomfortable, so she didn't pry any further. But, it seemed like Alpha fights were a lot more complicated than just family quarrels. She imagined, if a prince challenged his father, a king, didn't that mean the prince was trying to take the throne? And if the prince's coup failed, didn't that usually end with his execution . . . or his exile?

Gareth made it sound like he chose to leave his pack behind, but maybe his father forced him out?

"So you don't talk to them?" Maddy asked.

"I talk to my mom. My old man's a psychopath. Don't worry, you'll meet them all eventually, probably sooner than later. My brother Tony is coming out for the Alpha Challenge. He's going to be my second in the fight. In case anything happens to me, he'll finish off the duel with Marquis. At the very least, he'll keep you safe."

Maddy's mouth dropped open. She was surprised by this news, and a little taken aback by how medieval it all sounded. Gareth's brother was going to be her champion if he lost in the fight?

"Wait, you're kidding. No way. When is he going to be here?" she asked.

"Next week. He says Thursday but damned if I know."

"So it's just him? Or is the rest of your family coming?"

"I asked for him to come alone, but we'll see. Can't really control my brothers. The apple doesn't fall far from the tree."

Gareth shrugged. He looked uncomfortable again. Maddy went quiet. She tried to imagine meeting a family of werewolves. Gareth might have his reservations about his father, but she couldn't imagine anyone worse than Dean.

"Would your dad come out here?" she asked.

"Probably not."

"Well, at least your mom sounds nice."

"She's a sweetheart. I think you'll like her."

Maddy didn't say it out loud, but she was intimidated as hell. She didn't have parents of her own, or any strong family ties, so meeting Gareth's family made her feel extra vulnerable. As an orphan, sometimes she felt like the unwanted runt of a litter. People had a strange way of sensing her weakness and ganging up on her—Kaylee was a perfect example—and she didn't have a lot of people in her corner to fall back on.

Gareth's mom and brothers were his pack, his blood. They would have his back no matter what. And she was all alone on the other side. If she messed up, would they push her out? What if they didn't like her? Could they come between her and her lifemate?

Gareth interrupted her thoughts by pulling something out of a drawer next to the stove.

"Hold out your hand," he said.

She did so.

He dropped a key in the palm of her hand. It was one of those decorative keys with graphics on it. The hardware store had a machine that made them in the back. It was blue covered in little crescent moons.

"It's a house key," he said. "It works on the front and the back doors. Doesn't work on the garage door, though. I'll get you one for that later."

Maddy turned the key over in her hand, looking at the cute design. He must have picked it out personally for her.

"Moons?" she said, glancing up at him and grinning. He winked at her.

"*Mi casa su casa*. Make yourself at home, babygirl."

Chapter 15

Gareth sorted through a stack of unpaid invoices in the lobby of Jack's Auto Repair around seven o'clock on Wednesday morning. More tedious office bullshit. He really needed a secretary, but he couldn't afford to hire any extra help yet. A pile of outstanding bills from the previous month needed to be charged before the preauthorizations expired. But it looked like the credit card machine was down. Ugh.

For the third time, he reset the machine and followed the online instructions to reconnect to the network. A red light blinked. Shit. It kept failing. Was the machine broken? Did he need to call the company? What a headache. He should really switch to doing all this online.

Unfortunately, the broken machine did not keep his mind off the new threat of the werewolf hunter.

As he punched in the series of codes again to get the machine working, his mind dwelled heavily on the incident in the woods the day before. When he first heard the girls crying for help, he was already in his wolf form. He rushed to their side, thinking it might be the Grayridge pack. Stumbling upon a werewolf hunter was a surprise. It was a dumb move on his part. Now the bastard knew a big Alpha lived in the area, a prime target, and the bastard wouldn't be going home without a trophy.

With a sour grin, Gareth wondered if he could direct the hunter to Marquis? It would kill two birds with one stone, but he couldn't do that without putting himself at further risk. Approaching a werewolf hunter in broad daylight wasn't a great idea. So far, Gareth's only protection was his anonymity. This guy didn't know what he looked like in his human form. It meant the hunter wouldn't show up on his doorstep with a shotgun. The guild claimed to have a Code of Conduct, but it was all just for show.

The machine failed again. Gareth almost ripped it out of the wall.

"Fuck!" he growled.

He gritted his teeth, his pulse throbbing in his temple. Forget the credit card machine. Last thing he needed was some anti-shifter zealot from Hellstrom International snooping around his turf. He should remove the threat immediately, but where to start looking? Was the hunter staying in town? In Davenport? In the woods? He was sorely tempted to abandon the credit card machine, close up shop, and start investigating all the closed campsites in the area. Yeah. He should do that.

Then the business phone rang. Gareth glanced at the clock. It was still early. Technically, their doors didn't open for another two hours, but in weather like this, it might be an emergency. He picked up.

"Jack's Auto Repair, this is the owner speaking." He sounded a bit more gruff than he intended.

"Thank god I finally got through to someone. Do you have a tow truck? I'm stranded up near Elk Haven. I hit a pothole and blew a tire."

Gareth recognized the voice. He suppressed the urge to groan. It was Mrs. Mackovich. Last time she came by the shop, she got a free oil change out of him. He didn't like that. He also didn't like the way she looked at him, like seared tuna on the country club's menu.

He decided to throw out an outrageous price for the tow, to make up for that free oil change.

"Sure thing. Our hazard fee is an extra $12 per mile on top of our regular rate due to the weather."

"I don't care about the fees. Get out here ASAP. I'm running very late to a meeting."

Like that was his fault.

Mrs. Mackovich started rattling off details about her location. Gareth jotted down the information and ran a pre-authorization on her credit card. The machine didn't want to take it. With a sigh, Gareth took down the card info on a form to charge it later. He knew she was good for the money.

"We'll be out there in about thirty minutes," Gareth said.

"Can you get here sooner?"

"No, ma'am," he grunted.

"Well, try," she snapped. Then she ended the call.

Gareth straightened up and rolled out his neck, irritated. As he looked up, he saw Vin's black truck parking in front of the shop through the lobby windows. Perfect timing. He could get this job finished quick and get on with the rest of his day.

Gareth leaned out the lobby door as Vin jumped down from his car.

"Vin, we got a job," he said. "You up for a tow?"

The kid was eating a breakfast sandwich with his earbuds on. He popped one out.

"Sure thing, boss," he said. "Let me switch into my space suit."

That's what Vin called the gray shop coveralls that served as a uniform at Jack's Auto Repair. As he went into the employee break room to get changed, Gareth ducked into his office to grab the keys for the tow truck.

He locked up the garage. Then the two men headed back out into the rain.

***

Maddy arrived at school on Wednesday morning with her hood pulled up and her phone on silent.

A flurry of texts from Beatrice had awakened her that morning. Her best friend wanted to meet up before class, but Maddy didn't want to talk about their little adventure by the lake. Bea showed no sign of giving up her werewolf theory, and Maddy didn't like lying, but she really didn't have a convincing excuse for the black wolf's appearance. Half of Bea's texts were linked to articles online about modern day werewolf sightings. Maddy really didn't know what to say.

The power was back on, and it felt like Christmas around the school. Her teachers were all in a chipper mood, and the students seemed a lot more energetic than the day before. Black River High School was a small campus, and the student body was less than five hundred. Still, Maddy managed to keep herself isolated for the first half of the day. She avoided her locker and went directly to her homeroom. She spent the morning checking over her shoulder between periods, and using the bathroom behind the gym where nobody ever went. Luckily, she didn't have any classes with Bea until fifth period Earth Science. So far, so good.

During lunch, Maddy crept into the library, where she usually didn't go. Keeping her hood up and her head down, she skulked to the very back aisle, where it was dark and quiet. There, she found a vacant corner between the World History section and Foreign Languages, and sat down to nibble at a bag of chips. Forty more minutes to go, and then it was time for Earth Science class. She usually sat in the back row of lab stations with Bea. Maybe she could switch to the front?

"Hey! There you are!"

Maddy almost choked on a potato chip. She looked up with a gasp as her little Goth friend popped out from behind a bookshelf.

"What the heck, Bea?" Maddy demanded in a stage whisper.

At full volume, her little Goth friend asked, "What are you doing in the library? It doesn't look like you're studying. Hey, are you avoiding me?"

Maddy's mouth gaped open. She stuttered, "N-no!"

"Really? Because you've seen my texts but haven't responded. At first I thought you were out sick, but then I saw you on the PE field. Why aren't you eating at our lunch table? Look, I get it. Yesterday was pretty wild." Bea gave her a devilish grin. "Maybe you just don't want to talk about *werewolves*."

The library wasn't empty, and Bea was practically shouting. In sudden fear of the school librarian discovering them, Maddy leapt to her feet and grabbed Bea's arm.

"Ow! Let go of me!" Bea whined.

"Shut up! Follow me," Maddy hissed. "Keep your voice down!"

"This is *not* very Scooby of you," Bea grumbled.

Maddy dragged Bea to the girls' bathroom near the library's entrance. The bathroom only had two stalls, and both were blessedly empty. Maddy shut the door and locked the deadbolt. Then she released Bea's arm.

"Okay, we're alone," Maddy sighed. "What do you want to talk about?"

"You *know* what I want to talk about."

"No, I don't."

"Oh come on, don't play games with me," Bea said dramatically. "I spent all night reading about this stuff online. You know I come from a family of shamans. I totally overheard you guys in the kitchen. When were you going to tell me?"

Maddy felt a shiver of trepidation. "Tell you what?"

Bea crossed her arms, shifted her weight on one hip, and gave Maddy a piercing look.

"That Gareth is a werewolf, duh."

Maddy's eyes almost bugged out of her head. Her mind flashed to her conversation with Ms. Almut yesterday. If Bea had overheard them talking, then of course she knew the truth. Maddy didn't think she could get away with hiding it anymore.

"Alright, yes, Gareth is a wolf shifter. Did your mom tell you?"

"Oh my god!" Bea gasped. She clamped both hands over her mouth, her eyes like saucers. *"Gareth is a werewolf?"*

"Wait . . . huh? Were you lying? I thought you said you already knew?"

Bea rolled her eyes. "You dope, that was too easy! You're *so* gullible. Of course I didn't know. I was making an educated guess. But I mean, wow, you're dating a werewolf? Did he kill those men out by your trailer? Holy shit—*did he kill Dean?* This is too wild! I have a hundred questions."

Maddy wanted to slam her face into the bathroom wall.

"*You tricked me?* Bea, that's messed up, you're supposed to be my friend!"

"Yeah, well, you lied to me about the shifter thing, so let's call it even," Bea said with a sassy, arched brow. "Anyway, I didn't *totally* guess. I overheard some of what you two were talking about, but Joey kept interrupting. It was super annoying. Then I confronted mom about it later, and told her about the crazy guy in the woods. She was pretty worried, but she wouldn't tell me why, and that's when I knew the truth."

"Great," Maddy said weakly. "Well, that's cool your mom helped you out . . . sort of."

Bea puffed up a bit. "Really, it's not hard if you're paying attention. Think about it. There's a mysterious wolf that's been protecting you out in the woods. Then your sugardaddy's tattoos say 'Lobo Loco.' Vin sent me a pic of graffiti on the garage doors, 'Death 2 Alpha,' which totally screams werewolf. It's so obvious, now that I'm saying it out loud. Wow." Bea shook her head in amazement. "So he's the black wolf who's been protecting you all along?"

Maddy gave Bea an exasperated look. There was no way to deny it. Her little Goth friend might be a hidden genius, and she didn't seem at all put off by the idea of the paranormal.

"Yeah, he is," Maddy admitted. "I only found out this past Friday."

"So then, is he the only werewolf in the area? Is he responsible for all the killings?"

"Uh, not all of them," Maddy said slowly. Then she added, "There's a whole pack living down in Davenport that's been harassing him. They're responsible for most of it. Anyway, I'm new to all this myself. I only found out about Gareth last Friday after Fright Farm."

"That must have been quite a surprise, you being a virgin and all," Bea laughed into her wrist. "So did you fuck him in wolf form? Was there knotting?"

"What? No!"

"I'm sorry, I had to ask."

"No, I didn't have sex with a wolf. What's knotting?"

Bea looked genuinely surprised. "I have some websites I need to show you."

"What are you talking about?"

"It's definitely not safe for work . . . or school. I'll send them to you on Picplace. You can ask him about it."

"This better not be gross," Maddy groaned.

"Depends," Bea assured her. "So you had sex with a werewolf your first time? What's that like?"

"No, Bea, I didn't have sex with a werewolf. Like, he wasn't in *wolf form* or anything," Maddy said. "He was just . . . *a guy*. But before that, he Changed into a wolf. Then he Changed back."

"Got it, I think," Bea said, giving Maddy a suspicious once-over. "I think that's pretty wild, however it happened."

Maddy wondered if Bea thought she had lost her virginity to a big black wolf. She considered defending herself more, but if she protested too much, that kinda looked bad, too. Ugh!

A piercing whistle drifted through the closed door, interrupting their conversation. Maddy threw her hands over her ears with a wince. The bell system still wasn't operational yet, even though power was mostly restored to the school. The bells needed to be reprogrammed, and apparently only one janitor knew how to do it, but he was on medical leave, so they needed to call in a specialist. In the meantime, Principal Rodriguez was still using his whistle to herd children around the school. Maddy was surprised he hadn't incorporated a lasso into his routine.

"Let's talk about this later," Maddy said. "We have to go to class."

"Good thing we have Earth Science next," Bea reminded her, hooking Maddy's arm. "I can't wait."

The two girls left the bathroom together and walked out onto the quad. Principal Rodriguez strolled by in his leather cowboy boots, the whistle dangling from his mouth and his thumbs hooked in his belt. Maddy rolled her eyes at his back.

Bea dragged Maddy to their Earth Science lab in the new science hall. Rows of lab stations, each with its own sink, cabinet, countertop and power outlet, filled the room. Each lab station could fit four people, but the class size was so small, most stations only had one or two students. At the front of the room was an entire wall of white boards, a projector and a pull-down screen.

The lab didn't have assigned seating, so Maddy and Bea grabbed a station at the back. Meanwhile, at the front of the classroom, Mrs. Fleury started waving her hands for everyone to sit down. Then she started reading off roll call.

"Cell phones away!" Mrs. Fleury called. "Due to the power outage, I wasn't able to get the lab materials ready for our project today, so we're going to be working on the midterm study guides. Each study guide has fifty questions you can answer from the assigned reading . . . ."

As the students cracked open their books and began working on their midterm guides, Mrs. Fleury started handing back tests from last week. Maddy had completely forgotten about her Earth Science exam. She cringed when she saw her test score and tried to hide it under the table. It was a D-.

"You're going to have to try harder, Madeline," Mrs. Fleury said, staring at Maddy over the rim of her glasses with a stern eye. "Midterms are next week and you're not doing well. Make sure to study extra."

"Right, sorry Mrs. Fleury, I'll do that," Maddy mumbled.

Mrs. Fleury walked away, passing out more tests as she went.

"D stands for 'dick,'" Bea said, waggling her eyebrows.

Maddy rolled her eyes. She wasn't amused.

"Hey, you'll do better on the next one," Bea said, trying to reassure her. "Just keep reviewing this week, and you'll nail it."

"Yeah, we'll see," Maddy grumbled as she rolled up her test and shoved it into her backpack.

After a few more minutes, Bea leaned over and asked, "So, I'm curious, what if your sugardaddy bites you? Will you turn into a wolf, too?"

"Shh!" Maddy hushed her friend. Luckily, the students at the other lab stations were several feet away. They all looked busy. "We shouldn't talk about that here."

"Why not? Just pretend you're talking about a movie." Bea waved her off. "Anyway, have you thought about that? What if he turns you into a werewolf, too?"

"It doesn't work that way. It's genetic."

"That's not what the Upriver Paranormal Podcast said."

"Okay, well, who do you believe more?" Maddy asked, annoyed. "A podcast or a real werewolf?"

"I don't know. What if he's, like, ignorant or something?"

"Jeez, Bea."

"Look, we're arguing over werewolf facts, isn't there some room for interpretation?"

"No, there isn't!"

"Girls!" Mrs. Fleury scolded them from the back of the room. "What can possibly be more interesting than plate tectonics and geomorphology?"

"Sorry, Mrs. Fleury!" Bea called. "I was helping Maddy with a question in the packet."

"Less talking, more working," Mrs. Fleury called in a singsong voice.

"Sorry about that!" Bea repeated.

The teacher continued walking around the room.

After about ten minutes, Bea whispered, "So then, *are you* a werewolf?"

Maddy looked over at Bea, horrified.

Bea grinned at her shocked expression. "I told you, I've been thinking about this *a lot* since yesterday. I'm sure my mom talked to you about it. That hunter said his dogs were trained to chase werewolves, but they went after both of us, and I know I'm not a shifter, so . . . ."

"Look, I really can't talk about this now," Maddy said, pleading with Bea to drop it.

Mrs. Fleury's voice interrupted their conversation one more time.

"Madeline, Beatrice, if you two don't stop talking, I'll move you up here right next to my desk. Then we'll see if either of you have more questions about your packet."

"Sorry, Mrs. Fleury!" Maddy and Bea chorused together.

They shared a look. Bea shot her a little mischievous smile, and Maddy winced. She had a feeling Beatrice wouldn't let this go until she got a straight answer. Maddy expected a full interrogation as soon as school let out. She groaned inwardly. So much for following Gareth's "rules."

Then the two girls started working on their lab assignment.

Chapter 16

Gareth's towing vehicle was a white Ford F750 flatbed truck with a crew cab, diesel engine and 6-speed transmission. "Jack's Auto Repair" and his business number was painted along the door in rustic red letters. Vin called it "The Monster."

Gareth drove down a very wet, gray, miserable Highway 20 with Vin in the passenger seat. They were about a half-mile outside of Elk Haven when Gareth saw the black Mercedes G-550 SUV pulled over on the side of the highway. Not a great place to blow out a tire. Mrs. Mackovich was sitting inside her vehicle. She wore a big pair of square Gucci glasses and a floral patterned scarf around her head, like an actress from a 1950's movie. Her bangs were curled in a glossy, lemon-blond wave across her forehead.

Gareth parked his tow truck in front of the SUV. He jumped down from the vehicle onto the empty highway. He glanced upward. Both the sky and his bones told him another big storm was coming. The clouds looked darker-than-dark.

As Mrs. Mackovich got out of the vehicle, Gareth held out his hand.

"Safety first, ma'am. Probably best to stay inside the SUV. Low visibility with this weather."

"Right, that's an excellent point."

Mrs. Mackovich sat back in her seat and rolled down her window instead. She leaned out the window and glanced over Gareth with a little catlike smile, like they had some secret between them.

"You know, I heard down the grapevine that your autoshop is Veteran owned," she mentioned.

"Yes, ma'am, I'm a Vet," Gareth said brusquely. "Which side was the flat on?"

"The front right. Thank you for your service. I've always admired a man in uniform."

"Well, I haven't worn mine in a while."

Gareth stepped around the vehicle to inspect the flat tire. It looked shredded. He went around to the back of the SUV and checked under the car. He grunted to himself. Looked like a spare tire was secured under the vehicle, but Mackovich probably didn't know how to put it on.

Gareth went back to the driver's side window. He explained the situation and offered to switch out the damaged tire for the spare that was in the back, and forgo the tow fees. Mrs. Mackovich looked relieved.

Vin gave him a *"Really? Are you serious?"* look as Gareth got his tools out of the backseat of the cab.

Gareth gritted his teeth but didn't say anything. Yeah, he was giving up a fat invoice. He could've towed the SUV back to the shop and switched out the tire there. But if he brought Mrs. Mackovich to the garage, who knew how long it would take for her to leave. The drive down the mountain with her in the backseat would be excruciating. He just couldn't do it. Not today.

"I need my sanity, Vin," he said as he grabbed his tools. Then he pulled on his black baseball cap and stepped back out into the rain.

Despite his earlier suggestion to stay seated inside the car, Mrs. Mackovich got out of the SUV. She brought an umbrella with her and held it over Gareth while he worked on the flat tire. It was thoughtful, and he couldn't brush her off with his grouchiness. She stood around in the rain the whole time he was working. He caught her eyes roving over him more than once. He sighed inwardly and kept focused on the tire. When he finished up, Mrs. Mackovich handed over her business card with her Real Estate information on it, and her personal cell phone written on the back.

"I'm not looking to buy a house right now," Gareth said.

"Who knows? Maybe one day you'll be on the market. *Call any time.*"

She gave him a suggestive wink before climbing into her Mercedes SUV. Then she roared off down the road, spraying water and mud all up along the side of his tow truck.

Gareth watched her drive off. He shook his head slowly. She was good-looking for her age, and he knew a lot of men in Black River would take her up on that offer. But he wasn't interested. He flicked the business card into the bushes.

"That was the easiest tow we've ever done," Vin said as Gareth climbed into the truck. He laughed. "No free oil change this time?"

"Nope."

"Why did she give you her business card?"

"Fuck if I know," Gareth lied.

Vin raised his eyebrow but quit it.

The drive back to Black River wasn't too long, but the rain decided to kick up again as soon as they pulled onto the highway. Gareth turned the wipers on high and squinted out the windshield. He felt like they were caught on the backend of a waterfall. Lightning flashed across the sky as they rolled down the highway, and thunder roared across the mountain peaks. It was one hell of a sight.

Then Gareth cursed. He hit the brakes. The truck slowed down to a stop. Up ahead, a large pine tree had fallen over across the road. It was blocking both sides of the two lane highway. A little further past that, Gareth saw what looked like a fallen power line.

"Shit," Vin muttered. "Can we get around it?"

"Not without going over a cliff," Gareth grumbled, glancing over to their right, where a sheer drop ended about ninety feet down in the forest.

Just their luck, the tree must have fallen down a few minutes ago, because he didn't see any other stopped cars. Gareth pulled over to the side of the road. He threw the car in park. Then he reached behind him into an emergency kit he kept under the back seat. He dug out a few flares.

"What are you doing?" Vin asked.

"Some idiot is gonna come speeding through here and hit that tree," Gareth said. "I'm going to throw down some flares until they clear the road. You got cell phone service?"

Vin checked his phone. "No signal, and my battery's almost dead."

"My phone's internet isn't working either," Gareth said. "We're gonna pretend it's 1999 and use a map. You ever read a map before, Vin?"

"Uh, no, but I use GPS a lot."

"Great." Gareth opened up the glove compartment and pulled out a folded pamphlet, about the size of a restaurant menu. "Pretend it's an app. See if you can find us a detour."

Vin took the paper, a curious frown on his face. The kid was smart. He'd figure it out. Then Gareth jumped out of the truck and started lighting flares. He put them a few hundred feet up the road. After accomplishing his "good samaritan" duty, he headed back to the truck, drenched from his black hair down to his steel-toed boots.

Vin had the map spread out all over the passenger side of the cab. He was bent over, his finger tracing a line down a little byway that branched off of Highway 20.

Gareth climbed into the truck and glanced over Vin's shoulder. A tangle of unnamed forestry roads branched off Highway 20 through the mountainside. The map was only a few years old; he had picked it up at the gas station when he first moved to town. The roads probably weren't much different now. But which ones were kept clear, and which ones were abandoned? Hard to say.

"If we go back the way we came, past Elk Haven, there should be a detour through here," Vin pointed to the map. "Looks like a road goes through the mountains and comes out close to town."

"That looks like Old Highway 91," Gareth said, following the route with his eyes. The old highway was abandoned after they built Highway 20, but it was probably wider and safer than the forestry roads that spattered the wilderness. He agreed with Vin—it looked like the best detour to get back to Black River. Assuming the road was poorly kept, it might take them an hour or two to get back to town, but he didn't see any other option, other than waiting around for a road crew. This far into the mountains, who knew how long that would take? Besides, he had a spare canister of diesel in the back for these kinds of emergencies. The Monster could make it.

"Alright. Let's go," he said, and started up the truck.

Gareth drove back up the mountain. The white F750 sped past the gated community of Elk Haven, spraying muddy water at the iron fence and the faux-granite block walls. The entrance to Elk Haven looked like a fortress's battlements, built to keep out the downtrodden crackheads of rural America.

They continued up the mountain for another ten minutes or so, before Vin pointed out a sign that read, "Day Creek Road." Gareth turned at the last minute onto a one-lane road that curled up the mountainside. If Vin hadn't pointed to it, he would have missed it. A collection of mailboxes at the mouth of the road hinted at civilization. There must be properties up this way. But Gareth wasn't familiar with the area. Eventually, Day Creek Road connected to the old highway. He hoped the turn-off wasn't blocked.

They entered a vibrant tunnel of leafy branches and pine bows. The pine trees were a bright, minty green while the ancient beech trees were beginning to turn yellow and gold. The ditches to each side of the road were filled to the brim with rainwater. Up ahead, a miniature waterfall cascaded down the side of a hill right next to the road. The water overflowed the ditch and spilled across the street. It looked dangerous. Overflows like that could lead to mudslides.

"Hey boss?"

"Yeah, Vin?"

"Can I ask you something?"

Gareth glanced sideways at his younger employee. Vin was puffing on his vape with the window cracked, filling the truck's cab with an artificial purple-grape smell. It wasn't pleasant to Gareth's keen nose, but he didn't want to deprive the kid of his nicotine.

"Sure, Vin, what's up?"

"Let's say you have two girls . . . ."

Not what Gareth was expecting. "You got two girls, Vin?"

"Not, like, on purpose. But let's say you just got serious with the first girl. Like we just posted each other."

Gareth was listening, his eyes focused outside the windshield. He really didn't get the social media thing.

"You talkin' about Picplace?" Gareth asked.

"Yeah, like, we just went official."

"You kids take your apps way too seriously," he pointed out.

"*Kids?* You're like six years older than me."

"It makes a difference, Vin. Anyway, what was your question?"

Vin puffed and proliferated, "Right, so let's say you just got serious with a girl. But then you meet this really cool chick, who you vibe with more than anyone, and you can't stop thinking about her. Then the first girl wants to make plans with you, but you're not feeling it anymore, because you're really into this other girl—"

"Alright, stop there," Gareth said. "Does your main chick know you got a side chick?"

"No."

"Shit, Vin. Did you at least tell your side chick you're dating someone?"

"Yeah, she knows."

"She cool with it?" Gareth asked bluntly.

"I mean, not really. She said she doesn't play games like that. So I gotta break up with the first girl before we date. But if I do that, I'll hurt the first girl, and the second girl has already pulled back, so I might lose them both. I don't want to hurt anyone."

Gareth shrugged. "Well, it sounds complicated."

Vin looked anxious. "Yeah, it is. What should I do? Have you ever been in this situation before?"

"Nope."

Vin gave Gareth a once over. "I find that hard to believe."

"Why?"

"You just seem so . . . ."

"What, Vin?" Gareth turned and caught the younger man with a solid stare. "You think I'm some player, huh?"

"I see women throw themselves at you all the time at the shop, so I just assumed. Like, even Mrs. Mackovitch made a move on you just now."

"Stop, Vin, I don't mix business with pleasure."

Vin looked over at Gareth, still skeptical. Then he blew another puff of vape juice out the window.

"Alright, so . . . what should I do?"

"Sounds like you're gonna lose them both if you keep this up. I say pick one and stay the course."

"But which one should I pick?"

"I don't know, Vin, you gotta decide that on your own."

Vin fidgeted with his vape. "Like, how? Should I make a list of pros and cons?"

Gareth gave him a "*fuck no*" look. "That sounds tedious. Look, just think of the scariest motherfucker you know. Now imagine fighting him for this girl. Pick the girl you'd throw down for."

Vin considered it. "I've . . . never thought of dating that way."

"Yeah, well, in those terms, I think it becomes pretty clear."

The conversation ended. They drove in silence for a few minutes, the wipers creaking with each swipe across the windshield. Gareth turned on the defrost and squinted through the glass. Then he suddenly hit the brakes again, throwing Vin forward against his seatbelt.

"Hey, what the hell?" Vin gasped.

Gareth slowed down to a stop. A silver Nissan truck was parked on the side of the road in the mud. It didn't look like it had been sitting there a long time. Gareth's eyes scanned the vehicle and the surrounding area. The truck was empty and he didn't see anyone around. Where was the driver? There wasn't a building or a convenience store for miles.

Against his better judgment, Gareth pulled over. The weather was terrible. Maybe someone had stalled out here? Could be an emergency.

"Stay here, Vin," Gareth said.

"Do you think this guy broke down?" Vin asked, turning around to stare out the back windshield.

"I'm going to find out," Gareth replied.

He climbed out of the truck and looked around the quiet forest. He took a few deep breaths, opening his mouth slightly to taste the air. The rain dampened most smells, but using his werewolf senses, he detected a trace of human deodorant and fabric softener. Someone was here recently, probably within the last hour. Then he smelled something else unmistakable—wolfsbane.

The hair on the back of his neck prickled.

He scanned the forest again. He felt like someone was watching him. Maybe he was being paranoid, but he didn't think so.

Thoughts of the hunter and his dogs filled his mind. He turned in a slow circle, listening. The rain made soft pattering sounds on the canopy overhead. It was pretty noisy in the woods during a storm. Twigs snapping, branches falling, leaves rustling, birds and animals looking for shelter. But he didn't hear anything moving around that sounded as big as a human.

He started for the silver Nissan truck, his strides fast and tense. The stench of wolfsbane became stronger. It was coming from the truck.

Gareth tried the car door. It was unlocked. Alright. So the hunter must not be very far away. Probably didn't think anyone would be out in this kind of weather, driving around in the middle of nowhere. This might be his chance to discover the hunter's identity, if he could find an ID or car registration.

He searched around the cab for clues. A pair of birding binoculars hung from the truck's rear view mirror. They definitely looked familiar. But he didn't see any keys or wallet or identifying information lying around. He spotted a book entitled *Birds of New York Field Guide* by Stan Tekiela in the backseat. It looked well-loved, the front cover creased and the pages thumbed.

He slid into the car, leaned over and opened the glove compartment. His nostrils flared. He smelled the unmistakable stench of wolfsbane. He tossed aside an ancient car manual. Then he pulled out a teardrop-shaped leather pouch. It was fashioned out of yellow and black leather with a strange emblem embroidered on the front. He sniffed at it, then he wrinkled his nose. The leather was soaked in wolfsbane oil, likely the source of the stench in the truck. When he crushed it in his fist, the odor intensified. It made the palm of his hand itch. The pouch was filled with the noxious dried herb.

Underneath the pouch of wolfsbane was a plastic ID card tucked inside a slim leather holder. Gareth picked it up curiously. It looked like a driver's license, but it had the logo for Hellstrom International stamped across it: two outward facing crescent moons inside a hexagon. Two phrases in Latin ran along the top and bottom of the hexagon: *iustitia in tenebris* and *pax in morte*.

The top of the license read, "Official Hunter Badge ID #3120028." Beneath that was an initiation date. Then, finally, a name: Kevin Montgomery. A winged icon was stamped next to his name, which looked like some sort of special distinction, though Gareth couldn't guess at its meaning. He slipped out his phone and snapped a picture. He took out the ID from its leather sleeve and checked the back, but all he saw was a barcode. He snapped a pic of that too, just in case.

Alright, so this bastard, Kevin Montgomery, was sent out to Black River by the hunter's guild. Shit.

Crack!

A gunshot roared past his head.

Gareth ducked down, trying to flatten himself as low as possible. The trunk of the pine tree next to the truck exploded. The bullet missed the car by a dozen feet or so. It was a warning shot. The hunter must be nearby, and he wanted him gone.

Gareth jumped out of the vehicle, not bothering to shut the door, and ran back to the truck.

"Vin, you okay?" he called as he climbed into the driver's seat.

"What the fuck! Is someone shooting at you?" Vin exclaimed.

Gareth turned the keys in the ignition and threw the truck into gear. Then he took off, roaring up the mountain road, eager to put some space between himself and the mysterious Nissan truck. The Monster was not a speedy vehicle, and it had a lot of bulk. The flatbed truck slowly gained momentum as Gareth downshifted and pushed it uphill.

"You good?" Gareth repeated.

"Yeah, I'm fine, I'm not injured," Vin said. "Why do people keep trying to kill you?"

"It's not the same guy."

"Okay. But that doesn't make it better," Vin pointed out.

"Did you see where the bullet came from?" Gareth asked.

"No, but the gunshot sounded like it came from higher up the mountain."

"That's just the echo." Gareth judged the shooter to be level with the truck. The hunter was trying to avoid hitting the car—maybe it was a rental?—while sending Gareth a clear message at the same time. Gareth bit back the growl in his throat. He needed to contact Antony again, this time asking about Hellstrom's presence in Northern New York. If he could figure out where this guy was camped out, he could take the hunter head on. There must be a record somewhere of the guild's activity online.

Explaining the situation to Vin was out of the question. Vin might be into the Upriver Community Paranormal Podcast, but no way could he know the truth about werewolves. Gareth didn't reveal his identity to anyone. First rule of being a werewolf—never tell a human what you are. It was dangerous. Some wolves broke that code and ended up dead.

He ground his teeth, trying to calm the rush of vitality building at the base of his neck. He wondered if the hunter had gotten a clear view of him—if the hunter guessed what he was. His business's logo was all over the truck. Would Kevin Montgomery show his face at Jack's Auto Repair next? Shit, he hoped not.

The Monster ripped up Day Creek Road, higher and higher into the mountain.

"Do you think that guy's gonna follow us?" Vin asked.

"If he does, I don't have my gun on me."

"Fuck, this is insane." Vin opened the map and squinted at it. Then he pointed up ahead. "Turn left up here. That puts us on the old highway. It goes north for a ways, then it loops back downhill to Highway 20."

"Alright," Gareth grunted, turning between two large trees. Sure enough, a two-lane road materialized through the wilderness. It looked like the road hadn't been maintained in years. The cement was about as smooth as the surface of the moon, with crater-sized potholes, branches, rocks and slick patches of mud. The Monster could handle it, but Gareth wouldn't have risked his Camaro.

He cracked the window and pulled in a breath. A bit more calm, Gareth thought of Maddy. Here he was, trying to protect her, and a bullet in the backwoods almost blew his head off. Fucking irresponsible. What if that bullet had been a few feet farther to the left? It was a chilling thought.

What would happen to her, if some two-bit hunter got him? A little wolf girl all alone in the Adirondacks, going through the Change for the first time, her Alpha gone, no protection, surrounded by enemy wolves. She wouldn't survive.

That was the duty of an Alpha—to protect his pack. He was failing his duty.

What if her Change started while he was out here on the fucking mountain?

Gareth picked up his phone and checked it again. No bars. He typed out a text to Maddy:

G: *Hey, let me know if you get this.*

Got stuck on the mountain with Vin.

Bad signal.

We're heading home now.

Stay inside. Don't go wandering around.

He hit "send" on the off chance that the text might go through. But it didn't. After a moment, a notification popped up: *"Unable to send."*

"Fucking phones. You sure you don't have any signal?" Gareth asked Vin again.

"No. Sorry. It's a brick."

Gareth sighed. Wasn't technology supposed to make life easier?

The big tow truck lumbered through the wilderness, crawling at a snail's pace over potholes and boulders, as the two men carved their way through the woods, following the detour down the mountain to the highway.

Chapter 17

At three o'clock, Maddy dumped her books in her locker and met up with Bea outside the Administration Building, where the entrance to the school was located. As she walked through the school's front gates, her phone pinged. She checked it.

Gareth.

> Hey, let me know if you get this

> Got stuck on the mountain with Vin

> Bad signal

> We're heading home now

> Don't go wandering around

She frowned. When did Gareth send her the text message? She couldn't tell. If he had a bad signal, he might have sent it that morning. Her phone had been quiet all day, and now she knew why. She texted him back.

Got your message.

I'll hang with Bea after school.

Everything okay?

She sent it and waited for a moment, but no response. Then she slipped her phone back into her pocket. Well, if he was with Vin, it sounded more like a work emergency than a werewolf emergency, so probably nothing she had to worry about.

Bea was waiting on the sidewalk across the street from the school. She waved as Maddy approached. Then both girls flipped up their hoodies and walked quickly down the sidewalk. As they left the school and the crowds of students behind, Bea turned to Maddy excitedly.

"Okay, first thing's first. Knotting. I just sent you a bunch of links. Watch them when you're alone. You can hate me later for ruining your innocence. I'm sure you'll have *a lot* of questions for your sugardaddy."

"Um, okay?" Maddy said, still a little confused.

"So is it true? I mean, are you . . . ?"

"Am I what?" Maddy hedged again, though she knew well enough what Bea meant.

"Don't play dumb. I'm dying to know. I stayed up half the night thinking about it. Like, is my bestie a werewolf? Is she okay? Is she going to transform into a wolf monster and eat me?"

Maddy laughed. "No way. You didn't stay up all night worrying about me."

"Of course I did, you dumb bitch."

Maddy blinked, surprised by Bea's bluntness. "I honestly thought you were mad at me."

"Why would I be mad at you?"

"Well, I didn't exactly explain the wolf in the woods, and Gareth was pretty evasive about it . . . ."

"It's okay. I'll admit, I felt like a third wheel, but now that I know why, I'm not upset."

"Okay . . . Just so you know, Gareth told me not to talk about this stuff, but I guess I've already told you a lot, so, yeah . . . I'm a werewolf, too."

It felt like a huge relief to say it out loud. Maddy waited for Bea's exclamation of surprise—or total rejection—or some dramatic response. But her little friend hooked her thumbs under her backpack and kept walking, her gaze focused on the sidewalk ahead of them. She looked thoughtful.

"This is pretty wild," Bea finally said. "I get why you didn't tell me before, and I forgive you."

"Really? You don't think I'm crazy?"

"Hey, you believed me about the Beaumont ghost."

"I know, but that was a ghost. This is different, don't you think?"

"Not really," Bea shrugged. "I haven't seen you shift yet, but I saw that black wolf on the mountain yesterday, and that thing was *huge*. It definitely wasn't a 'normal' wolf by any standard, unless we're talking about dire wolves, and they've been extinct forever."

"You're taking this really well," Maddy said.

"I already had my freakout last night," Bea admitted. "Like, I almost called you about ten times. It's pretty amazing. My grandma used to tell me stories about shifters, but I don't really remember them anymore. I know some tribes call them skinwalkers. Sometimes they're thought to be evil spirits, but I'm not traditional like that." Bea glanced at her. "Why do you seem so bummed about it? What's wrong? Don't you like being a werewolf? Or is it about your stepdad? Are you sad? I'm sorry if I've been insensitive. You can talk to me about losing your dad anytime; I know grief is hard. If you want, I can try to contact his ghost."

Maddy blinked, a little surprised. Contact Dean's ghost? Oh god, she didn't want that *at all*. She hoped Dean's ghost was floating far, far away, down some eternal river into the afterlife. Not hanging out around the trailer, searching for an unopened beer.

"No, no, it's not Dean," she said hurriedly. "You're right, I'm not super excited to be a werewolf. It's kind of scary. I've never Changed completely, and from what I've seen, it looks painful and frightening. I've had moments where it starts to happen, but . . . I guess I'm kind of delayed."

Maddy felt a big weight come off her chest. She released a breath. It felt good to finally confide in a friend. Sharing the burden made it lighter.

"So how does that work?" Bea asked. "How can a wolf shifter be delayed?"

"I don't really understand it myself," Maddy admitted. "The first 'Change' is supposed to happen around puberty, but it never happened for me. Gareth makes it sound like being around him will trigger me to Change, but I don't know what to expect."

"So you've never fully shifted into a wolf?" Bea asked. "How do you know you're really a shifter, then?"

Maddy thought of her eyes turning yellow in the mirror back at the trailer, her heightened senses, and the hunter's dogs chasing after her.

"There have been a lot of signs," she said.

Bea looked thoughtful, like she had come across a riddle and needed to solve it. The two girls walked another block in silence as Bea digested all of this. Maddy wondered what her little friend was thinking.

Finally, Bea said, "I want to help you. You can't just take on all this by yourself. How can we get you to Change in a way that's safe and comfortable?"

Maddy was shocked; she didn't answer right away. Never in her wildest dreams had she imagined having a conversation like this.

"I don't really know," she admitted.

"Maybe you were supposed to shift when you were younger, but something stopped it. Maybe it's because your mom died and screwed up your schedule?"

Maddy stared at her little friend in awe. "Actually, that makes a lot of sense."

"Wow, I cracked it," Bea said with a little fist pump. "Alright, so your childhood trauma messed up your wolf shifter timeline. Hey, it happens. You're just a stunted werewolf. Or like, a delinquent shifter. I get that. My therapist said the same thing about my psychic powers."

"Psychic powers?"

Bea grinned. "She humors me, but she has no idea. My mom thinks that Becca inherited all the gifts in the family, but I think I got delayed when my dad got arrested. It really messed me up."

"I'm sorry, Bea, I can't imagine," Maddy said. Well, maybe she could, a little. "Do you keep in touch with him?"

"No, mom won't let us. She intercepts his mail if he tries to write."

They were almost to Bea's house. Maddy could see the big maple tree in her front yard down the street. The two girls kept walking as Maddy considered their conversation. So she was a delinquent shifter? It lined up with everything else in her life. She got held back in eighth grade and she didn't have a driver's license. She was super late losing her V-card, and now she was late to her first werewolf Change. The only thing she wasn't late on was paying her property taxes, but that was starting to look a little dicey this year, if the hardware store didn't bring her back on.

Bea continued, "Don't be too hard on yourself. But don't ignore the problem, either. If I found out I was a werewolf, I'd be trying to shift all day, every day. So maybe you just have to put your mind to it. Stop running away and embrace it, you know?"

Maddy nodded, warming up to the idea, but not quite convinced yet. Bea didn't know just how terrifying the Change actually was.

"Hey, I got an idea, why don't we practice at my house?" Bea suggested. "We can go behind the camper in the backyard. It's pretty private back there. I'll be like your body double."

"Body double? What's that?"

"It's an ADHD thing, but I think it's helpful for anyone with bad anxiety. I'll just hang out in the background while you try to Change. I'll help you focus and get motivated. Trust me, it works. My little brother is my 'body double' whenever we do chores around the house. It's great. Otherwise, I'll sit like a lump on the couch and scroll on my phone."

Maddy chewed on her lip, considering it. "I don't know, Bea, it could be dangerous. This isn't the same as doing chores or working out. The Change is pretty gruesome. It's not something pleasant to watch. Gareth said I might 'wolf out' and hurt someone."

"I guess it's up to you, but I think you should at least *try* to do something on your own, for yourself, you know? You shouldn't let your *boyfriend dictate your life.*"

Bea sounded unexpectedly sour, and Maddy was taken aback by the little jab. She glanced over at her friend with a concerned frown. Where did that come from?

"To be fair, Bea, I've done *a lot* on my own for the past five years," Maddy pointed out. "Life with Dean really wasn't easy, and it's nice having someone like Gareth around to look out for me. Why else have a relationship, if you don't take care of each other? I'm just trying to be considerate toward my boyfriend. He does a lot for me."

Bea scowled and kicked a pebble down the sidewalk. She still looked unhappy. Maddy watched her friend's reaction, trying to understand the sudden animosity.

"Are you . . . are you jealous, Bea?" Maddy finally asked.

"Why would you ask me that?" Bea grumbled.

"You just seem upset."

Bea looked conflicted. Finally, she admitted, "*Maybe* I'm a little jealous. I've never had a guy take care of me before. Like, my longest relationship was three months."

"Really?" Maddy gasped. "You're kidding."

"No, I'm serious. I know I call him your sugardaddy as a joke, but it's really cool how he takes care of you. I'd want a guy to treat me like that too, someday. I really thought Vin and I had a connection, but now there's this other girl, and it's really confusing for both of us."

Maddy gazed at her friend sympathetically.

Bea seemed uncomfortable with admitting so much. She rushed to change the subject. "Anyway, sorry if you felt attacked, I didn't mean it like that. Don't worry about the werewolf stuff scaring me off. I like horror movies and weird shit. Do you have any idea how cool this is? I've always wanted a pet werewolf."

"A *pet?*"

"I mean, a *best friend* werewolf."

Maddy released a bark of laughter. She admired her little friend's enthusiasm. Bea definitely had a passionate interest in the supernatural; she didn't seem concerned with her own safety at all.

"Okay, let's practice together a few times, just to see what happens," Maddy relented.

"Nice! You should come over to my place. We can use my backyard."

"Wait, you mean, you want to practice now?" Maddy blinked.

"Why not? It isn't raining. Is there a reason we shouldn't? Like, do we need to wait for a full moon?"

Maddy frowned, struggling with herself. She thought of the mysterious text from Gareth on her phone. Maybe spending a little extra time with Bea was better than heading home by herself.

"It just seems a little sudden, but I guess there's nothing stopping us. Alright, we can try it in your backyard. But you can't tell anyone, promise? It's our secret."

"Of course I promise! And my mom's not home, so she won't bother us."

They reached Bea's old craftsman house with the covered front porch. Instead of announcing their presence by walking through the front door, Bea took Maddy by the hand and led her down the side yard. Together, they sneaked into the backyard, past a pile of wooden pallets, a discarded bathroom vanity, a rusty tool shed and an old camper-trailer. A few forgotten tomato plants clung to one of the corners of the yard, along with a rogue squash plant overflowing a ditch at the back of the property. It looked like someone had started a garden at one time, but it was now abandoned.

They found a secluded spot between the camper and a row of scraggly, young birch trees. Maddy hung her backpack from one of the branches so it didn't get wet on the ground.

"Okay, so what do you know about the Change so far?" Bea asked.

"Well, Gareth said it's more likely to happen when your fight-or-flight gets triggered, so he told me to stay out of fights," Maddy said, thinking back to their conversation on Sunday night.

"I don't want to fight you, so is there another way?"

Maddy shrugged. "Not that I know of?"

"Maybe you just have to 'put your mind to it.' Maybe if you think really hard about the Change, you'll trigger it?"

"I guess it's worth a shot."

Maddy stood with her hands on her hips. She thought of the night at Fright Farm when she saw the Grayridge pack. She summoned to mind every documentary she had ever watched about wolves. She focused as hard as she could on her desire to Change. But nothing happened. She didn't feel any flush of fire rising through her body, or the telltale muscle spasms along her spine.

"Maybe you need to get your heartrate up, you know?" Bea suggested.

Acting as a coach, Bea made Maddy run sprints back and forth behind the camper, then push ups, then jumping jacks. Nothing worked.

After about an hour, Maddy gave up, feeling utterly defeated and exhausted. Her breasts hurt from all the bouncing around; she really wasn't wearing the right bra for this kind of workout.

"I suck at this," Maddy sighed, sitting on the steps of Bea's rusty old camper in the backyard.

Bea rubbed her back, trying to comfort her. "You'll get the hang of it. I'll do some more investigating online tonight. Maybe there's a trick to it. How about we practice tomorrow behind the bleachers? We can go after school. The woods go right up to the fence behind the football field. No one will see us. We can find a private spot and you can practice shifting there. Then if you Change, you can just run off into the forest."

Maddy considered it. She knew the place Bea was talking about. Kids went back there sometimes to smoke weed or whatever, but with the lousy weather, that probably wouldn't be an issue this week.

"What about the werewolf hunter?" Maddy said, gnawing on her lip. It seemed a little risky.

"I don't think that guy is going to hang around the school," Bea said. "Anyway, we know how to recognize him if he's around. I'm not afraid."

Maddy was still concerned, but Bea's enthusiasm gave her courage. Yeah, the werewolf hunter would have to be pretty bold to come after her at school. As long as they stayed close to campus, it should be pretty safe.

"Okay," Maddy agreed. "Let's try it tomorrow after school. But only for an hour. We'll see what happens."

"I think you'll feel better taking charge like this. I know I would," Bea said with her usual bravado.

Despite the risk, Maddy felt a bit of hope. Bea was right—she felt a lot better taking control of the situation, rather than waiting around for the Change to happen. This way, she would be able to defend herself against Marquis and the Grayridge pack. Mastering the Change meant that she could flee or fight when the time came. She knew she should tell Gareth about it, but she didn't know what to tell him. He definitely wouldn't approve. But a little practice couldn't hurt, could it?

Maddy checked her phone, thinking of Gareth. Her text showed "Unread." Was he still up on the mountain? It was getting late, and Buttercup was probably hungry. She needed to get home.

"I should get going," she said, picking up her backpack. "See you tomorrow."

"Bye!" Bea waved after her.

Maddy let herself out of the yard.

Chapter 18

When Maddy got home, she took out her new house key with the crescent moons and unlocked the front door. Gareth's Camaro wasn't in the driveway. As she let herself into the dark house, she tried not to worry about him. She felt like she should text him, but she suspected his phone still didn't have any signal. When she called it, it went straight to voicemail.

He's working, she told herself. *He warned you it would be a busy week.* Still, with everything going on, she felt a little concerned.

For the next half hour or so, Maddy went about the mundane tasks of starting a fire in the fireplace, feeding Joker and letting the pitbull puppy into the backyard to pee. Making a fire in the living room was somehow soothing. The trailer didn't have the best insulation, and she would make a lot of fires during the winter months. In a strange way, it made her feel like this was her house, too. Then she made herself a bag of popcorn, flopped down on the couch and went on her phone. She opened her text messages from Bea. She saw a long list of links.

Knotting. Right. So what did that have to do with werewolves?

Mildly curious, she clicked on the first link. It was a porn site. Ew, gross, why would Bea send her something like that? Was this some sort of a joke? She was about to close it when her eyes noticed the title of the video. "Bunny Gets Banged By Daddy Wolf." Okay?

A little hesitant, she hit play. She watched. It was animated, of course, and definitely not safe for work. The werewolf in the video looked like your stereotypical Hollywood wolfman, except he had a ridiculously huge cock, dripping with precum. It was a little ridiculous seeing that giant rod fit into the little bunny girl. Obviously pure fantasy. At the end of the short, forty-five second video, as the werewolf finished, she saw a big bulge swell up at the base of the monstrous cock. Heaving and growling, the furry wolfman worked that big, round bulge into the bunny girl, who seemed to enjoy it very much. With a wet pop, the bulge slipped inside, the bunny girl squealed, and the werewolf shot his load.

Maddy sat for a moment after the video finished. What the heck? She should give this up and work on her homework. But . . . .

After searching through several more links, the idea of "knotting" began to dawn on Maddy. And then she couldn't stop scrolling through the different websites. Holy shit. Her eyes grew wide. She crossed her legs as a warm little tickle started between her thighs. Wow. Really? How had she not known about this before? She had seen porn before, but only the normal kind, and she didn't find it very interesting. Dean never hid his porno DVD's around the house. She had learned to tune it out when he got home from the bar late at night and turned one on. She had never thought to look up any videos for herself.

Her mind wandered back to Sunday night, when she and Gareth had last had sex. It seemed like ages ago. She was a little self-conscious about that. Part of her wondered if he was backing off after her crying session, but it had been a busy week. How often did normal couples have sex? She had no idea, and if she was being realistic, they weren't exactly a normal couple. They slept together every night, so it seemed a little strange that he didn't try to initiate. She remembered the end of their session last Sunday, when she had collapsed on his chest, in his lap, with his thick girth jerking inside her . . . had she felt a knot?

Her eyes widened as she watched another video. Was the knot supposed to go inside her? How? His cock barely fit as it was.

Maddy's phone pinged, making her jump.

Have you checked out the links yet? [devil face]

watching now

Wtf Bea!!!!!

> *Why did you send me this???*

HAHAHAHA

Ask him1!!!!

Or don't.

Aren't you curious??

> *Oh gawd*

Maddy put her hands over her face and let out a soft, girlish sigh. Shit. She didn't think she was bold enough. How was she supposed to look a man like Gareth in the eye and ask him about a . . . a *knot?*

Alright, so maybe she didn't have to ask him directly. Maybe she would wait until the next time they had sex. Then she could confirm for herself just what kind of monster anatomy he was packing. And in the meantime, she had a slew of more videos to scroll through.

Maddy spent another hour glued to her phone until her eyes got dry and tired. Then she slid off the couch onto the floor and opened her backpack. She finished a few homework assignments. As the night deepened outside, her ears became tuned to every car that passed by on the road, but she didn't hear the familiar thunder of Gareth's Camaro down the street.

Finally, she got up and went into her new bedroom. She flipped on the lights. Her mother's box was sitting on the floor, undisturbed from where she had placed it the day before.

Maddy sat down on the thick, brown carpet. She placed her hands on the box's lid to open it, then she hesitated, as though an animal might jump out at her.

So . . . her mother was a werewolf. Or, a wolf shifter. Whichever.

That information sat heavily on Maddy's shoulders. Whatever she uncovered in this box, it might change her understanding of her mother and her family, forever. That was no small thing, but it couldn't be avoided.

Finally, she worked up the courage to pry off the lid. As she suspected, the box was full of manila envelopes and papers. The records went back a long time: insurance policies, credit card statements, bank statements, all sorts of stuff, and none of it very exciting. What did she expect? Hidden treasure? Adult life was nothing but bills.

With a sigh, Maddy started making a stack of all the documents she could throw away. She did that for about ten minutes before she lost her motivation. Then she set the stack of papers aside, put the lid back on the box and slid it under her desk. Ugh, what a disappointment. Maybe there was something important inside, buried between car insurance policies and pay stubs from work, but going through a bunch of old statements made her tired and depressed. She would tackle it again, later.

Still thinking of her mom's family, Maddy got out her phone and searched for her mother's name online—*Jonine Donovan*—trying to find any information she could on public records. The internet returned a hundred or more results for people other than her mother, of course. "Jonine Donovan" was apparently a popular name. Maddy sighed, frustrated. It seemed impossible to find information about someone who died before the age of social media. Maybe she should hire a private investigator to hunt down her mother's relatives? Well, that might work, if she had money. She felt a few angry tears slip down her cheeks at the futility of it all. She wiped at her eyes, but the tears kept flowing. With a deep breath, she finally succumbed, wrapping her arms around herself as deep sobs ripped from her throat. She needed to let it out.

As she cried, a burst of wind rattled the trees outside the window. It sounded like the storm was starting up again. A curtain of rain dropped from the sky, pounding on the pavement next to the house. Before long, tiny rivulets splashed over the gutters along the roof. Maddy's tears slowed down to a few hiccups, then she finally wiped off her face on the sleeve of her sweater. Her eyes were all gritty, and she needed to wash her face, but she felt a bit better.

Then Buttercup whined from the hallway, drawing Maddy's attention. She turned to look at the dog. The dog was lying just beyond the living room, panting and anxious. A crackle of thunder rumbled overhead. Maddy's eyes returned to the dark sky outside the window. A few more flashes of lightning split the night. It was pretty ominous.

Then Buttercup started to growl.

The hair stood up on Maddy's neck.

Buttercup stood up in the dark hallway, facing the front door across the living room. Her eyes were dilated and glowed like little lanterns in the light from the fireplace. Maddy had never heard a pitbull growl before. It was a shocking sound. Almost as terrifying as a wolf.

Maddy climbed to her feet as the blood drained from her face. The sound of the storm outside was too loud. She couldn't tell if someone was outside, or if Buttercup was just spooked by the wind. She crept to the doorway of her bedroom and peered into the hallway. The fire had burned low, casting warm red light through the living room. The curtains on the windows were drawn. She couldn't see the front of the house.

Then she heard the front door knob rattle. The bolt clicked, and the door swung open. A big, lumbering shadow stood on the threshold.

She recognized his scent.

"Gareth?" she gasped.

"Hey, baby."

Maddy launched to her feet. She darted down the hallway, through the living room, and threw herself in his arms. She pressed her head into his wide chest.

Gareth let out a surprised laugh. He pulled her into his big body. Then he walked with her into the living room, keeping his arms firmly wrapped around her. He shut the door behind him and bolted it. Then he buried his face in her hair and took a deep breath.

"I *missed* you," Maddy half-laughed. She almost burst out, "*I love you.*" Oh gosh. She couldn't say it yet.

"You missed me?" Gareth teased her, a grin in his voice. "Look at you, all attached."

"I just mean, I was worried."

"Worried, huh?"

Gareth bent down and gripped her legs under her ass. Without warning, he lifted her into the air. Maddy shrieked and clung to his neck, her legs wrapping around his waist. She hated being picked up, she was always scared someone might drop her, but he didn't seem at all bothered by her weight.

Then he carried her through the living room and dumped her on the couch. Maddy squealed as he climbed over her. He laughed all big and loud, kissing her exposed belly, then each breast, then her neck, then her lips. He was playful and affectionate and so, so physical. He sank his teeth into the soft flesh under her arm. Ran his tongue up her neck to her ear. Fondled her large breasts like he hadn't grabbed them in a year. Lifted her leg up and kissed her foot. He almost turned her upside down. She shrieked and laughed and giggled.

"Damn, it's good to be home," he said.

"Where were you? Why are you so late?"

"Let's just say Vin can't read a map for shit. Now give me your mouth."

Gareth's big hands cupped her face and he pressed his mouth to hers. His lips were warm and possessive. She felt herself slowly melting into the couch. Then Gareth broke the kiss. He licked her cheek. He pulled back to study her face. He reached up and placed his hand along her jaw, his thumb feathering over her soft skin.

"What's got you all upset? You been crying? What happened?"

"I was going through my mom's box, but . . . ." Maddy felt her throat constrict with tears. Then she blurted out, "Bea's mom—you know, the shaman lady—said my mom was a wolf shifter."

Gareth didn't seem surprised, as she suspected. He had probably already assumed her mom was a shifter. He searched her eyes, his brows knitted with concern.

"That must've come as a shock," he said. "You don't talk about your mom a whole lot. You doin' okay?"

"Yeah, uh . . ."

Tears welled up in Maddy's eyes again. Dammit, why did he have to ask her a question like that?

"How does Bea's mom know your family?" Gareth asked gently.

Maddy sniffled, trying to keep it together. "They used to work together at The B Joint. I guess they were kinda close. It's hard to talk about my mom," she admitted. "She passed away when I was thirteen."

Gareth's gaze filled with compassionate warmth. "I'm sorry that happened to you. That's a young age to lose a parent. So I gotta ask . . . did you find your mom?"

The question confused Maddy at first, then she realized what he meant. She didn't ever talk about that time in her life. After her mom died, Dean bottomed out. For a few weeks, the neighbors and townspeople brought over casseroles and groceries, but no one really talked to her after that. The trailer quickly devolved into a hoarder's home. Then the only people who came over were Dean's bar buddies.

"I, uh, I saw her that morning," Maddy mumbled. "I thought she was sleeping, so I just went to school, but I guess she was dead."

Gareth sighed. The silence stretched between them, filled with the sound of crackling wood from the fireplace.

"Fuck, Mads. Is there any part of your life that isn't heartbreaking?"

He pulled her closer to him and kissed her forehead, then the tip of her nose. She almost came undone at the gentle touch. She wasn't used to receiving kindness like this. It brought up a lot of pain.

"Did Bea's mom say anything about your bio dad?" Gareth asked.

"No. She didn't know anything about my mom's life before she moved to Black River. It's so fucked up. My mom didn't tell me anything about being a shifter, my grandparents, or anything like that. What if . . . what if my mom was a breeder?" she asked. "Like you told me, females are used for breeding, so . . . what if she was a breeder and she ran away?"

"It's possible. We won't know until we do a bit of digging. I know someone who can help us find more information."

"Do you think I should search for my mom's family on Picplace?"

"I think you should do whatever you feel like you need to do, Mads," he said, "but don't contact anyone until we know the full story, yeah? Your mom hid out here for a reason. Probably to keep you safe. So we'll figure that out."

"How?"

"I got resources," Gareth murmured. He sounded a little grim.

Possibilities filled Maddy's mind. Could she really belong to a wolf pack? The chance of having a family beyond Dean was like winning the lottery . . . unless they turned out to be even worse. That was a dark thought. So maybe less like a lottery, and more like a gamble. She would remain cautiously optimistic, she decided.

Who was her bio dad? Was he a werewolf? Was he an *Alpha?*

"Ms. Almut told me a bit more about werewolves," she said.

"Oh?" Gareth grunted, his voice deepening a notch. "What did the shaman have to say?"

Gareth sat up on the couch. He moved off of her body, giving her room to sit up next to him. He faced her, his head slightly tilted to one side, waiting. He didn't bring up the broken rule, how Maddy wasn't supposed to talk about werewolves with anyone. Still, his disapproval was written on his downturned lips. Belatedly, Maddy realized she had just boldly admitted to defying him. She felt a little unsure of herself.

"Well, uh, Ms. Almut said that Alpha wolves are dangerous, and, uh, that I should be careful."

Maddy waited for Gareth's reaction. His shoulders stiffened up a bit.

"I mean, she said Alphas are like apex predators in the supernatural world. She said a lot of the paranormal community won't tolerate them."

"Well, it's true, babygirl. But you don't gotta be scared of me."

"I'm not."

"Yeah? You sure you ain't afraid of a big bad wolf?"

"I know you'd never hurt me," Maddy said.

"Yeah, well, werewolves get a bad rap. Can't say it's completely undeserved. You've seen how Marquis handles himself. Lots of wolves have aggression issues."

"But you're not like that."

"Naw, babe, not really . . . well, sometimes . . . ." Gareth paused, and Maddy's eyes widened a bit. He cleared his throat. "You know what? Let me show you something. Give you an idea of who I am, besides all this Alpha stuff."

Unexpectedly, Gareth stood up and offered Maddy his hand. After a beat, she took it, slipping her fingers through his own. She felt a little jolt when she met his gaze, and her heart did a little ba-dump. She was suddenly shy.

Gareth led her down the hallway to his bedroom.

As he walked, he shrugged out of his jacket. He hung it on a hook behind the bedroom door. Totally normal. Maddy watched him quietly, struggling with her sudden, intense shyness. *Sometimes?* she thought. Her eyes flickered over his tattoos. He seemed so calm and restrained, especially when she was losing her shit.

Gareth crossed to his dresser and opened the second drawer from the top. It was full of phone chargers, headphones, various adapters, a few screwdrivers and other odds and ends. He took out a dark blue box.

What is that? she wondered.

It wasn't very large, maybe six by nine inches. It was covered in dark blue velvet. It looked fancy. Carrying the box in hand, Gareth returned to Maddy's side and wrapped his arms around her, getting all close and personal without hesitation. Then he sat down on the bed and pulled her into his lap. Maddy gasped at the sudden change of position. He was so strong, he lifted her against him like a plush pillow.

Sitting sideways in his lap, Maddy felt a giddy rush. She didn't consider herself a delicate, tiny woman, but he made her feel small. Sitting across his knees, her feet dangled in the air. She loved how he touched her with so much familiarity, no shyness at all.

Gareth brushed her hair to one side and kissed her cheek. Then he placed the box in her lap and opened it.

Her eyes widened. The inconspicuous velvet box contained a collection of military medals. She didn't know what the medals meant at a glance, and she didn't really understand their ranking or significance, but they were still impressive. Without thinking, she reached down to touch them. Her finger ran over the ridges of the letters engraved in each one. Curiosity filled her. She and Gareth had only been dating for about two weeks, though they first encountered each other five years ago on the mountain. There was so much she didn't know about him.

"Are these yours?" she asked.

"Yup. Earned by merit." A hint of pride colored his voice. Maddy glanced over her shoulder and caught his eye. He winked at her.

"This one is for the Iraq Campaign," Gareth explained, pulling out a medal with a tan ribbon. "Just means they shipped me out to the desert."

"What about this one?" she asked, pointing to the medal with the silver rifle on it.

"Ah. That's my Combat Infantryman Badge. I took a shot and the target shot back."

Her fingers grazed over a bronze medal attached to a blue, green and brown ribbon that read "Armed Forces Expeditionary Service" along the rim.

"And this one?" she pointed at the bronze star.

"I was doing something stupid and somebody saw it," he said with a grin. "That's a Commendation Medal for excellence in the line of duty."

"Wow." Maddy let that sink in. She had already known he was brave, and that he had a lot of skill with a gun. She hadn't known he was decorated, too. She tried to imagine him in the Army. With his werewolf strength, he must have made a formidable soldier, but with his long hair and tattoos, it was hard to picture him in the service with a shaved head wearing fatigues.

"I looked up NCO online when we first met," she mentioned. "So were you in charge of a group of other soldiers?"

"I took the lead on a few missions, yeah."

"So you're kind of a badass."

"Kind of, maybe. But there are way bigger badasses than me."

"I think you're just being humble," Maddy grinned. "Anyway, I saw a picture of you on Picplace from about eight years ago. You were wearing fatigues. Was that in Iraq?"

"Yup."

"Was it . . . was it hard, going to war?" Maddy bit her lip. It was a dumb question, but she didn't know how else to ask.

"I think the harder part was coming back," Gareth admitted. "I wasn't over there very long. Two tours. I resigned straight after. I really can't hold a candle to the guys who stay in the service for a few decades. Going to war definitely changes your perspective on things."

"Like how?"

"Some shit you just don't take that seriously anymore."

He kissed her nose, then he closed the box and slipped it out of her hands. Maddy moved off his lap and stood up. Gareth put the medals back in his dresser and shut the drawer.

"So?" he asked. "You still intimidated by your Alpha wolf boyfriend?"

Maddy went up on her tiptoes to plant a kiss on his cheek.

"Soldier or werewolf, I think I'm lucky either way," she said sweetly. "To me, you'll always be 'that hot guy I met on the mountain.'"

Gareth released a bark of a laugh. Then, with a wicked grin, he pulled her back down onto the bed.

Chapter 19

Gareth spent Thursday morning finishing the cleanup and itinerary he meant to do on Wednesday, before getting lost up on the mountainside for half a day. A few calls came in for tows up and down Highway 20. He asked if Vin wanted to handle them, and the kid agreed. He seemed to be in high spirits, despite getting shot at by an unknown nutter in the woods. He was glued to his phone most of the morning. If Gareth didn't know any better, he'd think Vin was talking to a girl.

Well, that was Vin's business, and Gareth really didn't need to know. He had his own issues to deal with. The hunter was on his mind. He had texted pictures of the Hellstrom ID badge to Antony last night, after putting Maddy to bed. He asked his brother to find him any information on the guy. This morning, his kid brother had already called him and left a voicemail.

Tony's message was short and to the point: *"You're fucked, bro. Call me back."*

Gareth had been waiting for a good time to call back his brother. Now with Vin gone and the shop otherwise empty, he had some privacy. Gareth shut himself in his office around noon, propped his leather work boots up at his computer desk, and returned his brother's call.

"Took your time getting back to me," Antony said. "I got some news for you. It's important."

Gareth stretched his big arms behind his head.

"Shoot," he said.

"I'll cut to the chase. Your picture's up on the hunter's guild forums. Nice hi-rez image on a private job board."

Gareth sighed. Well, that explained a lot.

His brother asked, "I take it you're not surprised?"

"Yeah, I had a suspicion. Some bastard took a shot at me yesterday."

"With a camera?"

Gareth grunted. "No, Tony, with a gun."

"Well, I suppose that's nothing new for you, right bro? Getting shot at?"

"For fuck's sake, Tony." Gareth sighed. "So how'd you get access to the Hellstrom forums?"

"I applied to the guild as a John Doe a few years back. Dad wanted me to keep tabs on them. Anyway, simple enough to spoof an account. You've been stepping in a lot of shit lately, brother. An Alpha Challenge *and* a hunter on your ass? That's a lot of bad karma. You want me to come out sooner?"

"Naw, I got the hunter handled. Just gotta figure out where he's staying. I don't know how easy it is for you to do this, but any chance you can check out hotels in the area? See if he's staying anywhere closeby?"

"Already did. No record of him at any hotels. I searched in a hundred mile radius from Black River, just to be safe. My guess is, he's staying with another guild member in the area, probably the guy who posted the job."

"Right. Or camping."

"I mean, yeah."

The brothers were quiet for a moment on the phone. Then Tony added, "Well, for your sake, I won't tell mom about this. She would lose her mind."

"Thanks," Gareth grunted.

"She wants to know how your little wolf girl is doing."

"You talked to her?" Gareth growled.

"Yeah. She doesn't want to call you. She thinks it'll scare you off if she starts prying. Come on, bro. You can't hint about a girl and then give her nothing. You know how she is. She's thinking about grandbabies."

Gareth sighed. "Alright. I'll call her with an update after I handle all this shit with the hunter. In the meantime, tell her the tea is working."

"What tea?"

"She'll know."

Gareth hung up. He took a moment to stretch out his shoulders and pop his neck. Then he opened an email Antony had sent him about the hunter. He opened the PDF attachment and started to read.

As he scanned over the document, he felt a headache coming on. Well, shit. Looked like Kevin Montgomery was an all-star killer. Almost twenty years with the guild. Awarded the Hellstrom Medal for excellence in the field. Gareth didn't really care. He had medals himself, legitimate ones, granted by the U.S. Army. He wasn't scared of some punk serving a guild.

His brother was thorough. Tony sent him a whole report full of stuff. No pic of the man's face, though, so maybe the hunter was a little savvy. No social media accounts or online presence, besides the guild forum. But it looked like Tony had mined a lot of information just off of the guild's online history. It looked like Kevin's first notable hunt was about sixteen years ago: the Redfern Massacre in Farmington, Maine. Working with a group of other Hellstrom hunters, they took down an Alpha and almost an entire pack of werewolves.

Gareth read that back twice. Redfern Massacre? Why did the name ring a bell? He tapped his fingers on his desk as he thought back. Then he remembered his mom telling their family about the infamous tragedy when they were kids. It had caused a wave of paranoia and fear to ripple through the shifter community. An entire werewolf pack had been ambushed by Hellstrom International and murdered in a town in Maine.

Gareth frowned. Maine wasn't too far from Northern New York. The massacre happened about sixteen years ago. Maddy would've been a toddler around that time.

"Shit," Gareth muttered.

He opened up a new browser page and navigated to the "wolf web." A black page loaded with a single login screen. It was a private internet service only used by werewolves. Pack affiliation had to be proven before receiving online credentials. His login was assigned back as a teenager. Actually, he was pretty sure Antony was part of the team that curated the wolf web, but his brother was pretty close-lipped about the projects he worked on.

Gareth logged into his account and pulled up a search bar. He typed in "Redfern Massacre." A handful of articles loaded on his screen from various different werewolf-affiliated webpages. So, legitimate sources. He started reading. It looked like the entire Redfern Pack had been ambushed on a full moon at their usual hunting ground just outside of Farmington, Maine. This was almost two decades ago, when the guild was growing in power. Twenty-eight werewolves and one Alpha were slaughtered by a group of hunters. It was the beginning of a chain of similar killings that led to the current paranoia in the wolf community, and part of the reason why shifters never revealed their identities to humans. Members of the guild were all across the U.S., even in rural small towns like Black River. All it took was a curious individual with a fear of the dark to sign up and pay dues to Hellstrom.

One of the older online articles was an obituary for the Redfern pack. Gareth read through it curiously, a frown on his face. His eyes caught on the name of the pack's Alpha at the bottom of the obituary: *Robert Donovan.*

Gareth's brow lowered even further. Wasn't "Donovan" also Maddy's last name?

He sat in silence for a moment. Then Gareth placed a hand over his mouth. He sank back in his office chair. Well, shit.

He might have just discovered the fate of Maddy's pack, and it was darker than he expected. He felt a sinking feeling in his gut. It looked like his little wolf girl was a survivor of the Redfern Massacre. It explained a lot. And it looked like she might carry Alpha blood. Of course she would. She was his lifemate. How could he assume differently?

This was a lot to take in.

Gareth stood up and began to pace around his office. He picked up a wrench off his desk and flipped it around in his hand, his thoughts furiously turning over this new information. Maddy's story was a lot sadder than he had ever anticipated. Her mother must have fled to Black River for sanctuary. The town might have been an agreed-upon bug out spot in case of emergencies. Except it looked like Maddy's mom was the only shifter to make it out. The articles on the wolf web didn't mention any survivors. Even if a few other wolves had escaped with their lives, they might have sought help from relatives or friends instead of coming to Black River. For whatever reason, Maddy's mom had reached Black River and decided to stay. It looked like Maddy's father was among the deceased.

Gareth sighed and tossed the wrench into a pile of scrap metal. It clanged loudly. He tried to think calmly; he wasn't sure what to do with this information. He couldn't tell Maddy all this yet, not until he knew for sure. He didn't want to drop another bomb on her life. She needed at least a little time to adjust to the whole werewolf thing. She hadn't started digging into her own past yet. Maybe there was more time for him to figure it all out, try to find another survivor, maybe someone who knew her family, or some other good news that wouldn't absolutely devastate her.

And what about Kevin Montgomery? By some cruel twist of fate, the hunter lurking around Black River had cut his teeth on that massacre. Kevin Montgomery was one of the hunters who murdered Maddy's family, maybe even fired the fatal shot that killed Robert Donovan. There was no way to know.

A mixture of rage and sorrow filled Gareth's heart. He was a rough man, but not unfeeling. Since discovering her werewolf heritage, Maddy had been given some sense of hope, like maybe she had a pack of her own out there, searching for her. And now he was the one who had to steal it away.

Well, it was stolen a long time ago by Hellstom International.

So maybe Gareth could make things right by killing this hunter. Maybe he could exact some sort of revenge for Maddy's father. He imagined the old Alpha of the Redfern Pack nodding sagely in agreement. An Alpha wolf like Robert Donovan would want to be avenged, and it was Gareth's honor to carry it out. That was werewolf creed: blood for blood, or sometimes, just blood.

Honestly, it was the least he could do. After blowing up Maddy's life, he could at least set this right. Gareth didn't consider himself a vengeful guy, but this was nothing short of karmic retribution. The universe must have some sense of justice after all . . . and if not that, then a healthy dose of irony.

***

Thursday morning passed by slowly. It wasn't raining, but heavy clouds filled the sky, preparing for the next downpour. In a daze, Maddy walked from one class to the next, preoccupied with blissful memories from the night before.

She had woken up in the middle of the night to Gareth's arms wrapped tightly around her body. She remembered lying on her side with the curve of her ass pressed flush to his pelvis. His hand was between her legs, his thumb brushing slow circles over her clit. Pleasure blossomed with each stroke of his thumb.

With a little gasp, she flexed her hips—he was inside of her.

The stretch almost broke her mind. She wiggled and whimpered, stuck on his wide cock. His hand probed her abdomen. When he pressed down, she could feel his thick head buried in her tight flesh. She gasped at the sensation. He kept doing it as he slid in and out of her, making her moan.

"*Gareth,*" she breathed. "*Ah!*"

He growled low in his throat. Fuck, he sounded like a beast. He rolled and pressed her down on her belly into the mattress, keeping her beneath him as his girthy, warm cock sank into her tight flesh another inch. Then he covered her with his body, crushing her with his weight. It felt good. Comforting. Secure.

He started grinding into her with slow, mind-bending friction. She gripped the bedsheets with a little sob. His big hands covered her own, his arms over her arms, his chest against her back, holding her down as he rocked into her.

She whimpered as her orgasm began to build. He bit the back of her neck, deepening his thrusts, murmuring into her ear.

"You're such a good girl . . . ."

When she came, she gushed onto the bed, her fluids dripping down her thighs. She couldn't cry out because his weight was so heavy on top of her, so she gasped and moaned brokenly into the mattress, writhing and grinding her hips.

He gripped her hands hard when he came, holding himself deep inside, their bodies locked together as one. She felt his cock pulsating from her lower lips to his thick head, snug against her womb. His seed spurted into her body, filling her up with a comforting glow. Her anxiety, which seemed like constant background noise, vanished in the calm after her orgasm. She felt comforted by his weight bearing down on her.

When he finished, he didn't bother cleaning up, but pulled her against him again, spooning her, enveloping her in the warm cage of his arms.

She was sweaty and sticky, and full of warm syrup. She felt no desire to leave the bed or even talk. It felt like a delicious dream, except it was real, which seemed too good to be true. Eventually she fell asleep, lulled by his steady heartbeat.

Now Maddy felt drugged. She floated through the morning with her head in the clouds. At lunch, she ate with Andie and Rachelle and listened to them complain about their AP History class.

Then Andie shared a pic of her Sailor Mercury costume, which she planned to wear to the Halloween Haunt at Devil's Tower. Bea also looked excited to go. The two girls discussed their plans for Saturday as Maddy munched on a bag of spicy pickle chips. Based on previous years, it sounded like the party was going to get pretty wild.

After the bell rang, signaling the end of lunch, Bea and Maddy headed to their Earth Science class together, where Maddy struggled to pay attention. She was eager for the day to be finished. Sixth period computer lab was predictably boring.

When the final bell rang at three o'clock, Maddy's cell phone buzzed in her pocket. She checked her texts as she gathered up her backpack.

> *Don't forget about werewolf practice.*

> *Meet me behind the bleachers.*

A little smile curled on Maddy's lips.

Heading to meet you now.

After throwing her books into her locker, she headed to the south side of campus. She passed by the PE locker rooms, then took a short staircase down to the sidewalk to skirt around the football field. The weather had turned the field into a mud pit, but the football team was outside doing their warm-ups. Football season was in full swing. Maddy watched the athletes stumble into each other as they ran through different routines, sometimes slipping in the mud or skidding across the wet grass.

The cheer squad and the colorguard were also out in full force, but they kept to the far side of the field near the gym and the PE lockers, where it was less muddy.

Maddy couldn't help herself. As she circled around the bleachers, she stared at the cheer squad until she spied Kaylee's curly blond head bouncing around. Several girls turned to glare at her as she walked by. When the coach wasn't looking, Amy Higgins flipped her off with a pink acrylic nail.

Maddy flipped her the bird, too. Then she pulled up her hoodie and kept walking.

On the far side of the football field, the forest abutted the last row of bleachers. It was a secluded spot. Beyond the bleachers was a chain-link fence, and beyond that fence, the woodland spread from the southeast side of town up into the mountains. It wasn't unusual to see the occasional deer or even a black bear wandering onto the football field during the summer. Maddy followed a walking trail that looped around the field and the bleachers, leading her away from the football players and off-key chanting of the cheer squad.

Behind the farthest row of bleachers, a fence stood at the border of the trees with a sign that read, "No Trespassing." But of course, students jumped the rusty chain-link fence all the time. The trees on the other side were scarred by pocket knives and ballpoint pens. Even Maddy had scraped her initials into one of the trunks. When she reached the fence, she saw Bea standing on the other side, sitting on an old log a few yards into the forest.

Bea pushed off the log and waved at her.

"Come on over!" she called.

Maddy glanced around one more time, but no one was closeby. Then she tossed her backpack over the fence and pulled herself up. She dropped down on the other side without an issue.

"So I think I found the perfect spot to practice," Bea said. She took Maddy's arm and led her a little bit deeper into the woods and down a slight hill. Curtains of emerald green pine needles hid them from view of the football field. It seemed like a safely secluded spot, but not so deep as to get lost in the forest. On the off chance that Maddy actually turned into a wolf, she could run into the woods rather than onto the football field. It seemed like a win-win.

"This is good," Maddy agreed. "So what now?"

"I looked up a bunch of stuff online," Bea said excitedly. "Granted, it's really hard to tell what information is real and what's fictional, so I made a note on my iPhone with all the stuff that looked legitimate."

"Why not ask your mom?" Maddy suggested. "She's a shaman, right? I bet she knows a few things about the Change."

Bea shrugged. "I tried to ask her about it, but, uh . . . ."

At Bea's awkward pause, Maddy crossed her arms.

"But what, Bea?"

"Well, I don't think she *needs to know* that we're practicing out here. Like, I don't think she'd be very cool with it. So we're doing this on our own."

Maddy wasn't truly surprised, but she was a little disappointed.

"So your mom doesn't want us practicing together?"

Bea shrugged. "She's just overprotective. She says shifter powers are unpredictable and it's better to drop the whole thing."

Maddy felt a slight misgiving, but pushed it aside. Learning to Change was important, and silly as it was, practicing with Bea gave her more confidence. Maddy slung her backpack down on the ground, out of the way, where she wouldn't trip over it. Then she placed her hands on her hips, facing Bea across a little patch of grass.

"So what did you find on the internet?"

Bea started to read off her phone: "Reddit's consensus is that you're probably going to have a hard time because you're delayed. Like, you might need something to stimulate the Change or trigger it. So I have a list of suggestions."

"Wow, did you really ask Reddit?"

"Yup. The r/werewolf boards are really helpful. Here's some of the suggestions for triggering your werewolf Change: full moon—"

"Well, that's out," Maddy grumbled. There wouldn't be another full moon for almost two weeks.

Bea continued to read her list: "—ghost pepper salsa, swim in a cold lake, ten minute headstand, LSD, bangin' sex, 'Rap God' by Eminem—"

"What?" Maddy laughed. "Are you serious?"

"Yeah, there's a few more: getting a tooth pulled without anesthesia, getting bit by another werewolf, fighting for your life, or getting tickled so hard you pee."

"Wow. So we're supposed to try all of those?" Maddy said with a raised eyebrow. "I mean, I'm a little skeptical about Eminem."

Bea shrugged. "It's just a list I found. Adrenaline seems to be linked to the Change. So the more you get scared or pumped up, the more likely you'll turn into a wolf."

"Great," Maddy said. Gareth had warned her to stay out of fights for that reason. "So you're going to try to scare me?"

Bea didn't answer right away. She turned on her cell phone's speaker and opened up her Spotify music playlist.

In a small, angry voice, Maddy heard the first few lines of "Rap God" by Eminem begin to play: *"Look, I was gonna go easy on you not to hurt your feelings / But I'm only going to get this one chance . . . ."*

Then Bea picked up a heavy tree branch lying on the ground next to her. It was about half the length of a broom handle and twice as wide. Without warning, she swung it at Maddy's head.

Maddy threw up a hand and blocked the heavy branch, taking the blow on her arm.

"Ow! What the hell, Bea!"

"Come on, Maddy! Get pumped up! I'm doing this for your own good. Maybe if you think you're in danger, you'll Change."

Bea started swinging the stick at her, harder this time. Maddy defended herself, taking blow after blow on her arms. Then she yelped when Bea caught her on the shin.

"Cut it out, Bea! Stop it!" she yelled, but her little friend kept swinging. The tiny Goth girl seemed to be enjoying herself way too much. Maddy started to get irritated. The sound of an all-treble "Rap God" blaring off the tiny phone speakers was super annoying. The song needed a subwoofer.

"Come on, you stupid wolf!" Bea yelled. "Fight back!"

"Fuck you!" Maddy roared.

Bea redoubled her efforts, swinging the branch harder and wilder than before. Maddy felt a little twinge between her shoulder blades. A bit of fire shot up her neck into the base of her skull. Was it the Change? Was it starting? With a roar, she grabbed the branch in mid-air and yanked it out of Bea's hands. She slammed the branch down on one knee and split it in half, then threw it into the trees. She glared at Bea and growled.

Bea froze.

The two girls stared at each other, about a yard apart. Maddy's angry breath created little puffs of vapor in the cold air.

"Holy shit, Maddy, your eyes flashed gold!" Bea gasped. "You're doing it! *You're Changing!* Let's keep going!"

"No," Maddy growled. Her voice had dropped to a husky alto, like a bluesy jazz singer. "No, I think we're done here. Your mom's right, Bea. This isn't safe."

"Oh. Okay." A little, disappointed frown knitted Bea's brow. "Are you sure? We're so close! Your voice is deeper and everything."

Maddy reached up and touched her teeth, feeling the sharp edge of her incisors. Then she thrust her hands into her hair. Her ears had little fuzzy tips. The Change had come on much faster than before. She could feel a fiery, burning energy in her arms and legs. It was kind of painful, kind of pleasant. But suddenly, she didn't want to go through with it. Gareth was right. The surge of energy was overwhelming. What if she lost herself to it?

"I need to use the bathroom," Maddy said.

"Alright."

Maddy went to grab her backpack. Bea didn't argue with her. The two girls walked back to the fence. Maddy's muscles felt super-charged and tingly; she practically leapt over the eight foot fence, she climbed so fast. Bea followed her at a slower pace.

"Are you feeling okay?" Bea asked as they started back around the football field. "You look kind of pale and sweaty."

"I'm a little dizzy," Maddy admitted.

Her voice sounded a bit more normal—good. As the Change started to reverse itself, a sense of nausea began to rise in her gut. Low blood sugar? She recognized the feeling from last week. Gareth's mom had sent her a special kind of tea that was supposed to help with it. She should probably eat something; she didn't want to faint. But first, she needed to get to the bathroom and splash some water on her face.

"Are you going to throw up?" Bea asked. Seeing Maddy's miserable look, Bea pointed to the basketball courts nearby. "The gym's bathroom is closest."

They started across the field at a fast trot. About halfway to the PE bathrooms, Bea's phone started to vibrate in her pocket. She fished it out and checked the caller ID. She groaned.

"It's my mom. Fuck."

"What's up?" Maddy asked.

"She probably thinks . . . well, she *knows* what we're doing at school so late. It sucks having a psychic mom. She asked me if we had any 'plans' before I left for school this morning. I know she's suspicious. Go on, I'm right behind you, I just gotta talk to her real quick."

Bea picked up the phone as Maddy surged ahead. Her nausea was increasing by the minute; she felt like she was going to throw up. She took off running around the football field, through the parking lot, then across the basketball courts to the PE bathrooms. The restrooms were still unlocked due to football and cheer practice. She rounded the little brick building, then she slammed through the door. She scrambled into one of the stalls as her stomach curdled.

Maddy hovered over the toilet, holding her hair back, gagging and heaving. Her lunch came up. Then a good amount of nasty yellow bile. Gross. She coughed and hacked a few times, then she flushed the toilet, feeling the burn of stomach acid in the back of her throat. She wiped off her mouth on a piece of tissue paper. Fuck, she didn't feel good at all. The strange fire of the Change was still circling in her blood, making her feel jittery and sick at the same time. Her body didn't seem to know what to do with itself.

As Maddy sucked in a deep breath and tried to quell the nausea in her gut, she heard the bathroom door open. A group of girls entered, their high-pitched voices echoing off the high walls of the restroom.

"I'm really sure I saw her come in here," one of the girls said.

"This is so bad, I can't believe we're doing this," another girl replied with a hushed giggle.

"Don't worry, this won't take long," the first one said confidently.

Maddy's eyes widened. She recognized that voice. Her stomach clenched.

Oh no, not now!

Chapter 20

Maddy opened the stall door and came face-to-face with Kaylee Mackovich.

A look of malicious glee passed over Kaylee's face. Her blond, angelic curls cascaded down her back in a celestine waterfall. She wore a bright pink turtleneck sweater under her black and red Varsity jacket. Her eyes were made even bigger and brighter by a pair of babydoll fake eyelashes. It looked like cheer practice had just let out.

Behind her, Maddy saw three other girls. She recognized two of Kaylee's cheer squad friends: Amy, the beautiful black girl who reminded Maddy of a Barbie doll, with blond braids woven into her thick dark hair. Then a third girl, Jaylen, who was basically Kaylee's less attractive clone.

As she sized them up, a fourth girl lumbered in through the bathroom door. With a scowl, she shut the door behind her and locked it. Maddy didn't recognize her. This girl was new. She was tall, broad and curvaceous, with big shoulders and wide breasts. Her eyebrows were drawn-in with a sassy arch, and her hair was pulled back in a strict braid. She wore a color guard uniform. She stood a head taller than the other three girls, and she was wide enough to block the doorway. She looked confident, gorgeous and spitfire mean.

"It stinks in here," Kaylee sneered.

"Yeah, smells like *trash*," Barbie echoed.

"We're talking about you, *Muddy*," Kaylee added.

"Fuck off," Maddy snarled, feeling a little nervous. She wondered if Bea was still outside talking to her mom. The four girls were standing between her and the exit. It looked like they meant to block her from leaving. Maddy wanted to groan—it wasn't anything new. Ganging up on her in the girl's bathroom was Kaylee's original scare tactic. The last time it happened, Maddy got suspended for a week after a fist fight, while Kaylee got a slap on the wrist.

It looked like Kaylee was back to her old ways, except this time, Maddy couldn't fight them. Not with the Change burning in her blood. It was a really bad idea.

She glanced around the bathroom: three stalls, a scuffed tile floor, metal plates on the wall instead of mirrors, and two narrow windows set far off the ground, near the ceiling. She was trapped in a box. She felt claustrophobic inside the confined space with so many girls. She felt a sinking feeling. She didn't want to fight Kaylee. Not now.

"Look, let's just drop this childish bullshit, okay?" Maddy said, trying for a peace talk. "You want my wallet? Here, take it." She slung down her backpack and started unzipping it. "You can have my ID, my money and whatever else you want. Take my phone, I don't care. I just don't want to fight."

"Fuck your dirty stripper money," Barbie spat. "We're not here to steal your crappy phone."

Jaylen giggled in the back. She sounded a little nervous. Then she piped up, "Hey, I want to know who that hot guy is, the one who picked you up from school last week. The guy with the Scorpio tattoo. Does he live around here?"

"Yeah, he does," Maddy said, feeling a spark of rage at the mention of Gareth. Now she felt protective. "He's my boyfriend."

Kaylee looked like she had swallowed her tongue. Then she released a shriek of derisive laughter. "You? A *boyfriend*? Hah! Giving a blowjob to some guy doesn't make him your boyfriend, you dumb slut."

Maddy's hands balled into fists. She felt her face growing red with anger. "At least I didn't lose my virginity in a treehouse like a baby," she shot back.

Kaylee looked shocked.

"Oh, that's low," Barbie growled. "That's like, too far."

"Too far?" Maddy demanded. "And spreading rumors that I'm a stripper is okay?"

"They're not rumors. You work at Sapphire," Kaylee said.

"Stop lying!" Maddy shrieked. Fuck, she was losing her mind.

"Anyway, that's not what this is about," Kaylee cut her off. "This is payback for breaking Adam's nose. If you don't want us to break *your* nose, then you should come with us. We'll make it super easy on you, if you do what we say."

Maddy glanced back and forth between the four girls warily. She honestly wasn't sure if Kaylee or any of the girls in the bathroom were capable of breaking her nose, but she didn't want to find out. The new girl in the back looked pretty mean and tough. She considered her options, but she didn't have very many. Her back was against the wall, but she didn't want to wolf out at school.

Then Amy Higgins reached into her pocket and took out a pair of metal handcuffs. They looked like real police handcuffs. Maybe her dad was a cop?

Kaylee giggled when she saw the cuffs, unable to hide her amusement.

"Oh, this is *so* good," she laughed, sharing a grin with Jaylen.

Maddy glanced around their group again. This was unexpected. She didn't want to go with Kaylee, but she didn't want to fight, either.

"Why the cuffs?" Maddy asked suspiciously.

"Come with us," Amy said. "You'll find out."

"You might even like it," Jaylen giggled.

Ugh. Maddy wanted to roll her eyes. Jaylen always sounded like a twit. She wondered what mode of torture Kaylee's crew had in mind for her. Gritting her teeth, she allowed Barbie to put the handcuffs on her wrists. Then, like a prisoner, the girls led her out of the bathroom.

Outdoors, it was starting to rain again. Maddy noticed Bea approaching across the basketball courts with a cigarette in her hand. It looked like she had finished up the phone call with her mom and was taking her time getting to the bathroom. The little Goth girl caught sight of them and gasped visibly. Her eyes met Maddy's across the open space, but Maddy shook her head, warning her friend not to interfere. Bea didn't listen, of course, and started walking faster in her direction.

Kaylee and the Varsity jackets escorted Maddy to the door of the boys' bathroom. It was only about ten feet away from where they were originally. Maddy hesitated before she followed them in.

The boys' bathroom was blessedly empty, but it wouldn't remain so for long. Maddy could hear whistles blowing out on the football field. With the rain coming down, practice would probably end early. Then the boys' PE locker rooms and bathrooms would be full of randy, post-workout, Red Bull fueled football players.

Maddy was forced to walk forward as the girls crowded behind her into the restroom.

"Alright, what's all this about?" Maddy demanded. Her voice hitched. She was more than a little freaked out.

Kaylee fixed her with a glare. "Strip."

"What the fuck?"

"Strip naked, you slutty bitch," Kaylee repeated.

"I'm not going to strip!" Maddy said, feeling her temper rise again. "My hands are cuffed, dumbass."

"You can take off your pants," Jaylen pointed out.

Maddy was shocked. "Wait, *what?* Why did you bring me in here?"

"We're going to handcuff you to a urinal like the whore you are," Kaylee said gleefully. "Don't worry, we'll leave a tip jar."

At her signal, Jaylen removed her backpack and took out a jar labeled "Tips" in black Sharpie marker. It was decorated with little stickers and sparkles, like a craft project for Home Ec. Maddy almost laughed when she saw it. Were they serious?

"Do you like it? We made it in my *treehouse*," Kaylee mocked her evilly.

"Are you insane?" Maddy gasped. "You're psychotic! Let me go!"

"I'm *psychotic?*" Kaylee demanded, as though she were actually offended. "You're a disgusting stain on my life, Muddy. You flaunt your tits around like you're hot shit, but you're just a slut. So what if all the guys want to fuck you? Now they can fuck you for free. Jesenia, lock the door," Kaylee commanded.

"Done." The big girl reached behind her and turned the latch. Then she crossed her arms and looked at Maddy menacingly. She planted herself in front of the door like a bouncer to a club.

Maddy stared at Kaylee in disbelief. Did all of Kaylee's animosity stem from *jealousy*, because some of the boys on campus thought she was hot? *Really?* Because in some alternative universe, Kaylee perceived her as competition?

"Punishing me isn't going to make Trace go out with you again," Maddy pointed out, as she backed farther away from the girls.

"Don't you dare speak his name to me. We were *in love* and you *ruined it* with your nasty giant tits," Kaylee snarled. "*You deserve this.*"

"Hey, I thought this was about Adam's broken nose," Barbie pointed out. She frowned and gave Kaylee a side-eye. "I thought you were over Trace."

"Does it fucking matter?" Kaylee screeched. "Let's get this over with before a teacher comes."

The three girls advanced on her. Jesenia was blocking the exit. Maddy was trapped. She started to panic. Her heart began to pound. Her ears started ringing. She tried to repress the power of the Change, but a rush of fire flooded her body. It began in her toes and moved up her legs. Her nausea was replaced with a burning, manic sort of energy.

She felt a crazy urge to bodyslam her way through the girls to the exit. She was pretty sure she could make it past Kaylee and Jaylen, but the other two girls were bigger and more aggressive. Barbie stood in a wide stance with her buff arms folded across her chest.

Jesenia blocked the door like a troll. She probably weighed twice as much as Maddy. She wouldn't be easy to topple.

Then, bubbling up from her throat, Maddy released a terrible growl. It didn't sound human. Her skin felt itchy. Her mouth hurt. She felt her teeth getting larger. Her muscles bulged in her arms. When she looked down, she saw long red fur covering the backs of her hands.

Her eyes widened in alarm. Oh no. *No no no.*

When Maddy looked back up, the four girls were staring at her in shock.

"What's wrong with her?" Jesenia asked from the back.

"Her eyes are yellow," Jaylen gasped.

"What the fuck?" Barbie yelled. "Is she growing *fur?*"

Maddy caught sight of herself in the mirror. Her face was bulging and disfigured from the big fangs filling her mouth. Her lips looked all puffed out. A dusting of red fur covered her forehead and the bridge of her nose. Her eyes were bright yellow.

Two tufted, fuzzy wolf ears stuck out from her red hair.

Well, shit. She needed to think fast, before the Change completely overtook her. Maybe she could scare them off? She couldn't do much with these handcuffs on her wrists. With a roar, her arms straining, Maddy broke the chains in half. *Snap!*

Jaylen screamed.

Then Maddy turned and grabbed the bathroom sink, desperate to scare off the girls before the confrontation escalated. Metal shrieked and tore. Porcelain tiles shattered. Water gushed out of a broken pipe. She channeled all of her strength into her arms. Maddy pulled the whole basin off the wall and threw it on the ground, where it broke into several pieces.

The girls all screamed and ran for the exit. Jesenia unlocked the door and threw it open. The heavy metal door slammed into Kaylee's face, who was right behind her, and knocked the skinny blond girl on her ass. Kaylee howled and sobbed. Jaylen and Amy grabbed her by the arms and hauled her to her feet. Then all three girls scrambled outside, shrieking like a flock of parrots.

Maddy hunched over the broken sink, trying to control the insane fire rushing through her body. She hunched her shoulders, her breath heaving, sweat pouring down her brow.

No! she thought. *No, go back, be human!*

Pain shot up her neck as her muscles cramped. She was fighting the Change with all her might. She couldn't turn into a wolf here in the student bathroom. It simply couldn't happen! But the fire was burning through her whole body.

"Ah!" Maddy groaned in agony.

Then someone joined her side and boldly took hold of her arm.

"Holy shit, Maddy!" Beatrice exclaimed. "What the hell—"

Maddy met her friend's gaze. Bea's eyes widened. The two girls stared at one another. Then Bea shrugged off her jacket and threw it over Maddy's head.

"Fucking hell! Maddy, come with me. Hurry!"

"What . . . where are we going?" Maddy mumbled, but her elongated incisors made it almost impossible to talk. Her words sounded garbled.

"Holy shit. *Holy shit*," Bea repeated. "Just come with me!"

Maddy couldn't see anything as Bea led her outside. They dashed around the PE locker rooms, avoiding the busy basketball courts. Bea ushered her behind the band room, then across an open area of grass, beyond the auditorium. Kaylee's crowd of flying monkeys had disappeared. It seemed like not even a janitor was around. Bea pulled her down a staircase and across the quad. They slipped through the corridor next to the new Science Hall, then past the Administration Building. They found the sidewalk.

Maddy could only see a few inches in front of her feet. She struggled not to trip as bolts of agonizing pain shot down her spine. It was torture. She wanted to collapse on the ground and scream. Somehow, they crossed the street. Bea kept her jacket thrown over Maddy's head. Maddy walked, doubled over at a limping sort of jog, in utter agony.

Bea led Maddy through an empty, vacant lot. They were away from the school, now. Maddy saw mud and wet grass beneath her feet. Then she saw asphalt and gravel as they entered the residential streets of Black River. She peeked out from under the jacket and recognized Bea's neighborhood.

A few minutes later, they reached Bea's hundred-year-old craftsman style house. Her tiny friend led Maddy up the driveway and unlocked the gate to the backyard. The gate creaked loudly as she swung it open, like nails on a chalkboard to Maddy's sensitive ears. Then Bea led Maddy across the yard to an old, bullet-shaped camper, surrounded by overgrown grass and abandoned yard furniture. Bea yanked open the rusty door and ushered Maddy inside.

The camper was maybe ten feet long and half as wide. A few steps led up to a tiny table and a chair covered in cracking red leather. Behind the little table was a miniscule bathroom, the size of an airplane restroom, and behind that, a twin-sized bed. It looked like it was used for storage. A bunch of random boxes and black bags blocked the narrow walkway back to the bed.

Then Bea pulled the jacket off.

"Oh my God, your face!" she gasped as Maddy looked up.

"What . . . what the fuck?" Maddy groaned. She had a throbbing headache and her whole body was sore. She felt another muscle spasm in her back. She released a cry of pain.

"Oh my gosh, are you okay?" Bea exclaimed. "Holy shit, of course you're *not okay*. You're shifting! Maddy, you're shifting into a werewolf!"

"I'm trying not to . . ." Maddy's words were cut off as another groan of pain escaped her lips.

The camper trailer had a little mirror hanging up in the bathroom. Bea took it down and held it in front of Maddy's face.

"Look!" she said. "Just look at you!"

Maddy didn't see a redheaded girl staring back at her. But she didn't see a wolf, either. She saw something horrifically misshapen, her nose pushing forward into a snout, her mouth bulging with teeth, her eyes bright yellow. Fur completely covered her face in a red and white mask. Her long red hair spilled past her shoulders. Two foxy ears stuck out of her hair like a bad costume. She looked like a live-action version of a furry cartoon character.

"Your ears are kinda cute," Bea pointed out.

"Are you kidding me?" Maddy exclaimed, though it came out all grumbly and garbled.

"You scared the shit out of Kaylee. Those girls probably peed themselves. Haha!" Bea stopped to laugh. "Shit, Kaylee hit her head *hard* on the door. Serves her right, that bitch. I can't believe they cornered you in there. Did you hear me trying to get in?"

"No, I didn't," Maddy said, recalling her fierce surge of adrenaline when she realized what Kaylee and her friends intended to do.

"So, can I get you anything? Ibuprofen? A beer? Weed? I have gummies." Bea started to look worried. "How long is this supposed to take? Should I call your sugardaddy?"

Gareth.

Fuck. He was supposed to pick her up from school today. She had told him to come around four o'clock because she had "tutoring." Right. What would he do when he saw her?

"I'm . . . I'm trying to reverse it," Maddy groaned.

"Can you do that?"

"I don't know."

If she calmed down, regained some control, maybe she could force the monster back inside.

Her left hand started cramping. With a grimace, Maddy looked down and saw long claws at the end of each finger. Her hands were covered in reddish, whitish fur.

"What can I do to help?" Bea said worriedly. She started petting Maddy's head soothingly, like she was a dog. It actually felt kind of nice. "Wait, my mom's home, this is her day off. She knows a bunch of shaman stuff. I'll go get her. Maybe she can help?"

Maddy groaned. The pain was too much. She couldn't speak.

"Alright, I'll go get her. Sit tight," Bea said.

Then she jumped out of the camper and ran across the backyard. Maddy tried to stand up. She wanted to follow Bea into the house, or maybe go out onto the grass. The tiny trailer felt suffocating. But she collapsed when she tried to stand, her legs unable to carry her weight. Something was wrong with her spine. She couldn't stand up straight. It was a nightmare come to life. What if she couldn't Change back? What if she remained disfigured like this forever?

Five minutes felt like an hour. Maddy was in so much pain, she barely noticed Ms. Almut return with Bea. The door to the camper creaked open again. The shaman lady cursed softly under her breath when she saw her.

"She's too far along in the Change. There's nothing I can do," Ms. Almut said. "We should keep her here for now, for her own safety. Maddy, sweety? You need to call your Alpha. Now."

Maddy groaned. A garbled, inhuman sound issued from her mouth, not like words at all. She fumbled with her cell phone, dragging it out of her hoodie and trying to unlock it in her clumsy, clawed hands. Bea stooped down like she meant to help, but her mom grabbed her arm and dragged her back.

"No, honey, don't touch her," Ms. Almut said. Then she called gently, "Nothing personal, Madeline, but we need to keep a safe distance!"

"I get it," Maddy croaked.

The muscles in her hands were rigid. Her fingers felt like rubber bands. She somehow managed to open her text messages and select Gareth's name.

> Hey, I'm at Bea's
>
> Can you come get me?

Her phone buzzed almost immediately.

> Why? You okay?
>
> Something wrong?

Maddy didn't know how to answer that.

> I sorta attacked Kaylee

> I started to turn into a wolf at school.

She sent the text message. When she read it back, she saw all sorts of spelling errors. It didn't really make any sense:

> I attaxed Kayle

> strted trn aasloi wulf azkuul

There was a long pause. Maddy tried to type out another text, but her fingers were clumsy and her vision kept blurring.

> OMW

"Did you text your Alpha? Is he on his way?" Ms. Almut asked.

Maddy nodded. Then, with a groan, she doubled over onto the floor. She let go of her cell phone and it went tumbling across the camper. Bea chased after it and dragged it out from under the table. She checked Maddy's last message sent with a little frown on her face.

"Wow, how did he read that? Hah! Yeah, he's on his way," Bea confirmed.

Maddy couldn't speak. Her mouth was all misshapen and full of unfamiliar teeth. Her tongue was too long and wouldn't shape the right vowels. She opened her mouth and started panting. Fuck, it was hot. Why was it so hot in the camper?

"What should we do?" Bea asked her mom.

"We're going to leave her in here for now and wait for the Alpha to come," Ms. Almut said.

"I'll hold onto this for you," Bea called to Maddy helpfully, waving the cell phone in front of her.

Bea hovered for a moment, all jittery and eager to help. Then Ms. Almut took her daughter by the arm and pulled her out of the camper, closing the door behind her. Maddy overheard her little friend talking excitedly at her mom as they crossed the backyard to the house. Bea sounded like Christmas had come early.

"I can't believe there's a real werewolf in our backyard! I can't wait to see her wolf form! Her ears are so cute!" Bea's voice reached her, before the two women went into the house.

Unfortunately for Maddy, the horror had just begun. The power of the Change surged again. A wave of fire swept over her body. Her back arched and contorted. Her neck popped. She screamed, but the sound came out a gurgly sort of howl. She curled up on the floor, her body racked by uncontrollable tremors. Was she having a seizure? It was the most painful thing she had ever experienced, worse than getting stitches in the ER back when she was fifteen.

She threw back her head and howled.

Chapter 21

"Where is she?" Gareth demanded.

He strode through the front door of Bea's house and scented the air. It stank like herbs and tonics. These old homes in Black River were built for small people, or so it seemed, with tiny, compartmentalized rooms and a million doorways. His head almost touched the low ceiling. The living room was crammed full of bookshelves, arm chairs, and a scratched-up coffee table in front of a big green couch. But he didn't see Maddy anywhere, and he didn't smell her closeby.

Bea and her mother both stood in the living room near the front door. Ms. Almut was clutching her shawl nervously while Bea cringed slightly behind her. Both women looked a little shocked.

Gareth folded his big arms across his wide chest and looked down at the two women. He could see his reflection in a mirror hanging over the fireplace, and his eyes were bright yellow. He reminded himself to calm down and chill out. He was a large man and he looked a little rough around the edges. He didn't want to frighten the two women any worse.

"Hi Gareth," Bea said nervously.

"Hey. How's it going?"

"Good. Uh, this is my mom." Bea stuck her thumb out at the older woman, who was wrapped up in a gray shawl that matched the weather outside. Gareth looked the woman up and down. She was built small and stocky like her daughter, with thick hair and a pleasant, oval face. He guessed her to be in her mid-forties.

"Nice to meet you," Gareth rumbled in his deep baritone.

Ms. Almut seemed to recover herself. She smiled at him, displaying a straight row of coffee-stained teeth.

"Hello, Alpha," the woman said in a placating voice.

Gareth was a little taken off guard. *Alpha.* He wasn't used to being addressed like that.

The woman continued, "My name is Thea Almut. Please call me Thea. We've met before, but only in passing. I've seen you drop by The B Joint with the lunch crowd. I'm one of the bartenders there."

"Right. Good to see you."

"You run the auto shop up on Highway 20, right? I've known about you for a while now," the woman said. She stuck out a smooth hand. "Nice to meet you officially. I knew Maddy's mother, too, but that was a while back."

Gareth took Thea's hand in a brief, firm handshake.

"You're a shaman?" he asked.

"I dabble. Nothing too impressive. I haven't taken clients in a while."

"I see." So this was the woman who had known Maddy's mother back in the day, and had told Maddy about her shifter heritage. He wondered what else the shaman lady knew about this small town. Maybe she knew something about the werewolf hunter? Nothing prevented a shaman from joining Hellstrom International. She might be an informant for the guild.

Gareth glanced around the living room again, sniffing the air. He didn't smell any wolfsbane, but he was still on edge.

"Where is Maddy? Is she safe?" he asked again.

"Yes. I'll take you to see her."

"I have her phone," Bea said, handing Gareth a black cell phone with a cracked screen. "She, uh, can't really use it right now."

"Thanks," Gareth grunted. He slipped Maddy's phone into his pocket. This didn't bode well. He glanced over at Bea, who was walking next to her mother, keeping her long black hair pulled over her face. She looked guilty. He could smell it on her. Something was up.

Thea continued, "Maddy had an adventure today, or so Bea tells me."

"What sort of adventure?"

"Bea was trying to help Maddy with her Change," the shaman said.

"*What?*"

"I take it you weren't aware of this?"

"No."

Gareth's eyes narrowed on Bea again, but the little Goth girl looked studiously down at her feet as she walked. He came to a halt by the backdoor. The two women took a few more steps, then stopped as well, turning to face him.

"Maddy asked you to help her?" Gareth asked Beatrice in a gruff tone.

"No, I . . . I offered." At least Bea looked a little ashamed, though Gareth wasn't too sure if the girl felt any remorse. He recalled Bea dragging Maddy through the haunted house at Fright Farm, chasing after the Beaumont ghost. Seemed like she was more keen on getting Maddy into trouble than looking out for her best interests.

"So she started to Change at school?" he asked. "What were you doing?"

"Nothing too extreme," Bea hedged. "I might have . . . taken a branch and swung it at her."

"What the fuck?" Gareth muttered.

"I just wanted to help!" Bea explained. "She seemed really scared about the werewolf thing, so I thought I could get her to be bold, you know, *embrace* it. Build her up a bit. She has, like, no confidence. The internet said that adrenaline can trigger the Change, so I was just trying to help Maddy figure it out. Um, it was kind of my fault. We were practicing out behind the bleachers—"

"*Practicing?*" Gareth groaned.

"Yeah, well, it made sense at the time. Anyway, she started to feel super sick, so she went into the bathroom. I really didn't expect her to tear a sink out of the wall—"

"*What?*" Gareth and Ms. Almut both chorused together.

"It was self defense! Kaylee Mackovitch had her cornered. She's always targeting Maddy!"

Thea Almut jumped in, chiding her daughter, "That sounds *very* dangerous, Beatrice! Wolves can be unpredictable on their first Change. She could've attacked you! You're lucky she didn't hurt Kaylee or anyone else. This kind of reckless behavior is exactly why I haven't . . ." she stopped herself from finishing that sentence.

"What? Exactly *what*, Mom? Is this why you won't teach me about shaman powers?"

"Not now, Beatrice. It's a bad time."

"Well, I think it's the *perfect* time."

"Well, *it's not*," Ms. Almut snapped in her "*that's final*" mom voice. Then she whirled on Gareth, too. "You should keep better control over your pack, Alpha. If something like this happens again, I won't take it lightly. I realize Bea had a part to play in this, but Maddy put my daughter in danger. She never should have agreed to practice the Change at school. She could have killed a student."

"I realize that," Gareth bristled.

"Luckily, Bea was able to get her to safety. We have Maddy out back in our camper. But just think of how *wrong* this could have gone! If it happens again, I will have to take action."

Gareth glared down at Ms. Almut, a bit of fire running up the back of his neck. He didn't know what Thea Almut meant by 'take action,' and after a beat, he suspected she was bluffing. He could smell her fear. The shaman woman might be more like her daughter than she realized. She barked loud, but Thea Almut's powers didn't hold a candle to his own Alpha strength. He should play it civil. No need to threaten a couple of women in their own home.

"I'm a peaceful guy," Gareth reassured her, flashing his white teeth. "I'll have a word with Mads. She knows better."

"Thank you, Alpha."

Gareth released a slow breath. Maddy *should* know better, but it sounded like she was making some misguided decisions. He would need to address it like an Alpha once they had some time alone. She needed to learn to respect the pack.

Gareth followed the two women outside, stepping through the backdoor into the brisk, early-evening air. It looked like Ms. Almut's house sat on a half-acre lot similar to his own: long and narrow. Her back deck was only half built. He glanced over it.

"You need a hand with this?" he asked.

"My boyfriend and his son are building it," Ms. Almut replied.

By the look of the wood, Gareth guessed it had been standing unfinished for at least a season. But he didn't point that out. He followed the two women down the half-built steps into the backyard. The Almut lot was covered in birch trees and uncut raspberry bushes. A bullet-shaped camper was half-swallowed by the overgrown bramble. Now Gareth could smell Maddy's scent on the wind. His nostrils flared and his head went up. Her scent had changed. It carried wolfish undertones. He wondered what state he would find her in.

Gareth found his strides lengthening. He overtook the two women on his way to the camper. The sweet smell of his lifemate filled his lungs. Maddy's scent reminded him of everything soft and warm. He felt a stirring beneath his belt. A wave of protective feelings washed through him.

"Stay back, Beatrice," Ms. Almut said as Gareth approached the door to the camper. He paused with his hand on the handle, trying to calm himself down, lest he Change too. It was a powerful moment. He needed to remain in control.

Then he threw open the door.

***

Maddy was lying on her side in a strange place. She didn't remember how she had come to be there. She tried to think back, but her entire mind seemed focused on the current moment. At best, she could summon an image of her school, but even as she focused on that memory, it slipped away.

She rolled to her feet, but she couldn't stand up straight; instead, she hunched forward on all fours. She licked her left paw, which was a little itchy. Actually, she itched all over. She scratched the soft fur behind her left ear. She wanted to roll around in the grass, but she couldn't. She was trapped inside a metal cage full of interesting smells.

She shook herself off, creating a little cloud of fur inside the camper. Then she turned around in the cramped space and started sniffing through the old boxes of junk. She could smell rat piss, mold, old tobacco, dust mites, pennies, and countless other nameless things. Her tail was too long and bushy, and seemed to have a life of its own. She kept smacking it into things and knocking stuff over.

She stopped to sniff the air. She was ravenously hungry. She started sniffing around the metal cage for something to eat. Something smelled kinda good in one of the black bags. She ripped it open with her teeth. The bag was full of plastic bottles and paper containers. She found a cardboard pizza box with a bit of cheese inside. She licked it. Salty.

Then the door to the camper opened.

Maddy bared her teeth and growled, her hackles immediately going up. A man stood at the door who she didn't recognize. He smelled like a male wolf, but he didn't look like one. His strong pheromones and wolflike scent confused her. She whined a bit when she saw him, feeling an instinctive urge to submit. Her ears went back against her head. She ducked down until her belly touched the floor. But when he stepped into the camper, his bold movements startled her. She jumped back and growled again, scared of his size and testosterone.

"Is Maddy in there? Is she okay?" a higher pitched voice came from outside.

"She's fine," the big man boomed. "She got into the trash."

"Oh wow, really? That's hilarious. So, is she a wolf now? Can I see?"

"She's not fully Changed. Looks like she got stuck a little more than halfway," the man said.

"What does that mean, halfway? Is that bad? So she's like an anthro animal? Like *Zootopia?*"

"Something like that. Just means she wasn't quite ready to go full wolf." The man gazed down at her, a flash of sympathy crossing his face. Then he glanced over his shoulder and growled to the young human girl, "That's why you don't go out and *practice*. It's gotta happen naturally."

"Oh, uh, I didn't realize." The small female was standing at the door of the camper, trying to see past the larger male. "Is she hurt?"

"Probably not. Her memories are there, but not on the surface. I'm gonna take her home."

Maddy understood most of the words they said, but she didn't understand the context. Human? Full wolf? Neither concept meant anything to her. She was simply a creature. Her hearing was crystalline clear. Her sense of smell was so keen, layers of information filled each breath. She knew the bottom of the camper was covered in mold and rust, and a family of rabbits had lived under it last summer.

The man smelled good. She really liked his scent. Spicy, peppery, woodsy. She recognized it. But when he moved toward her again, his size scared her, and she bared her teeth in confusion.

"She's lost in the Change," the man said. "Stay back. I'll get her."

He climbed fully into the trailer. Maddy shrank back, tripping over her gangly, awkward arms and legs, trying to bury herself under the bags of trash and clothing. Her elbows and knees didn't bend the way she expected. She floundered just as the big man lunged. He caught her by the back leg. Maddy twisted and growled. She bit down on the man's arm and got a mouthful of flannel jacket. The man hissed and let go. Maddy scrambled to the back of the camper again.

"I hate to ask," the man rumbled at the two women outside the door, "but you got a leash or a collar or anything?"

"I do," the older woman replied. "I'll be back in just a minute."

Maddy waited, her heart pounding, as the man crouched before her, blocking the door. Nothing happened immediately. He gazed at her. Hazel eyes. She was confused again. He smelled like a wolf, but he didn't look like one.

"You're a pretty girl, huh?" he said in his gruff, low voice. "Red fur. That's rare. Looks like you got some white markings. You sure you ain't a little fox shifter?"

She whined and thumped her tail. She liked his voice.

The man grinned, a flash of white teeth in his tan face. His calm presence put her at ease. Then a black-haired girl leaned inside the metal cage. She stared at Maddy curiously over the big man's shoulder.

"Oh wow, she's really pretty. Like, I'm not even a werewolf, and that coat is gorgeous. She's the color of the Maple tree in the front yard."

"Yup," the man grunted. Maddy caught a strong whiff of dislike coming off of him. He wasn't fond of this girl.

"This is, like, *so cool*. Can I take a pic with my phone?"

"No."

Maddy heard someone else approaching outside the camper. The older woman returned with a collar and a rope-style leash in hand. She offered it to the male.

"Here you go," she said.

"Wow, is that Barney's old leash?" the girl asked. "He died like five years ago."

"Found it in one of the boxes in storage. Auspicious timing," the older woman said. "We'll leave you two alone now, Alpha. I'm sure you've got your work cut out for you. Take good care of our Maddy. You can go out the side yard, the fence is unlocked."

"Thanks."

"Come on, Beatrice."

The younger girl craned her neck for a few more seconds, staring at Maddy intently, then her mother dragged her away from the camper door. The two women walked back across the yard. Maddy listened to them leave, her fluffy red ears perked forward. The man stayed with her in the metal cage.

"You gonna let me put this on?" the man asked. "It's only for a little while."

Maddy eyed the man warily. She didn't know what he meant to do with her. He knelt down so they were eye level. He locked eyes with her, so she was forced to stare into his burning hazel gaze. He had eyes like a wolf. She sensed his dominance through his gaze. Again, she became confused. She knew he was her Alpha, but he was a human. How was that possible? Then he reached into his pocket. He pulled out something that smelled delicious. He unwrapped a stick of pepperoni and offered it to her.

Saliva filled her mouth. She was starving. Maddy crept forward on her belly and sniffed at the stick of dried meat.

In a flash, the man slipped the collar over her head. She yelped and scrambled backward again, but it was too late. The stinky collar tightened around her throat. She hated it. She rolled around and scratched at her neck, trying to get it off, but she was horribly clumsy with her stubby, clawed fingers.

The leash snapped onto the collar and tugged tight.

"Alright, girl, we're gonna get you home safe," the man said. "Then I'm gonna teach you a few things."

Keeping the leash tight so she was forced to walk next to him, the man led her out of the bullet-shaped camper into the yard. At first Maddy tried to walk upright like a human, but her back legs wouldn't support her weight. Then she tried to walk on all fours, but her hind legs were too long, and her front legs too short. She settled for a hunched, rambling sort of gait, something like an ape in a zoo. It was not elegant in the least.

Maddy walked behind the man across the mushy green grass. The yard and the sky smelled like rain. She wanted to run around and explore, but when she pulled away, the man caught her fast by the leash. She choked, then put her ears down. She had no choice but to follow his lead.

A wooden fence separated them from the street. She didn't want to go that direction. She didn't like the stench of car exhaust and cement pavement. It smelled like poison. She tried to turn away, but he redirected her leash with a firm hand. He unlatched the gate and pulled her down the side yard toward the road. Then he led her to a car parked across the street.

The sky overhead was dark and cloudy. A cold wind blew off the mountain, carrying with it a flurry of leaves. Some soda cans and papers littered the ditch next to the house. The pile of litter rattled in the breeze. Her eyes traveled up to the mountain that loomed over the town. Its lonely, mysterious presence seemed like a beacon for lost souls. The sight of it struck a chord in her heart. It was her hiding place. Her home. She belonged there. But when she leaned toward the mountain, the man dragged her back. He opened the car door and guided her into the backseat. Oddly enough, she could smell herself inside the vehicle, as though she had been there just yesterday. She relaxed. This was familiar, too.

The man climbed into the driver's seat in front of her. She poked her head over the seat and sniffed at his hair. She licked his ear. He laughed in a deep, loud, rumbly way. He reached up and scratched her behind the ears. She liked that a lot. It felt really nice. She leaned into his hand.

"Good girl," he murmured, scratching the thick fur on her neck, then rubbing her throat. "You're warming up to me, huh?"

She licked his cheek, feeling his rough stubble against her pink tongue. It tasted like aftershave.

"Alright, little half-wolf, let me drive," the man laughed, pushing her back. "Let's get you home. But I gotta warn you, you're not gonna like me when you come out of your Change."

Maddy didn't understand what he meant. She whined in the back of her throat and tried to lick his cheek again.

The man cracked the window to give her some fresh air, then he started the vehicle. The roar of the motor was obnoxiously loud. Maddy's ears flattened back against her head. Then she pushed her snout outside the window. She sniffed the fresh, rain-scented air. The cold wind moved across the car as they started down the street.

After a few minutes, Maddy started to feel a little dizzy. She pulled away from the window and laid down across the back seats. She was suddenly very tired. Her eyelids felt heavy. Her vision began to swim, and then everything went dark.

Chapter 22

Maddy woke up with a headache and her stomach in knots.

She was lying on her back on a leather couch, staring up at the popcorn ceiling of Gareth's living room. The heater was on, and a fire burned in the fireplace, filling the room with cheerful golden light. She could hear Buttercup whining from the laundry room. A fuzzy blue blanket covered her body. Beneath the blanket, she was dressed in her hoodie and her panties, but her jeans and shoes had disappeared. She didn't remember taking them off.

With a flash of memory, Maddy recalled her altercation with Kaylee and the cheer squad in the boys' bathroom.

"*Oh no*," she muttered. She started to sit up, then she groaned. Her muscles ached. She felt like she had the flu.

"Easy does it," Gareth's voice reached her.

He circled around the couch and set a cup of warm tea on the table. By its green, earthy scent, it was the tea his mom had sent her. It was supposed to help with symptoms of the Change. Then Gareth disappeared again, presumably back to the kitchen. She caught a glimpse of his long black hair, which hung loose and wet down his back, and a big bandage wrapped around his left forearm. A bit of blood stained the bandage near his elbow. Was he injured?

With a groan, she sat up, this time more slowly, and set her feet on the brown carpet. She reached for the tea and took a sip. She hissed. It was hot.

"Am I sick?" she mumbled, feeling weak and dizzy. She didn't remember how she had come to be at Gareth's house, and that bothered her.

"No, babygirl, you're just having a rough time of it," Gareth's deep baritone rumbled from the kitchen. "Your body wants to Change, but you don't got enough vitality built up yet."

"I don't get it."

"It's like you ran out of gas halfway to Vegas."

"I've never been to Vegas?"

"Right. Southwest joke. So you ran outta gas halfway to NYC." Gareth emerged from the kitchen and crossed the living room again, this time with his own mug of tea in hand. His cup smelled like mint. He came to sit down on the coffee table across from her. He used the short table like a chair. He faced her with a stern expression.

Maddy's vision swam a bit as she tried to focus on his face.

"What happened?" she asked.

"You don't remember anything?"

"I remember I was at school. . . ." A flash of pain seared across Maddy's forehead. "Uh . . . ."

Shit, werewolf practice. The Change. Kaylee. Her eyes widened. She met Gareth's gaze.

"The way Bea tells it, you almost went full wolf at school," he growled, his voice pitched low in his throat. He sounded stern, but he didn't seem angry. "I picked you up at Bea's house. You were in her camper. Do you remember that?"

"Not really? I remember reaching her house . . . ." Maddy frowned.

She recalled Bea ushering her into the camper, but after that, her memories became fragmented and fuzzy. Then, in a flash, she remembered the excruciating pain as her body became contorted and deformed. Ah, so that's where her pants and shoes must have gone. She remembered wrestling off her tight jeans in agony.

A little shaky, she set down her mug of tea and reached up to touch her face. She didn't feel any fur growing on her cheeks, and her nose was a normal shape. Then her fingers crawled up to her ears. Her eyes widened as her hands ran over her head once, twice, three times. Was she imagining it, or did she still have furry, pointed wolf ears protruding out of her hair?

She almost jumped up and ran to the bathroom, but then she thought better of it. Did she really want to know what she looked like with wolf ears?

"This is crazy," she gasped. "What the heck?"

A glint of amusement entered Gareth's eyes. "Fluffy ears on a cute girl? I'm into it," he grinned. Then he leaned forward. He placed a big hand against her cheek. He searched her gaze briefly as he leaned in close. Then he kissed her.

Maddy's stomach squeezed. She felt like she would melt into the couch. His tongue slid between her lips, soft and skillful, exploring her mouth, running over her slightly-sharpened teeth. The play of his lips captivated her. She felt a pleasant tingling sensation in her breasts. She leaned forward into his touch.

When he released her, his eyes were bright yellow. The wolf was showing. As they gazed at each other, his expression became serious.

"Mads, we need to talk. Bea told me you two were practicing the Change."

Maddy glanced away. She felt nervous. She knew she was in trouble. A quiet tension filled the room. At that moment, he very much seemed like an authority figure, and she felt very young. Their ten year age gap stretched between them.

"Yeah, we were practicing this afternoon, after school," Maddy admitted.

"So tell me honest. Did Bea talk you into it?"

"I mean . . ." Maddy hesitated, which told Gareth everything he needed to know. "It's not her fault!" she rushed to say. "It was Bea's idea, yeah, but she only meant to encourage me. She just wanted to help. Isn't it a good thing to practice shifting? I mean, I should probably figure this out sooner rather than later. What happens if you lose the Alpha Challenge? How am I going to defend myself against Marquis? I have to be able to fight."

Gareth grunted. He didn't seem surprised by her sudden outburst.

"So you thought it was a good idea to break the rules and lie to me?" he pointed out.

"Bea figured out the werewolf thing by herself. Her mom's a shaman. Their whole family believes in paranormal stuff. She even saw you as a wolf in the forest, that day we went to find Buttercup. It's not like you were being discrete."

"Alright, I see your point. Still, Mads, you should've denied it."

"And lied to my best friend?"

"Yup."

Maddy's face turned from angry to pleading. Tears stung her eyes. Shit, her plan had totally backfired. And she had almost attacked Kaylee. She searched Gareth's eyes, suddenly scared. Did he know about that? Did he know that she tore a sink out of the school bathroom?

In a deep voice, he chided her, "First, babe, I'm not gonna lose to a chump like Marquis. I fought in a fucking war—you think I'm scared of some backwoods Alpha? He doesn't stand a chance and he knows it. Secondly, protecting you is my job. I can teach you self defense if you want, but you don't gotta worry. Nothing bad is gonna happen to you. That's why my brother is coming into town. Why didn't you tell me you're scared?"

"I . . . I don't know," she admitted. "I'm used to doing things on my own. I want to stand up for myself."

"Sure, Mads, but forcing yourself through a preemie Change isn't *that*."

"A preemie Change? You're kidding me."

Gareth reached out and ran a hand up one of her soft, velveteen ears, as though to prove his point. A little shiver of pleasure went down Maddy's spine. *Ooo!* Alright, no one had warned her about that. It felt really nice. No wonder dogs liked being scratched behind the ears so much. Her cheeks heated as he stroked her ear again. It felt intimate. She blushed and glanced down at her hands clasped in her lap, trying not to melt.

His expression softened as he watched her.

"You didn't go full wolf, Mads," he said, his voice gentle. "You didn't have the vitality to sustain it. You got stuck halfway. It happens. Less so as you get older and stronger. But in the beginning, you gotta be careful."

He really made it sound like she was a car low on gas. Her eyes darted to the bandage on his forearm. A bit of blood was leaking through the thick padding, staining the white medical tape. She frowned.

"Did I . . . did I do that?" she asked.

"Yup."

Maddy felt a twinge of horror. "Really? I bit you?"

"You lost yourself in the Change, babe, it happens. Don't worry about it."

Maddy felt ashamed. She hadn't thought herself capable of biting anyone, let alone *him*.

Gareth continued, "I wasn't going to do this, Mads, but I think we need to pull you from school."

"What? You mean, disenroll me?"

"Yeah."

Maddy stared at him, her mouth falling open in shock. Her fluffy ears perked forward at attention.

"You can't do that!" she burst out. "You're not my legal guardian!"

"You're right, but I'm your Alpha and your lifemate. If I tell you to disenroll, you're gonna do it. You broke the rules, Mads," he said, reading the petulant look on her face. "I told you there would be consequences. No more practicing with Bea. I mean it. Cut that shit out. She can't help you with this, and it's too dangerous for her if something goes wrong. Did you consider what would happen if you wolfed out? *You could have killed your friend.*"

"I thought, if I learned how to control it—" she jumped to defend herself.

"You can't 'learn to control it' until you experience the Change on its own, full wolf, baby. That's how it works. Can't learn to swim by standing on the side of the pool. You gotta dive in first." He sighed, his irritation bleeding through his words. "I'm trying to be patient, Mads, but how am I supposed to trust you now? I mean it. I'm gonna have to pull you out of school."

Maddy felt an anxiety attack coming on. "You can't do that! You can't force me to disenroll."

"You're staying home until you complete the full Change and learn how to control it."

"Are you threatening to lock me up in your house?"

"Someone's gotta protect those students. I'm not putting those families at risk."

"*I'm* not a risk!" Tears stung her eyes. "They don't need protection from me. I would never hurt another student!"

Gareth fixed her with a firm glare, and Maddy stared back in defiance, even though she knew she was lying to herself. She had no control over the Change. She couldn't deny the bandage on his arm; she had bit him hard enough to break the skin. She had almost wolfed out on Kaylee in the boys' bathroom, and she had torn a damn sink out of the wall. As much as she hated to admit it, she was in over her head. Maybe he was right. Maybe she should exile herself from Black River High.

But damn, she hated how he was forcing her to make a decision, like he had some authority over her life.

"Tomorrow, I want you to go into the admin office first thing and disenroll," Gareth repeated sternly.

"Just like that?"

"Yup. You're over eighteen. Sign whatever you gotta sign and walk away. Then you're staying home until all this passes. You can sit on the couch and play videogames all day, I don't care. We'll figure out the GED thing. You can still go to community college if you want." He reached out, lifting her chin to look at him. He searched her eyes with a commanding gaze. "You lied to me and you broke the rules. You endangered Bea and probably other students, as well. I told you there'd be consequences. You're homebound, little wolf girl. You ain't leavin' this house without me knowing. There's a hunter on the loose and the Grayridge pack is sniffin' around my doorstep. So you're gonna stay put. Obey your Alpha. Respect the pack."

Maddy's hands balled up into fists. She glared into his eyes, unable to look away from him, as he kept a firm hold on her chin. Staying home and playing videogames all day wasn't exactly corporal punishment, but he was taking away her independence. Treating her like a child. Forcing her to obey. She wasn't going to submit that easy, belly up, like a puppy desperate for approval.

Was it just her imagination, or did she feel her incisors sharpen in her mouth? She ran her tongue over her teeth, wondering if her simmering anger could trigger the Change again. She tried to pull away from his hand, but his grip tightened on her jaw. She glared into his eyes, feeling the wolf swim beneath her skin. She felt like a mask was slipping from her face. Beneath the mask, she was raw and bloody—a feral beast that wanted to rage. She didn't know if she was angry at herself, Gareth, Kaylee, Dean or every part of her life, but she couldn't rein in her temper anymore.

"Fuck you! You can't control me!" she finally snapped, her voice thick and hoarse. "I don't care if you're an Alpha. I'll never obey you! I'll run the moment you turn your back. Maybe I'll call up Marquis, see what kind of life he can offer with the Grayridge pack. He promised '*pleasure I've never experienced before.*' I should take him up on that. *I don't need you. I can leave whenever I want.*"

Gareth's face grew dangerous. Oh shit. It seemed like her words had struck a nerve. She could sense his Alpha vitality flare between them, heating up the room. Her breath hitched. She should have been scared, considering how much stronger he was than her, but she leaned closer toward him, eager for a fight. Maddy felt a surge of adrenaline. Her fluffy, pointed ears folded back against her head, a clear sign of aggression.

Gareth's hands gripped her wrists with sudden strength. It shocked her. "If you want to be someone's breeder bitch, then I'll breed you right here."

Without another word, he dragged her up to her feet. Maddy snarled at him like an animal, and he bared his fangs, snarling right back. For a moment they stood like that, his big body towering over her, their faces inches apart, gazes burning, growling like two beasts ready to fight. Then he pulled her down the hallway, caveman style, to his bedroom.

Maddy resisted, even as her heart quickened, and a strange, warm flush of anticipation flooded her body. She dug her feet into the ground and twisted away, but it was futile. She couldn't hope to break free.

Once they reached his bedroom, he ripped a leather belt down from his wardrobe, almost tearing out the whole closet with it. Maddy finally managed to wrestle away from him. She lunged at the door, but he caught her arm and threw her down onto the bed. She landed with a soft '*oof*' on her stomach. She started to scramble away, but he leaned over her, pinning her with his weight. He easily looped a leather belt around her wrists, tying her arms behind her back, restraining her. Then he bent over her on the mattress, pressing her belly down against his bed.

With a sharp *crack!* his hand smacked her round, plump ass. The sharp sting reverberated through her flesh. Only a thin pair of panties created a barrier between his palm and her jiggly ass cheeks. Maddy shrieked, more from surprise than pain. He swatted her ass again for good measure. *Whack!* She gasped, her back arching slightly. When she tried to pull away, his hand gripped the belt around her wrists, holding her captive.

"You're such a *fucking* brat," he snarled.

"I hate you!" Maddy yowled, turning her head to one side, trying to see him over her shoulder. A lock of red hair fell against her face, obscuring her eyes. *"Fuck you, fuck you, fuck you!"*

Whack!

"Ah!" she yelped as he spanked her again with the flat of his palm. He wasn't fucking around; his hand carried a message. Maddy was shocked by a sudden gush of moisture between her legs. She didn't expect that. She trembled, feeling the warm sting of her ass cheek spread down to her lower lips. Heated blood pooled between her legs; her clit tingled. For real? No way. She was *not* going to get turned on by this crazy foreplay.

"You can't treat me like an animal!" she yelled.

"I will if you act like one," he snarled back.

Gareth dragged down her panties, yanking them over her round cheeks, letting the scrap of clothing fall to the ground. Then he slapped her ass hard again, her body singing after each strike. He spanked her on the same cheek, over the same meaty area, again and again. Then he paused, giving her a moment to rest.

Maddy lay on the mattress, panting, beads of sweat collecting on her brow. She had never imagined anything like this. She rubbed her thighs together, irritated by her own lusty reaction. She shouldn't be turned on right now, not like this, not considering her history. But his dominating presence made her instantly wet. His hand pressed lovingly over her stinging skin, soothing her. Maddy breathed heavily, tension running through her body, waiting in anticipation for what he might do next. He petted her softly, his touch suddenly gentle after his firm discipline. The loss of control was pure torture. She grew wet and frothy down below. Fuck, she was dripping. Did he know this would turn her on?

Her flesh buzzing, he squeezed her tender cheek with his rough hand, rubbing and massaging where his palm had bruised her. He rolled her tender, humming flesh in his hand. A little whimper escaped her throat. When he leaned over her, she felt his rock hard erection nestle between her ass cheeks and press into her lower back. Fuck, he was so long. The weight of his muscular body made her spine tingle.

He murmured into her ear, "You know what I think, sweetheart? I think you've lived too long up on that mountain alone. You're used to doing things your own way. Nobody raised you. Nobody taught you better. But that ends tonight."

"*Fuck you.* I don't need you to *raise* me."

"Oh yeah? Cuz I'm gonna."

His hand traveled down the curve of her naked buttocks again. Then his fingers dipped between her lower lips, testing her wetness. He grunted when he felt her frothy arousal, and he hummed his approval into her ear. "*Such a brat,*" he murmured.

Then he pushed his fingers into her. Maddy gasped at the brutal way he probed her insides, like he owned her body, like she truly was a breeding slave. Two fingers pushed into her flesh, opening her from behind, flicking the sweet bundle of nerves deep in her core. He massaged her G-spot, and she quivered and moaned, gushing around his hand.

He shifted his position, pressing his hips against her ass from behind. Her legs trembled. He rested the palm of his hand over the stinging red marks on her flesh, gripping her, toying with her. She flinched, biting her lip, unsure if he would spank her again.

"Good little bitch," he murmured.

Maddy clenched her teeth, a snarl lodged in her throat. She couldn't help it. "Fuck you, I'm not your bitch," she growled.

"Oh, you're gonna be, sweetheart," he said in his terrible, dark voice.

Her eyes widened when she felt the length of his girthy erection press against her ass. He was fully engorged, as long and thick as her forearm, his head almost as wide as her fist. He passed his thick, mushroom-shaped head over her asshole, teasing her, pressing against her back door like he might slide right in. Maddy wanted to grip the bed sheets and scream, but her wrists were bound behind her back. She pressed her face against the cool mattress. She was completely in his control. But then his head slid down to her lower lips, settling against her cunt. She knew he meant to fuck her until she Changed, and while he was at it, he was going to make her a little obedient wolf girl—a mindless slave for breeding. Did she want that? Shit, maybe. Her wet core ached to be filled. Being his mindless slave for a while might be a relief. She didn't want to think anymore.

"Now, if you want to be a wolf so bad, baby, I'll get you there."

With a deep groan, he mounted her from behind, just like an Alpha wolf claiming his mate. He got the head into her tight canal, lubed and slick. Then his hands gripped her ass cheeks. She felt him arrange her hips, lining her up with his cock. He pressed forward, guiding himself into her. She felt her flesh begin to part. God, it was happening. He was going to fuck her.

As he pushed into her juicy little cunt, he layered himself over her body, his arms landing on either side of hers, his chest against her back. Her clit was so sensitive, she instantly started to come, her muscles fluttering and gripping around him, little whimpers and moans slipping from her throat. The fullness was addictive. He carved a path through her tightening flesh with his meaty, engorged rod. Her body started twitching and shivering. Maddy felt like tiny fireworks were bursting between her legs. She started to pant, unable to comprehend the sensation. It went beyond pleasure, beyond pain.

Fuck, she wanted to feel him deeper.

"More," she whimpered, blushing in humiliation.

"More?" he growled. He pressed his hips forward. "This deep?"

"*More*," she gasped. "*Please*, all of it."

He rumbled his approval. The sound was like a wolf's growl. Then he sank down with his full weight, burying himself until his hips rested against her, firmly sheathed to the hilt. Maddy felt herself opening in delicious ways. He held himself there for a moment, their bodies locked together as she twitched and gasped, trembling from the onslaught of little orgasms. She waited for him to move, anticipating the sweet friction of flesh against flesh.

Then he murmured into her ear, "Say *daddy*, and I'll give you what you crave, baby-girl."

Maddy squirmed beneath him, shame burning in her cheeks. Fuck, she wanted to submit to him, but she was embarrassed. She held back.

"Say it," he encouraged her, shifting his hips against her ass, letting her feel his full length stretching her inside, coarsely rubbing against her G-spot. His hand brushed over her furry ears. She moaned. From behind, he stroked the soft triangles of velvet with his strong fingers. Tendrils of bliss flowed down her spine, making her breasts swell pleasantly. He slid a half-inch deeper as her muscles loosened.

"Ah . . ." she gasped, arching her back in a puppy pose, fully humiliated. "*Ah . . . daddy . . . please . . . .*"

"Good girl," he murmured.

He withdrew, and she felt the drag of his flesh departing. She gasped as he thrust back in, sliding his full length into her tight slit. He started humping her with short, firm thrusts. She moaned as her hips bounced against the pillows. He ground against her, stirring her flesh, then pumped into her vigorously, asserting his dominance. His hand sank into her hair. He gripped the back of her head, holding her down as he pleasured her roughly. Her body started trembling, overwhelmed by the sweet friction. Her eyes grew wide and glassy, fixed on the edge of the mattress. A vision flashed in her mind of a big black wolf. She wondered if this was what it felt like, being mounted in the wild, pinned down and utterly at his mercy. She was mated to a monster. Shit, what if she Changed while he was fucking her? She should be afraid, but all she could think about was his delicious seed filling her womb.

"*Gareth*," she whimpered. Her body jiggled with each thrust. She arched her back, her mouth slightly open and drool on her lips. She rocked back to meet him, eagerly taking his cock to the hilt, succumbing to the pleasure.

Gareth grunted his approval—he was enjoying this. She felt a shiver pass through his body into her own, something unexpected that she hadn't felt before. Vitality. Gareth groaned again. She felt his body growing rigid. At first, she thought he was going to come, but then her eyes widened. Fuck, was he Changing?

Maddy tried to look over her shoulder with her hands still bound behind her back. She managed to turn a little onto her side, trying to see the monster behind her. Gareth's chest was fully flexed, his muscles bulging, veins standing out against his pectorals and biceps. He gazed down at her with blazing yellow eyes, his jaw clenched and teeth bared. Fangs out. He looked fierce, exotic, masculine and rugged. No fur, no claws, but . . . .

His cock felt different. Wider in some places, bulbous in others. She felt it grow and Change inside of her, expanding, making her squeal and squirm. Was this "breeding?" Gareth leaned over her body and started humping at a vigorous pace, a long tongue hanging out between sharpened teeth, his hips pressed to her ass. Maddy mewled, a little primal sound of shock. She lifted her face toward him, and his long tongue entered her mouth, his saliva dripping down her throat. It wasn't really a kiss, more of a *claiming*. His tongue filled her mouth like his cock filled her wet sheath, and she sucked on it, drowning.

Then she felt his: a bulge the size of a large apple. A hard, fleshy mound at the base of his cock pressed against her. She rubbed herself against it, enjoying the friction on her lower lips. She could feel him pulsing through her tight canal, dumping little spurts of werewolf precum into her body. His seed stimulated her, adding to her arousal with its drugging effect. Fire burned through her veins, making her tits swell. Fuck, she wanted more. She wanted to feel him split her in half.

She felt the massive knot pushing against her tight hole. She would break in two if it entered her, but she still wanted it. Her legs spread wide and she flared her hips, pressing backward, offering herself to him.

Gareth's breathing grew ragged, his thrusting erratic. Grunting, he ground his hips against her, gripping her ass, working his wide knot inside her soft flesh. Maddy's pussy strained as she gasped and moaned. Finally, with a strong thrust, it popped inside of her. She yelped. Her body opened just enough to accept him.

"*Aah*," she sighed. She felt paralyzed. She was obscenely full.

Gareth licked her cheek. He wasn't done. Keeping his body layered over her, he gripped her ass firmly with his hands, panting and grunting in primal pleasure. He kept his knot inside and used shorter thrusts to stir up her tight, young cunt. Maddy wailed helplessly as his hard knot tugged and pulled at her flesh. She was plugged up tight. She could feel his heavy balls against her ass, twitching as he neared climax. Gareth's cock ballooned up, distending her abdomen with his size. Then with a jerk, he began to fill Maddy's womb with his druglike seed. He eased the knot into her more securely, pumping her full, his teeth grazing the back of her neck possessively.

Gareth deposited his fertile semen inside of Maddy's squishy, warm body. His hips hunched over her again and again, fucking her with little thrusts as his wolf seed spilled out, shooting deep in her womb, overflowing and gushing out of her cunt. His balls twitched and clenched with each spurt. It went on and on. The pleasure was immense. Maddy came multiple times from the feeling of his seed filling her up. Each time she tightened around the knot, she started sobbing in pleasure, unable to handle the fullness.

"*No no no*," she murmured mindlessly, her fuzzy ears pressed back against her head, her ass thrust high, utterly overcome by the sensation. She flexed her hips, rocking his monster cock deep inside, bowing her spine, spreading her knees apart, pushing her tits against the bedding, trying to adjust to his size, the angle, her bloated belly. But it was impossible. Her abdomen became swollen and distended, poking out like she was pregnant. He dragged the knot against her swollen, sticky flesh, stimulating her in the most obscene way.

"Yeah, you can't handle being bred, little wolf," he growled, the first he had spoken during their mating. "Look at your little body losing control."

Maddy finally collapsed, too exhausted to remain kneeling. Gareth laid down on top of her, his cock still embedded inside. She felt him loosen the belt around her wrists, freeing her arms, but when she tried to shift beneath him, his knot was still wedged inside, pinning them together. Her movement summoned another spasm of cum from his quivering testes. He shot deep into her flesh. She groaned; she felt so full. He must have emptied a liter into her womb already.

It took a few minutes for the swelling of his cock to go down. He finally slipped free with a groan. Then Gareth picked her up in his arms and maneuvered her onto the bed, onto her side, spooning her from behind. His hand squeezed her red ass cheek. He gave her a little love tap, reminding her of his discipline. Maddy groaned, delirious. She felt the head of his cock nudge between her legs again. Her muscles trembled. She looked up, gazing into his golden eyes. Wolf eyes. He looked like an animal.

"Gareth," she mumbled, half pleading, "I'm so full . . . ."

He brushed a damp strand of hair back from her forehead. He kissed her temple. Then his fingers went to her fluffy ears again, where he rubbed her gently, soothing her. Ah, it felt so good. She thought she might begin to purr.

"A breeder doesn't choose," he rumbled with a slow, seductive grin. "Until you Change, little wolf, this is what you get."

"But . . . how many times?"

"Until we howl at the moon."

With his seed dripping between her legs, making her body flushed and warm, he slid into her much more easily. His one hand stimulated her clit with dexterous fingers. His other hand clasped her throat in a firm, dominating grip. Maddy was overcome. The stretch as he filled her to the brim was delicious.

As he rocked his hips against her, another orgasm came on her like a slow tidal wave, pushing her up and up and up. She started panting heavily. When the wave finally crashed over her body, she thought she might have howled.

It was the last thing she remembered.

Chapter 23

M addy woke up on Friday with no sense of time or place. Her body felt like a sandbag, heavy and cumbersome, her muscles spent and stiff. She groaned, sat up halfway, and collapsed back onto the mattress.

"*Aah,*" she moaned.

Her mind flew to the night before, and a wave of heat curled through her body. Her nipples were still swollen and sensitive, her thighs covered in little bruises and love-bites. She was still aroused. Her body felt . . . *different.* Used in so many ways. Sore in places she didn't want to think about. Fuck. Last night, Gareth had ravaged her without restraint. She smelled like him. Her muscles were so, so relaxed. Her anxiety was nonexistent. She felt, in a word, *blissful.*

And really fucking sore.

Maddy relaxed against the mattress for a few more minutes, feeling the sweet warmth of Gareth's seed in her body, lost in arousing memories of the night before. A pool of semen had leaked out during the night to stain her thighs. She reached down to check between her legs, then raised her hand up, inspecting the sticky substance between her fingers. She remembered Gareth making her drink it down, even after they had made love so many times. He had filled every part of her with his vitality, marking her as his own.

Consequences, babygirl.

Absent-mindedly, she licked her fingers clean. Then she sat up with a sigh.

It was Friday. Technically a school day, but she had no idea what time it was.

Then she groaned again for a different reason. Right. The whole reason she had fought with Gareth returned to her mind. She was supposed to disenroll from school. The thought of refusing him seemed less attractive now. She was a wolf girl, and he was her Alpha. She felt branded. Did she really want to test him again? She shivered pleasantly—maybe she did.

Then, with a loud groan, Maddy rolled clumsily out of bed, her limbs stiff and uncoordinated. She winced; her core muscles were utterly spent. Her thighs trembled when she climbed to her feet. She took a moment to catch her breath after standing up.

"Fuck you, Gareth," she breathed heavily, meaning the words.

She glanced at the clock above his bedroom door. It was past ten o'clock in the morning. She had to get to school.

Maddy wandered into the bathroom. She brushed her teeth and, snagging on several knots, ran a hurried comb through her hair. In relief, she saw that her ears had returned to normal. She ran her hands through her hair, then over her round pink human ears, remembering the shivers of pleasure her wolf ears had given her. She kind of missed them.

Then Maddy threw on a clean outfit from her closet: skinny jeans, a blue T-shirt with a yin-yang symbol, and her favorite black hoodie. She applied some of Gareth's deodorant and hoped for the best. Then she grabbed her backpack from the living room and headed out the front door.

Surprising her, Gareth's Camaro was parked in the driveway. She stared at the car in confusion. It was unexpected. Her lifemate was usually at work by now—it was late in the morning. The trunk was open. As she stood there stupidly, Gareth exited the garage with a big duffel bag slung over one shoulder. He threw it into the back of the car, then he shut the trunk and locked it. Buttercup was in the backseat. She whined when she saw Maddy and wagged her tail furiously.

Maddy stared at her Alpha. Gareth leaned back against the side of the car, his arms crossed over his broad chest. He wore a red-and-black checked flannel over a gray T-shirt, ripped jeans and tan hiking boots. Casual, but his square jaw made it look like fashion. His expression seemed a little smug.

She didn't know what to say. Last night, he had done things to her body that shouldn't be mentioned in the light of day.

"Hey," he said.

"Uh, hi," she mumbled, her cheeks turning bright pink.

They gazed at each other for a beat. Maddy had no idea what to say, and in truth, she didn't really want to speak to him. Last night, she had melted into a primitive, incoherent mess of herself. She didn't think she had cried, but she had definitely begged, multiple times, for him to do very explicit things to her body.

"Surprised to see you walking," he flashed her a white grin.

Maddy groaned. Did he have to say stuff like that? She rolled her eyes, and Gareth laughed. He seemed to be in a good mood. He opened the passenger side door and motioned to the car. "Get in."

"Uh, where are we going?" Maddy asked as she dumped her backpack inside the car and climbed into the low seat.

"Taking you to school," Gareth said. "Then we're going camping."

"Oh." The sound of his voice did something strange to her body, and Maddy felt a sense of warmth bloom in her belly. She felt especially attuned to him now, even more than before. Just the growl of his deep baritone sent a tremor of arousal racing through her blood.

His gaze sharpened. With his werewolf senses, he undoubtedly smelled her body's response to him. Maddy avoided his gaze as she buckled her seatbelt. She could feel the heat growing between them. It seemed like the fire from last night hadn't burned out yet, but remained simmering beneath their casual interaction.

Gareth shut her door, then he crossed to the other side of the car and got in behind the wheel. The Camaro's engine choked to life. The muscle car slid out of the driveway, then cruised down Bickford Ave toward Black River High School. Gareth was quiet, but not in a bad way. He looked thoughtful. Maddy gazed out the window, avoiding his eyes, trying to make herself immune to his presence. But she couldn't help it—she kept seeing him from the night before, outlined by candlelight, his hair long and wild, his warrior's physique flexing above her on the bed.

Buttercup whined in the backseat and snuffled at Maddy's hair. She reached back to scratch behind the dog's ears, still thinking of the erotic way Gareth had stroked her wolf ears the night before. It was pretty wild.

"Is Buttercup going camping with us?" she asked.

"I'm dropping her off with Vin. He's gonna watch her for the weekend."

For the weekend? So Gareth planned for them to be gone for a few days. She wondered where he was going to take her. Camping seemed like a much better idea than staying locked up in his house. She had no doubt what he intended. Last night seemed to have started a chain reaction. His vitality was burning in her blood, but it wasn't enough to invoke the full Change yet—otherwise, she would already be a wolf. She hated to admit it, but she wanted more. And he intended to give it to her.

As Black River High School appeared down the road, Maddy's thoughts cooled a bit, returning to everyday life. She needed to go into the Administration Building and disenroll from school. It was a bit intimidating. Her entire life revolved around school—she had never imagined the alternative. Dropping out felt like giving up, in a way. But she knew it was for the best.

"Pull over here," she said to Gareth, pointing across the street from the school's main building. They were maybe about a half block away from the front doors. Gareth parked along the curb and turned off the car.

"You need me to come in with you?" he asked.

"No, I'll handle it," Maddy said. "It's just paperwork."

She got out of the car and crossed the street, her backpack slung over one shoulder. No traffic. No kids on the sidewalks. A light drizzle was sprinkling down from the gray sky. As she walked across the empty road, Maddy checked her phone. She had kept it on silent that morning, but her lock screen showed a few unread notifications from Picplace. That seemed unusual. No one ever contacted her on Picplace. She wondered if Bea was asking her about the fallout from yesterday, or possibly sharing more news about the party at Devil's Tower.

She opened the Picplace app. Over one hundred unread notifications?

What? She almost tripped over the curb. She came to a halt before the front steps of the admin building. What the heck?

Maddy blinked at her cracked phone screen. For a moment, she thought she had logged in accidentally to someone else's account. She turned up the screen light just in case she had read that wrong. She barely had any followers on Picplace, but now, in the span of a few seconds, it said one-hundred-and-one unread notifications. Huh? Did somebody hack her account?

Maddy tapped on her feed. It looked like she was tagged in a public post. Why would someone tag her? She started to feel a sick wave of anxiety rising in her stomach. She thought about Kaylee and the incident in the boys' bathroom. Had the Varsity jackets caught her partial werewolf Change on video? Could this be it? Her big internet debut? *No, no, no!*

With a sinking feeling, Maddy clicked on the post. It was a video reel. Yup. She was screwed. She recognized the username on the account: *PmpkinSpicePrincess.* Oh god, it was Kaylee. A blue "Verified" badge with a little check mark showed up next to the username. Maddy rolled her eyes when she saw it. She used to think the "Verified" badges meant someone was a famous celebrity. Then Kaylee got one, and now she knew anyone could buy a "Verified" badge for as cheap as $15 per month.

Her worst fears were confirmed. Kaylee would tag her in a post only for one reason, and that was to humiliate her. It must be a video reel of Maddy turning into a werewolf.

Shit. Her thoughts raced. It was close to Halloween. Maybe she could say it was a prank?

As the thought crossed her mind, she saw a text message arrive from Bea.

> hey r u at school?

> Emergency flying monkey alert. It's really bad.

> Call me when u get this.

> I'm serious. Don't go to your locker.

Maddy swiped away Bea's text message and kept scrolling through the notifications. As she read them, her face grew paler and paler. The comments didn't seem to be about werewolves. Kaylee posted the video last night at 7:03pm. It was twenty-seven seconds long. She had tagged Maddy's account in the description.

Maddy hit "Play."

Kaylee Mackovich was sitting on her bedroom floor in a cute pair of black silk pajamas from Stacy's Closet, an online lingerie boutique. In the background of the video, Maddy caught a glimpse of a white dresser with crystal knobs, a plush white rug, and a cute farmhouse-style bed frame that probably cost two grand on Wayfair.com.

Kaylee Mackovich spoke into the camera with big tearful eyes. Her hair and makeup was perfect, of course, but her mascara and powder didn't hide the swollen black eye or bruises spreading across her cheek.

Kaylee sobbed beautifully.

"Hello friends and followers. Today's post is going to be a little different than our usual makeup tutorial. I'm just asking for your support. I was physically attacked at Black River High School by Maddy Donovan. I want to expose her as a bully and an abuser. She has anger issues. She's really dangerous. Today she punched me in the bathroom at school. Just look at my eye."

Kaylee paused to pull back her hair, displaying the dark purple shiner.

"My career as an influencer is ruined. How can I post videos if my face looks like this? There might be permanent scarring. Please, if you hate bullying, leave a comment below and upvote this video to raise awareness. . . . Remember, hurt people hurt people. Maddy Donovan is a damaged person with a lot of problems. Encourage her to seek help by sharing

this post with your friends, or reach out to her directly here on Picplace. I tagged her profile. Tell her to get a therapist."

Well, that explained the 59 direct messages in Maddy's inbox. The DM's were probably from people "reaching out" to help her, or more likely, just being nosy and cruel. She didn't dare open any of the personal messages. She didn't want to see who had contacted her. Maybe some kids from school, but more likely a bunch of random strangers from the internet spewing their usual garbage.

Kaylee glanced down at her silky pajamas as though just noticing her cute outfit.

"Oh, right!" she gasped. She angled the phone screen for a better shot. She wasn't wearing a bra. Her perky B-cup breasts were clearly outlined through the black silk nightshirt. *"Since we're here, this cute lingerie is from Stacy's Closet. It's their new Fall line called Black Bunny. It's super comfortable and smooth on my skin. I can't wait to sleep in it tonight. You can use my coupon code to get 50% off your own set. Make sure to share this post with your friends, and follow my account for more great deals."*

Maddy's mouth gaped. Her ears were ringing. The video started to replay as soon as it finished. Maddy hit the mute button and watched Kaylee brush back her curly blond hair again, displaying the dark bruising across her left cheekbone. Big tears rolled down her face. She was trying very hard to look pretty even as she cried. Her performance was pretty believable. Maddy wondered how many times Kaylee had recorded her little speech before she got the perfect take and posted it. It was sickening.

The video already had over 100,000 views, and it was still climbing. Jeez.

"And the award for best actress goes to . . ." Maddy mumbled, still in shock.

She thought back to Friday afternoon, trying to remember their confrontation in the P. E. bathroom. She remembered Kaylee smacking her face into the door when she ran outside. Did she really hit herself that hard?

Maddy played back the video a second time and paused when Kaylee showed the closeup of her black eye. Some of the bruises looked like makeup, but it was hard to tell in the bedroom's low lighting.

Unable to stop herself, Maddy started to scroll through the comments posted under the video. Kaylee had almost 10,000 followers, almost ten times the population of the whole town. Maddy was pretty sure the young influencer had bought most of them. More importantly, Kaylee was followed by half the school, including several teachers and the cheer coach. So even if a lot of her followers were fake, a handful of important people might still see the video. Enough people to ruin Maddy's life.

A long list of comments were posted under the video by Kaylee's fans and fellow students. Some of the comments were hateful and obscene, but the worst comments were the sympathetic ones:

"You're so beautiful, Kaylee! I hope you keep posting videos. I love your makeup tutorials."

"I know this girl, Maddy, she has a lot of problems. I hope she gets help before she hurts anyone else."

"I blame her parents. They should be ashamed, raising a daughter like that."

"Maddy obviously needs therapy and medication. She's psychotic."

"I hope you can recover from this trauma, Kaylee. I love you!"

After scrolling through a few dozen similar comments, Maddy closed the app, feeling sick to her stomach. Psychotic? Well, shit.

Ahead of her, at the end of the block, loomed the school's administration building. Class was already in session, so the campus felt empty. Maybe that was a blessing in disguise. The comments on the video were so hateful, she wondered if other students would try to confront her. Probably. They would feel pretty righteous about it, too. This was way worse than the condom incident last week. If the whole school thought she had attacked Kaylee, what could she do to defend herself? Kaylee had successfully instigated a witch hunt.

Maddy didn't know how she managed it, but she forced herself to climb the steps to the front entrance of the Administration Building. As she approached the glass front doors, she saw a security guard leave his post and walk toward her. Great. That didn't take long.

"Are you Madeline Donovan?" the security guard asked.

"Yeah," Maddy said.

"Come with me. Principal Rodriguez wants to see you. Unfortunately, you're not allowed on campus unescorted at this time."

Maddy nodded. She felt numb. She followed the security guard inside. The women working in the admin office looked up when she entered. They stared at her. Nobody said anything. Maddy felt the overpowering urge to pull her hoodie up over her head. She caught the eye of Julia Miller, a front desk clerk who was nice to her in the past, but Julia looked down at her desk and pretended to be busy.

The security guard led Maddy up the hallway to the principal's office. Maddy was dismayed to see a police officer standing at the end of the hall, talking to Principal Rodriguez. The two men were chatting outside his office.

"Ah, here she is. Looks like she came to school after all. Thanks for waiting, officer. You're tardy, Madeline," Principal Rodriguez pointed out when he saw her.

"Yeah, sorry," Maddy mumbled. Her eyes traveled from Principal Rodriguez to Officer Malone, who was standing in the hall. He was a young man, maybe a few years younger than Gareth, with a blond buzz cut and a wholesome face. Maddy knew his younger brother, a senior in her same class.

"Come on in. Let's have a chat," Principal Rodriguez invited her.

With a sense of foreboding, Maddy stepped past Officer Malone into the principal's office.

Principal Rodriguez was a stout man with a wispy gray combover and horn-rimmed glasses. He fancied himself a cowboy. Today, he was wearing a plaid button-down shirt with a string tie around his neck. A big, flashy silver buckle adorned his leather belt, where he hooked his two thumbs, his hips shifted forward pompously. The medallion-sized buckle had a buffalo head emblazoned on it. A pair of leather cowboy boots completed the ensemble.

Maddy half expected Principal Rodriguez to flash a star-shaped sheriff's badge at her before starting the conversation.

"Have a seat, Madeline," Principal Rodriguez said, indicating one of the uncomfortable metal chairs in the corner of his office. He sat down behind his desk in his high-backed office chair. Maddy slung her backpack down on the ground and took a seat. Her leg bounced nervously; she couldn't stop fidgeting. A million excuses and explanations for Kaylee's bruises flashed through her mind.

Rodriguez continued, "Officer Malone is here to take down a statement. No one is pressing charges at this time, but we do have some questions. Were you aware of the bathroom sink being vandalized in the boy's P.E. locker room?"

Maddy gulped. This was not what she expected. At all.

"I, uh . . . what do you mean, vandalized? Like spray paint?" Maddy stalled.

"The sink was damaged and the bathroom flooded," the principal explained. "The water pipe was pulled clear out of the wall . . . ."

As he further described in detail the damages to the bathroom, Maddy glanced around the principal's office. She took a breath and held it, trying to calm down. She noticed a couple new pieces of cowboy memorabilia since last semester: a statue of a bucking bronco on the principal's bookshelf, two horseshoe bookends, and a painting of a desert sunset. A bowl of succulents rested on a little table beneath his office window.

Behind his desk, a motivational poster with "Cowboy Wisdom" hung on the wall. Advice #3 on the poster read: *"There are two theories to arguing with a woman. Neither one works."*

Principal Rodriguez finished his description of the damages with, "Several witnesses stated they saw you going into the bathroom with some girls from the cheer squad, before the flooding occurred. Can you tell me what happened? Why were you girls in the boys' bathroom?"

Maddy couldn't think of an excuse. She was tongue-tied. Then she finally stuttered, "Uh, Kaylee was trying to play a prank on me. Nothing happened."

"And the sink? Was that part of the prank?" Principal Rodriguez watched her with an inquisitive look on his amphibian face.

She couldn't tell him about the werewolf Change, obviously. But how else could she explain a sink being ripped out of the wall? With Officer Malone standing right behind her chair, she felt it was wise to keep her mouth shut, rather than try to fabricate an excuse.

"I don't know," she said, shrugging. "I don't remember anything happening to the sink."

The principal leaned forward on his elbows. "What do you mean, *you don't know?* You were in the bathroom when it happened. We have several witnesses."

"I don't know how the sink broke," Maddy repeated.

"Alright. Then maybe you can explain how Kaylee Mackovich got a black eye? The girls from the cheer squad say you punched her in the bathroom. Was there a fight, Madeline? I know you've had problems with those girls before. You can tell me the truth. I want the full story."

Maddy glanced down at her lap. "I don't know."

"Did those girls threaten you? Why don't you tell us your side of events? I have three written statements right here about what happened yesterday after school. But it seems like no one can agree on *why* you all went into the boys' bathroom."

Maddy glanced over her shoulder at Officer Malone, then back to the principal. She started picking at her left thumbnail. She was sorely tempted to launch into a tirade about Kaylee threatening her in the bathroom and trying to make her strip. She wanted to recount every single shitty thing Kaylee had done to her since eighth grade, and throw it all in the principal's face. But she had tried to report Kaylee's behavior before. She had tried and tried. It always backfired somehow. Kaylee denied everything, and Maddy never had enough evidence to back up her claims. Mrs. Mackovich was on the school board and the PTA, and with her helicopter-parenting, it seemed like Kaylee was untouchable.

That's why Maddy kept her mouth shut.

"I don't know," she repeated.

Mr. Rodriguez looked like he was about to lose his cool. "Did Kaylee hit you first? Did you give her that black eye?"

"No. I didn't. There wasn't a fight."

"There must have been some sort of fight, Madeline, because a student is injured!"

Mr. Rodriguez slammed his hand down on the desk, his face growing flushed. Maddy had witnessed his temper before. The principal acted like a nice guy, always joking with the new Freshman, doing a little do-si-do in his ridiculous cowboy boots. But Maddy knew better. He was a volcano waiting to blow.

If Officer Malone hadn't been standing in the office, Principal Rodriguez probably would've started screaming. Instead, he cleared his throat and straightened his tie.

"I know you threw the first punch, Madeline," he said. "We've discussed your anger issues before. I understand your stepfather recently passed away, and you're going through a difficult time. I've spoken to Mrs. Mackovich on your behalf, and convinced her not to press charges, considering your current situation. But I cannot abide you staying on campus as long as you are a danger to other students."

Maddy's lips tightened. She gripped the arm rests of the metal chair. The principal obviously wasn't interested in her side of the story, except to pin the crime on her. When she didn't answer based on his script, he blew up. That's how it always went. Mr. Rodriguez didn't want to *hear* her—he just wanted an easy target.

Proving her point, the principal brought out a thick file and placed it on top of his desk.

"Madeline, this is a folder containing every infraction, tardy slip, complaint and incident since eighth grade, when the problems started. Unfortunately, considering your record of violence and misconduct on campus, I have no choice but to suspend you indefinitely. Your case will go before the school board next month, and depending on their verdict, you will be permanently expelled from the district. Damaging school property and physical assault are both criminal charges. I'm warning you now, it's very unlikely you will attend another class at Black River High."

Maddy nodded, her jaw clenched. "And if I disenroll?"

"Disenroll?"

"Yeah. If I withdraw from attending school, will I still get expelled?"

"Well, no. We couldn't expel you, if you were already disenrolled."

Maddy clacked her nails against the metal chair. "Then I'd like to do that. I'd like to disenroll."

"Oh." Principal Rodriguez blinked at her over his thick glasses. He looked surprised. "Really?"

"Yes."

The principal considered her for a moment. Maddy assumed he was supposed to give her some sort of speech, resources or intervention to stop her from dropping out of school. But he didn't. He reached down and opened a desk drawer. After some rummaging, he took out a form and slid it to her, then placed a fancy fountain pen on top of it.

"This is a form stating your intent to withdraw from attending the school. Just fill it out and sign it at the bottom. Since you're over eighteen, we don't need a parent's signature or letter of notification."

"Okay."

Maddy filled out her address and her name, then signed at the bottom and included the date. Then she slid the paper back across the desk. She stood up.

"There. Are we done, now?" she asked.

Principal Rodriguez picked up the paper and looked it over, his brows lowered over his glasses. He looked a little relieved, a little shocked. "Yes. We're finished, Madeline."

"Good."

Maddy stood up, and the principal climbed to his feet as well.

As she picked up her backpack and turned to leave the office, Mr. Rodriguez added, "You're over eighteen, Madeline. Jail time is a real consequence. We will continue to investigate the vandalism of the student restroom."

"Alright. But just so we're clear, I didn't punch Kaylee Mackovich."

"Right." The principal stared at her for a beat. He seemed at a loss for words, which was refreshing. Then he grumbled, "Well then, a security guard will escort you to your locker. You will no longer have access to your locker once you leave campus today, so be sure to get everything you need."

Maddy's jaw was clenched so tight, she could feel her pulse in her neck. She was angry, but she didn't want to show it. So what if she already planned to disenroll? That didn't make the situation any less affronting. She just needed to get out of the school before she put her fist through a wall, or through someone's face.

Before leaving the office, she glared at Officer Malone.

"Do you need anything else from me?" she snapped.

"Nope, thank you, Ms. Donovan," the policeman said professionally.

Then Maddy walked out the door. The security guard was waiting for her in the hallway. He walked with Maddy to her locker. Class was in session, so she didn't encounter any students along the way, though she did pass a few open doors where heads turned curiously toward her.

Maddy cringed when she saw her locker. No wonder Bea had told her to stay away. Trash littered the ground around her locker, and wads of gum were stuck to the door. Someone had taken a sharpie and written "PSYCHO TITTIES" across her locker door in black ink, and drawn a pair of tits. Maddy felt a hysterical urge to laugh. Had she finally graduated from Porno Titties to Psycho Titties? At least being a psychopath made her somewhat interesting. So Kaylee Mackovich had finally gotten her revenge.

Maddy emptied her locker into her backpack. She didn't have a whole lot. Just a few pens and pencils, some crumpled homework assignments and a half-eaten bag of Flamin' Hot Cheetos. She left behind her books; she didn't feel like returning them to the library. Then she left the campus.

The security guard escorted her to the exit. As they walked through the empty halls of the school, he said, "You know, I got expelled when I was in senior year. It's not the end of the world. Word of advice, whatever makes you blow up at people, take it out at the gym. That's what I do."

"Thanks," Maddy said. "I didn't get expelled. I disenrolled."

"Right. You want my number? I'm a good listener if you want to talk."

Maddy looked the guy up and down. For real? Was she getting hit on right now?

"No, I'm good."

"Well, I hope your situation gets better. Have a good day."

The security guard left her at the school's entrance next to the admin building. He gave her a little wave, then he walked back to the high school. Maddy thought about his sage words of advice: *take it out at the gym.* Maybe that's why Gareth worked out so much. His tattoos read "*lobo loco*" for a reason. She wondered if he had ever been expelled from school.

Shit, Gareth.

Her eyes found the Camaro across the street. She could see him through the windshield scrolling on his phone. What was he going to think about all this? He might look like a hardass, but he wasn't some rebellious teenager. Far from it. She thought of his military medals, his successful business, his house on Bickford Ave. Maybe he was a rebel in his youth, but he was all rules and responsibility now. He wanted her to disenroll to protect the other students from her werewolf Change—not because she was a shining star of excellence deserving early graduation.

How would Gareth react when he heard about this? Would he get angry? The school might charge her with assault and vandalism. Gareth was a bonafide hero, and his new girlfriend-slash-lifemate might already have a criminal record.

Shit, she was a real fuck up, a total mess. She really didn't deserve him.

Her phone pinged. When she checked it, she had a ton of texts from Bea.

> *where are you?*

> *did you check Picplace?*

> *oh god don't check it*

> *if you check it, call me*

it might be better if you don't come to school today

just stay home

everyone is talking about what happened to Kaylee

it's total bullshit

Her fingers trembling, Maddy texted back:

I saw the video

Kaylee Bitchovich strikes again

I just talked to Principal Rodriguez

I disenrolled

Oh shit!!!!

Really??? Is that permanent?

So you're not coming back to school?

I would call you but I'm in class

What are you going to do?

It's okay

guess I don't need to study for midterms

Gareth is taking me camping for the weekend

maybe I'll get through the Change

next time you see me, I might be a real werewolf

She texted Bea a smiley face, trying to lighten the mood. Then another flood of texts arrived from Bea:

if you do go full werewolf, you should bite Kaylee's face off

I'm going to figure out how to fix this

I'll go tell Principal Rodriguez the truth

Kaylee better watch her back at the party this weekend

she lied about all of this. She's not even at school today

If that black eye disappears, I'm gonna give her a real one

Maddy's eyes widened as she read Bea's threats. Shit. The last thing she needed was her little friend confronting Kaylee. If Mrs. Mackovitch decided to press charges, then Maddy could find herself in a lot more trouble.

it doesn't matter

I disenrolled

it's over

I have a bad record, remember? teachers won't believe you

just stay out of it. They're still doing an investigation. I might get charged don't put yourself at risk

whatever

I mean it

you should bite Kaylee's face off

Maddy felt a little sour grin twist across her lips. Yeah, biting Kaylee's face off would feel pretty good about now. She sent Bea a "wolf" emoji and a laughing face.

have fun at Devil's Tower this weekend!

be safe and stay out of trouble

I'm heading out with Gareth, chat later

Then she put her phone on silent and slipped it into her pocket. She was grateful for Bea's support, but she didn't think her friend could do much to help at this point. Principal Rodriguez had been trying to get rid of Maddy since Freshman year. He was never going to let her re-enroll, and Maddy didn't want to return to school, ever.

For a moment, she imagined how satisfying it would be to wolf out on Kaylee Mackovitch. The vision was shockingly vivid in her mind: Changing into a wolf, leaping at Kaylee's throat, snapping her skinny neck and ripping her head off. She could almost taste the bitch's blood. A silent growl lodged itself in Maddy's throat. Shit. She wondered if all the vitality in her blood had something to do with her sudden, violent thoughts. It scared her, how good it felt to imagine her revenge.

Maddy pulled in a deep breath, trying to cool her head. Then her feet turned toward the Camaro. Her eyes traveled to the forested mountain peaks, and the gray wooly clouds hanging over the trees. It would be a good weekend to get out of town.

As Maddy slid into the passenger seat of the car, Gareth looked up from his phone.

"All good?" he asked.

"Yeah."

She glanced at the phone in his hand, a sudden sinking feeling in her gut. Then she met his eyes. "Did you . . . I mean, are you on Picplace right now?"

He didn't answer immediately. Then he nodded. Maddy stifled a groan. She had added him as a friend on Picplace last week, so their accounts were linked. That meant he could see any photos or reels she was tagged in.

"Kaylee posted this video . . . ."

"Yeah, well, we can forget about her now," Gareth said, and slid his phone into his pocket.

Maddy felt a tear escape from her eye and slide down her cheek. Gareth reached over and caught it with his big hand. She leaned against his warm palm.

"I'm so done with the Mackovitch bullshit," she said.

"Yeah, me too. Mother and daughter both got serious issues. You ready to get out of town?" he asked.

"I've been ready for the last five years. Let's go."

The Camaro started down the street with a sputtering roar. Maddy gazed out the window, struggling with a sense of regret. She struggled not to think of the week ahead. Kids would show their parents that video. Parents would show their neighbors. What if the story reached Archie Hawkins at the hardware store? He might never bring her back on staff. The Mackovitch family owned half of Main Street. Assaulting their daughter was a very big deal.

Maddy considered she might have to delete her Picplace account and all of her social media. Maybe that was a good thing. In a way, it would be freeing. At least then, nobody could hurt her over the internet. But her reputation in Black River was also irrevocably destroyed. So what was she supposed to do now?

As the Camaro cruised down Main Street to Highway 20, her eyes returned to the mountain. She thought of the events of the day before: werewolf practice with Bea, the power of the Change, her bulging muscles as she ripped the sink out of the wall. She wanted to feel that fire again. To claim what was rightfully her own. She wanted to be strong to protect herself. She wanted to Change.

Gareth had given her a lot of his vitality the night before. Her whole body was vibrating with it. She was ready. The fire of the Change burned beneath the surface of her skin, urging her onward. She just needed a bit more time with him in the privacy of the woods. Then, she would become a wolf. The thought was more appealing than ever before. Her heart yearned to run free. The forest was expansive. Endless. Thousands of miles of wooded groves, unnamed rivers and hidden places. She could explore them all. Howl at the moon. Free herself from society, from Kaylee, just *be free*.

She wasn't bound to the trailer anymore, not since Dean's death.

She didn't have work. She didn't have school. Her entire life had fallen to pieces within the span of a week. Besides Gareth, what was keeping her in Black River?

She could quit being a human and become a wolf.

Maddy glanced over at Gareth. They were headed deeper into the mountains. She didn't know where he was taking her, but she knew what he intended. He was going to finish what he started last night, and she was going to enjoy it immensely.

She reached over and placed her hand on his leg. His right hand covered her own. He glanced at her. She met his eyes. Heat sparked between them.

"I'm really looking forward to this," she murmured, her voice low and lusty.

He raised an eyebrow and bared his teeth. "Oh yeah?"

"I'm ready to Change."

"You sound like you know what you want."

"I do," Maddy said, a grim little smile on her face.

Gareth growled low in his throat. He glanced over her again, his eyes lingering on her breasts, his desire apparent in his burning gaze. A sexy little smirk rested on his lips. Then he looked back at the road.

If a dark voice in the back of her head whispered of revenge against Kaylee Mackovitch—in the bloodiest, most terrifying way imaginable—she didn't say it out loud.

Chapter 24

Gareth took a quick detour to drop off Buttercup at Vin's trailer. Maddy had never been to Vin's place before. He lived in a three-season camper off Mohen Road, a forested street at the edge of Black River next to a junkyard. He was drinking a beer in a lawn chair out front, under a blue tarp he had strung up like a canopy in front of the trailer. He raised his beer in greeting when the Camaro pulled up the muddy, weed-covered driveway. Maddy assumed Gareth must have given Vin the day off, since he wasn't at work.

If Maddy had to guess, it looked like Vin was renting the camper. A rundown house stood far back on the property, but the overgrown yard made it look less than hospitable. White sheets covered the windows. A few broken-down trucks littered the yard. Maddy couldn't tell if anyone lived there or not.

After Gareth parked, Maddy got out and opened the back door of the Camaro. Buttercup ran up to Vin the moment she saw him, wagging her tail. It seemed like the big pitbull puppy remembered him from their visit to the auto shop the weekend before. Maddy was pretty sure Vin had fed the dog some of his meatball sub. He laughed and petted the dog, then gave her a potato chip from a bag in his pocket. Buttercup was in love.

Vin seemed to be in a good mood. He looked excited to dog-sit for the weekend. Gareth handed over a ziplock bag of dog food, Buttercup's leash and a few other supplies.

"Where are you guys going camping?" Vin asked. "I can recommend a few spots. I think a bunch of local sites are closed, though."

"We got a place," Gareth said briefly.

Vin looked over at Maddy. "So you're not going to the Halloween party tomorrow at Devil's Tower?"

"I thought that was supposed to be, like, top secret," Maddy grinned. "No, I'm not going. Did Bea invite you?"

"Yeah, she mentioned it," Vin shrugged, suddenly acting disinterested. "I might go. I don't have a costume, though."

Maddy felt like she should say something to help out Bea. "Just wear a lampshade on your head, or like, a funny T-shirt. Costumes don't really matter anyway," she pointed out. "I'm sure Bea would be excited to see you. She might need a ride. Maybe you guys can go together."

Vin hesitated. For a moment, Maddy wondered if she had said too much. The young man scratched the back of his neck, a little bit of pink rising in his cheeks.

"Yeah. She's cool. I mean, I'll probably go."

Vin swigged his beer, but he still seemed bashful. Maddy glanced away with a little grin. Hopefully the Halloween party would give Bea and Vin an opportunity to sort out whatever was between them. Part of her wished she could go to the Halloween Haunt, just to be a fly on the wall. But she knew that wasn't an option.

Gareth seemed eager to hit the road, so they didn't stay long. After about twenty minutes, Maddy found herself back in the muscle car, flying up Highway 20, climbing higher and higher into the Adirondacks. They passed by Elk Haven and a few smaller, nameless burgs. Then Gareth exited the highway and turned onto a dirt road. They drove on for a while longer. Maddy checked her cell phone. Spotty service. She had never explored this part of the mountain before. The terrain was brand new. It was kind of exciting. She felt like they were going on an adventure.

She wondered if she should tell Gareth about her plan to live in the woods. She didn't want to return to Black River, ever.

"So . . . you saw the video," she said.

He glanced over at her. He didn't say anything.

"I didn't punch Kaylee. I'm pretty sure the bruise was mostly makeup."

Gareth was quiet. Then he asked, "What about ripping the sink out of the wall?"

This time, Maddy went quiet.

"Bea told me," Gareth explained. Then, with a little smirk, he added, "I guess the boys' bathroom needed a new drinking fountain?"

Maddy snorted, trying not to laugh. "I didn't hurt anyone," she pointed out.

"Don't worry. I believe you." He reached over and put his hand over hers. "Past is past, babe. You're not enrolled anymore. You don't gotta deal with any of that shit."

"And if the school presses charges?"

"Then we'll figure it out. But I don't think they will. How are they gonna explain a girl ripping a sink out of the wall? Anyway, they got insurance for that shit. Trust me, it'll blow over."

Maddy nodded. She felt a little better, but still nervous. She wanted to tell him about her plan to live in the woods, but the words faded from her lips. She would bring it up eventually. Probably when the weekend was over and it was time to go back to his house. Yeah. That's when she would explain. She was going to live as a wolf from now on. As soon as she figured out how to Change all the way, she was going to live in the woods forever.

Then they passed a rusty chain-link fence and a big red sign that read: "PRIVATE PROPERTY. KEEP OUT. NO TRESPASSING." A big metal livestock gate blocked the road ahead. Gareth threw the Camaro in "Park" and jumped out before Maddy could say anything. She watched him undo the heavy-duty chain that held the gate closed. Then he pulled the gate wide open. He returned to the driver's seat. The Camaro rolled through. They paused again so Gareth could close the gate, and then they continued up the dirt road.

"Where are we going?" Maddy asked, a little concerned about the "private property" sign. "I thought all the campsites were closed around Black River."

"They are. We're going to my cabin."

"You own a cabin? Wait, is this *your* property?"

"Yup. Twenty acres of undeveloped land in the middle of nowhere," Gareth said with a wry grin. "Any werewolf's dream."

Maddy was amazed, to say the least. Twenty acres? That was as big as the whole Fright Farm theme park. Did he really own that much land?

"So . . . this is all yours?" she asked, still unable to believe it.

"Yup. Nobody's gonna bother us up here, babygirl."

They drove on for a while longer. Eventually, Gareth pulled over at the side of the road. The engine cut off and Gareth climbed out. Maddy followed his lead, carrying her backpack slung over one shoulder. Gareth opened the trunk and took out his duffel bag and a large box full of supplies: cans of chili, instant noodles, water bottles, extra blankets, LED lanterns and the like. Then Gareth led her into the woods. At first, Maddy saw no discernible path. Then a trail emerged between the ferns and bramble. Gareth led her up a dirt path as the clouds broke open and the sun climbed higher into the sky. It was turning into a chill, brisk autumn day.

"It's very remote," Maddy commented.

"So much bullshit going on, I didn't have a chance to show you this place yet," he explained.

She wasn't familiar with this side of the mountain at all. They were probably around eighty miles outside of Black River. It was a long way to walk back to town if they needed help. But with Gareth by her side, Maddy felt safe. She didn't think it was very likely to encounter the Grayridge pack way out here, in the opposite direction of Davenport, and the werewolf hunter seemed like a distant concern.

At the end of the trail, a cabin appeared through the trees, set far back in the woods. It looked like Gareth had converted a twelve-by-twenty-foot shed into a tiny home. The cedar siding was still unpainted. The shingles looked brand new, and moss had yet to gather on the roof. She saw a metal chimney flue with a shiny aluminum cap on top. The roof's overhang sheltered a small porch and a white front door. It looked like a sturdy piece of work. He took out his keys and unlocked the door. Maddy stepped inside and cautiously looked around. The cabin wasn't much bigger than Gareth's living room. She saw a wood-burning stove, a few cabinets, a full-sized bed and a small table under a window. It was neat and clean, but a little musty, like it hadn't been occupied in a while.

Gareth tossed his duffel bag on the floor at the foot of the bed. Then he started unpacking the box of supplies and putting things away in the cupboard.

"Got an outhouse with a composting toilet behind the cabin," he said. "Make sure to take toilet paper with you. No plumbing or running water. Got a big bottle of hand sanitizer over here, and there's a 5-gallon portable shower around back."

It seemed like they were well stocked for the weekend. Maddy was impressed. She glanced up at the peaked roof overhead. The walls were a little taller than average, which gave the cabin a lot more headroom than she was used to. Gareth was a big man, so he probably designed it that way.

"This is really great," she said. "You built all this? It's like luxury camping."

He flashed her a grin. "Bought most of the materials from Hawkins' Hardware."

Maddy thought of all the times he had come through the hardware store, purchasing nails, drill bits and screws. Was he building the cabin back then? Actually, she half-remembered an order for cedar siding he put in last summer, so this construction must be pretty new.

After he finished putting their supplies away, he turned to face her. He was holding something in his hand. She frowned. It looked like a leather collar, a lot thicker and stronger than what she would typically use for a dog. Maddy was taken aback. She had seen cute black collars for sale at places like Hot Topic, and she was pretty sure Bea owned a few as part of her Goth wardrobe. But this was a double-paneled, studded leather dog collar for a very large breed, made for utility and not style.

He held it out to her like it was the most normal thing in the world.

"What is that?" Maddy asked, feeling a sense of trepidation.

"Exactly what it looks like, babe."

"You're going to put a collar on me? Really?"

"Yup." Gareth raised an eyebrow. "It's nothing personal."

"I mean, it feels a little personal?"

"Alright. Think about it. What if you go full wolf and try to take a bite outta me? This'll help me drag you off if things get outta hand."

Maddy shrugged uncomfortably, eyeing the collar. It felt demeaning putting something like that around her neck, like she was his slave. Then her eyes traveled to his left forearm. She recalled the bandages from the day before. The wound had already healed thanks to his Alpha vitality, but . . . what if she bit him again? She didn't know what she might be capable of as a wolf. She might take off his hand.

With a resigned sigh, Maddy took the collar and turned it over in her hands. It was thick and strong, appropriate for a large animal like a wolf.

"Is that why you brought me here? To get me through the Change?" she finally asked. She already knew the answer.

"Yup."

Maddy gazed at him, waiting for him to acknowledge the tension between them. All morning, her breasts had felt swollen and sensitive to the touch. Gareth looked devastatingly handsome in his casual flannel and jeans. Her eyes swept over him, hungry. They were alone in the woods. They could get a little wild.

She remembered his words from Sunday at the Black Bear Diner: "*. . . maybe I should take you back home and fuck you until you Change.*" He meant to deliver on that promise. Her encounter with Principal Rodriguez had cooled her heels a bit, but now her desire ignited once again. She undid the collar and fastened it around her neck. She struggled a bit with the buckle, and he pushed her hands away, taking a step forward.

"Here, let me do it," he murmured.

He fastened the collar so it wasn't too tight, estimating the fit for her wolf form. Then he hooked one finger under the collar and drew her toward him. She took a step, emboldened by the heat of his gaze. Then she reached up and placed her hands on his shoulders, running her palms over his chest. He let out a slow breath, a growl rumbling in his throat. Maddy leaned up and placed her lips to his rough jaw. She couldn't quite reach his mouth, so she kissed the underside of his jaw, his throat, the delicious indent between his collar bones. His skin tasted warm and a little salty. Her hunger grew.

Then, unexpectedly, his hands sank into her hair. He ran his fingers over her round human ears, a reminder of the night before.

"Let's continue where we left off, little wolf girl," he murmured.

"Yes," she breathed.

Gareth's eyes flashed yellow. When he grinned, his incisors looked a little sharper and longer than she expected. Then he leaned down and claimed her lips in a deep kiss. Fire bloomed in her belly. Heat flared between them. With sudden urgency, Maddy found herself dragging off her shirt and bra. Her breasts sprang free, her nipples swollen and perky. She started to pull off his flannel overshirt. He shrugged out of the long sleeves, then helped her drag off his gray T-shirt. He tossed both articles of clothing onto the floor.

Fuck. His muscles. He grinned at her reaction.

"You like the view?" he asked, noticing her gaze.

Her eyes swept over his powerful chest and smooth skin. Her eyes continued down his six pack to a trail of dark hair leading into his pants. She gazed up at his body, over six feet of solid muscle. His six pack was so close, she could lick it. What was stopping her? Maddy felt a little thrill of excitement. Yeah, she was going to take a taste.

She leaned forward and kissed the line that traveled down the center of his torso. Then she kissed the flat terrain beneath his bellybutton. He sucked in a quick breath. His abdomen tightened. Then her hands went to the belt of his jeans. He watched her undo the buckle and drop the belt to the ground, then the zipper. She slid his pants and boxers down. His cock was at half-mast. Under her lusty gaze, his member began to swell and harden to its full length. Her mouth went a little dry. She didn't think she would ever get used to seeing his full size.

Gareth sat down on the side of the bed, and she knelt before his thick cock. No knot, perfectly human—she wondered if it would come out again, maybe in the heat of passion. One hand went to cup his weighty balls, while the other stroked up and down his considerable length. When she took him into her mouth, she felt a flood of power and excitement. She liked giving him pleasure like this, and she was eager to taste his cum again. She experimented with his cock, sucking on it at different angles, until she took it deep into her throat. Gareth's groan of pleasure was the sexiest sound she had ever heard. A ribbon of precum spurted into her mouth. She drank it down, feeling a warm flush to her cheeks and breasts.

When Gareth withdrew from her mouth, his shaft was slick and glistening with precum. Then he took her large breasts in hand and rolled them around in his strong palms, like he was kneading dough. Maddy gazed up at him with big eyes, her lips swollen and slightly parted. His handsome, angular face was stern, his dark eyebrows drawn low. He pinched her pink nipples. He cupped her breasts in his hands and squeezed them like he meant to milk her tits.

Then he started rubbing his cock between her breasts. Precum leaked from the head of his cock, adding lubrication to her soft skin. Maddy watched, utterly aroused, as he pleasured himself with her body. Gareth groaned deep in his throat. It didn't take him long to cum. After a few minutes, his cock swelled and stiffened. His hand went to her hair, and he pulled her mouth down on his head, ejaculating down her throat. Maddy knew he meant for her to absorb his vitality. Every last drop brought her closer to her Change. She drank him down, struggling to keep up. His load overflowed past her lips and chin. He watched her. Maddy watched his face grow gaunt as every muscle in his torso flexed. His shoulders went rigid, his arms bulged. Fuck. He was a monster.

After he finished, he leaned over her, breathing hard. Then he kissed her mouth, his hands cupping her face. His fingers hooked her collar again, and he gently pulled her onto the mattress. He layered himself over her, trapping her with his big arms. She felt his member grow rigid against her soft inner thigh, already erect and hard. She felt the swelling at the base, the werewolf knot making its debut. Yeah, he was very aroused.

Barely a sentence passed between them for the rest of the afternoon. Gareth feasted on her body, bringing her to multiple shattering orgasms. She didn't notice when the sky grew dark, and the rain started on the cabin's roof. The room grew cold, but she didn't feel it. Her skin burned and her body throbbed. As she received more and more of his vitality, she felt a sense of power flooding her limbs, flowing up and down her spine, skittering across her skin. At one point, Gareth reached up and stroked her ears. Maddy gasped in pleasure; she hadn't noticed them Changing. Her triangular, red wolf ears were soft and fuzzy once again.

"Almost there, baby," he encouraged her in his gruff voice.

This time when she took his knot, she was riding on top of him on the bed. He held himself deep within her, watching her expressions as he shifted his hips, torturing her from below. She felt his wide head nuzzle up against her womb. She gazed into his golden eyes, vulnerable and overwhelmed. He rocked her back and forth at a sensual pace, letting her feel his full length and the fleshy, hard anchor pinning them together. Fuck. She couldn't hide from him like this. She whimpered and sobbed and bit her lower lip. Ah, he was so deep. She felt like he was penetrating her mind, body and soul.

She lost track of how many times he emptied himself into her. He pinned her against the headboard and pounded into her with short, hefty thrusts. Moan after guttural moan slipped from her mouth. Fuck, he was strong. The friction on her clit was devastating. She felt the moment her mind broke. She gave herself over to him, primal heat throbbing in her veins as the power of his vitality filled her. Too many orgasms, too much sex, too much passion. He kept going. Eventually, she passed out.

***

It was close to evening when Maddy next opened her eyes.

She was alone in the small, square cabin. She shook herself out, then she climbed to all fours and jumped to the floor. She started sniffing around. She investigated every corner. The room was clean and dry. No rodent nests or droppings. The bedding smelled like *him*, but he wasn't there now. It seemed like the hut was empty and she was alone.

As the thought crossed her mind, the door opened and the man stepped inside with an armload of firewood. He was fully dressed and showered. He kicked the door shut behind him and deposited the wood in a basket next to the stove. Maddy sat on her haunches and watched. Her tail thumped on the ground twice. She didn't really remember who he was, but she was happy to see him.

Then he turned to face her. "I see you're awake, little wolf girl," he grinned. "Wasn't that a better way to Change? You slept right through it. I leave for ten minutes and you've gone full wolf."

Maddy whined low in her throat. She understood some snatches of his sentences, but not the whole thing. The cadence of his voice was soothing. He paused after dropping his jacket on the table and came to stand before her. He reached out and placed his hand on her head. He scratched her ears. It felt nice. She leaned forward a little, letting his big hand run down her neck where he stroked her thick reddish-brown fur. Then down her back to her haunches.

He grinned down at her, his eyes flashing gold.

"Pretty girl," he murmured. "We're gonna run all this energy out of you. Then I'm gonna show you how to Change back."

She cocked her head to one side, trying to understand.

Then the man opened the door of the cabin and shooed her outside. Maddy trotted through the doorway and into the woods. The stormy afternoon was already dimming into a murky purple-gray twilight. Deep shadows gathered beneath the pine trees. The air was thick with moisture and the trill of birdsong. The forest was peaceful and quiet after the rain. She heard the music of frogs croaking and crickets chirping.

She lingered at the edge of the trees. She gazed into the forest, then she looked back at the man, who was standing in the doorway of the cabin.

"Go on," he said. "Take off. Run around. I'm just gonna set up a few things for when we get back. I'll be right behind you, babygirl."

Then the man went back into the cabin and shut the door. Maddy heard him rummaging around, but no indication that he would return soon.

She turned back to the woods. Her fluffy red ears perked forward as she explored the rich undergrowth of the forest. The evening's song drew her attention: owls hooting, frogs croaking, a chorus of crickets and gurgling streams. Enticing, mysterious smells. Minty, musty moss. Rich, dark earth. The *green*. It called to her.

She started running. The smells of the forest were very strong, and she felt like all of her senses were heightened. She detected the little rustles and murmurs of the underbrush with acute clarity. Her eyes, too, were keen in the gray gloom. Splashes of intermittent rain sprinkled down from the darkening sky. The calming scent of spruce trees embraced her. She continued through the woods. She followed a familiar trail for a little while.

When she reached a grove of balsam fir, she cut left. After a few yards, she found another trail wandering through the wilderness. She didn't think it was a path made by people passing through. It was hardly six inches across. By the scent marks on the ground, it might be a rabbit run. She followed the little trail downhill, through bunchberry dogwoods and snowberry bushes, until she came to a gurgling brook. The water was crystal clear, and multicolored rocks lined the bottom of the stream like colorful Easter eggs. She lapped up a few mouthfuls of fresh, chill water.

Maddy followed the little stream. It led her to a hidden meadow deep in the woods. The deep grass was speckled with painted trillium and white, delicate starflowers that seemed to glow under the moon. A colony of frogs lived in a pond at the edge of the meadow, where the stream emptied. She paused. The frogs were excited about the rain. They jumped back and forth from one lily pad to another, then onto the logs by the bank. She tried to catch one of the frogs in her clumsy paws. She missed a few times before she settled back to watch, her ears pricked curiously forward. The frogs croaked and chuckled at her, laughing at her clumsy attempts. *Good luck, little pup.* If she watched long enough, maybe she could catch one. But they were too fast, and she grew bored after a while.

She wandered into the trees, searching for another hidden trail through the forest. She craved deer meat, and she could smell a herd somewhere nearby, not too far away. But she didn't have a pack to hunt with.

Where was her pack?

The question troubled her deeply. Why was she alone? Her bones were singing with the desire to see her packmates. Yet with a wistful sort of sadness, she felt like she hadn't seen them in a very long time.

As the evening twilight deepened, she came upon a rocky overlook. Below her, a valley stretched between two mountain ridges. A stream ran down the center of the vale. The torrential rain of the past week had flooded part of the valley, while the other half was alive with movement. Maddy saw a herd of deer milling about. She felt a little *zing*. Instantly, her ears perked forward and her nostrils flared. The scent of warm blood and fresh meat made her hunger sharpen in her belly.

But she had no pack to hunt with. Hunting a large deer by herself was a foolhardy risk. If she were wise, she would return to the woods and fill her belly with rabbits and voles.

Another gust of wind blew across the valley, carrying with it a different sort of smell. Maddy raised her head and sniffed the air. It was an enticing scent, stimulating her in a strange and unexpected way. Spicy. She liked it. A lot. It made her feel frisky and giddy. Another wolf was in the woods. The wind blew again, carrying with it a flood of information. It was a male wolf in his prime, a strong Alpha, virile and dominant.

With a sudden flash of certainty, she recognized her Alpha.

She turned around. Her eyes searched the edge of the woods behind her as she sniffed the air. A dull whine started in her throat. Yes, her Alpha was nearby. The scent was unmistakable. She knew it in her bones. Her tail raised up and her ears perked forward. She waited expectantly. He was coming for her, she knew.

Then a big black wolf stepped out of the forest. He was a handsome beast, built long and thick through the neck and shoulders, with a glossy coat and paws the size of dinner plates. His size alone revealed his supernatural nature; he stood taller and broader than some of the deer in the meadow below. His pelt was the color of blue-black raven wings; his eyes were a deep amber-gold; his fangs were white and gleaming. His long body tapered down to his haunches, ending in a bushy tail that brushed the ground. His scent enticed her: delicious, dark and peppery.

They gazed at each other, their eyes locked, scenting the air. She was a sleek young female, built swift and dainty, with a coat the color of autumn leaves. A white mask framed her delicate muzzle and wide, fluffy ears. Maddy felt a little shiver as she inhaled his scent again. There was no mistaking it. He smelled like home. Like pack.

Like . . . her *lifemate.*

A sudden jolt of electricity traveled through her whole body. *My mate.*

A low whine started again in her throat. Maddy was entranced by the black Alpha. She couldn't look away. He was her other half. Her future. Her home. Her pack.

The two wolves stared at each other. The big male held himself in a confident stance, his head raised and chest thrust forward. He expected her to submit.

Cautiously, she approached him with her ears back. He waited, his head held proudly. She sniffed his neck and shoulders, learning through smell more than she could ever explain in words. She could smell his calm temperament, his self-control, his patience, his strength. Then she gently licked the black wolf's chin. The big male returned her gesture of affection. He sniffed her ears, her face, then down the rest of her body, appreciating her with little licks and nuzzles. Maddy wiggled a bit as he inspected her, trembling with excitement. She couldn't get enough of his smell. His presence gave her a sense of security that made her forget her hunger.

The two wolves spent several minutes investigating each other. Then the big Alpha nipped Maddy's hind leg to get her attention. He took a few steps forward, inviting her to run with him. Then he bolted down the side of the hill, into the valley below, his long black tail streaming out behind him.

Maddy followed with a little leap. She was small and swift, and she flew down the rocks, at times dropping almost twenty feet to the next ledge along the valley's rim. Once she reached the valley floor, she followed the black wolf through the tall grass. The deep twilight shadows hid them from the herd of deer. Maddy followed the black wolf's lead, keeping her belly low to the ground and her head below the line of tall grass. Together, they stalked the herd.

The black wolf snuck up all close to his unsuspecting prey. She remained a few yards behind him and watched for his queue. He selected an older doe with a slight limp and graying haunches. Then he lunged. Maddy scrambled after him with a low growl.

The herd broke apart, fleeing before the two wolves, the deer forming two rivers of silent movement across the valley. The big black Alpha easily overtook a limping doe that trailed along at the edge of the second herd.

Maddy followed his lead. The doe stumbled as the Alpha sank his teeth into its neck. Maddy leapt on the doe's back. The beast went down seemingly without struggle, as though accepting its fate.

For the first time, Maddy tasted the hot, rich blood of a fresh kill. Her nostrils flared at the heady scent. She felt a fierce, primal satisfaction.

If she hadn't been his lifemate, the big Alpha would have backed her off his kill. She would've been made to wait to eat. But the black male moved aside to let her worry and rip apart the corpse. He allowed her to feast next to him on the steaming flesh. Maddy filled her belly, gulping down mouthfuls of sweet deer meat. Full night closed in as they devoured their kill.

The deer herd was long gone and the valley empty by the time Maddy looked up again. Full night had fallen. No moon or stars illuminated the sky, and a heavy layer of storm clouds covered the mountain. Her belly full from her meal, she settled down on a cushion of wet grass to clean her paws. The big Alpha joined her and started cleaning her face, his tongue laving over her snout like a mother would clean its cub. Maddy whined, then nuzzled and licked him back, returning the favor.

After grooming each other clean, the black Alpha sat up. He raised his noble head and howled a haunting song into the night. Maddy felt her spirit stir at the sound. Raising her head, she howled with him, her own voice higher and gentler as she joined him in wolfsong. They sang for several minutes together, their voices rising and falling together.

After the song was finished, Maddy felt a little frisky. With a full belly, she was in a playful mood. She ducked down into a play bow, her tail swishing back and forth suggestively.

Can you catch me? she seemed to ask.

The black wolf cocked his head to one side, considering her. Then, without warning, he lunged. She yipped and took off at a fast run, and the big Alpha chased after her, the two wolves racing back to the forest.

Under the trees, Maddy saw clearly in the dark. What appeared as vague shadows to a human eye stood out in sharp relief to a wolf. Her nose helped guide her. Before long, she found her way back to a familiar part of the forest. She remembered the meadow and the pond with the frogs. From there, she could follow a stream to a rabbit trail, and then back to the river and her trailer . . . .

She needed to check her phone. Someone was coming to meet her . . . .

A jarring pang of pain split down the center of her head. *Ow.*

Maddy stumbled suddenly. She slowed down, her head throbbing. Something was wrong, but she didn't know what. She felt like she had forgotten something important.

Then the big male overtook her. With a soft growl, the black wolf tackled her from behind, toppling her into a bed of ferns. Maddy yelped, more out of surprise than pain. She lay on the ground beneath him on her back, her belly exposed. The black male stood over her, his paws planted on each side of her head. Their size difference was a little absurd. Even by wolf standards, he was a hulking beast.

Her ears went back as she displayed her soft belly. *Okay. Okay. You win. I'm done playing.* Submissive.

His head dipped down and his teeth grazed her belly. She quivered at the feeling of his hot breath, waiting for his acceptance. If he chose to, he could rip open her belly and kill her in an instant. But he didn't. Of course he wouldn't, she was his lifemate. His teeth grazed her pink skin, but he didn't bite. He licked her, and she felt instantly soothed. An Alpha's acceptance meant his protection. She waited until he was finished, when he finally stood up and gave her room. She rolled onto her feet, keeping her ears pressed back submissively.

She followed the male wolf until they reached a brook swollen with rainwater. He guided her down the edge of the stream for a quarter mile or so, until they reached a massive, ancient tree that towered over the surrounding pines. Instinctively, Maddy recognized this as a sacred place of the forest. The Mother Tree was hundreds of years old. Mounds of white mushrooms and curtains of moss covered the decaying wood. Its massive roots spread far out around its trunk, almost fifty feet in diameter, creating a cavern at the tree's base. The ground appeared to be dry beneath the ancient tree, and a bed of soft pine needles filled the little cave. It was the perfect place for a den.

Exhausted, Maddy slunk into the heart of the ancient mother, down into the womb between the roots. The scent of pine wood engulfed her. She explored the burrow, kicking up leaves and pine cones with her paws, but she didn't find any unfriendly critters.

Designating it safe for sleeping, she collapsed on the soft earthen floor, exhausted from her long run through the woods. It was good to be out of the cold, wet forest.

The big male entered the hollow tree after her. He circled the space, his tail lazily sweeping the ground. He sat down next to her, nuzzling his head against hers, wrapping his body around her own. She curled against his neck, their two bodies creating a yin-yang of warmth and security. He began licking her fur dry.

After resting for a while, she raised her head and began to do the same, cleaning his ears, neck and belly, burying her face in his fur. After a time, she looked down at her white paws.

I'm a wolf.

Another painful throb split down her forehead. She felt like she was waking up from a dream. Except somehow, she was still in the dream.

She blinked and looked at Gareth.

Holy shit. I'm a wolf.

Then, in a flash, it came crashing over her: she was a wolf girl, and she had Changed.

Maddy gasped, but with her wolf jaws, it turned into a nervous yawn. When she looked down at herself, curled up in a little ball next to Gareth, she saw a shiny pelt of reddish brown fur blending into her white paws. Her hearing was very sensitive. She could hear a little vole burrowing through the weeds outside their den, almost twenty paces away. She had Changed and now she was in the woods.

Maddy felt a sudden pressure on her chest. Was she going to have a panic attack? She opened her mouth and started panting.

Gareth noticed her sudden change of mood. He raised his head and nuzzled her neck. His golden eyes caught her own. The awareness in his gaze was self-evident. His intelligence. His understanding. He saw her flicker of awareness. They couldn't speak to one another, but through his gaze, she felt him compelling her to calm down.

She was a wolf. It wasn't a dream or a vision. Her life in Black River would never be the same. She didn't want to go back. Kaylee. The video on Picplace. Disenrolling in school. As a wolf, it all seemed so far away, so insignificant. She had a whole mountain to explore. Why care about social media? It was just bondage of a different kind. Here, in the woods, she was free.

Maddy's brief moment of awareness began to slip away as her wolf-senses reclaimed her. Her breathing became regular again as simple, lupine thoughts filled her mind: memories of the deer hunt and their wolfsong. She had found her lifemate. Finally, after all these years of solitude, she knew her pack. She had a full belly, a cozy den, and a big male by her side. The night was calm and peaceful outside, and it was starting to rain. She had nothing to fear.

In the private darkness of their new den, the two wolves snuggled close together. The black male and the little female curled up in the dark, blissful womb of the tree.

Chapter 25

When Maddy opened her eyes again, she was lying on a soft, furry bed inside the massive trunk of a hollow tree. It was pitch black. The scent of pine needles and rich earth filled her nose. Outside, she heard the percussion of raindrops pattering on wet leaves. She was very warm.

Her hand traveled over her breasts, then over her gently rounded stomach to her curvy hips. She was totally naked. Not even a sock or a hair tie. What the heck?

For a moment she was disoriented. She raised up one hand and held it in front of her face. She couldn't see her fingers, it was too dark. She wiggled her five digits and made a fist. She felt human fingernails bite into her palm. A sense of relief flooded her. She moved her lower limbs, then she ran a hand down to check between her legs, just in case. She sighed. Alright. Definitely human, and not an anthropomorphic half-wolf. Most importantly, she was all in one piece.

It was nighttime, and it was raining outside. The storm gently murmured outside the hollow tree. She listened to a chorus of frogs singing in the dark woods. An owl hooted. It was soothing. The forest felt like home.

Then she noticed the quiet shush of slow breathing. Gareth's scent filled their little cave. A knot of tension eased from her brow. His wolf form was curled around her, asleep, like the biggest, most comfortable stuffed animal she could imagine. So warm. She nestled deeper into the thick fur on his chest. His tail was curled against her back. If she lay very still, she could hear his heartbeat. It was pleasant. Soothing. His soft pelt tickled her breasts and thighs. It was like a high-quality blanket.

Maddy put a hand to her forehead. No way. Did she actually transform into a wolf? She remembered running through the undergrowth on all fours. The deer. Then . . . a big black Alpha. Maddy put her hand up to her mouth. *Gareth.*

The intensity of recognizing her lifemate washed over her. Goosebumps ran down her skin. Her stomach clenched. As a little red wolf, she had been utterly entranced by the big Alpha: his scent, his presence, his strength. She couldn't explain how or why, but she felt their bond instinctively.

He's my lifemate, she thought. She understood it, now. The mountain gave him to her. She belonged to him, and he belonged to her. He was her home. She rolled over, snuggling deeper into his warm, furry body. He shifted, curling tighter around her in a half-moon position. She was cuddling with a giant wolf. Her protector. Her Alpha.

I did it. I Changed.

She was a wolf girl. She even ate raw deer meat. If she thought too much about that, she felt a little sick, so she glossed over that memory. She chose to focus instead on the beauty of the wilderness: the incredible, exhilarating freedom of running through the woods at night. For a few wonderful hours, all the bondages of society had fallen from her shoulders. No thought of bills, school work, Dean, Kaylee or anyone else. She had been free. She never wanted to return to Black River. She was going to live out the rest of her days in the wild with her lifemate.

As that thought sank in, her sense of excitement began to grow. No more bills. No more classes. No more goals. No more worries over homelessness or career or education. She could live in the woods with Gareth. She didn't need anything else. With that realization, Maddy felt a rush of relief. She scrunched up her nose, telling herself to Change back. *Be a wolf!* she told herself firmly. She wanted to Change back into her little red body and live the rest of her days out on the mountain.

But nothing happened.

Why couldn't she Change back? She wished and wished, tensing up her face so hard it hurt, focusing her thoughts, but she remained in human form. A little groan of frustration slipped from her throat. *Please Change back!* she begged her body, but only the slightest stirring of vitality answered her call.

Her big furry cushion started to move. Gareth's breathing changed, a sign he had woken up. He raised his wedge-shaped head and looked at her. She was curled up along his side, her head nestled against his chest, his tail draped over her like a blanket. He sniffed at her face. Then he licked her cheek. His wolf head was so huge, he could have opened his mighty jaws and swallowed her skull in one bite. But she wasn't afraid.

"Hey," she said softly.

She raised a hand to his silken muzzle, gently running her fingers over the fur on his face. His golden eyes glinted down at her. She hadn't spent any time with Gareth in his wolf form like this before. It was . . . intimate. Finally, she felt like she understood his world. It didn't seem so strange or frightening. She was a werewolf, too.

He nuzzled her cheek with his snout. She was draped between his big wolf paws, belly up, unintentionally submissive. He sniffed her face, her hair. His rough tongue lapped twice at her exposed belly. Then he settled his head between her breasts with a contented sigh. Maddy wrapped her arms around his neck, just like holding a stuffed animal. She fell asleep like that, lulled by the sound of the rain.

***

When Maddy woke up again, gray light was funneling between the roots of the tree. She could hear the sound of morning birdsong. She sat up with a groan. She was covered in mud, twigs and dirt. It wasn't a good look, but there really wasn't much she could do about it. She pushed a hand halfheartedly through her wild witch hair. She stank like a dog.

I'm disgusting, she thought. But she felt great.

She looked around. She was alone in the earthen den under the tree. Her heart skipped a beat in her chest. At first she was filled with concern. Where was Gareth? Was he coming back soon? Why would he leave her alone?

Then she heard rustling from outside. The footsteps were unmistakably human. She scented the air and felt the tense knot in her stomach loosen.

When Gareth appeared, he was fully dressed. Maddy glanced over her mate's appearance, a little disappointed. In comparison, she felt like a grungy urchin child caught living in a cave in the woods, while Gareth looked like any other Latin-American outdoorsman. He wore khaki shorts, big hiking boots and a black tank top that showcased his full sleeves of tattoos. His hair was clean, parted down the middle and tied back from his face. The stubble along his jaw was darker than she was used to, but other than that, he looked ready for the day.

"Hey there, wolf girl," he said with a grin. "You look like you've had a night."

Maddy blushed awkwardly. Then she ran a tired hand over her face.

"So?" Gareth asked. "How was it?"

"How was what?"

"Your first Change."

Maddy blinked a few times and slowly shook her head. "Pretty wild. Not at all what I expected. Um, did I imagine eating a deer, or . . . ?"

"Nope, you didn't imagine it. You did good on your first hunt," he said with a glint in his hazel eyes. "Think of it like our *second* first date, wolf style."

Gareth's enthusiasm was infectious. He didn't seem bothered at all that she looked like a cavewoman and stank like a sweaty trash heap. Despite herself, Maddy started to smile. Then she laughed in earnest.

"It was a lot of fun," she admitted.

"See? Being a werewolf ain't so bad."

"It's really not."

Maddy took a moment to marvel at that. She felt . . . *whole*. Like she had only been living half of her life up until that moment. Part of herself was missing before, but now, she felt complete. No wonder she had struggled to fit in for so long with the normal human population of Black River. She was a wolf girl. How had she not realized it before?

Perhaps without intending to, Gareth had restored an essential, missing part of her life. Without him, she never would have discovered this part of herself.

"I owe you a lot," she blurted out, unsure how to voice her feelings. "I . . . uh, thank you for all this. I had a really good time last night. Thank you for sharing it with me."

"Ah, you're cute, babe," he grumbled in his deep voice. "You don't owe me anything."

On weak legs, Maddy climbed to her feet. Hunched over so as not to hit her head on the tree, she walked to the entrance of their den. Gareth reached out a hand and helped her find her footing, then he supported her as she climbed out from under the tree. When she was standing next to his side, he kissed her cheek firmly.

"I'd do it again in a heartbeat," he said. "You're a fast runner for a little wolf, you know that?"

"It took you a while to catch me," she grinned. "Will you take me hunting again?"

"Of course."

She grinned, feeling shy. She unzipped her backpack and started pulling on her clothes. When she was finished dressing, she glanced over her shoulder at the giant, hollow tree.

"This is a cool spot," she said. "Did you find this place?"

"I found it a while back, when I first built the cabin. It's a good place for the Change. Nice and secluded."

Gareth brushed a bit of dirt off of her butt, then gave it a friendly smack.

Maddy gasped. "Hey!" she exclaimed.

He laughed all big and loud.

"Let's get back to the cabin. It's not far from here. We can eat some human food. Then I'll teach you to control the Change."

"Yeah, I'd like that. I desperately need a shower."

"I figured you might. I got the solar shower setup behind the cabin. Got some shampoo, too. The water might even be warm by now."

"Good enough for me," Maddy agreed.

Their hands clasped together, Gareth led Maddy through the rainy, wet woods. The mountainside was full of little streams and unexpected waterfalls from the heavy rain. He helped her through the slippery mud, then he led her around big rocks and over fallen logs.

Maddy didn't recognize anything about the forest. It felt brand new. All the little trails and woodland secrets she had discovered as a wolf were veiled to her human senses. She didn't understand how Gareth could navigate the terrain so well. Maybe with practice, she would be able to keep her wolf senses in human form?

Hand in hand, they walked about a mile through the woods, then the cabin came into view. Maddy was relieved to see it. Being naked in the woods was not as freeing as she had first imagined. The ground was rough against her soft feet, and she kept scratching herself on little branches and bushes. Thankfully, Gareth led her around the worst of the raspberry thickets.

He walked with her up to the cabin's front door and opened it. Then he ushered her inside. He handed her a towel and a bottle of shampoo from the box of supplies.

"I'll get the stove going. You want tea or coffee?"

"Coffee, thanks," she said.

Then Maddy walked around behind the cabin, where a woodpile and rain catchment system were located. The solar shower was ready to go. It was no more than a black bag with a little hose hanging from a tree branch not far from the outhouse. It was simple enough to turn on and off. Maddy cleaned off as much of the rain and mud as she could. After she finished shampooing her hair, she wrapped herself in the soft towel and returned to the cabin.

Gareth tossed her a pair of his pajama bottoms and an oversized T-shirt when she came back inside. Two hot mugs of coffee were sitting on the table. After a cold night in the wet woods, the dark brew smelled delicious. Maddy picked up her mug eagerly and took a sip.

"I didn't bring any decent clothes for camping," Maddy pointed out.

"Don't worry about it. Prepare for a long, naked weekend, babygirl. No sense getting dressed if we're going to be practicing the Change. I got a jacket for you if you get cold."

Maddy sat down at the small wooden table and pulled Gareth's heavy flannel jacket around her shoulders. It looked like he was making breakfast over the stove. He was frying a couple of eggs in a cast iron skillet. A kettle was boiling on the second burner. Maddy wrapped her cold hands around the mug of coffee. She couldn't help but appreciate the view as Gareth moved about the cabin. Her eyes trailed over his muscular back, visible through his T-shirt, down to his chiseled torso. She shivered as a bit of warmth spiraled through her belly. She got a clear view of his tattoos running up each arm. His long black hair was loose. It hung down his back in a glossy, silken sheet.

He glanced back at her, catching her look; his hazel eyes glinted. She found herself smiling at him. *Lifemate.*

Then Gareth slid two plates of eggs and sausage onto the table. He sat down across from her and started eating. Maddy was ravenous. She dug into her plate with gusto.

Gareth talked around a mouthful of eggs: "It's Saturday, so we have another day before we gotta head back to the real world. I'll teach you how to control the Change. It'll be hit-or-miss at first, like riding a bike. But once it clicks, you're good."

Right. The real world, the land of homework and property taxes. Maddy bit back a groan.

"Can't I just live as a wolf forever?" she asked, testing the waters to see how he would react.

"So now you wanna be a wolf?" Gareth teased. He obviously wasn't taking her comment seriously.

"Actually, yeah, I like it *a lot*. It's freeing. I think I like it even more than being a human."

The smile melted off of Gareth's face, to be replaced by a thoughtful frown.

"What do you mean?" he asked.

Maddy struggled to explain herself. "I mean, this past week, my life has been completely . . . *destroyed*. Dean was murdered, I've lost my job and I'm not in school. Everything is different. As a wolf, I don't have to deal with any of it. I can just live in the woods and eat and sleep."

Gareth cocked his head to one side, as though deeply considering what she had to say. Then he reached over and brushed his thumb over her left nipple. With a little gasp, Maddy straightened up an inch.

"I'd miss these, if you stayed a wolf," he grinned at her.

"Gareth!" she exclaimed. "Jeez. You're such a guy."

The devilish grin stayed on his face. He rested a hand on her shoulder and gave her arm a gentle squeeze. He didn't seem satisfied with the simple touch, so he scooted his chair around the table next to her. Then he pulled her against his body. He rested his chin on her head protectively. She sagged against him, feeling unexpected tears sting her eyes.

"I hate my life," she groaned. "This is the most fucked up week ever. It's beyond words."

"I know. A lot has changed for you in a short time," he agreed. "Look, Mads, I know you've had it rough. But it's gonna get better now. When we get back to town, we'll make small, reasonable goals. Sign you up for the GED. After that, you can hit up community college or trade school next year, if you want. You got options."

"I don't have a car," she pointed out.

"Yeah, but you'll have a license soon. The car will come. We're working on that. I'm gonna help you. No one makes it through life alone, baby. You got me now. I'm not goin' anywhere."

"And Dean? The Grayridge pack? The hunter?"

"Well . . . all that's gonna shake down. Dean's gone. Can't do anything about that, except hold a funeral for him when the time comes, if you want. Or we can dump his ashes in the woods. I don't care, baby. But whatever happens with the trailer and the bills, we'll figure it out together."

"Together," Maddy echoed.

"That's right."

Maddy opened her mouth, then shut it. She really didn't know what to say. He was her lifemate; he wasn't going to abandon her. In a way, it was like they were already married. And she hadn't even said *"I love you"* yet. The thought struck her numb. All she did was moan and complain, and he was always there to help her. How could she be so self-absorbed?

"I-I-I'm sorry," she stuttered.

"For what?"

"For not believing you about the lifemate thing."

"I told you, babygirl, you got nothing to apologize for."

Maddy put down her cup of coffee. She leaned over and hugged Gareth, hard.

Lifemates.

All those years he spent checking on her in the hardware store, finding her on the mountain, leading her through the woods on those dark nights, he had known they were fated for one another.

"It's instinctive . . . like two lost souls coming together by fate. There's some special power involved. I don't know how it all works myself, but maybe we can figure it out together."

Two lost souls brought together by fate.

Nothing could break that bond.

Maddy took a deep breath. Whether she understood a big concept like "fate" or not, she believed they were meant to meet each other. She was supposed to find him and move in with him. Everything was unraveling as it should.

"You doin' okay?" Gareth asked, noticing the shimmer of tears in her eyes.

Maddy nodded. She rubbed her face into his chest, inhaling his delicious smell. She took a deep breath. Then she released him and sat back in her chair.

"Fine," she sighed. "I'll live out my days as a human girl, but only if I can live with you."

Gareth released an unexpected laugh. "You're sweet, baby. But I got bad news. Shifters can't stay in wolf form forever. Eventually our vitality runs out and we Change back."

"Oh. Really?"

"Yeah, I know, it sucks. Some werewolves try to live in the wild, and they make a good run of it, but eventually their vitality runs out and they're forced to return to society. Tale as old as time."

Maddy felt crestfallen at that news. Her sense of euphoria faded a bit. So she wasn't going to be freed from her human obligations, after all. She should have guessed. It was way too easy and convenient to just disappear into the mountains. She should have thought about that before.

Maddy picked up her fork and kept eating. She wanted to find out more about being a werewolf. Maybe she could work out a system, living half in the woods and half in the world.

"I want to practice my shifter power," she said as she ate. "Changing into a wolf is a lot more intense than I thought. I totally lost myself. I'm really glad you were with me."

"That's how most of us Change the first time. A few people retain awareness, but I think they're prepped by their pack. I'm gonna teach you how to control the Change this weekend. But it's not gonna be simple, Mads. The reason I couldn't teach you before now, is because you gotta *remember* the Change in order to manifest it. That's how you summon your vitality—by memory. If you've never experienced the Change even once before, how are you gonna remember it?"

"I, uh, well, I hadn't thought of that," Maddy said with a little frown.

"That's why you need a teacher who knows what he's talkin' about." Gareth poked his thumb in his chest. "Trust your Alpha."

She laughed. "Alright. Yeah."

"After we get back to town, the rules still apply, understand? There's a lot I'm gonna have to teach you about the shifter world, not just about the Change, but about our laws. But that'll come as we go."

"Got it. I figured there would be more to learn than just shifting."

He grinned. "Smart girl. Remember, just because you can summon the Change with your thoughts, and come out of it alright, doesn't mean you won't still be triggered. You gotta keep working on your self control. The Change can hit randomly if you get too angry or frightened. Hell, sometimes I get triggered, and I've been practicing for fifteen years."

"Fifteen years?" Maddy gasped. "You're so old."

He rolled his eyes at her. "Brat."

She gave him an impish little smile.

"Listen, Mads," he cautioned her in a low voice, "the wolf is unpredictable. You might still forget you're a human sometimes when you Change. This ain't a linear road. I just want to make sure you got a handle on it while we're here. Sounds good?"

"Yeah, I get it."

"Good. So we'll practice a bit until you're confident. Eat your protein. Then let's get to work."

Chapter 26

Maddy came out of her Change curled up at the base of a fir tree, panting and sweating. She groaned as a cool breeze teased her nipples. A shiver passed over her bare, pink human skin. She was freezing. Changing into a fluffy, doubled-coated werewolf was *a lot* more pleasant than transforming back into a human girl.

It was early Saturday evening. Beginning early that morning, Gareth had run her through the Change a half-dozen times. Her joints ached and her muscles were tired. But she was starting to get the hang of it. She could summon the Change with her thoughts now, and when she willed it, the fire of her vitality was quick to rise. It wasn't all that difficult. In order to summon her vitality, she needed to focus on the memory of her first Change. Then she grabbed hold of that flame and fanned it, until the burn traveled from her feet to her knees, to her hips, to her breasts and shoulders, then to her head. The fire kept building until the Change took over. It wasn't pleasant, and it wasn't without pain. But Gareth explained that it would eventually feel good, like a runner's high, with more repetition.

Now she could retain a good amount of her human awareness during the Change. She still felt the pull of the wolf's mind, but Gareth had taught her a trick. All she needed to do was keep a touchstone memory at the front of her thoughts, someone who was important to her, to remind her of her humanity. She picked her mom. Whenever she felt her mind falling into the wolf, she thought of her mom and kept a firm grip on herself, and it was surprisingly effective.

Overall, Maddy felt good about her progress over the course of a short day.

She heard footsteps approaching from beyond the tree where she was sitting. She recognized Gareth's scent.

"Water," he said as he circled the large trunk. He offered her a canteen of fresh mountain runoff, which she raised eagerly to her lips. To Maddy's parched mouth, the fresh spring water tasted like candy. Then Gareth sat down next to her in the shade of a pine tree. He was fully dressed and showered, and he smelled delicious. It had rained most of the afternoon, but now a few orange sunbeams were breaking through the clouds. Rays of golden light sparkled against a dove-gray sky. A beautiful sunset was poised to strike over the mountains.

"I didn't get lost in the wolf this time," Maddy said. "I remembered who I was."

"That's great progress, babe. Sounds like you're almost *out of the woods*."

"Hah. Very *pun-ny*."

Gareth's warm hand landed on her knee, giving her an affectionate squeeze. His words of encouragement brought a lift to her heart. She glanced away, trying not to show how pleased his praise made her. She had to admit, she was proud of herself. Considering how traumatic her first Change was in Bea's camper, she had come a long way. She was starting to feel a lot more confident. Wolf-Maddy was a bit of a blend of human and beast. While she was in her wolf form, she could remember her human life with some detail, but she still reasoned like a wolf and relied heavily on her instincts to navigate the forest.

"It's getting late," Gareth said, glancing at his stainless steel wrist watch. "You ready to head back to the cabin?"

"One more try?" Maddy begged.

"You got stamina, huh?"

"I'm a little tired, but . . . ." Maddy's eyes returned to the forest. Her heart yearned to stay within the trees. "Just one more time. I want to see if I can keep my memories again. Twenty minutes?"

"Alright, babygirl. But then we gotta head back to the cabin. Time to make dinner and rest up for tomorrow."

Maddy climbed to her feet. Her hair was a tangled mess from Changing so many times into a wolf. She felt a bit like a magical wood nymph; she had almost gotten used to walking around *au naturel* in the forest. It was kind of scandalous, but she loved it.

"Aren't you going to join me?" she asked.

"Naw, I just showered. Don't forget—twenty minutes."

"Alright," Maddy agreed, a little disappointed.

As Gareth walked back to the cabin, Maddy focused her mind on the memory of her first Change. She grabbed onto that red heat, beckoning to the wolf within. The flood of shifter vitality came much easier now. Fire gathered in her toes and ran up her legs. It flooded her arms, her hands. Red fur sprouted from her skin, up her spine and neck, across her cheeks. She felt shoots of pain start in her legs as her bones began to shrink and reshape themselves. She felt her hips shift, her spine bend. She hated this part the most. She clung to the vision of the wolf in her head and tried not to think of all the weird things going on with her organs and various bodily systems.

Then she stood on all fours in the grass.

She turned to look at Gareth. He was watching her about twenty feet away.

"All good?" he called.

She wagged her tail like a dog and huffed twice.

"Alright, don't be long."

Maddy turned around and took off through the forest at a fast run. She loved running as a wolf. She flew over the ground, easily finding a trail through the ferns and undergrowth. She passed a rabbit's burrow and a den of raccoons. The forest was teeming with wildlife. As a wolf, nothing escaped her keen senses. She could hear the buzz of a hornet's nest thirty feet away through the trees; the trickle of an underground stream hidden beneath her paws; the creaking roots of a great forest giant. It seemed like the whole mountain was breathing and moving.

If she had a choice, she would stay there forever, exploring all the mysterious nooks and crannies of the mountain.

Maddy ran downhill for a while. She splashed through a familiar stream. She decided to follow the winding brook into a grove of dogwood trees, then circle back to Gareth's cabin. But as she entered the copse of ancient dogwood trees, her steps slowed. The forest felt different here. Quieter. A certain tension lay over the woods.

Maddy's footsteps slowed to a halt. She sniffed the air, her ears perked forward, listening.

Then she heard the sound of barking dogs.

At first she was confused. The dogs seemed out of place. Was she imagining it? What were domesticated pets doing this deep in the wilderness? The fur on her neck prickled, standing on end. The frantic baying sounded familiar. The wind shifted and she raised her nose to sniff the air. She caught a whiff of something pungent and foul: wolfsbane.

A flash of human memory interrupted her thoughts: the man by the lake with his three dogs. The werewolf hunter. Was it him?

Maddy turned in a slow circle as her heart quickened in alarm. The echoing mountain cliffs confused her hearing. She couldn't tell which direction the dogs were coming from, but they were getting closer and louder by the second.

Her wolf instincts kicked in. At first Maddy turned to run back to the cabin, but then she thought of Gareth. What if she led the dogs straight to him? If the hunter found their cabin, Gareth might be shot on sight. The thought made her blood run cold.

Maddy picked the opposite direction from the cabin and ran, panicked, through the woods. She found a rocky trail that led up the side of the mountain. She followed it. The climb was steep and perilous, studded with sharp rocks and sudden holes. She thought the hounds would be too uncoordinated to follow her up the cliff. But, the dogs were relentless. They kept after her, slowly closing the gap between them.

As Maddy ran on, the sky darkened to night. A thick layer of clouds overhead obscured the silver moon. She climbed into the high country of the mountains, where the ground was covered in sharp rocks, spongey lichen and creeping sarsaparilla. Her paws were sore and bleeding from the rough terrain. A perilous drop hedged her in on either side, and behind her, the dogs were coming. She didn't know which direction she was running, and she felt thoroughly lost. It was difficult to navigate in the dark, and she feared the dogs would soon catch up to her.

Growing desperate, Maddy threw back her head and howled. The sound ricocheted off the rocky cliffs and echoed through the forest. The dogs increased their barking. They heard her fear and exhaustion. They would soon corner their prey. Maddy howled twice more, hoping her message would reach Gareth. He must have noticed her missing by now; she had been running for what felt like a long time.

Then, from the darkness behind her, a dog leapt out of the brush. It was a thin, wolfish male with a masked face. He had a mean, narrow snout full of gnarled fangs, and a matted gray coat. He stank like wolfsbane. The ugly dog snarled at her. Maddy growled back, her hackles rising. As a wolf, she topped the hound by several inches and maybe forty pounds of muscle. She felt pretty confident that she could take the lighter male. Maddy snarled, preparing for a fight. Adrenaline surged. She saw red.

The two canines lunged at each other. The vicious male got her by the leg with strong jaws and Maddy squealed in pain. She had no choice but to use her teeth. She twisted around and bit into the male's neck, but the dog's fur was thick and wiry. Maddy couldn't seem to find any flesh buried inside her thick ruff.

Desperate, Maddy tackled the masked dog to the ground. The fight happened in a flash. They rolled for a moment, snarling and scratching at each other, then Maddy's jaws found the underside of the male's throat. She sank her teeth down into soft, bitter flesh. It wasn't a pleasant taste. She ripped and tore with all her might, desperate to win. She might have gone a little overboard, because she heard bones snap, and then the dog went limp.

Holy shit.

Maddy released the dog's throat, her mouth full of blood and foul bits of flesh, and she limped a few paces away. Her foot was wounded and it was painful to walk. But she couldn't stay near the corpse of the dead dog. She had to keep going. She could hear the hunter's other two hounds approaching in the near distance. She glanced down at the hound's body, horrified at her own survival instinct. Then she continued on through the high country, seeking a place to hide and lick her wounds. The bitter taste of the hound's blood stayed in her mouth.

A few more minutes passed with the hounds gaining ground behind her. Maddy's wounded leg slowed her down considerably. She didn't think she could fend off the other two hounds if they caught up with her. She needed to find help.

Then Maddy's ears perked forward. Was it her imagination, or did she hear music? The heavy throb of bass reverberated in her chest. It sounded like someone might be camping out on the mountain. She had no sense of her location, or which direction she was running. Was she close to the highway or Elk Haven?

Desperate, Maddy followed the sound along a narrow trail, traversing the edge of a rocky cliff. As she circled around the hillside, she saw glowing lights in the forest down below. Bonfires? Then the trail came to a sudden end. Maddy found her way blocked by a cement wall that loomed out of the darkness. It looked like an old cement structure built into the side of the cliff. Her eyes combed over the strange building in the dark. The block walls were smudged from decades of dirt and rain. Moss caked the cracks between the stones. The old cement factory stood out against the forest, a series of boxes and rectangles stacked in tetris-like patterns against the cliff face, crumbling from weather and wear. The clouds broke open at that moment, and silver moonlight illuminated the decrepit, graffiti-covered walls of Devil's Tower.

Most of the building was covered in long sheets of moss. A long corridor stuck out of the north end of the building and disappeared into the woods; it might have contained a conveyor belt at one time. A single tower protruded from the top of the factory, looming ominously overhead. With the moonlight shimmering down, it was an eerie sight to behold.

Beyond the sprawling maze of cinder block and rusted metal, Maddy saw bonfires glowing merrily in the forest. She heard music blaring from giant speakers. A row of cars and trucks were parked farther down the hill on an asphalt road that led to and from the tower. As her eyes adjusted to the firelight, she saw the bouncing, jittery forms of dozens of bodies. The chatter of voices and laughter drifted to her on the wind. It was Black River's legendary Halloween Haunt!

Somehow, she had found her way from Gareth's cabin to the Devil's Tower, all on the same night as the super-secret Halloween party.

She felt a ray of hope pierce her panicked thoughts. Wasn't Bea supposed to be at the party? And Vin? Maddy's heart leapt. Maybe she could take shelter with her friends and Change back into a human girl? She could blend in with the rest of the party goers. Then, even if the hunter caught up with her, she doubted he would fire his gun into a big group of people.

Of course, she would be naked if she shifted back into human form. But if she could reach Bea, maybe her friend could help her find some clothes?

With careful steps, Maddy maneuvered down the side of the cement building, leaping from one part of the shaky roof to the next. She avoided areas where the roof sagged or groaned beneath her weight, and kept to the rafters and braces that supported the building. Finally, she leapt the remaining twelve feet or so to the ground, to land in a pile of moldy leaves. Then she started circling around the edges of the party, avoiding the light of the bonfires, looking for her friends.

***

Gareth was splitting a few logs for firewood out behind his cabin as he waited for Maddy to return from her run. He was pretty satisfied with the weekend so far. She was a fast learner. Very fast, actually. For most wolves, it took about a week to begin shifting at will, but it seemed like Maddy already had a grasp of it. He was proud of her. He could tell she really wanted to master the Change as fast as possible. At first she had been scared of the Change, but now her attitude was completely different. He liked seeing the wild come out of her like this. She seemed a lot more confident just within the past day or so.

He suspected she carried Alpha blood from her father. Her wolf form was smaller than his, but it was a good sight bigger than most female wolves. She was quick on her feet, and her coat was an unusual russet red, almost auburn. Her own Alpha vitality was growing now, which probably explained her exceptionally fast progress as a shifter.

He caught himself wondering what their cubs might look like, if they would take after him or her, and he stopped himself. They had a lot to get through before that happened. He still hadn't told her about the Redfern Massacre and her father's death. He hadn't found the right words yet. Considering everything she had endured over the last week, he didn't want to dump more on her. He really wanted to tell her at the right time. He just didn't know when that would be.

His thoughts were interrupted when a distant sound reached his ears. He turned his head, listening to a faint wolf howl. Shit. Was it Maddy? Her voice sounded again, this time unmistakable. He would recognize his lifemate's howl anywhere. She sounded distressed. Something was wrong.

He abandoned the wood pile, tossing his ax on the ground, and ran into the woods without hesitation. He kicked off his boots so he could run faster. He summoned the fire of the Change and fell forward onto all fours, his muscles bulging, his spine elongating, his mouth filling with sharp teeth. Leaping over fallen logs and dense brush, he shifted into his wolf form as he was running downhill.

Using his wolf senses, the big black Alpha raced through the woods after his mate. He tracked Maddy's scent to a grove of ancient dogwood trees. There, he discovered a different set of tracks through the muddy forest floor: the hounds.

Three of them. They stank like wolfsbane.

Gareth growled low in his throat. The hunter. How did this asshole find them? Gareth's cabin was an hour outside of Black River, almost unreachable from the roadside. When they drove out, he kept a careful eye on the road, and he wasn't followed. It shouldn't be possible for the hunter to find them here . . . unless the bastard somehow put a GPS tracking device on his car.

Well, shit. Maybe. GPS trackers used to be considered "high tech" when he was growing up, the stuff of *James Bond* and *Mission Impossible* spy movies, but now any fool could buy one for $20 online and sync it to a phone app. Had the hunter put a tracker on Gareth's car? He would have to investigate the Camaro later. But first, he needed to reach Maddy's side. He hoped he wasn't too late.

Maddy's trail led him out of the woods and uphill, over barren, rocky land covered in shrubs and lichen. There, he discovered a few smears of blood on the rocks. He recognized her scent. The pads on her paws weren't tough enough yet to handle this kind of terrain. It only made him more worried. As he gained elevation, the forest became less prominent. The orange and gold leaves of autumn fell behind him, to be replaced by flat stretches of rock, spiny dwarf shrubs and moist alpine soil. The wind was a lot stronger this high up, whipping across the flat rocks with a vengeance. Above him, the sky darkened from purplish gray to deep indigo. A layer of low clouds gathered between the mountain peaks. It was going to be a cold, clammy night.

Unfortunately, Gareth was in too big a hurry to enjoy the panoramic nighttime views, or to appreciate the glint of moonlight shining off a distant, ribbonlike river. As he continued across the high country under a dark, expansive sky, his ears caught the sound of barking dogs. He broke into a run.

He came across a stream of stormwater runoff, roaring deep and fast down the mountainside. It looked like Maddy and the hounds had forded the riverlet a little ways downstream, where the water was less deep. Gareth crossed it in one mighty leap.

When he reached the opposite side, he heard the crack of a rifle through the cliffs.

His army training kicked in. Still in wolf form, Gareth threw himself down on the ground and rolled behind a rock. He remained crouched for a long minute, unmoving. He listened. No second shot was fired. But he felt certain the hunter was nearby, likely on the cliff above him. Gareth felt a silent roar of rage lodge in his throat. The hunter was stalking him. Sending his dogs after Maddy was just a way to draw Gareth out.

In Alpha form, he remained behind the large boulder, hidden behind a screen of low-growing mountain ash.

Gareth considered his options. The baying of the hounds continued in the distance. He could follow the hounds to Maddy. Or he could take out the hunter. He pondered the situation. He felt certain the hunter had positioned himself upstream a ways, on a higher ledge uphill, where Gareth would be an easy target if he tried to approach. The hunter was skilled; he used the terrain to his advantage. Higher up, there wasn't any tree cover for a big Alpha to hide. The moment Gareth left the shelter of the boulder, he would be an open target.

Which meant, it would be smarter for him to run downhill, back into the denser woods. There, he would follow after his mate.

Nothing else for it. Gareth leapt to his feet and lunged downhill, running like the wind. Another gunshot roared behind him, and a bullet ricocheted off the ground near his feet. Then Gareth leapt down a cliff, dropping about twenty feet into the woods below. He crashed through branches and vining plants, taking a few hard knocks to the ribs. Then he dove into a copse of paperbark birch trees.

Under cover again, he paused to catch his breath and assess his injuries. Nothing major, just a few scratches along his ribs and flank where stubborn branches had scraped him. Then his ears twitched. Behind him, farther up the mountain, he heard the static of a walkie-talkie. It took him back to his days in Iraq. Despite himself, Gareth paused to listen, his wolf ears perked.

"First attempt failed. I got a few shots off, but he was too fast. He's heading to you now," the hunter said. "He's pursuing the female, like we thought."

So, did the hunter have help?

With a blast of static, someone responded on the walkie-talkie: "Roger that, I think she just arrived. Everything according to plan . . . ."

Then the wind picked up and muffled the words, making the conversation difficult to discern. Still, it sounded like a woman's voice, if he had to take a guess. Which meant the hunter was working in a team. It confirmed his suspicion: they were using Maddy to bait him. Without a doubt, a surprise would be waiting for him when he reached her side. He would need to stay vigilant and look out for traps.

Then he heard the low rumble of an engine, the stench of gasoline and the crunch of rolling tires. His eyes traveled up the mountainside again. It sounded like a truck. The hunter was on the move. There must be a forestry road up above him, near where the hunter was camped out. If Gareth had to guess, he figured the hunter was heading to his mysterious partner's location, wherever that might be.

It didn't matter. Gareth's first concern was reaching Maddy to protect her. The wind shifted again, and he caught her sweet, summery scent through the woods. She had passed by this way not long ago. He didn't think she was too far off now, either.

Gareth started through the dark woods, working his way north and west. There wasn't much else he could do except follow his lifemate's trail through the forest, accompanied by the distant baying of the hounds.

Chapter 27

Maddy stalked around the edges of the party. The decorations were sinister. She saw big inflatable spiders hanging from spruce and fir trees; silver, black and orange balloons; fake cobwebs, streamers and flickering lights dangling from tree branches. A big pile of jack o'lanterns created a pyramid at the center of the party, where a bunch of beer kegs and tables full of snacks were set up. She saw a wide range of ages: lots of teenagers, college kids, and a pocket of folk who might have been closer to Gareth's age. So far, nobody she recognized. She saw students dressed in a variety of costumes: witches, superheroes, zombies, vampires and fairies. People were dancing to music, taking selfies and drinking a variety of different kinds of alcohol.

The smell of beer, tequila, vodka, weed and wine made her nose burn. She kept to the trees, away from the light cast by the bonfires and flickering Halloween decor. She was getting a little desperate by the time she caught Bea's scent. She recognized the soft, vanilla-esque odor of her friend's perfume from Fright Farm Haunted Manor. She zeroed in on the smell and followed it around the edge of the party. The trail of perfume led her to a secluded spot in the woods near the Devil's Tower. That's when she overheard Bea's voice.

"So let me get this straight—you haven't broken up yet?"

Bea sounded upset. Maddy hunkered down between the ferns at the edge of the woods. She could see Bea silhouetted by a string of pumpkin lanterns. The dark-haired girl was wearing a devil costume: a red leotard, knee-high black boots, a pitchfork and little horns. Maddy didn't see Andie anywhere. She was supposed to be dressed up like Sailor Mercury. Maybe she was hanging out with another group, or talking to a boy. Hard to tell.

Vin stood across from Bea. He was wearing skinny jeans, a studded leather jacket and combat boots. Very punk rock. Maddy could smell a hint of oil on his clothing, a memory of the garage where he worked with Gareth. The skinny punk kid was puffing on his vape in agitation while Bea sucked down a cigarette.

"Look, this situation is a little confusing," Vin said. "I didn't expect to fall this fast."

"Right. I've heard that line before."

"It's not 'a line.' I have real feelings for you."

"But you haven't broken up with this girl yet."

"No, we aren't broken up *yet*," Vin admitted. "I told her I was having second thoughts and I needed some space to figure things out."

"So you want to date me, but you're not even single? That's not a good look, Vin."

"I know. She's not a bad person, and you both have good qualities. I don't want to hurt anyone . . . ."

"We *both* have good qualities? Wow. Must be pretty hard for you to choose." Bea rolled her eyes. "I *really* don't need to hear this right now."

Bea looked ready to storm off. Her cheeks were flushed from vodka shots, and she was twirling her plastic pitch fork around in her hands in a dangerous way, like she might stab Vin through the gut with it. Actually, she looked very drunk.

"If you really want to go out with me, then break up with her right now."

Vin groaned. "Alright, but then you'll think I only did it because you forced me to."

"True, but it's still shitty that you won't do it."

Maddy's ears went back. She wondered how to get her friend's attention without scaring her. Bea might recognize her in her wolf form, but she was drunk. What if Bea freaked out? Vin wouldn't know what to do, either. And if she shifted back into human form, she would be completely naked, which was almost worse.

Maddy hesitated, wondering what she should do. She didn't want to be butt naked in the woods, surrounded by a hundred strangers. Yeah. Probably not a good idea. And she was starting to feel tired. She didn't know if she had enough strength to Change back into a wolf after this. Maybe if she looked around, she could find some clothes? Maddy padded away from Bea and Vin, and started back toward the main party. Someone must have brought a change of clothing, right? Maybe she should check around the parked cars for any bags.

Then a high-pitched shriek of laughter caught her attention.

"Come on, I dare you to go in there!" Kaylee Mackovitch screeched.

Maddy's head swung up. Her ears perked forward, and a little snarl pulled at her lips. The sound of Kaylee's obnoxious voice was unmistakable. She saw a crowd of five or six girls and boys standing outside the entrance to the Devil's Tower. Her interest piqued, Maddy slunk closer through the woods.

As she approached the group of kids, she recognized the "Varsity jacket" crew. It looked like Kaylee was hanging out with her usual group of flying monkeys. Appropriately, they were all dressed up like different characters from Wizard of Oz. Kaylee was Dorothy; Jaylen was the Good Witch of the East; Amy was the Wicked Witch of the West; Adam was the cowardly lion. She didn't recognize the rest of the kids, but she guessed they were all cheerleaders or football players from school.

Memories from Thursday afternoon in the boys' bathroom filled her head. She felt a surge of rage as she remembered the tip jar and the handcuffs. Then Maddy's mind flashed to Kaylee's pathetic, attention-seeking video on Picplace. She bared her teeth, a soft growl rumbling in her throat. She was in wolf form, and she didn't think she could sustain the Change much longer. Now was the perfect time for revenge.

A reasonable thought broke through her anger. The hunter might arrive at the tower soon. Maybe she should focus on finding clothes and joining her friends? But Maddy wasn't feeling very reasonable at the moment. She didn't know if she would ever get another opportunity like this one again.

On impulse, Maddy stalked through the undergrowth toward the Devil's Tower.

"I dare you to go inside!" one of the boys laughed. "Come on, let's look around. It's supposed to be the most haunted site in Jefferson County."

"I thought that was the Beaumont Manor," one of the girls pointed out.

"The Beaumont family made up that story to sell tickets to their Halloween carnival," Amy said. "I'm ready for a *real* scare. Come on, let's go to the tower!"

"I'll *only* go if Kaylee goes," Jaylen whimpered. She grabbed hold of Kaylee's arm, and the two girls shared a big-eyed look. Then Maddy watched the group tiptoe into the abandoned cement factory, red solo cups and phone lights in hand.

Her tail swished slowly back and forth. Maddy imagined the look on Kaylee's face if a big wolf suddenly appeared in the abandoned cement factory. Oh yeah. This was going to be fun.

She entered the cement factory behind the group of kids. Maddy followed them for a few minutes through the bowels of the drippy, moldy building. Graffiti murals covered the walls in a vibrant array of color. Trash littered the ground, and the building stank of mildew. Maddy padded silently behind the kids, keeping about a hundred paces between herself and the group. They discovered a giant graffiti mural on a wall that was almost fifteen feet high. There, they stopped to take a bunch of selfies. Then they started down one of the long, dark corridors toward the staircase to the Devil's Tower.

At the end of the corridor, the group stopped. A second hallway led them around a left turn or up a flight of stairs, but they couldn't continue straight.

"Do you think we should go back?" one of the boys asked. "This place is a lot bigger than I thought. I don't want to get lost."

"I've seen enough," Jaylen whined. "My skirt is getting muddy."

"Yeah, it smells like shit down here, I bet homeless people poop all over this building," Kaylee sneered. A burst of derisive laughter came from Amy, and the other kids joined in.

Maddy decided it was time to spring her trap. A rumbling growl started in her throat. It echoed eerily off the block walls, just like in a horror movie. The kids froze up ahead of her. They started looking around left and right. Blue cell phone screens bobbed in frantic circles.

"Do you hear that?" Jaylen gasped. "It sounds like an animal."

"Is it a dog?" Amy demanded. "Is that a stray dog growling?"

The group didn't see her until she was right in front of them. Then Adam screamed. The kids whirled around, frozen in horror as the big red wolf loomed out of the darkness. Maddy pressed her ears back, the fur on her neck and shoulders bristling, and released a ferocious roar.

Kaylee screamed bloody murder and ran into Jaylen. The two girls cracked their heads together. Solo cups went flying. At least two cell phones clattered to the ground. Then Kaylee and her group of flying monkeys took off running down the hallway. Their screams echoed off the old cement walls, magnifying the sound a hundredfold, creating a cacophony of panic.

Maddy took off down the hallway after Kaylee, howling and snarling, snapping at the hem of Kaylee's blue dress. The other kids were faster than her and pulled far ahead. Kaylee screamed at the top of her lungs. Maddy smelled the sharp scent of urine. If she was human, she would have laughed. Oh, what glee! Kaylee had pissed herself. Fucking brilliant. She was enjoying this way too much!

"Wolf!" Kaylee shrieked. "Help! Help, it's the killer wolf!"

"Run! Run!" Amy and Adam chorused together from the other side of the hallway.

"Killer wolf! Killer wolf!" the group took up the cry.

The hallway ended at a big hole in the building where one of the exterior walls had collapsed. Kaylee tried to jump over the rubble to make it outside, but her foot caught, and she fell to the ground. Amy and Jaylen appeared by her side, pulling her up by the arms, their eyes bugging out of their heads. Scrambling madly, they escaped through the hole in the building. Maddy stopped at the edge of the collapsed wall to watch them go. She didn't follow the girls outside. If she was in human form, she would have been laughing uncontrollably. She memorized the sight of Kaylee and her flying monkeys running panicked into the woods. Brilliant. She could finally die happy.

Feeling pretty good about her little prank, Maddy turned around and trotted back down the hallway. The factory was a maze in the dark, but she followed her own scent back to the building's entrance. Time to nab some clothes, go find Bea and Vin and shift back into her human form.

When Maddy reached the entrance to the old factory, however, she found the whole party in an uproar.

The cry of "Wolf! Killer wolf! There's a killer wolf in the Devil's Tower!" echoed through the forest, taken up by the rest of the partygoers. Mass panic ensued. People threw down their drinks and ran to their cars, abandoning the music and decorations. It looked like no one wanted to risk encountering a killer wolf in the woods, especially with all the recent animal attacks. Within minutes, the bonfires were abandoned, left to burn out unsupervised, while a hundred drunk party goers ran down the side of the mountain to jump into their cars and leave.

Maddy watched the chaos with a sinking feeling in her gut. Shit. What had she done? Now the hunter would be sure to find her. She needed to track down Bea and hitch a ride back to Black River, before her friends left the party. But how was she supposed to do that as a wolf?

As the thought crossed her mind, Maddy felt a strange sensation overcome her body. Her legs weakened and her vision blurred. She felt suddenly dizzy and nauseous. A foul taste entered her mouth. Maddy groaned and sat down on her haunches, hanging her lupine head toward the ground. Ugh, she didn't feel very good. Without intending to, she felt herself shifting back into her human form. Something was very wrong. When she came out of the Change, she was lying on her side, a fever burning in her cheeks and the venomous taste of wolfsbane in her mouth. She tried to climb to her feet, but she felt so dizzy, she almost threw up. Her mind flew back to the hound in the woods. When she bit the dog's neck, she got its blood in her mouth. She hadn't thought much of it at the time, except for the unpleasant taste. But now she felt a sinking sense of dread. Was she poisoned?

Maddy placed a hand to her burning cheeks. Either she had suddenly come down with the flu, or yes, she was poisoned. She didn't know what to do.

Suddenly, she heard footsteps. Someone was approaching her. Maddy's heart raced. She was totally naked, with no good explanation how she got to the tower. She knew she needed to run away and hide, but she could barely sit up. Then someone was standing over her, gazing down at her with their arms crossed. She saw a pair of women's boots and a warm burgundy coat. She squinted up at the person next to her, trying to discern their face in the flickering light of the bonfires.

"Sarah?" Maddy gasped.

Then she swooned and collapsed on the ground.

Chapter 28

When Maddy woke up, her head was throbbing. She was lying on her side on a grungy, cold cement floor. She was naked and covered in goosebumps. She shivered uncontrollably. Her wrists were tied behind her back at an uncomfortable angle. Her skin chafed against the rope. Her left hand was numb.

She rolled over and puked, but only a little bit of yellow bile came up. Ugh. She felt sick, and her cheeks were still warm and flushed with fever. How long had she been asleep? She sat up and looked around. It seemed like she was still in the Devil's Tower, and it was still nighttime. She guessed only a few minutes had passed since she had fainted at the factory's entrance. She felt sick. Her gut churned from the wolfsbane poison. She didn't know if the dose she had swallowed was deadly or not. Hopefully it would pass like bad food poisoning, but she couldn't be sure.

As more minutes passed, Maddy took stock of her surroundings. It seemed like she was lying inside a large pit on the lower level of the factory, perhaps in a basement of some kind. She guessed it was the basement by the damp air and the heavy scent of wet earth, which hinted at the underground. She could hear a scratchy-scritching sound in the darkness. Probably rats. Ugh. She *hated* rats. It looked like the floor above her had collapsed at some point, creating a hollow sort of pit where she was being held captive. She saw no hallways, doors or exits on her level of the building, just piles of trash and puddles of soiled rainwater. A pile of rubble stood at the far end of the hole where the floor must have collapsed long ago. Maddy's eyes roved over the chunks of concrete and twisted rebar leading up to the floor above. It looked a lot easier to climb down than to get back up. She didn't know how she would manage such a feat in bare feet with her hands tied. That was probably the point.

Then Maddy heard footsteps from up above. A bobbing yellow light revealed two shadows across the cement wall. Then two figures appeared at the edge of the hole.

"She's up now," a woman's voice said. It sounded familiar. Sarah? Maddy sucked in a breath of surprise. So she hadn't imagined it. She recognized her coworker's red hair, brilliant even against the harsh LED lanterns.

Then a man answered her, "Ah. So the little bitch is awake."

A middle-aged man, probably in his 50's, appeared next to Sarah on the ledge. He had a gaunt, leathery face and brownish-grayish hair. He wore a camouflage-colored vest over a green hoodie and khaki pants stained with mud. A bigass black rifle was slung over his shoulder. She recognized him. It was the same bastard who treed her and Bea out near the lake. Maddy felt viscerally sick. Shit. The werewolf hunter.

"I suppose you're wondering why you're here," the man continued, staring down at her with intense eyes, his hand on his gun. Maddy was reminded of her nudity and tried to curl away from him. "I've been watching you all week, Madeline, and I know what you are. Do you know why I'm in Black River?"

"You're a werewolf hunter," Maddy spat.

The man leered at her, unblinking. The LED lantern glinted eerily off his eyes.

"I'm surprised. You look like a bimbo, but you're a smart little bitch."

Maddy's lips tightened. She was a bit offended. "You're just a nasty, desperate old man who's stalking me," she spat.

The hunter threw back his head and guffawed. The derisive laugh reminded her of Dean.

"I'm definitely not interested in a female wolf. I'm after your Alpha, little bitch."

Maddy felt another chill run down her spine. Shit. So then, Gareth was the real target?

"Then why did you capture me?" Maddy asked.

"Why else? I can't run down an Alpha wolf on foot. That's absurd. But I can lure him out . . . using his *mate*." The man leaned forward with a sickening grin. Then he started to climb down the pile of rubble into the hole. Maddy watched him approach, a sick feeling of dread in her gut. Her eyes traveled to Sarah, who was standing with her arms crossed uncomfortably. Maddy felt a stab of betrayal. Her mind shot back to the hardware store and the strange, hushed conversation in the office. Were they lovers? Maddy felt like she wanted to vomit all over again. It all made sense now.

"Sarah, are you helping him?" Maddy demanded. "It was you, wasn't it? You reported me to the guild."

"Hi, Maddy," Sarah mumbled, sounding embarrassed. "I know what this looks like, but believe me, it isn't personal. I didn't know you were involved. I reported *the wolf attack* near your trailer to the guild. I thought it was suspicious. They sent Kevin out here to track down the Alpha, and well, it led us to you."

Sarah still wouldn't meet her eyes, even as she answered Maddy's question. The woman obviously felt guilty, seeing a teenage girl tied up like livestock. She looked pained. She glanced from Maddy to the hunter. "Can't we at least get her some clothes? I have a spare jacket in my car."

The hunter snorted. "She's not a girl, Sarah, she's a *creature*. She'll Change the moment we loosen her bonds. It's too dangerous. Besides, the Alpha will be here soon."

Kevin stared at her, his gaze lingering on her exposed breasts. Maddy felt her lips pulling back into a phantom growl. If she was in wolf form, she would have snarled. *Dirty old bastard,* she thought. He might claim to have "no interest" in a female wolf, but his eyes were more than telling.

Well, she didn't have to tolerate this sort of treatment. She was a werewolf, after all. She could shift into wolf form. At least then, she would have some protection. Maddy focused her mind on the memory of her first Change. She stirred the flames, just like Gareth had taught her, and waited for her vitality to rise. Waited. *Waited.* She felt a little flicker of something, but . . . it slipped away. The taste of power wasn't enough to begin her shift. She tried again, but this time, she felt nothing at all. Maddy ground her teeth in frustration. Had she run out of juice? Had she burned up all her vitality for that day? Or was the wolfsbane poison somehow interfering with the Change? She wanted to howl in frustration. Shit, she was stuck here until Gareth came for her, and it sounded like the hunter meant to shoot him on sight. How did she warn her lifemate?

Then the hunter started to move. With a crunch of boots, he climbed down the pile of rubble into the pit. Then he approached her across the dirty cement floor, splashing through a puddle of putrid water before he reached her side. Maddy turned away from him and cringed back. She didn't know what to expect.

The grizzled man drew a knife from a sheath under his vest. He circled around behind Maddy. For a terrifying moment, she thought he was going to slit her throat, end her life right there on the cold ground. Instead, she felt a fiery flash of pain as he ran the blade down the underside of her arm. Maddy screamed at the stinging, burning sensation. Hot blood trickled down her elbow to her wrist. She couldn't see the size of the gash or how deep, but it felt excruciating.

"What the hell are you doing?" she yelled.

The hunter wrapped a towel around the wound, soaking up the blood. He squeezed her arm too tight, inflicting a bit of extra pain. Maddy shrieked and flinched to one side, but he held her in a firm grip. She couldn't squirm away.

"I'm gonna use your scent to lure the Alpha straight into my trap."

"*Fuck you*," Maddy seethed angrily. She felt the fire of the Change growing within her, fueled by the burst of pain and accompanying adrenaline. She could feel her pulse in her forehead.

"This wasn't part of the plan, Kevin," Sarah protested, her voice soft. Her eyes passed over Maddy's naked body. She still looked uncomfortable. "I told you I'd help you as long as you didn't hurt her. You said Maddy would be safe with me while you hunted down the Alpha."

"She's safe, isn't she?" the hunter barked. "A little cut on her arm ain't gonna change nothing. She'll heal right up in a jiffy. Trust me, I know werewolves. We'll use her blood to lure the Alpha out. He'll be here soon enough. Now that we got the bitch, all you gotta do is stay out of the way until it's finished."

"And then you'll let her go, right?" Sarah asked.

A malicious glint entered the hunter's eye. "Right. Then I'll let her go."

Sarah relaxed a little bit, but the hair stood up on Maddy's neck. She could smell the lie on the hunter's rank breath. She knew a threat when she heard one. How could Sarah trust this bastard?

"You're an asshole," Maddy snarled at the hunter. He laughed at her. Then he reached up to pull out a stainless steel chain from under his flannel shirt. A single wolf fang hung from the end of the necklace. It was very long, curved and discolored with age. It looked like it might have once belonged to an Alpha. The hunter grinned at her, displaying a missing incisor on the front left of his jaw.

"See this?" he rasped. "I kept it as a trophy from my first kill. Twenty years ago, now. A big ol' Alpha with a black stripe from head to tail."

"That's sick," Maddy glared, but she couldn't take her eyes off the tarnished fang. It looked like it had once belonged to a giant beast. So this hunter meant business, and he had a lot of experience. It only fueled her fear. In disgust, Maddy wondered if he planned to add one of Gareth's teeth to his necklace. She had to stop him somehow.

Then the hunter put the tooth away under his shirt. He stood up, tossing the bloody rag on the ground at Maddy's feet. It was soaked with her blood.

Then the hunter walked back to the pile of rubble. He started climbing back up to the first floor, using the twisted metal rebar like handrails. Maddy felt desperate tears sting her eyes. The reality of the situation crashed down on her. This could all end with a bullet to her head, and she wouldn't be able to defend herself. She needed to get free somehow and reach Gareth before it was too late.

Pleading, she cried out, "Sarah, please, you can't do this! We've known each other for years. Gareth might be a werewolf, but he's also a person. He runs Jack's Auto Repair. I know you've taken your car there before. Come on. This is *murder*."

Sarah's lips tightened. "Werewolves are dangerous monsters, Maddy."

"That's not true. I'm a *shifter*. I'm not a monster. You know me, Sarah. I'm still the same person. I only just found out about werewolves last Friday. This is all new to me too!"

"Okay, but what about the men who died outside your trailer, Madeline?" Sarah asked coldly.

"The men outside my trailer?" It took Maddy a moment to remember the incident, so much had happened since then. "You mean, those thugs who broke in two weeks ago? They tried to rape me! They were werewolves, too, Sarah!"

"Werewolves? Huh? What do you mean?" her voice caught.

"Those men who got killed outside my trailer *were all werewolves*. They tried to rape me. Gareth saved my life. Please, Sarah, I know you don't understand all of this, but the hunter is lying to you. He's not a good person. There's two sides to every story. Please let me go."

"Shut the fuck up, you little bitch!" the hunter roared. "Don't listen to her, Sarah. These monsters are all the same. The moment you turn your back, she'll jump on you. She's just trying to save her own skin."

Sarah looked conflicted and miserable, but she dropped her eyes again, refusing to respond to Maddy's plea.

As the hunter reached the first floor, Maddy heard the distant sound of dogs barking. Kevin swung his rifle up into his hands. Then he strode out of sight.

"Do you think the Alpha is here already?" Sarah asked, walking after him, her boots crunching over the debris-covered floor.

Maddy listened as Sarah's footsteps receded down the hallway. Her two captors disappeared from Maddy's line of sight, but she could still hear their conversation echoing off the cement walls.

"Oh yes, the hunt is on!" Kevin said with a sinister sort of excitement. "Hunch down and stay out of sight. I'll be down the way a bit and over to the side. Once he's in the hole, he'll be an easy target. Douse the lights. Don't make a noise, or you're dog meat."

"O-okay!" Sarah said. She sounded terrified.

Then the LED lantern went out.

Maddy's eyes had grown accustomed to the harsh white light. When it blinked out, she was plunged into total darkness. Fear gripped her. She could barely breathe. The barking of the hunter's dogs was getting louder and closer.

"No!" Maddy yelled, her voice hoarse and panicked. "No, wait! Stop! Gareth, it's a trap! *It's a trap! Stay away!*"

Maddy's words echoed off the cement walls, but she felt like no one could hear her.

Chapter 29

Gareth barreled headlong through the mountain wilderness. Branches, vines and bracken scratched at his coat and caught on his paws, but he tore through the underbrush without mercy. His mind remained focused on Maddy. Encountering a hunter on her first Change was a dangerous, "worst case" scenario he hadn't prepared for. Now, to help her, he had to keep a cool head. The hunter could very well be luring him into a trap, but he couldn't abandon his lifemate. His body might be that of an Alpha wolf, but his mind was that of a soldier deep in enemy territory.

Gareth reached the site where Maddy had encountered the hunter's dog. He slowed down to investigate, surprised by the sudden sight of a dead hound. The canine's body lay in a bloody heap beneath a hawthorn bush. The stench of wolfsbane filled the area, along with a spatter of Maddy's blood. Anger surged, and fierce protectiveness. She was injured. Shit. Someone was gonna pay.

Nose to the ground, he followed her trail along the ridge of the mountain. He moved quickly, a black beast of supple power sprinting through the night. Eventually, the trees parted and the ground leveled out, and Gareth found himself at the Devil's Tower.

The abandoned cement factory was about five miles away from his cabin. Gareth was somewhat familiar with its location, even though he had never explored the area. It was a long distance to run through the woods. Covered in jade green moss and vibrant graffiti murals, the cement factory held an eerie sort of beauty. Gareth was a little superstitious when it came to abandoned places. He believed in hungry ghosts, and he didn't like the vibe of the tower. It seemed like an easy place for anyone to slip and break their neck.

The area was closed off to the general public, with big "No Trespassing" signs posted all over, but it looked like someone was throwing a Halloween party. By the number of guests and decorations, it was a real rager. He smelled the sharpness of alcohol on the wind, and somewhere down the mountainside, big subwoofers were blasting heavy beats. The base punctuated the night like cannonball blasts, making his lupine ears throb.

Then the music cut off. Gareth hesitated behind a screen of spruce trees, watching. Through a screen of pine needles, he saw people packing up and heading down the mountain. Some people were running. Others looked confused. Was the party already over?

He caught a few voices: *"Do you really think there's a wolf?"*

"No, I think those kids just scared themselves in the tower."

"That sucks. It was a good party. Now everyone's going home."

"What should we do about the bonfires?"

His ears perked at that word, "wolf." Someone must have seen Maddy and freaked out—he could smell her all over the area. She must have wandered around for a little bit before slipping off. Did that mean she was inside the tower?

Gareth decided to investigate. The wind teased his nose again with Maddy's scent, accompanied by the tang of blood. He couldn't ignore it. She was closeby, and she was injured. He needed to reach her side. If it was a trap, then so be it.

He climbed down the side of the old cement factory, following Maddy's scent trail, then circled around to the front of the building.

That's when he came face-to-face with the hunter's hounds.

Gareth didn't hear any barking or baying, but suddenly the stench of wolfsbane caught his attention. Then two big, hairy dogs ambushed him at the gaping, mawed entrance of the old cement factory. They lunged out of the shadows between two crumbling walls, growling and snarling. The dogs jumped upon him in a hurricane of teeth and claws.

Gareth was taken off guard—but he was ready for a fight. Full of pent-up rage, he threw himself on the two dogs, taking them both at once. He sank his teeth into the largest one's neck, getting a mouthful of fur. He redoubled his strike and bit down harder, his long fangs piercing the dog's flesh. He ripped open the hound's jugular vein. He felt the beast perish between his jaws as hot blood gushed into his mouth. His tongue went numb. The blood was bitter: wolfsbane. It was poison.

Gareth released the body of the first hound and let it drop, lifeless, to the earth. He shook his head, trying to spit out the nasty taste, but a good amount had already slid down his throat. Wolfsbane was toxic to werewolves. He didn't know how poisonous these dogs were. But he couldn't back down now. The second hound was on him. He didn't have any other choice but to fight.

The last female was vicious and fast. She darted between his legs and clamped her fangs down on his neck. She missed the soft fleshy underside of his neck, where she might have struck a fatal blow to his jugular. Instead, Gareth turned at the last second, and her teeth sank into the corded muscle between his neck and shoulder. Snarling, her jaws locked down. Gareth roared at the sting of sharp teeth piercing his skin. He twisted, but the bitch had strong jaws and wouldn't let go. There was no easy way to dislodge her. He rolled across the ground, crushing her with his body weight. Finally, with a mighty shake, he flung her off. She took a chunk of flesh with him. *Fuck.*

The female dog flew into the darkness of the cement factory, launched by the force of Gareth's throw, to collide with a pile of rubble and scrap metal. The impact made a horrible clanging sound. Gareth bared his teeth, his ears perked forward, his eyes scanning the shadows. He waited for his opponent to reappear, but the female dog didn't get back up.

Gareth stood for a moment, panting. Blood matted his fur, streaming down his left shoulder and across his chest. He felt a little dizzy. He didn't know how much wolfsbane he had ingested from both dogs' blood, but it was enough to make his jaw numb and his vision a little blurry. The poison would continue to spread through him, possibly causing paralysis, helped by the thundering pace of his heartbeat. If he was smart, he would find a safe place to hunker down until the poison worked its way out of his system. But he wasn't feeling very smart at the moment. His head burned. He needed to reach Maddy's side.

He started through the shadowy halls of the abandoned cement factory, his nose to the ground, following Maddy's scent. He caught a whiff of the hunter, too. He recognized the man's peculiar stench from the hiking trail. The scent made him furious. Gareth felt himself giving into the wolf, his mind full of fire, his thoughts bullish and violent. A heady mix of poison and adrenaline throbbed through his veins. The risk of being shot by the hunter didn't seem to matter. He needed to reach his mate. He would rather die by Maddy's side than keep living on in this world alone. Their story couldn't be finished yet. Not when it was just beginning.

***

Maddy screamed and yelled until her voice died in her throat. Then she lay in the darkness of the pit for an excruciating amount of time. It felt like hours, but couldn't have been more than twenty minutes or so, waiting breathlessly for Gareth to arrive. Her hands were numb, and fever burned in her cheeks. She struggled to stay conscious and upright. Whatever happened, she couldn't let herself collapse.

Then the dead, chill air of the factory seemed to shift. It was a subtle change, but her head lifted. A flurry of movement seemed to be approaching on the floor above.

Then a giant black Alpha wolf came barreling out of the darkness, hurtling over the edge of the pit. Gareth landed with a splash in the dirty water pooling on the basement floor. Maddy stared at him in shock. Even with her eyes adjusted to the shadows, he was almost invisible in his wolf form. All she could see were a pair of sinister yellow eyes glowing through the darkness.

In a blur of movement, he crossed to her side, almost bowling her over backwards. Her gasp of relief was quickly replaced by terror, because she knew that the hunter was approaching from above them.

"Gareth, no!" she said, trying to find words. Her voice was cracked and dry, a mere whisper. "No, *no,* you have to leave!"

His jaws found the ropes binding her wrists. He tried to split them with his teeth. One of his sharp fangs grazed her skin. She flinched. He could very well bite off her hand if he wasn't careful. She could sense his frustration as he tried again. His teeth grazed her soft skin, scraping her again, even though he tried to be gentle. A tear leaked down her cheek.

"Please, please run away . . . ." she begged him. "Just forget about me, Gareth!"

Then a bright LED lantern suddenly switched on. A beam of light shot down into the pit, striking Maddy's eyes. She went blind for a moment. She curled away from the harsh white light. She squinted. Looked up. Sarah was holding the lantern up high, like a spotlight, trained on Gareth's Alpha form. Her lifemate was fully illuminated in the dark pit. He was monstrously huge, his coat matted with dirt, blood staining his long fangs and dripping down his majestic throat. Shit. Maddy cringed. He looked fearsome and deadly.

Gareth left Maddy's side and approached the bottom of the ledge, near Sarah's feet. He looked terrifying, foaming at the mouth, his eyes red with rage. The hunter appeared next to Sarah on the ledge, a big black rifle propped up on one shoulder, taking aim. His weathered face stretched into a wide grin.

Maddy braced herself. Gareth stood in the hunter's crosshairs, unphased. The Alpha snarled up at the hunter.

"Aha!" the hunter crowed. "The perfect shot. Look at that pelt. What a handsome beast . . . you'll make *quite* the trophy. Half a mil, at least. At this distance, I can get him right between the eyes."

"Just take the shot! Before that beast jumps up here!" Sarah cried. She sounded terrified. Indeed, Gareth looked large enough to leap out of the pit in a single bound. Maddy expected him to spring up at any second.

Then, suddenly, the rhythm of pounding footsteps echoed down the hallway. Maddy looked up at the sound. Sarah almost dropped the lantern. The hunter seemed startled, too. He started to turn around. Then, in a whirl of movement, someone leapt out of the shadows.

"Hey you!" Vin yelled. He swung a big metal pipe at the hunter's head and beamed him. With a cry, the hunter stumbled over the edge, his gun falling out of his hand, arms windmilling, a frantic look of terror crossing his face. Then, with a shriek, Kevin fell into the pit. Gareth lunged at the same time, his jaws opened wide, a monstrous snarl emitting from his throat.

Maddy screwed shut her eyes and ducked her head, cringing away from the scene, rolling into a ball. She didn't want to see the hunter's fate, but she heard the wet sounds of ripping flesh. The gun went off twice; the bullets ricocheted off of metal and steel; she didn't see where they landed, but she counted herself lucky she wasn't shot. In the cacophony of echoes and screams that followed, she thought she heard Bea's voice cry out, "You crazy bitch! Give me that flashlight! Fuck you!"

Where did Bea and Vin come from? Why were they in the Devil's Tower? Maddy couldn't wrap her mind around it. She heard Sarah's voice mixed in with the rest. It sounded like a second fight was happening up above. Then the flashlight fell into the pit with a plastic rattle. Sarah screamed some profanities. Then Maddy heard the familiar patter of Sarah's boots on the cement floor. It sounded like the Hawkins' secretary was running away. Hopefully far, *far* away.

When Maddy dared to open her eyes again, she found herself staring at the cement wall of the basement. The harsh white light from the LED lantern only illuminated a thin slice of darkness across the bottom of the pit. Her eyes widened marginally at a giant mural on the wall behind her, which she hadn't seen before, because of the darkness. The word "ALIVE" was spray painted across the wall in bright teal green and orange lettering.

Yeah. Alive.

Her eyes followed the light from the LED lantern. The pool of muddy water on the basement floor was stained deep red. The hunter's body lay in the shadows on the other side of the pit, near a crumbling cement wall. She glanced away quickly. She thought, maybe, the body was missing a head. But she didn't look very close.

She looked around the black pit. Shadows engulfed every side of her beyond the lantern's thin white glow. She didn't see the giant black Alpha wolf anywhere. Her heart skipped a beat. Shit. Where was Gareth? Was he alright?

Then a man's silhouette emerged from the darkness. Maddy stared at Gareth in awe. He was fully nude and blood smeared his chest. His hair was a tangled, matted mess, falling down past his shoulders. A gruesome, terrible wound was oozing blood on his left shoulder, the flesh near his neck mangled and bruised. Her stomach churned. A small whimper escaped her throat, but she couldn't summon words.

Gareth carried the hunter's gun over one arm. As she watched, he removed the bullets from the rifle and tossed them into the darkness. Then he knelt down behind Maddy and untied her wrists.

In a rough voice, like two rocks grinding together, he asked, "Can you walk?"

Maddy tried to stand up. Her calf was scratched up by the hound's teeth, but the bleeding had already stopped. Her arm was sliced up from the hunter's knife and the graze of Gareth's fangs when he tried to untie her in his wolf form. The wounds burned and stung, but the pain seemed more like background noise. Mostly, she felt a little hazy and flu-ish from the wolfsbane poisoning.

"I think I'm alright," she mumbled.

Gareth knelt next to her. She glanced down at the ground, averting her eyes from all the blood that stained his chest and shoulder. He took her hands and rubbed her wrists for a moment, working the blood back into her fingers. Then he helped her to her feet.

Maddy was surprised that she could stand up. She thought she would be exhausted, but adrenaline still coursed through her veins. Shivering and naked in the underground cavern, she started walking through the bloody water toward the pile of rubble at the side of the pit.

Then Gareth stumbled.

Maddy's arm went around his waist. Her hand found the long, bloody gash along his ribs. It was bleeding profusely.

"Oh my god!" she gasped. "Gareth, were you shot?"

"It grazed me," he grunted.

Maddy stared at him in awe. How was he still conscious after enduring all that? Well, considering his miraculous healing powers, maybe she shouldn't be surprised. Arm in arm, they started across the pit again to the pile of rubble, where they could climb back up to the first floor.

In the light of the LED lantern, something on the ground caught Maddy's eye.

"Wait," she murmured.

Gareth slowed down as Maddy stooped to pick up something off the ground. Her fingers groped for a moment in the darkness, then she snagged the chain of the hunter's necklace. She fished it out of the pool of muddy rain water. She tried not to wonder how it had come free of his neck, since the chain was still intact.

She squinted at the curved fang of the long-dead Alpha, a sense of pity filling her heart. She felt connected to this unknown Alpha wolf who had died at the hunter's hands. Maybe because Gareth had just escaped a similar fate. She didn't want to leave this tooth behind, to be forgotten in a dank place like the Devil's Tower. She would have slipped it in her pocket, if she was wearing clothes. Instead, considering her nudity, she pulled the necklace over her head. It dangled down between her breasts, a little on the long side, like a medallion.

When she looked back up, she noticed Gareth watching her, a grim expression on his face. His eyes were dark gold. His gaze flickered to the unknown fang. Then he took her hand and together, he led her back toward the pile of rubble.

The LED lantern was lying near the edge of the debris pile. Maddy picked up the lantern as they passed it. Together, Gareth and Maddy traversed the pile of rocks to the first floor of the building. Gareth went first, testing the cement boulders and loose shale as he climbed up. He paused at each twisted rod of rebar they passed, reaching back to help her up the hill. They used the bent rebar to pull themselves up the steeper parts. Maddy winced as the sharp cement bit into her soft feet.

Bea and Vin were both standing at the top of the pit, waiting for them. Maddy tossed the LED lantern to Bea. Vin was holding a length of metal pipe in his hands. He looked totally amped.

"I can't believe it," were the first words out of Vin's mouth.

At the same time, Bea said, "Holy shit, are you two okay? Wow, you guys are . . . *very naked*." Then, with a blush, Bea made an about-face and gave them her back.

Vin stared at Maddy for a second too long before he shrugged off his spiked leather jacket and tossed it to her. Then he also averted his gaze, a pink tinge to his cheeks.

"Oh, thanks!" Maddy mumbled as she pulled on the jacket. It smelled like strong cologne. Her voice was croaky and dry from screaming. She sounded like an old woman. "Uh . . . sorry . . . about all this. Um. How did you guys find us?"

"Are you kidding? Kaylee came screeching out of the tower like a bat out of hell. 'Wolf! Wolf! Killer wolf!' The whole party blew up. Everyone ran off. We were going to leave, too, but then I saw a big black wolf run into the tower . . . I thought it looked like *your* wolf, Maddy." Bea glanced significantly over her shoulder, briefly meeting Gareth's eyes, then she turned away again.

"That was the hunter, wasn't it?" Bea asked. "I think we passed one of his dogs on the way in here. It looked . . . uh . . . ."

"It was dead," Vin supplied.

"Yeah," Bea sounded more disturbed by that than the dead man in the pit. "So was that guy going to shoot you?"

"Fucking wild," Vin muttered.

Gareth didn't say anything. Honestly, he still looked pretty feral, all blood-smeared and blazing eyes. Maddy could feel the vitality rising off of him in a wave of supernatural heat. It seemed likely he would Change back into his Alpha form at a pin drop. Probably a good thing. He still had enough energy to protect them, despite the battle he had just survived.

Gareth handed the rifle to Vin, startling the young man when the weapon was thrust into his hands.

"Thanks," Gareth grunted, briefly meeting Vin's eyes.

The young man stared at Gareth, speechless.

Then, without any other explanation, Gareth shifted back into his wolf form. Maddy watched his face begin to change and elongate, his chest thrust forward, fur run up his neck, his arms grow long and narrow. Maddy watched in fascination. By now, she could appreciate his skill and control. He almost made the Change look beautiful.

Vin gasped, his eyes like saucers. "Holy fuckin' Frankenstein's monster!" he stuttered as Gareth strode past him in his Alpha wolf form. Then Vin looked back at her, all wrapped up in his jacket. He blushed again and turned away quickly. "Holy shit," he said again.

"Yeah," Bea agreed. "That about sums it up. Best Halloween party *ever*."

The big black wolf took the lead. Gareth kept his ears perked forward and his tail down low as he started through the Devil's Tower. Maddy fell into step behind Bea and Vin. She was grateful to have a jacket to hide under, but she still didn't have any pants, which was a little—okay, *a lot*—weird. Luckily, Vin's jacket felt a little past her waist, like a very short dress. As long as she didn't walk too fast, she probably wouldn't flash anyone by accident. Though she supposed, by this point, it didn't matter. She felt so shocked and numb, she could have strode out of the Devil's Tower naked in broad daylight, with a whole crowd outside, unphased.

"So then . . . then it's true," Vin said as they walked. He sounded pretty freaked out, but also excited. He gripped the big gun in his hand, slinging it over one shoulder. "It's *really* true. You guys are werewolves. Both of you."

"Yeah, uh, that's right," Maddy confirmed, her voice a soft echo compared to his.

Vin seemed appropriately amazed. He stared at Gareth's Alpha form with a good amount of admiration on his face.

"I saw that big black wolf run in here, too," he mused, "but I never would've followed it on my own. If Bea hadn't taken off into the tower like some crazy obsessive fangirl—"

"Hey! Don't make it sound like my fault. You didn't have to come," Bea snapped.

"*Of course* I had to follow you. I'm not going to let you get jumped by some crazy crackhead in the Devil's Tower. Or eaten by a killer wolf, for that matter. I'm not afraid to throw down for you. I'd totally fight off werewolves, junkies, or like, some psycho with a semi-automatic rifle. No lie. I hit that guy with *a pipe*. Just look at this gun he was carrying!" Vin called up ahead to Gareth, "You were about to be Swiss cheese, you hear that boss? That's twice I've saved your hide. This time, I *really* want a raise."

Gareth's ears twitched, the only sign that he had overheard Vin's little speech. Beatrice glanced over at Vin, a catlike little smile on her lips and a glint in her eye. The look was fleeting, but Maddy caught it. She thought, maybe, her friend liked Vin's act of heroism very much.

Maddy felt the urge to giggle. Vin's enthusiasm was contagious, and she was starting to feel a little hysterical. Actually, their whole group seemed a bit manic and unhinged. Bea was nervously humming to herself. Vin kept switching the rifle around in his hands. Maddy felt lightheaded. And yet, it felt good to be surrounded by friends. A man had died, and she was pretty sure she'd have nightmares for the rest of the year, but she was safe now, and Gareth had survived.

After a long walk through the dark, they reached the entrance to the Devil's Tower. The forest outside the abandoned building was mostly empty. The music was silent. Someone had dumped water and sand on the bonfires. All that was left of the Halloween Haunt party was a table of snack food, a handful of jack-o-lanterns, some holiday streamers and a bunch of abandoned decorations. Maddy was grateful for the lack of witnesses as they made their way down the hill through the forest, leaving the solemn tower far behind. She rescued a picnic blanket abandoned underneath a tree and wrapped it around her waist. There. Finally, not naked.

The black Alpha wolf led them to a gravel road where Vin's truck was parked. When they reached the vehicle, Gareth ducked into the trees briefly, then reemerged in his human form. Vin unlocked the back door and tossed him a pair of swim trunks from under the passenger seat. Maddy felt that ridiculous urge to giggle again.

"Should we drive you guys to the hospital?" Vin asked, glancing at Gareth's bloody chest.

"No hospitals," Gareth grunted as he pulled on the pair of blue swim trunks. They were a bit too short. He winced, openly adjusting his balls, obviously too tired to care about company.

Maddy crossed to his side and gripped his arm, steadying him. He looked a little off balance. It concerned her.

Then, unexpectedly, Gareth said to Bea. "Does your mom know how to treat wolfs-bane poisoning? Can she brew an antidote?"

Bea frowned. "Probably. She knows a lot of stuff. I'll call her once we get down the mountain a little ways. I don't have cell service this far out."

"Alright. Let's go there first," Gareth said.

Gareth helped Maddy climb into Vin's truck, kissing her on the forehead as he packed her into the backseat. Then he slid in next to her. As they settled next to each other, Maddy got a better look at Gareth's wounds in the cab light. Alarm filled her, and she gasped. Black veins spread from the gash on his shoulder up the side of his neck. Shit. It must be the wolfsbane. Sweat dripped down his forehead. Even without touching him, she could feel the fever burning in his skin.

"Gareth?" she asked softly, as Vin started up the truck and pulled onto the road. Gareth's golden eyes, bright with wolf power, slid to her. His gaze was quiet, steady, but she saw a tightness in his expression she hadn't seen before. He was in pain.

His hand wrapped around hers in the backseat, his fingers threading through her own.

Maddy pressed her other hand to her cheek, wondering at the extent of her own poisoning. She had also ingested a small amount of wolfsbane, but beyond a vague fluish feeling, she seemed okay. She wondered if she had similar black marks on her skin, but without a mirror, she couldn't be sure.

A few minutes later, they were roaring down the side of the mountain in Vin's truck, leaving the dark forest and the Devil's Tower behind.

Chapter 30

Maddy woke up on Sunday morning, tangled in a pile of blankets on Bea's floor. She groaned. She felt like she had a hangover, even though she had never drank a beer in her life. Her head throbbed. Her mouth was bone dry. She licked her lips. The bitter aftertaste of Ms. Almut's wolfsbane tonic lingered in her mouth.

She put a hand to her forehead and sighed. What a wild, *wild* night. Her dreams had been full of the Devil's Tower: dark, echoing corridors filled with rats, trash, broken glass and debris. She had run down hall after hall, pursued by the hunter, a cold pit of dread in her stomach. Twice she had woken up, convinced she had been shot dead. She could hardly believe she had survived such an ordeal. Without her friends, she and Gareth might not have made it out of the tower.

Her mind returned to memories of the night before. Vin had rushed them down the mountain to Ms. Almut's house, where Bea's mom had met them at the door. The shaman was ready for them with two mugs of herbal tea and plenty of towels. Luckily, Ms. Almut knew how to brew an antidote, but it took a bit of time. The cure for wolfsbane poisoning was brewed from the same plant, but using a different part of the roots, which Ms. Almut kept in her workshop. Within an hour of drinking the tonic, Maddy's fever had broken and she started to feel a lot better.

Gareth's treatment was a much more serious ordeal. He had ingested a much larger dose of the poison. He was almost unconscious by the time they reached Ms. Almut's house. The shaman lady had spent two hours drawing the contaminated blood out of his wound before giving him the healing draft. It was a stressful time. Maddy sat with Gareth in Ms. Almut's cramped workshop as she performed an archaic sort of surgery on his shoulder. She used some sort of reiki healing during the process, passing her hands over the wound several times while humming a strange chant deep in her throat. Her words were powerful—they made Maddy's skin itch and her ears tingle. Gareth endured the procedure without novocaine, with his usual stoicism, but Maddy wasn't fooled. By the time it was over, he was pale with exhaustion, his face gaunt and brow creased. He looked ten years older.

Ms. Almut put Gareth to sleep on the couch in the living room, in front of a roaring fire, where she could check on him throughout the night. Maddy had gone to sleep up in Bea's room, but not before she spied her little friend saying goodbye to Vin in the driveway. Curious, Maddy had overheard a few snatches of their conversation through the open window.

"A wise man once told me to choose the girl I'd throw down for," Vin said as he got down on one knee in front of his truck. He held Bea's hand between his own. *"I'm sorry for all the bullshit, Bea. I'd do anything for you. Werewolf, militia or vampire, it doesn't matter, I'll always fight to protect you. Will you be my girl?"*

Maddy was pretty sure Bea started crying, but that's when she had shut the bedroom window to give them both privacy. Then she crawled onto the pile of blankets on the floor. She didn't remember Bea coming into the room or climbing into bed. Maddy was already asleep.

After tossing and turning for a few minutes, Maddy wearily climbed to her feet. It was still early in the morning, but she was wide awake. She didn't want to go back to sleep, where more nightmares would plague her about the hunter and his hounds. A layer of fog obscured her view outside of Bea's window. It looked like a cloud bank had settled over the town of Black River. The yard below was covered in a veil of white mist.

Bea let out a loud snore. Her little friend was snuggled up in bed, wrapped around a panda-shaped body pillow. It was kind of adorable—the body pillow was bigger than her little friend. Maddy tiptoed to the bedroom door and let herself into the hallway. The house was silent. She was wearing a borrowed nightgown from Ms. Almut, since Bea's clothes were too small for her curves. Shivering in the cold air, she made her way downstairs to check on Gareth.

In surprise, she found the couch in the living room empty. By the pile of cold cinders in the hearth, the fire had burned out hours ago. With a pang of concern, Maddy wondered where her lifemate had gone.

She started her hunt through the house. As she passed through the kitchen, her eyes spied a full pot of coffee on the kitchen counter. It was reassuring. If Gareth was healthy enough to make himself coffee, she probably wouldn't find him collapsed in a hallway somewhere. She followed Gareth's trail to the back door. She opened the slider and stepped outside in her bare feet. A wall of mist embraced her. The boards of the half-built back deck were damp and slick with nighttime dew. She couldn't see the camper or the back fence, the fog was so thick.

Gareth stood at the end of the deck wearing borrowed clothes from Ms. Almut's closet. The t-shirt was a size too small, and the pajama bottoms were a little short in the leg. He stood in his bare feet at the edge of the half-built deck, a mug of black coffee in hand, looking across the misty yard. A fat white bandage created a lumpy shape on his shoulder, where the dog had bit him. His eyes seemed far away.

Maddy approached his side. He lifted his arm automatically and she slid under it. He pulled her against him. His warmth was instantly comforting.

"You doing alright?" Gareth asked.

Maddy nodded. "I'm okay. Pretty bad nightmares, but that's the worst of it."

"Sorry about that, babygirl." Gareth sighed. "I'm just glad you're safe."

"Hey, I was worried about you, too," Maddy pointed out. "That wolfsbane poisoning looked really bad when we left the tower. I'm glad Bea's mom could help us."

"Yeah, well, I owe her big time. She really downplays it, but she's a skilled healer. I'm pretty sure she saved my life last night."

Maddy was shocked. She blinked up at him, remembering the black veins on his neck. She hadn't realized the poison was that strong. A bit of darkness tainted her mood as Gareth sipped on his coffee. Ugh. No. She didn't want to think about how close they had both come to dying. She didn't need to relive it.

Trying for humor, she asked, "So what are you going to do to repay Bea's mom? Free oil changes for life?"

Gareth barked a laugh. "Yeah, something like that."

"So what's the plan for today?"

"Plan?" He mussed up her hair, then rested his big hand on top of her head. "Get Vin to drive us back out to the cabin. Clean up the place and pick up my car. Then I dunno . . . you wanna go fishing?"

Maddy snorted. "Fishing? Really? In this weather?"

"The mist will burn away by noon. The weather report seems to think it's going to turn into a nice day." Gareth glanced upward at the sky, as though he could see the sun through the layers of clouds. Then his voice grew more serious. "Mads, I gotta ask, why'd you pick up that necklace from the tower last night?"

"Oh, this thing?" Maddy reached under her shirt and drew it out. She had almost forgotten about it. She had fallen asleep with it on, and now it was tangled in her hair. She picked at the strands of red hair ensnared in the chain, then she held it up. The hooked fang was stained yellow with age. It was longer than the palm of her hand. "The necklace belonged to the hunter. He said it's the fang of his first Alpha kill. I felt bad leaving it behind in the tower. I don't really know why. Just seemed wrong."

"Gotcha."

"Why do you ask?"

Gareth sighed and took a sip of coffee. "Well, babe, I found out our hunter was part of the Redfern Massacre back in the day."

"What's that?"

"It happened about sixteen years ago. Hellstrom International ambushed the Redfern wolf pack in Farmington, Maine. Killed every last one; I couldn't find a record of any survivors. But . . . it happened around the same time you moved to Black River with your mom. I think you woulda been around three or four."

"Okay." Maddy stared up at Gareth's face, curious why he would bring it up now. "Do you think this fang is from the Redfern Alpha?"

"Probably." Gareth paused. A long silence stretched between them. Maddy sensed there was more he wanted to say, so she waited. Finally, in a low voice, Gareth said, "I did some digging, and the Alpha of the Redfern pack was named Robert Donovan."

Maddy felt a chill run down her spine. She stared at the fang again, then back to Gareth's face. "Wait . . . Robert *Donovan?* That's weird . . . my last name is Donovan."

Gareth watched her face. His hand brushed over her cheek gently. "Yeah, well, you share the same name. I don't know if that's a coincidence, but the Redfern pack was known for their reddish coats."

Maddy didn't know what to think at first. Her hand tightened around the necklace. She struggled with this new information. She looked back down at the yellowed fang. For some reason, her mind wasn't putting all the pieces together. Then it finally clicked.

"So my last name is Donovan, and I'm a red wolf," she repeated.

"Yup."

"And my mother showed up in Black River the same year as the massacre," she said, her voice growing more quiet. At first it seemed like a stretch, but the more she thought about it . . . the more likely it seemed . . . that her mother was a survivor of the attack.

Maddy felt numb as the full implication of Gareth's words settled over her shoulders. She sucked in a breath, her teeth sinking into her bottom lip. Alright. So Robert Donovan, Alpha of the Redfern pack, might have been her father. And this very fang hanging from around her neck might have belonged to him. Her hand started to shake where she gripped the long tooth. Holy shit. Was she holding a part of her father's body right now?

Her knees grew a little weak at that thought. Gareth wrapped his arms around her and pulled her into his chest. Maddy felt tears filling her eyes.

"But how can I know for sure?" she asked. "How can I find out the truth?"

"His name might be on your birth certificate, babe," Gareth said gently. "Have you thought of looking at that?"

"I . . . I mean, I haven't really . . . ." Maddy felt dumb. Her teen years were spent in survival mode, terrorized by Dean's alcoholism and physical abuse. She had never wondered about her father's true identity; it was a forbidden topic around the trailer. Now, finally, it seemed like she had a chance to discover her true roots.

"How do I get a copy of my birth certificate?" she asked.

"We'd need to find out which hospital you were born at."

"I don't know where I was born."

"We'll figure it out together, babe. There must be some info in public records. Or we can call around. I say we start around Farmington, Maine."

Maddy wrapped her arms around Gareth's waist. She felt the bandages under his shirt where the bullet had grazed him. This man would take a bullet for her. Shit. How did she get this lucky?

"Thank you," she said.

"For what, babe?"

"For finding out all this. And . . . for saving me."

Gareth grunted low in his throat, then he gripped her hard. "I'll always come for you, baby," he murmured into her hair. "Nobody's gonna get you long as I'm around."

They held each other like that, pressed close together, for a long moment. Then Maddy glanced up at him with a bashful little grin.

"You really want to go fishing today?"

"Yeah, why not? We can grab some sandwiches and chill by the lake."

Considering the events of the week, relaxing by a lake with a fishing pole sounded like a much needed vacation, even if it was only for a few hours. How Gareth could act so calm and nonchalant after such a harrowing night, she didn't know. But she was beginning to suspect it was in his nature. He was her rock. She thought back to the first time she had met him on the mountain, when she was fourteen. Even then, she had sensed his strength, his protectiveness. He was her Alpha. They were meant to find each other.

"I love you, Gareth," she said, unable to hide the shy smile from her face.

He leaned over and kissed her forehead. "I love you too, babygirl."

About the Author

Meet A. Mariposa!

A. Mariposa's first series, BLACK RIVER MOON, is a bit like Shameless with were-wolves: "slice of life, heavy on the spice." Ms. Mariposa grew up traveling between Los Angeles, CA and Washington State, which gave her a love of diversity, Southwest culture, big forests, rainy weather, and a fascination with weird little historic towns. Many of her own life experiences make their way into the fantastical world of Black River. She currently lives in Seattle, WA with her husband and two fur babies.

Listen to the Podcast!

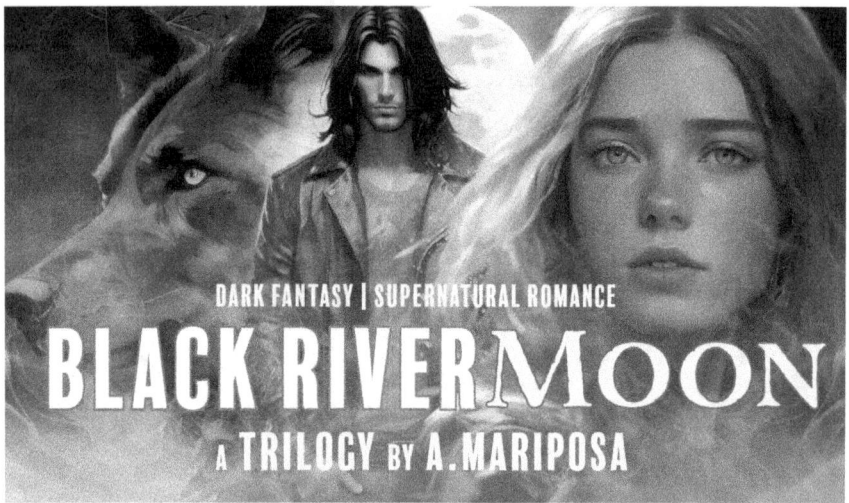

With over **150,000 views and 1M** watch hours, BLACK RIVER MOON is an entertaining dramatized podcast available for Free on Youtube.

www.ingramcontent.com/pod-product-compliance
Lightning Source LLC
Chambersburg PA
CBHW070540260626
47161CB00002B/464